The Possession

There was nothing else she could do but step into his arms, and Lord Kerry embraced her, pulling her against his chest.

Katherine clung to him as their lips meshed and melted together and parted with his persistence. She succumbed willingly to this devasting intrusion, a strange warmth flooding through her, demanding more, demanding to be touched, demanding things she could not put a name to.

"My kitten has grown up," Kerry whispered huskily. "You are a woman now, Katherine. I will have to start treating you as one. . . ."

Lady Sorceress

Passionate Historical Romances from SIGNET

Lady Sorceress

PATRICIA RICE

A SIGNET BOOK

NEW AMERICAN LIBRARY

NAL BOOKS ARE AVAILABLE AT QUANTITY DISCOUNTS WHEN USED
TO PROMOTE PRODUCTS OR SERVICES. FOR INFORMATION PLEASE
WRITE TO PREMIUM MARKETING DIVISION, NEW AMERICAN LIBRARY,
1633 BROADWAY, NEW YORK, NEW YORK 10019.

SIGNET TRADEMARK REG. U.S. PAT. OFF. AND FOREIGN COUNTRIES
REGISTERED TRADEMARK—MARCA REGISTRADA
HECHO EN CHICAGO, U.S.A.

SIGNET, SIGNET CLASSIC, MENTOR, PLUME, MERIDIAN AND NAL BOOKS
are published by New American Library,
1633 Broadway, New York, New York 10019

First Printing, June, 1985

1 2 3 4 5 6 7 8 9

PRINTED IN THE UNITED STATES OF AMERICA

THIS IS DEDICATED . . .

to the one I love

AUTHOR'S NOTE

The characters of this novel are entirely fictional, including the governors and lieutenant governors of the Carolinas. However, the story does follow history as accurately as is possible. The governors of the Carolinas were not always a scrupulous lot and there have been periods when they went ungoverned entirely. I have attempted to keep my novel within the confines of history at this period of time, with some condensation of the years for the sake of the story. Any deviation from historical detail was entirely intentional.

December 1732

FIRELIGHT sent shadows flickering across the room, playing against the tall cloaked figure settled uncomfortably on the high stone hearth, his black-draped shape a shadowed mass in the darkened room. Outside, a winter storm howled, rattling the shuttered windows and sending currents of cold air to chill the room and fan the fire. Icy snow spit shivering tattoos against the panes. Muttering explicit curses, the apparition pulled the cloak tighter around broad shoulders while staring into the dimly lit room, letting his eyes adjust to the darkness as he searched the shadows.

The man's face was a formless blur in the ill light of the fire, but he could have been the devil himself seated at the entrance to hell and the room's only other occupant would not have denied it. Terror hid in her pounding heart, compounded by the torments preceding this moment, magnified by visions of what was yet to come. Shivering, her teeth chattering, she cowered in a far corner as far from the dark specter as she could hide, but totally aware of his every movement, like any small animal cornered by a hungry predator. The silence between them mounted.

His gaze settling on her cowering figure, Kerry cursed silently. It had been a long and revolting evening; he should have left as soon as he lost sight of that ass Derwentwater, instead of lingering to discover the fate of that unfortunate creature in the corner. Now here he sat, freezing in this filthy attic, when Derwentwater was probably home warm in bed with whatever bed companion he had found in that ghastly farce downstairs. Kerry was beginning to wonder wearily just which one of them had been the ass.

"Get over here and let me see just what my purse has bought." He spoke curtly, gesturing toward the spot in front of the fire. His cloak fell free with his movement, exposing a glimmer of immaculate white lace at chest and wrist. When the slight figure did not move, he added irritably, "Have you suddenly turned shy?"

The creature crept a pace or two forward, propelled more by curiosity than fear at the sound of the mellow voice, so different from the crude sounds grating her ears earlier with their jeering obscenities. Catching the green glint of his eyes, she stopped to consider its nature, wondering what fury or depravity it might denote.

"I still cannot see you. Move over here in front of the fire where it is warmer." Kerry's voice lost its irritation, but retained its command. If appearances weren't too deceiving, he was dealing with a child, but one in her profession could scarce have claim to shyness.

Fearfully the girl moved closer, shivering, until the fire-light captured the blue sheen of her best gown. Torn now, its worn and mended bodice ripped from her tiny bosom by the contemptuous hands of the men below, the gown hung tattered across her shoulders, exposing the creamy skin beneath. Holding it clasped together as best she could, she stepped into the firelight, coming to a halt inches from the knees of the man who was now master of her fate.

Could it have been only a few short hours ago that she had stood—cold and shivering and free—in front of this monstrous building, staring longingly at its lighted warmth while she dared herself to make this final debasement to keep body, if not soul, together? But she had not understood then that it was body and not soul they desired; although she had known figuratively what she was doing when she offered herself to the highest bidder, she had not known what it meant literally. She gathered the tattered remnant of her gown closer over bruised and aching breasts, hugging her shame inside.

It had been the gnawing hunger in her belly, the freezing numbness of uncovered fingers and ill-shod toes, and the desperation of knowing she had no warm place to sleep that night, that had driven her in the fury of the winter storm to stand before that doorway despite her knowledge of the depravity lurking within. It had taken only one strong gust of icy north wind to blow her that fatal step through those portals to hell.

She had been struck at once by the strong stench of unwashed bodies, masked by the odor of smoking lamps and tobacco, but it was warm, and once in, there had been no turning back. With undisguised derision they had hustled her onto the platform, adding her to the line of more experienced "merchandise" hoping for a warmer berth or a few extra shillings for a mug of gin.

Shocked by the sight of nearly nude females parading brazenly before the drunken revelry of a hundred men, she had frozen in the background, gazing in horrified fascination through swirls of smoke at the dimly lit scene. But then hot hands had fallen on her, dragging her forward while stripping away her soaked and clinging gown to a chorus of hoarse yells and drunken profanity, her naked, defenseless protests only bringing jeers.

Standing in front of that audience of drunken revelers while the auctioneer ran callused hands up her skinny thighs, she had suffered the humiliation of being pinched and raped by the fingers of a dozen men, their derogatory comments burning her ears while tears scorched her eyes. Mindlessly clinging to the remains of her gown, she had searched frantically for some reprieve until her terrified gaze fell on a distant pair of cool green eyes. Through her misery, she focused on what she imagined to be their compassionate concern, until suddenly she realized that he too was bidding on her, and she had sunk into the black depths of despair, unable to face the reality of her insanity. Until now, when she was faced by her nameless purchaser.

With half-cynical scorn, Kerry watched the tremors shaking the frail body before him, scorn at his stupidity in falling for the frightened eyes of this child-actress, scorn for the child at her performance. That was no white slave market down there: the women were all willingly sold, flaunting their wares and jeering their buyers into higher bids in order to earn a higher percentage of what they brought the house. This infant would not have been down there if she had not long ago shed her innocence, and any fear he had seen was purely imaginary on his part, or superb acting on hers.

"You're a scrawny, plain wench. I can see why you would find slim pickings on the street." Shadowed eyes swept scornfully over the small figure in the firelight, her soaked gown gradually drying but still bedraggled, a child's gown and not the seductive fashion of the street. She had made some attempt to style her hair in the elaborate bewigged fashion of her betters, but unpowdered and wet, it fell about her ears and throat in limp, damp curls.

Kerry found himself pulling on one of the long tendrils, stretching it to its full length. "You would do better to hide these. I had a spaniel once about this color, and with much the same smell." He wrinkled his nose at the musty odor arising as the heat of the fire steamed damp clothing and hair. A trick of firelight sent a shimmer of gold down the strand of filthy hair wrapped about his finger.

The girl jerked her head away, painfully pulling the curl from his grasp. "You would smell too, had you only the Thames for your bathing place, and that in the midst of winter." She stepped backward defiantly, safely out of his reach.

"Ahhh, the shy kitten bares her claws at last." Surprised, the girl's first words betraying a startling lack of the uneducated gutter speech he had expected, Kerry looked up into the most amazing pair of violet eyes he had ever encountered. Those eyes had bewitched him from the first, but he was a fool if he thought them frightened. She glared at him now with passionate fury.

Gad! She stood skinnier and straighter than any schoolboy, scarce tall enough to reach his shoulder, and he was no giant, but those eyes! Where did one get such wells of emotion in so few short years?

"How old are you, child?" Kerry pulled his cloak back around him and retreated into the shadows, shocked at his reaction to one so young.

"Fifteen," she muttered sullenly, clenching the torn material tighter. She had seen the flicker of interest in his eyes despite his derisive words, and her thin body rebelled at further intrusion. But it was submit either to this one man or to the many down below, and this thought quenched any further rebellion.

From the looks of the wench, Kerry doubted she reached even this claim to age, but he did not dispute it. "How many of those years have been spent on the streets?" he asked disdainfully, striving to maintain disinterest.

For a moment, confusion clouded petite features, and she became childlike again, staring at his feet nervously rather than face him. "It depends on your meaning, milord," she finally admitted.

Puzzled by the change in her demeanor, Kerry clarified crudely, "How long have you been selling yourself for a living? You scarce look old enough to take a man."

To his amazement, a blush spread from the girl's white throat to her pale face, accenting frail features with their first hint of color. She continued to stare at his feet.

"You will not send me back if I tell you?" she whispered hesitantly.

"I doubt if they would take you back. Looks to me like they were well rid of you; you are my problem now. Unless you tell me you've been prostituting yourself for fifteen years, I fear you won't amaze me."

Again that slow blush as she continued to contemplate his boots. Surely the child could not be such a consummate actress as to produce a blush on command?

"No, milord. This . . . this is my first time." The words came hesitantly at first; then, as fear-filled eyes finally looked up to his, she plunged on urgently. "You will not send me back? Please—I could not go through that again! I will learn quickly, I am a very fast learner. Please, do not send me back!"

The agony was all too real in her startling confession, but Kerry refused to believe the evidence of eyes and ears. What she had said was totally unthinkable in this time and place, contradicting all rational notions.

"That is utter nonsense. Do I look to be such a fool as to believe that tale?" Whipping his cloak back impatiently, he rose, towering a full head over her, though he stood less than six feet in height. Firelight flickered over high cheekbones and an arrogant jaw, his wide brow revealing the source of the intelligence lighting emerald eyes. The light played against the copper coloring of hair pulled back in an unfashionable queue, the severe style only emphasizing the strength of his face. He did not look to be a man easily fooled.

The girl did not flinch at his abrupt motion or under his cynical glare. So close she could count the threads in his lace jabot, she simply clenched her fist tighter and stared back at him.

"It does not matter to me whether you believe or not. You will find out soon enough." At this mention of her coming fate, she blanched, but held her ground. At least this one was not drunk or corpulent, as were so many of the others, although he was of uncertain temper and sardonic humor.

Still angry at finding himself in this situation, Kerry could find no taste for making love to this wretched child, virgin or not, and for the hundredth time he wondered why he had made that final bid. He had no use for another woman in his bed; the ones he had were trouble enough.

"If what you say is true, why did you not make that fact plain? You would have fetched a far higher price for your virtue than any fancy coiffure you make claim to." His hand flicked contemptuously over the maligned object of his attention.

A startled look swept across her young face as she searched his eyes. Ignoring his insult, she questioned, "Why? I have been told often enough these last months that experience is needed for employment. Why would they pay more for my inexperience here?"

Caught by surprise at this evidence of her naiveté, Kerry stared back at her in total amazement that quickly turned to laughter. His features softening with his mirth, his good

humor temporarily restored, he whipped his cloak off and
pulled it about the girl's bare shoulders, completely engulfing
her pitifully slender figure.

"I find it hard to believe such innocence exists in this day
and age, but if you are not being truthful, you are the most
adept liar I have ever faced, and this comes from the descendant of a race renowned for its farfetched tales." Switching
to a faint brogue, he grinned and asked, "Would you be
tellin' me your name, lass?"

Gratefully snuggling into the warmth of his cloak, unable
to understand the change in his mood, the girl returned his
smile hesitantly. "Katherine Devereaux. My father called me
Katy."

His eyebrows rose slightly, whether in surprise or disbelief, she could not discern.

"Well, Katy it is, then. And where is your father now?"
He sat back down at the fireside and studied the huddled
figure in front of him, his broad shoulders straining the fine
material of his well-tailored coat, light flickering across the
highly embossed brocade of his long waistcoat.

Too worried about her own predicament, Katy did not
question the reasoning for a man of his looks and obvious
wealth to be purchasing a mistress. She studied her hands as
she replied obediently to his questioning.

"He is dead, sir, some three months ago."

The auburn head nodded slightly. "And your mother?"

"She died when I was very young."

The catechism continued. "And where have you been
staying since your father died?"

"With friends or neighbors. But times are hard, and they
cannot afford another mouth to feed . . ." She shrugged
lightly beneath the heavy cloak.

"So you thought you would find a lover to support you. A
very romantic notion indeed." Kerry smiled faintly. By Gad,
he was almost coming to believe her. Preposterous as her tale
might be, she did not have the look of a well-used urchin and
her speech was certainly not of the streets—he thought he
even detected a trace of French in her accent.

Katherine lowered her eyes, the fine sweep of lustrous
lashes contrasting with the drawn childish features. "A friend

of mine came here. The man who . . . bought her is most kind. She always has enough to eat, and he keeps her in pleasant rooms. Of course, she is much prettier than I, but still . . . I had hoped, maybe . . .'' The effort of making this much of a confession drained her, and she faltered. Already she knew the foolishness of her hopes; those men down there were not the kind, lonely gentlemen she had imagined, but vicious brutes. Which left her to wonder what perversity brought this gentleman here.

Kerry frowned. ''You thought to set yourself up in comfort as some man's fond mistress and never have to work again, except in bed, of course. Could you not have found more honest employment elsewhere? Had you no relatives to call on? Did you not know the fate of most of those poor creatures down there? Your fate, if I had not bid against that panderer?'' His voice had suddenly turned cold.

''No, sir,'' she replied weakly. ''I have tried these three months or more to find work at anything at all. They look at me and say much as you have tonight. They ask my age and say I am too small or have not enough experience. Why you bid for me, I shall never understand.''

''If I had not, you would have gone to that monstrous piece of humanity who owns one of the most notorious whore-houses on Saffron Hill. Within six months, if you survived, you would be thrown back out on the street, riddled with pox, crippled by the bestiality of his more frequent customers, and wishing you were dead if you retained any sense at all. That was the life you chose when you so idiotically chose a life of leisure.''

His harsh words terrified her. The smoke-filled room below swept through her memory: the stench of unwashed bodies, cruel hands touching her in private places, the knowing smirks on painted faces—these and other images too painful to recall passed swiftly before her eyes, and they widened with horror at the new meaning his words gave the scene.

Kerry watched as violet eyes darkened to near-black. Then, before he knew what was happening, the girl began to sway, violet eyes closed, and she pitched forward in a swoon.

With the swift reaction of an active man, he sprang to catch her, his strong arms encircling her tiny form entirely.

"Devil take it!" he muttered, searching the room for a place to lay the child. "Wake up, lass, I'm not one to be carrying smelling salts or pots of water about me."

Feeling the thin arms beneath his fingers, aware now of smudges under fine eyes and the unnatural frailty of her form, he guessed her faint to be caused as much from hunger as the terror he instilled in her. Whether her tale was true or not was no matter; her dire need was no lie.

She stirred slightly, and he held her closer, as he would a frightened pup, hoping to revive her with his warmth. A man nearly twice the girl's age, he had never married nor held a child in his arms, yet he reacted naturally to the helplessness of this one. As her thick lashes flickered, he was caught in the spell of her youth and knew there was no other choice. He could not bring himself to turn her out in the cold, and it was not a matter of money lost on her purchase.

The coach ride through darkened, snow-clouded streets was a silent one. They sat together for warmth, huddling under a blanket of fur, close, but not touching. Only knowing he could not turn a child loose on a cold night in the midst of an inhospitable London winter, Kerry thought no further.

Katherine was too frightened and confused to think coherently at all. She was cold. It seemed like she had been cold for months, that she would never be warm again. Even the large well-built man beside her, radiating health and vitality, failed to warm her in any way. She tried to imagine what it would be like to lie under his trim, muscular body, but she could not get past his clothing. She was too much in awe of his fine appearance to imagine herself associated with him, even as an object he had bought for his own personal use, to be discarded if unsatisfactory. She hoped he would at least give her a meal before discovering how unsatisfactory she really was. Her belly growled in sympathy.

The driver stopped at a small but fashionably elegant town house, only a dim light in an upper window giving any indication of occupancy. After giving the driver instructions concerning the horses, Kerry guided the girl inside and up the darkened stairs, using a single candle to light the way.

Entering the apartment, Kerry used his candle to light several others, and the room flickered into view. Sparsely furnished with a settee, several comfortably masculine chairs, a beautifully wrought rosewood table, and an overcrowded desk, the room still conveyed its owner's casual wealth and unaffected good taste. Candelabra and several small oils provided the only ornamentation, but the dying fire was the only object of any interest to Katherine. She hurried to warm her hands at its side.

A door opened and a servant entered carrying a bedroom candle. A portly man of about Kerry's height but some thirty years his elder, he seemed surprised to find his master returned and did not notice the small, silent figure hovering by the embers.

"Lord Kerry, sir, I did not expect you back at this hour. Did you persuade young Derwentwater from his foolishness? Let me stoke the fire for you."

As the man turned to his task, his face registered surprise, then went blank at the sight of the huddled, ragged figure on the hearth. At the servant's mention of Kerry's name and title, she had turned enormous eyes of awe to his presence, but remained silent. Now she took the poker from its hook and began to stir the fire while the servant turned questioningly to his employer.

"Well, Betts, it looks as if I not only did not persuade the young gentleman from his foolishness, but fell into some of my own. If you would be so good as to fetch some water to my room, the young lady is in dire need of a bath. While she washes, will you see if there are the makings of a cold supper for us? And you had better see to a cup of hot chocolate for the child. For myself, I fancy something stronger." Kerry moved to the liquor cabinet and poured himself a liberal brandy to prove his words, gulping the first few drinks indiscriminately as he eyed uneasily the small figure now studiously ignoring him.

Warm water and towels were produced, and with an uncertain glance, Betts led the girl to his master's bedroom, removing a long faded green waistcoat from Lord Kerry's wardrobe to cover the girl. With sleeves well below her fingers and buttons only partially down its full length, it would display a scandalous amount of leg, but it would have to suffice under the circumstances. She would be displaying a good deal more than leg before the night was over.

The waistcoat held a distinctly masculine odor and the faint smell of cigar smoke as Katy folded it over her arm. With hesitation now that they were out of his lordship's presence, she dared to question the servant. "Mr. Betts, sir, is he truly a lord?"

At her childishly upraised eyes, the man's features softened. "That he is, miss. Younger son of the Duke of Exeter, and baron in his own right, owing to his mother's estates in Ireland. Will that be all, miss?"

Katherine gulped and nodded, dismissing the servant. Why would a member of the nobility frequent that seamy warehouse of prostitution when there were so many fashionable women available for mistresses? Could he have tastes not easily satisfied by more discriminating women? Knowing only that degrees of perversion existed, she had no knowledge of what they might be. She who had never lain with a man could not even imagine this most natural of acts, and she shivered at the thought of what lay ahead.

It would not do to wonder much, and he had mentioned supper waiting. Quickly stripping, she washed thoroughly, and then immersed her tangled knot of curls in the remaining hot water. He would not be so insulting once her hair was clean.

Upon the child's reentrance to the main room, Kerry rose, brandy glass in hand, and scrutinized her carefully. Katy squirmed under his long gaze.

"I see Betts has found something more comfortable for you to wear," he commented wryly, his eyes lingering overlong on neatly turned ankles. He gestured toward a chair at the now cloth-covered table, its top laden with a variety of cold dishes.

Katy sat, hastily sliding her legs beneath the protective cloth away from his gaze. She was not yet ready to contemplate that part of their bargain. Eyeing the fare hungrily, she waited politely but impatiently for her host to join her, not hearing anything he said while considering which dish to choose first.

A sharp laugh from behind abruptly returned her attention to his words.

"You have not heard a single word I've said, have you? I'll save my lofty speech for some other time. Go ahead, eat, I am not particularly hungry tonight." He gestured shortly at the food, then continued his pacing about the room.

Kerry watched with concern, then amusement, as the child packed away more food than he had seen his sister eat in a week. When her hunger seemed to be somewhat satiated, he returned to sit across from her.

"Would you mind answering a few questions while you eat?"

Katy nodded acknowledgment of his question and waited for him to continue.

"Have you no relatives who would look after you if they knew your plight?" Kerry watched the girl's solemn face for some trace of truth. For all he knew, he was harboring the front for a criminal ring and would be robbed blind by morning, but she looked more the frightened child than the sultry seductress who would first tempt, then drug him. He would take his chances on his judgment.

Katy returned his stare with as much bravery as she could summon. "None that I am aware of, milord. My mother was . . ." She halted, searching for an appropriate phrase. ". . . illegitimate, disowned by both families. Her mother died at childbirth, and she was raised an orphan."

"I see. And your father. You spoke of him earlier. I trust that means you were born in wedlock?" His expression did not change as he thoughtfully examined a piece of cutlery with his fingers, keeping his eyes on the girl's face.

"Yes, sir. Of course, sir." She was irate, but bit her tongue, keeping her anger to herself. "It was because he insisted on marrying my mother that his family disinherited him. My mother once told me he was of a noble house in France, a younger son with no property to his name."

Encouraged by his apparent interest, Katy continued. "I don't know all of it. My mother told me when I was very young, and my father refused to speak of it, so perhaps it was more of a daydream of mine or my mother's. But my father never communicated with his family and I doubt if they even know of my existence, any more than I know of theirs; they are more a myth or rumor not to be believed.''

Kerry nodded. ''You have the speech of a person well-educated. Who taught you?''

''My father. He was a very educated man—he could speak both English and French fluently. He loved books, so much so that he made them his living when he found all else closed to him.''

It pained her still to speak of him. Theirs had been a close relationship, and love glowed in her eyes.

Kerry saw the gleam lighting her pitiful face and knew his judgment was not faulty. He spoke softly, encouraging her to continue.

Hunger appeased, coldness fled, Katy took advantage of the first friendly interest she had received in months to pour out her childish paean to a father who had given her love and learning and little else. A man whose intellect comprehended the words he read, but with neither wisdom nor courage to follow them, leading his wife and daughter deeper into poverty while continuing to lead the scholarly life he had led before marriage, unable to make the transformation from thinker to doer.

Surrounded by the books he loved, he hated to part with them. His wife's death while Katy was still young left a gap he filled unsuccessfully, plunging the shop into a morass of debts in his inefficient operation. Lack of any business acumen whatsoever, coupled with his faith in the classics, led him to scorn the romantic novels and pornography that were the mainstay of his competitors, and days would go by without a customer. During this period he began to teach his daughter all the lessons he had learned as a boy, a much broader education than most women ever received.

Living above the bookshop in a dark London back street, watching their income slowly dwindle and their larder disappear, Katy quickly learned the practicalities her father never had the incentive to learn. But by the time she was old enough to apply them, it was too late. Her father's death after a long, debilitating illness left the shop and Katy penniless, the remaining stock and all the cherished personal pieces of her parents' past sold to pay the enormous debts that were her only inheritance. Their creditors were generous enough to leave what few articles of clothing she could wear, relics of a better day cut down to Katy's size, and now even those were gone, pawned for the few small coins needed to eat. She had saved the best for last, hoping to make a good impression while looking for employment, and finally hoping its soft silken material would be seductive enough to attract attention, not realizing how it would be torn to tatters along with her hopes.

Kerry listened quietly to her tale, reading behind her words of love to see the true character of the man she called father, hearing the desperation in her voice as she spoke of these last few months without him. There were probably similiar tales by the thousands out there in the streets, just waiting for someone with the time and interest to listen, but only this one came to Kerry's ears, and it rang with truth.

Exhaustion darkened the circles under the girl's eyes as her story came to an end, and Kerry did not have the heart to question her further.

"I think you had best be off to bed, kitten, before you fall asleep at the table." He tried to speak paternally, realizing he had given little thought to the girl's expectations when he brought her here, knowing she had heard none of his earlier words of reassurance.

Katy did not rise, but continued to study the dregs of her chocolate cup. "May I be allowed one question in return for all I have told you?"

With some amusement, Kerry granted her request, and she looked up to meet his eyes, ignoring the laughter lying just below their surface.

"Why did you buy me?"

The laughter disappeared, and he frowned speculatively as he contemplated the small image occupying the seat across from him, her stare containing more courage than her stature warranted.

"That, my colleen, I cannot readily tell you. Perhaps it was because you have the finest set of violet eyes in all of London, or mayhap I was so sick of such depravity by the time they brought you forward that I had to fight for self-respect. If neither reason is satisfactory, you may search for

one of your own. It could be just as close." He spoke
teasingly, with the faint trace of an Irish lilt he assumed on
such occasions, but his eyes remained reflective.

She looked at him curiously, then returned her attention to
her cup, tilting it sideways and swirling it gently as she
studied its contents. Apparently not finding what she sought,
she set it down sadly, her eyes darkening.

"Are you a witch that reads her future in the bottom of her
cup?" he questioned smilingly.

"An old woman taught me once, this and other things.
Some called her witch, but I found her mostly lonely." She
eyed his brandy glass distastefully. " 'Tis a pity you did not
have tea. I would read you a fine fortune."

He laughed and rose, giving her his hand. "I am after
thinking if you are not a witch, you are a witch's familiar in
the form of a kitten. You have bewitched me enough for one
evening. In the morning you may read all the cups you like."

With his assistance, she rose, carefully keeping the coat
about her, avoiding his eyes. She felt their burning gaze as
she traced her footsteps back to the bedroom alone.

Folding the satin waistcoat over the arm of a chair, she
crawled naked and shivering between the cold sheets. Dry
now, her hair spread in pale golden cascades across the
pillows, but her mind was not on the appearance of her hair.
Almost quizzically she touched her budding young breasts,
but the hard bones of her rib cage were more pronounced.

Mentally comparing herself with the women she had seen
tonight, their voluptuous curves daringly displayed in a variety of poses and states of undress, she knew herself to be
unformed and unappealing. Her fingers tentatively traced
lips that had never been kissed, had never had a desire to try.
She could not understand this need of men for women, and
wondered if this lord would teach her. She should be stirring
with excitement at the thought, but the only need she felt
within her was that for sleep, and as she waited for him to
appear, she succumbed to its call, falling into the untroubled
slumber of youth.

When Kerry appeared in the doorway much later, restless
and unable to sleep on the hard settee, he found an angelic

image of innocence curled on his pillow, her hair forming a golden halo about the smooth face, lined only by the dark length of lashes against her cheek. He smoothed the covers more tightly about her shoulders and gently closed the door.

December 1732–October 1733

THE NEXT DAY, Katherine woke to the luxury of sunshine and the astonishing discovery that she was alone. Her hands flew over her untouched body with joy, and then her gaze fell on the undented pillow next to her, and she knew Lord Kerry had never been there at all.

The day became a constant stream of revelations after that. Finding a gown of fine printed rosebuds and a matching underskirt beside the bed, Katy dressed hastily in its luxuriant folds, smoothing the tiny laced bodice over her small figure, reveling in the amazing fit and the exquisiteness of the lace flounces.

A benevolent Betts served her breakfast at her appearance in the main room, and a remarkably jovial Lord Kerry joined her shortly thereafter, flinging his cloak and hat to the floor with a cheery greeting, his expression triumphant at the sight of his new protégée rapidly entrancing his solemn manservant.

"Miss Devereaux, you look enchanting this morning. Have you had breakfast?"

Delighted to find this jolly creature replacing the sardonic one of the night before, Katherine replied with equal good humor, "I am just beginning, thank you. Do I not still remind you of your spaniel, then?"

Kerry choked on his drink, and Betts, knowing his master's penchant for bluntness, made haste to depart, a grin growing on his broad face. The tyke showed some sign of spunk after all.

"I can see you have quickly overcome your shyness," Kerry observed dryly, sipping his tea. "Perhaps I should find a better topic. As I understand it, you have a smattering of learning, but not enough to earn a living as a governess, even if you were old enough to try. By the way, what was the date of your birth?" he asked casually, still uncertain as to the truth of her age.

"May 22, 1717, and I have a baptismal certificate to prove it," Katy replied defiantly, guessing his disbelief.

"Do you now? And would you be hiding it in your petticoat perhaps?" His eyebrow quirked inquiringly with a hint of amusement.

Katy blushed gracefully at this reminder of the state he had found her in. He was well aware of how little she possessed. "No, milord, I hid a few books and trinkets from the auctioneers and left them with a friend. My parents' marriage papers and my baptismal certificate are with them. I would not lie to you."

"All right, Katy, I believe you. You will have to tell me how to find your friend, and I will have someone retrieve them for you. I do not wish you to be parted from your few possessions."

Her eyes widened. Did this mean he intended to keep her after all?

Kerry read her expression and chose to ignore it. Charmed by this spectacle of childish naiveté in a room where he had entertained the most sophisticated and jaded of society's ladies, Kerry could not resist continuing his little game. "Go tend to your hair. We have an outing to make and I am growing impatient to be off."

A wise child, Katy took him at his word and hurried to tie her hair into some semblance of order. The whims of nobility were well known and best obeyed; she was in no position to quarrel. Still, he did not look too cruel, and his humor had improved remarkably overnight.

Surreptitiously, from behind lowered lashes, she studied the sculptured contours of Lord Kerry's face as they descended the stairs to the waiting carriage. Perhaps he wasn't handsome in the classic fashion: his reddish hair in its unforgivable queue prevented that, and the greenish glint of his slightly slanted eyes detracted from any suave attempt at good looks. He appeared to be always laughing quietly at whatever he observed, and the small wrinkles at the corners of his eyes only served to confirm this impression. But his square jaw and thin, firm mouth told of a stubborn and probably proud character. No, she wouldn't wish to try his temper too far.

To Katy's fascination, the afternoon was spent in a hectic whirl at a mantuamaker's. Following Kerry's insistence on simple styles and materials, the seamstress hastily basted a variety of small gowns and undergarments while attempting to pump Katy on her relation to his lordship. Not knowing herself, Katy could not satisfy the woman's inquisitiveness. When asked for decisions on laces or materials, she was at a loss to reply, until finally, so many questions had to be forwarded to Lord Kerry that he stormed the cubicle to point out materials and patterns, consenting to most of the suggestions made except the more extravagant and unsuitable. He seemed to take no notice of his embarrassed, half-dressed protégée until, the last suggestion agreed upon, he turned to leave with a roguish wink in her direction.

Supplying the trunk for those items ready to be carried off, Kerry directed its placement in the carriage before returning to a thoroughly flustered Katherine. Clad now in a simple serge mantle instead of Kerry's cloak, she took his offered arm and ascended silently into the waiting carriage. As the carriage pulled away, she turned to a smiling Lord Kerry with tears of despair in her eyes. Kerry's benevolent smile faded.

At his questioning look, she replied, "I do not understand, your lordship. Last night you condemned my poor choice of occupations and made no use of the services your money purchased, yet today you have spent more money on me than I can ever hope to repay from my wages in any other employment. Would it be too presumptuous of me to inquire about your intentions?"

Surprised by tears instead of the smiles of joy and gratitude he had anticipated, it took Kerry a moment to recover his thoughts. Then, realizing he had met a street cynicism to match his more cosmopolitan one, he understood her difficulty. Her golden hair still hung about her shoulders in a natural disarray, and he shook his head in amazement that such angelic innocence could cover so wordly a mind.

"My dear suspicious kitten, let me attempt to allay your suspicions as you have mine, then perhaps we can be friends." Bright violet eyes fastened intently on him as he spoke.

"Some friends of mine, old retainers of the family, actually, have asked me if I know of anyone who could assist in their shop." This was just a small lie; he had asked first, and they had agreed they could use more help, but he felt the end had justified the means. "Mary Dublin is probably one of England's finest pastry cooks, and George is a good man, not overly educated perhaps, but he runs his bakery well—well enough to need some occasional assistance while his wife bakes. They have no children of their own, and they were delighted with the idea of a live-in assistant. I believe they will be fine company for you, and at the same time provide you with the employment you need. Do you have any objections?"

Violet eyes widened as she stared up into his, their lashes suddenly growing moist with tears. "No, your lordship," she whispered. "But what of the money you have spent? How can I ever repay you? I have given you nothing in return for all your kindness."

"A mistress would have cost me a good deal more than you have, kitten, and would have been considerably more trouble. Let's just call this a favor from one younger son to another. Your father may be in no position to return the favor, but perhaps his daughter can pass it on someday." He smiled benevolently and tugged a golden curl to produce a returning smile.

The remainder of the ride was spent in silence as Katherine attempted to compose herself and become accustomed to this unexpected turn in her destiny. The night before, she had

been prepared to give herself and her virginity to this imposing nobleman who sat beside her, and now—after having
slept in his bed, accepted his hospitality and his costly gifts—
she was to make herself a stranger to him once more. She had
no illusions about her place in society or his offer of friendship; she was so far below him as to make the opportunity of
meeting him again almost nil. This thought inexplicably sad-
dened her.

Their arrival in a modest bourgeois side street of shops and
taverns was almost an anticlimax. With little fanfare, Katy's
box was unloaded and she was introduced to Mary and
George Dublin and shown to her new room. When she returned downstairs, Lord Kerry was gone.

Suspicions allayed by Lord Kerry's assurances, Katherine
delved into this new life given her, with the fervor of one
rescued from the certainty of hell.

The Dublins treated her as a long-lost daughter and she
returned their affection with equal measures of eagerness and
ability. Rising before dawn to help in the kitchens, she spent
afternoons selling the wares she helped bake in the mornings.
In return, the Dublins urged her to eat well and often created
special treats just for their new "daughter," to "fatten her up
a little bit."

Under their care, Katy's childish frailty blossomed into
young womanhood, and by spring she was letting out the bod-
ices of her new gowns to accommodate her new development.

Still, despite her new maturity, Katy's height remained
diminutive, and she frowned at the delicately drawn features
reflected in her tiny mirror. Her pale coloring and overlarge
violet eyes would never reach the perfection of the magnifi-
cently powdered and painted beauties of society, nor even the
wanton vividness of the girls on the street.

Ruefully inspecting her small upturned nose and dainty
pink mouth framed by unruly wisps of fine spun gold, Katy
tried to imagine a daring beauty patch placed right between
these tiny features and laughed heartily at the image. If her
destiny were to be clerk or governess, her looks were well
suited to the part.

The arrival of two handsomely bound gilt-edged volumes
of Swift and Voltaire on her birthday, along with a note from

Lord Kerry to his "kitten" with comments on the reasons he chose the cynical satires to send to a sixteen-year-old, instead of more conventional romantic novels, brought a crisis of homesick tears which Katy fought valiantly.

With characteristic decision, she sent a polite letter of thanks accompanied by a small sketch of a smiling kitten in witch's pointed hat curled about a volume of Voltaire while gleefully perusing an open page of Swift. A short note at the bottom of the sketch explained the accompanying letter was for public consumption and if Lord Kerry wished her real opinion of the aptness of the gift, he would have to wait until she read the books. With the same mischievousness that gleamed in the kitten's eye, Katy added she was certain Voltaire—being French—would have more appeal than any upstart Irishman.

The impulsive note was quickly forgotten in the rush of days and her absorption in the biting satire of Swift (who, despite her words to the contrary, she read greedily). Lord Kerry remained an enchanted reprieve from a frightening nightmare, though the Dublins' constant gossip and tales of his family painted a more realistic picture.

Katy listened to the stories of Lord Kerry's aristocratic family with the same spellbound interest she had given to her father's fairy tales. The Dublins had worked for the powerful duke under both his first wife and his second, Kerry's young Irish mother. They had left soon after the birth of Kerry's younger sister, Brigitte, but they retained their avid interest in the family's doings.

So it was that Katy heard of all Lord Kerry's rakish escapades and wondered at the difference between the kind man she had met and the dissolute rakehell of the gossip. His appearance at the opera with two ladies on either arm, one the prince's mistress, kept tongues wagging most of the summer. Before that particular night was over, he had broken the bank at a high-stakes gaming table, been challenged to a duel by the brother of one of the ladies he accompanied, and settled it by choosing flagons of ale as the weapons and drinking the other man under the table. Katy did not find the tale as amusing as the remainder of London did.

But whatever her doubts about her protector's character,

they quickly fled at Lord Kerry's appearance at an unreason-
able hour early one brilliant October morning. It was evident
even to the unsophisticated sixteen-year-old that his lordship
had been out all night, the shadow of his beard staining his
cheeks, his stockings mud-spattered, and the heels of his
buckled shoes showing the effects of city streets. But his
forest-green coat and white satin waistcoat were neatly but-
toned and topped by faultless linen, the fall of lace at his
sleeves only slightly the worse for wear.

Taking a step inside the doorway, he switched his ebony
walking stick to the opposite hand and let the brilliant morning sunshine fall on the girl behind the counter. In contrast to
himself, she personified the freshness of the morning, her
open, inviting smile greeting him like the dawn. Her crisp
cotton gown was sprigged with small green flowers and
cinched in by a rose bodice, unadorned by either neckerchief
or fichu, leaving the creamy skin of her oval neckline exposed to his gaze. Not expecting his call, she had allowed her
hair to go unpinned, and it hung now in gilded curls about her
shoulders.

The sun from the doorway struck the fine gold hairs about
her face, emphasizing dark eyes wide with astonishment, and
the faint blush of color staining her cheeks from the heat of
the bakery. Kerry came to a sudden halt in almost total
amazement.

Quick inspection revealed the curves straining at the girl's
laced bodice and he realized the child he had dropped at the
door nine months before was rapidly becoming a most interesting young woman. His intentions of erasing a night's
debauchery with the innocence of the purveyor of "notes for
public consumption" quickly evolved into a determination to
sweep the slate clean and start afresh.

"Top o' the mornin', kitten," he proclaimed grandly with
a wide, sweeping bow, a cynical quirk to his brow as he noted
her confusion. "I trust you've had sufficient time to judge the
superiority of Swift to Voltaire?"

With sudden nervousness at this apparition of her fantasies,
Katy colored deeper. How presumptuous he must have thought
her! The note had seemed appropriate at the time, but the

dashing, aristocratic gentleman before her with his air of bored dissolution was not the man she remembered.

Still, he waited, hat in hand, for her reply, and she stuttered nonsensically, "I regret my impertinence, milord. The gifts were most appreciated."

Kerry grimaced and advanced further into the shop, studying her bent head with more than casual interest. "I did not come to see the author of notes for public consumption, but the wicked artist of the kitten sketch. Where have you hidden her?"

Katy glanced up quickly and caught the mischievous gleam in his eye and her heart raced a little faster. The laughing gentleman had returned, disguised behind that air of dissolute nobility. She did not know what had prompted his surprising visit or what he had been doing with himself, and she did not want to know. She only wished to express her heartfelt gratitude for the kindness that had placed her here.

"She's much too wicked to appear in public, milord. How can I extend her thanks without being any more presumptuous than I have been?"

The waking smile on rosy lips and in violet eyes brought sunrise to a dismal night and Kerry threw sense and caution to the winds. "You can thank me with one of those tempting pastries and your company. The stench of the city offends me on a day like this. Would you care to take a ride to the country?"

It wasn't much of a decision. Katy discarded her apron and disappeared into the kitchen, returning with George Dublin. He gave Kerry's dissipated state a thoughtful glance, but the young lord had his rights, and he only nodded a greeting of respect. Kerry met this stern greeting with a grim glare, then returned his attention to Katy's graceful quickness as she gathered pastries and bread and wrapped them carefully.

The baker watched silently as his lordship led the young girl to a waiting carriage. As they lurched off, he prayed the wench knew what she was about.

Katy prayed the same thing when it became apparent Lord Kerry's mood ran dangerously near some unseen precipice. He raced the mettlesome thoroughbreds through city streets just beginning to wake with life. Shop clerks and market peddlers dashed out of his way as he drove over mud-caked cobblestones with the single-mindedness of a prisoner bent on escape.

The outskirts of town were a dismal hell of darkened narrow streets and wide open lakes of sewage, breaking into mud flats and hovels of a dangerous nature. Kerry paid no heed to the dangers of cutthroats and thieves, but raced madly onward toward the ripening fields of farmland beyond.

Never having been outside London in her life, Katy eagerly turned her attention to the sight of harvesters gathering sheaves of golden wheat in the surrounding fields. The day was too exhilarating to be disturbed by the nobleman's madness, and the wild rush down country lanes suited her mood. She hung on while the wind whipped at her hair and a smile of delight lit her face as she let the day wipe away past terrors.

As the city fell behind them, Kerry allowed the horses' pace to slow to a canter and cast a sideways glance at his companion. Her enchanting smile as she handed him a pastry brought the world back into perspective again, and Lord Kerry accepted the flaky offering hungrily.

When they had totally consumed every crumb of the tasty meal, Kerry relaxed and sought to draw out the silent figure beside him.

"Have they been treating you well, then, kitten?"

Violet eyes reluctantly pulled away from the harvest scenes at the roadside to rest cautiously on the angular profile of the half-Irish nobleman. She feared the mocking devil in his eyes and remained wary of his intentions, but his expression now contained only interest and a touch of amusement. She replied with her usual frankness.

"The Dublins pamper me, my lord, as if I truly am some pet kitten. I do not know what you told them, but to return their affections I feel I should purr, only I would much rather earn my keep."

Kerry chuckled. "You look well fed and content. I scarcely recognized the scrawny kitten I remembered."

"And you, my lord? Are you content?" she asked cautiously, sensing the troubled spirit behind his rakish exterior. He seemed a man to have everything—wealth, looks, intelligence, and a loving family—but he seemed far from content with his good fortune.

Kerry cast her a quizzical glance, then, noting the sincerity of violet eyes, shrugged lightly. "That is an odd question for a young girl to ask on a pleasure outing. Are you reading fortunes again?"

"Pardon my rashness, my lord. I knew the nobility lived loftier lives than the rest of us, but I did not realize that your world is not so beset with problems as ours," she replied scornfully.

"You have the mind of a wizened monk disguised behind that innocent facade, Miss Devereaux. My life is no more noble than yours—less so, if the truth be known."

"Then why do you not change it? Surely the whole world must lie open at your feet, to choose from as you would."

A wry smile twisted his lips as he looked down on the golden head at his side. "A younger son must make his own way in the world, kitten. He is expected to represent the family in the military or in politics and to marry a wealthy heiress to breed potential heirs and support him. Those are the choices from which I must choose."

Katy mulled that over for a while, imagining the highly volatile and half-wild Lord Kerry as a ramrod-straight officer of the cavalry or a dark-suited, smooth-spoken politician, and the picture made her smile. When not on the field of battle, she suspected the officer would spend most of his time in the stockade. The politician would let his tongue fly once too often and find himself counting pigeons from the Tower's loftiest cells.

"You do seem to be in a bit of a predicament, my lord," she replied softly, attempting to hide the grin flirting at the corners of her lips.

Kerry caught the amusement in her voice and broke into a wide grin. "You've divined for yourself, then, that I am not of the military cut of life? You must be a witch indeed. Or have the Dublins been carrying tales of my brief sojourn with the army in the colonies?"

"I have heard few tales of that part of your past, but your present has been much related, at least those parts thought suitable to a maiden's ear. I dare not imagine what is kept from me.''

"My behavior has been inexcusable," he agreed in response to Katy's dry words. "When I first came to London from looking after my Irish estates, while still in my idealistic youth, I thought I could institute some reforms by going into politics. But I pride myself on not being a stupid man, and it did not take long to discover that unless I was willing to court royalty, I would never have any power."

"And with a tongue like yours, you could never court royalty, even if you had the patience, which you don't," Katy concluded for him. "And if asked for an opinion, you would give your own and not the one expected of you. You would be a valuable man if they would only listen."

"Thank you, my dear," he replied gravely. "I will use your recommendation if I should ever amend my way of life." Drawing the carriage to a halt at a small roadside inn, he excused himself and promised immediate return.

Katy stared around her with curiosity, wondering if she had learned anything at all. She was miles from town, in a totally unfamiliar environment with a man she could scarcely claim to know, with no one to turn to for help. What madness was this? Yet though she stood outside the door of one of the notorious wayside inns of which she had heard such terrible tales, she was not afraid. She greeted Lord Kerry with a trusting smile as he came out.

"I have a surprise for you." With a grin, Lord Kerry caught her waist in his broad, capable hands and lifted her clear of the carriage, swinging her lightly to the ground. Then, stripping off his elegant coat, he threw it back in the carriage and began on the buttons of his waistcoat.

Still tingling from the ease with which he had handled her, Katy stared at this undressing with growing wonder. "Milord, have you taken leave of your senses?"

Stripped to his shirt sleeves, Lord Kerry threw the reins to the innkeeper, who had waddled out after him, and then caught Katy by the waist again, guiding her across the road and away from the inn, much to her relief. He was grinning more like his old self when their feet reached a grassy hillock on the other side and they began to climb. "What's the matter, fair Kate, are you regretting having trusted me this far?''

"No, milord, but you must grant you have given me cause to wonder. Where are you taking me?'' She was grateful when he released her waist and took her hand instead, afraid she would have to quit breathing if he continued the previous arrangement much longer.

"To the fair, Katy, as every good countryman should this time of year. I could not go wearing that getup, now, could I? Now I shall be the miller and you can be the dairy maid and we will go the fair together.'' He helped her over a rocky ledge, strolling to the top of the hill hand in hand.

Below lay a patchwork plaid of colors, dusty lanes striping the tuffets of green grass dotting the spaces between the motley assortment of colored tents and canvases. Roaming among the squares of amusements were small, colorful figures, the reds and yellows standing out in vivid array from this distance. Carnival music drifted up to reach their ears, and the barking of dogs and yells of the peddlers barking their wares intertwined with it. It was a gay panorama of movement and noise, and the most fascinating palette of colors Katy had ever seen.

The breeze billowed out Kerry's light linen shirt, erasing the lines from his face as he took Katy's hand and raced her jubilantly to the bottom of the hill.

It was a day Katy long remembered. Captivated by each new exhibit, she had to be pulled away to be shown the next. She examined the carefully sewn and embroidered linens and bonnets, let Lord Kerry buy ribbons for her hair, had her fortune told by a palm-reading Gypsy that Kerry swore was not a Gypsy at all but a pickpocket in disguise, crowed happily over the horse corral until one farmer became convinced he had his best pony sold, sampled the meat pies and ale with a hunger she had not felt in months. Through it all, Kerry acted as her tour guide, finding the most succulent pies, the prettiest ribbons, the most interesting sights, entranced by the giddiness of genuine delight she displayed at these simplest of pleasures. It had been a long time since he had found a lady so easily pleased.

Her hair bedecked with ribbons, her hunger satiated with

an overabundance of pies, her gaiety enhanced by a trifle too much ale, Katy easily agreed when Kerry suggested it might be getting late and time to leave. The sun lingered low in the western sky as he led her one more time past the gaudy displays, waving their farewells to the barkers who had successfully sold wares to the handsome couple. Clinging to Lord Kerry's hand, stars spinning in her eyes, Katy looked up to her benefactor and gave him a sultry, dazzling smile of happiness.

"Sweet Katy, with a smile like that you have repaid me every coin I have spent. Would that every lady I pleased would smile on me like that. Would that I could please every lady so easily," he added ruefully.

"Any lady who failed to be pleased with you, sir, has no right to be called a lady. I deny womanhood to anyone finding you lacking in any way," Katy proclaimed grandly.

Kerry laughed. "You have probably stripped half London of its sex by that statement, innocent. What are the men to do now?"

"You have such a large following and they are all displeased with you? You have been naughty, haven't you?" She tugged at his hand, grinning impishly. This was heady excitement loosening her tongue, and she would not take back a word of it.

"It is only at being naughty that I am good. There is no pleasing the fairer sex, or so I thought until today." He swung her hand freely, not caring that his title required her respect and his dignity.

"Then you have been seeing the wrong ladies, milord. May I suggest that the stuffy drawing rooms of society are the wrong place to be looking?"

"You may suggest what you will, minx, but it is in those stuffy drawing rooms that I am required to find a wife. My family grows impatient with my dilatoriness. But what of you? How many beaux have you gathered with that breathtaking smile you have just bestowed upon me?"

"I must remember to smile more often, for I have gathered no beaux at all, only the grocer's son, and he must be half-blind to find any attraction in a skinny, plain wench such as I." Katy loosed his hand and ran tauntingly down the street, for he was getting daringly near to a touchy subject. Men turned to stare as she passed, their faces alight with laughter at the teasing glint in her eye, and a cheer went up when Kerry quickly shortened the distance between them and grabbed her firmly by the waist.

"I will turn that skinny, plain wench over my knee if she repeats that stunt. There is danger here, as anywhere, for such plain wenches as you." Now that his hand was about her waist, it lingered there with a will of its own while Kerry gazed down into dancing violet eyes. "Are you trying to tell me that you have reached the ripe old age of sixteen and have never been kissed? I find that hard to believe."

"Believe what you will, milord, but I will tell you now that the grocer's son has not got beyond wishing me a good morning, and that after seeing him every day for months. Not everyone is so forward as you, milord." She tossed her hair peevishly.

"Right you are, miss, and to show how forward I am, I intend to rectify a situation that should have been remedied some time ago. You have grown much too audacious, and if the grocer's son will not give you satisfaction, then I shall." With a firm grip and a swift movement, Lord Kerry spirited her into an alleyway between the last two tents, away from the tumult of the crowds and into the shadows.

"All right, Katy Devereaux, are you prepared for your next lesson?" His eyes were twin green lanterns in the darkness as he faced her, both hands completely encircling her waist.

Suddenly shy at this quick turn of events, Katy tried to move away, but her back came against the tent pole, and he held her too firmly. "I am always willing to learn, milord, but I do not think this lesson is quite proper, is it?"

"Nonsense, every sixteen-year-old should know how to kiss. Do you not have any curiosity at all?"

Kerry spoke with all the authority of his position and she bowed her head shyly at his tone. "I admit to some curiosity, of course, sir. What do I do first?"

The tip of his finger caressed her chin as he lifted it until her eyes met his. "Nothing at all, my love." And he lowered his head until their lips touched and held and a shiver went through them that should not be. With a shudder of half-understood distress, the kiss ended, and Katy's head fell weakly to his shoulder. Lord Kerry rested his chin on the golden nimbus of curls he had been given to protect, and stared bleakly into the nothingness beyond.

Regaining his senses, he moved reluctantly away from the tiny frame resting in his arms, his hand falling back to hers. Silently they retreated to the safety of daylight.

Convinced the emotions summoned by one small kiss had been a momentary aberration brought on by too much malt and too much sun, they soon fell back into their friendly camaraderie, and the ride home found them singing nearly naughty folk songs that Lord Kerry taught her a verse at a time. Giggling as she realized he was making them up as they went along, Katy scarcely knew when they entered her home street, and they made a scandalous arrival at the front door by finishing their verse after the horses came to a stop.

Swinging Katy down from the carriage with growing familiarity, Kerry escorted her into the dusky gloom of the Dublins' front parlor. Any who may have noticed their return gave no sign of it, and Katy moved uneasily from under the glowing lanterns of green eyes. At times like these, his gaze made her exceedingly nervous, though he did nothing to justify the feeling.

"I think, kitten, that I have neglected a very valuable asset among my many possessions. With a little polish, you would grace the finest of homes," he murmured half-teasingly as the sun's last rays set fire to a tendril of gold when she moved away. "Have you given thought to what you want out of life, Katy?"

Katy swung around and regarded him cautiously. "I wish only to make an honest living, milord. I have not thought past that."

"Your wit and beauty are wasted behind a bakery counter, surely you must realize that?" Kerry asked with curiosity, knowing full well the vanity of other women with half her looks.

"Since when have spaniels become the vogue, milord?" Katy asked wryly, not certain if he teased her still.

"I can see you will easily become uncontrollable if not

tamed. I must put my mind to it at once. Come here and
practice today's lesson. A lady who has enjoyed a day's
outing ought certainly to reward her escort.''

Kerry caught her quickly while she hesitated, his hands
sliding with practiced ease about her slender waist. Auburn
hair glinting against the room's dusk, he bent his head until
his lips met Katy's, and her hands slipped of their own accord
about his neck.

His mouth seared like a burning brand against hers, an
instant's work, but a lifetime's seal. Without pressing for
more, Kerry lifted his head, smiled deeply into bewildered
violet pools, and departed in the same manner as he had
come.

Katy was left with the heat of his touch impressed upon her
memory forever and nothing stronger to grasp.

October–December 1733

KERRY'S PARTING WORDS came back to her full force a few days later when Mary Dublin called her to the parlor and introduced Katherine to a thin-lipped, plain-spoken spinster by the name of Belinda Greene.

"Lord Kerry says ye're to mind Miss Greene and learn what she has to teach ye." Mary Dublin smiled approvingly as the tutor looked over her new student and made arrangements to visit each afternoon. Neither woman expressed any surprise at his lordship's generosity, and Katy stared between them with growing apprehension.

Under Belinda's expert questioning, Katy revealed her fluency in French, her command of literature, and her woeful understanding of math. The latter provided no concern, since a lady had no need of such knowledge, and Katy's aptitude for drawing more than compensated for her lack of other talents. Based on a sound foundation from her father's extensive art library, Katy's lightninglike strokes produced remarkable caricatures and sketches whose wicked nature was not in the least childlike.

Deciding polish was, indeed, all Katy lacked, Belinda

concentrated on her knowledge of the social graces. If Lord
Kerry wished a well-turned-out young lady, dance, manners,
and etiquette were of the utmost importance.

During this time, they had no word from Lord Kerry, and
there were no further tales carried of his revelry. Rumor had
him attending all the appropriate social functions with a lady
not his mistress.

Katy mused over these rumors, remembering Kerry's scorn
for the ladies of his acquaintance. If only she could meet
these women he escorted, she could tell him whether they
were right for him or not, but he would never believe such
sorcery. Only Katy believed in her ability to see characters as
other people see paintings. But where Kerry was concerned,
she was convinced if anyone could see clearly the woman to
love him, it would be herself.

So Katy greeted the letter that came at the end of October
with as much delight as did Belinda, but for entirely different
reasons. In it came Lord Kerry's instructions for Katy's
introduction to the opera, his box to be available to them one
night a week, his carriage at their call, and Katy to be
gowned appropriately. For Belinda it was a chance to see her
beloved opera once again, an opportunity not often open to
her. For Katy it was a chance to meet the women Lord Kerry
must choose among for a wife. It was too good an opportunity to reject, even if it meant entering that society she
scorned.

Gowned in a royal-blue velvet mantua, its sumptuous folds
falling back over a white satin petticoat embroidered in matching blue silk, the tightly cinched bodice broken by a fall of
fine lace from the low neckline to her waist, Katy dressed for
the opera as simply as Belinda would allow. Like Kerry, she
disdained powder and wigs, and only a pinner of white lace
crowned the halo of golden curls.

They arrived early, unlike the more fashionable *beau monde*,
who continued to arrive throughout the next act. By that time
Belinda was too enrapt in the familiar story to point out the
new arrivals to Katy, leaving Katy to study them alone. She
had already devoured the program and dismissed the Italian
opera as hopeless, for she had no interest in the elaborate
costumes or the exaggerated arias of the singers, and the story

line was too nonsensical to consider. So she bent her attentions to sorting out names and faces and placing them in the
gossip she had garnered from Belinda and other sources. But
her knowledge was too limited and the theater too dark and
she was finally forced to admit defeat. If she could not do
better than this, these trips would be useless except to pacify
Belinda, which was probably his lordship's intention after all.
She sighed resignedly to herself.

Kerry's unexpected arrival in their box at intermission sent
Katy's heart skipping erratically, but his nonchalant reference
to the lady waiting below brought her eyes around in the
direction indicated. Two angry faces looked upward at her,
and under Katy's steady gaze the older woman began to
whisper furiously to the younger, whose beautiful cold countenance looked quite peeved.

Uneasily Katy turned to Lord Kerry. "Are you displeasing
the ladies again, or am I the one they are frowning at?"

"Both, my colleen, but don't let that bother you too greatly.
Lady Elizabeth presumes too much on our rather nebulous
relationship. She will soon learn her jealousy entices me
not."

He gestured to Belinda, indicating two smirking ladies
trying to capture her attention. "Bring them up, Belinda, and
let's get this over with. We shall establish Katy's reputation
properly."

In amazement, Katy listened as his lordship introduced her
as his ward to the two old gossips and their escorts. They
made effusive compliments on the "lovely young woman
they had heard so much about," but Katy scarcely heard
them. Ward? Who would believe that? Kerry was neither so
old nor so trustworthy as to be justified in placing a young
girl in his hands as ward. But he was surely aware of that.
She waited for the next blow to fall.

Other minds were quickly coming to these same conclusions, and they were not so reticent as Katy. The baroness
spoke her doubts first.

"You can't tell me, your lordship, that anyone would leave
this lovely creature in your care. Why not your father's? Or at
least Burlington's?"

Lord Kerry smiled, his hand resting lightly at the back of

Katy's seat as he spoke. "My brother finds our joint duties tedious and time-consuming, since he cannot be in London often, but you are right, Miss Devereaux is the ward of James as well as me. Her late brother was a friend of ours and he left the remainder of his father's estate rather impoverished, but we promised to see to her education, and dear Belinda has come to our aid. I do not know what we would do without her." He bowed gallantly in the direction of the astonished governess.

Katy was no less astonished at this acquisition of a brother as well as an estate of any kind, but she continued to smile demurely with downcast eyes as Lord Kerry spun his tale. What his brother would say when he found himself guardian to a girl he barely knew existed, she could scarcely contemplate.

Curiosity momentarily satisfied—until they located Lord Burlington, at least—their visitors soon departed, leaving Lord Kerry smiling serenely over his invited guests.

"Thank you, Belinda, your friends never fail to amuse me." His tone was caustic, but it changed as he turned to his silent protégée. "Well, kitten, you are now fairly launched into the edge of society, and your reputation will be what you make of it." He spoke softly, as if only to her, his eyes holding hers for a moment.

Blue darkened to violet as she frowned up at him. "Lord Kerry, I have no wish to be launched anywhere, especially at the mercies of such lies. It does not matter to me what people think, so long as I know I am not guilty, but to be party to your lies would not leave my conscience clear. What will happen when your brother finds out about his supposed guardianship?"

"Damn, I had no idea I was dealing with a pristine conscience." Kerry raised a quizzical eyebrow while regarding the origin of this new development. "To all intents I am your guardian, and, my little saint, my brother knows of my tale. He is vastly amused and will keep quiet so long as my intentions are honorable. Those were his exact words. Now, are you satisfied?" He leaned on his walking stick and stared down harder at her.

Bravely Katy returned his gaze. "I have no brother or

estate and will say so if asked. Perhaps I had better stay home
with the Dublins.''

Kerry sighed exaggeratedly and turned to Belinda. ''You
will see that she attends the opera as directed and behaves
herself accordingly. Someone has to show her that life exists
outside those confounded books of hers. Now the curtain is
about to go up, so I must leave. Good evening.'' And without
a backward look at Katy, he left.

In the following weeks Lord Kerry's behavior toward his
''ward'' was all that polite society could wish, consisting of a
circumspect visit during intermission at their once-weekly
public appearance. Katy's cool demeanor and Lord Kerry's
aloof politeness almost convinced the wary Belinda that her
original suspicions of her cousin's intentions were unwar-
ranted. But she quickly became sensitive to the silent current
of communication flowing between the disparate pair.

Always eager for any new diversion, a steady stream of
society's curiosity seekers made themselves known to this
amusing new obligation of the Southerland family. Confirmation by the staid and upright Lord Burlington of Katy's
guardianship gave her a foot into aristocratic circles, and
many were those who wished to take advantage of it. Upon
Lord Kerry's advice, any invitations Belinda accepted from
these social climbers were for herself and not for Katy. The
one night a week at the opera was sufficiently educational for
a girl in Katy's position. She was not marriage material, and
young gallants who began to attend her knew it.

To be the temporary toast of bored young men was amusing, but Katy found few worth sharpening her wits on. Their
flattery leaving her unimpressed, their gossip of little interest,
she declined their invitations with little regret. She knew
where they would lead and she had no desire to give up her
present life for that of mistress—she was no longer that
hungry. Lord Kerry observed these debates placidly, with a
hint of secret amusement, but said nothing to encourage or
discourage her suitors.

These intermissions swiftly became a game to the bored
nobleman and his quick-witted protégée. With all society

watching their every move and word, including the disapproving Lady Elizabeth and her mother in their box, they
could say or do little to compromise the relationship they had
forged for the public eye. Instead, they communicated subtly,
capturing nuances of expressions or tones, making plays on
words that only the two of them could understand, leaving
their companions to gape in bewilderment when they broke
into laughter for no discernible reason. Only Belinda suspected the truth, and she frowned with disapproval at each
outburst.

As the weeks wore on, Belinda's nerves wore to a frazzle,
in the certainty that Katy was headed for a disaster she could
not divert. The youngster was no match for the audacious
Lord Kerry, who dangled his unannounced fiancée on a string
while playing with his latest toy. Yet all the governess's
admonitions about Kerry's formal courtship of the Lady Elizabeth fell on deaf ears.

Katy had no need of Belinda's subtle warnings. The Lady
Elizabeth possessed title, wealth, and beauty, and Kerry courted
her with every intention of making her his wife. Of this, she
did not have to be told. But the Lady Elizabeth also had a
spoiled disposition and an evil temper, and if Lord Kerry
were to marry such a termagant, he would need a sympathetic
listener. In gratitude, she would serve his lordship in any way
she could.

Belinda gave up the battle with a sigh. These deft character
portrayals of Katy's were becoming notorious, even beyond
her small circle. The time she refused to speak anything but
French to one of England's worst rakehells, driving that
obnoxious young gallant from the box in an embarrassed
fluster, had sent Lord Kerry into whoops of laughter. Having
complete comprehension of the outrageous lies Katy had
spouted in French, he reprimanded her for her bilingual hy-
pocrisy, and promised to lie only in French himself from now
on. But he found continual amusement in producing various
characters for Katy's discerning judgment, and stories of her
accuracy quickly swept the coffeehouses of London. Whether
she be witch or no, none dared question, but one rogue
never dared show face in that box again, and several others

avoided it assiduously. The Lady Elizabeth's shallow character never stood a chance among such competition.

Yet, in a way, it was Lady Elizabeth who eventually brought about Katy's downfall, though the good lady would never come to know it. It began innocuously enough when the door to Katy's box swung open at the end of intermission before Lord Kerry had time to leave.

Kerry's irritated greeting caused Katy to turn. In the doorway stood a tall, rather ungainly young gentleman dressed in white. His haughty expression was enhanced by his manner of looking down his large and slightly hooked nose; protuberant icy gray eyes completed the unpleasant impression.

Katy shivered under his gaze and scarcely heard the flow of conversation over her head until she realized Kerry was making introductions.

"Miss Devereaux, I don't believe you have had the pleasure of meeting Mr. Joshua Halberstam, son of Sir Robert Halberstam." Casually Lord Kerry gestured to the waiting gentleman. "Joshua, this is my ward, Miss Katherine Devereaux."

Appraising eyes swept over Katy's low décolletage and tiny waistline before coming back to rest thoughtfully on violet pools. "Charmed, I'm sure." he bent briefly over Katy's hand, the coldness of his touch sending shivers up her arm.

As he turned that icy gaze to Lord Kerry, Katy suddenly understood the true nature of the stranger's coldness, and she froze into immobility as the two men continued their conversation.

"And what shall I tell the Lady Elizabeth?" Halberstam barely disguised a grimace of distaste as he faced his opponent.

"Tell her I'll return when I'm damned good and ready. If she does not choose to meet my ward, she will have to bide her time until I am done." Perched on the railing, Lord Kerry made no motion to move as the curtains of the next act began to rise.

Halberstam's expression at this curt dismissal was quickly hidden in polite farewells, but Katy refused to meet the eyes of either man as he took his leave. Even after he was gone and Lord Kerry turned to ask her opinion of this character, she continued to stare out into the darkened theater.

"If your lordship does not mind, I would prefer to keep my opinion to myself."

Belinda sighed in exasperation at this sudden reticence. Even she knew Lord Kerry detested Joshua Halberstam. The two had been at constant odds since childhood, starting with an argument over Halberstam's ill treatment of a puppy and continuing on in competition over the same fickle females, whom Lord Kerry inevitably won. Joshua had deliberately set about undermining anything Kerry accomplished, his sharp tongue carrying most of the malevolent rumors following Kerry about. Only excessive caution on Joshua's part in avoiding insulting his rival to his face had prevented Kerry from calling him out. Kerry was well known to be the better of the two at swords, and pistols were to the taste of neither man. Katy could have criticized this one to her heart's content without offending anyone.

But Lord Kerry did not let her off the hook so easily. "His lordship does mind; he wishes for an honest opinion from his talented sorceress. What do you make of Joshua Halberstam?"

With indignation at this demand, Katy faced him abruptly. "I will give you my opinion, milord, but I do not promise you will like it. That man has a devious nature, as convoluted as yours. In your case, I am willing to trust the depths; in his case, it would be deadly to do so. The man is a menace and a danger to your well-being, if not to your life. Will that satisfy your lordship?" she asked sharply.

For once, Kerry was silenced. Looking down into the elfin face whose angelic innocence was so deceiving, he studied the grim expression behind the violet eyes and the stubborn set of her chin. Then he nodded. "Yes, that answers my question. I believe I asked for that. Perhaps I had best join the ladies before my devious friend implies more than my message intended. Good night, kitten." And without further word, he departed.

"Have I offended him again, Belinda?" Katy asked quietly, not understanding the turmoil she felt whenever he left like that.

"I think not," Belinda answered brusquely. "But I am

beginning to wonder if you are not the sorceress he claims
you are," And with that oblique remark she explained the
relationship between his lordship and his so-called "friend."

Subdued by her last encounter with Lord Kerry, anxious
when he did not appear when they next attended the opera,
Katy sought solace from her troubled thoughts by drawing
closer to Belinda. With better care than before, she practiced
the lessons her teacher set for her, and their rebellious relationship slowly developed into a strange friendship.

When Katy's disrespectful attitude toward the society to
which Lord Kerry had introduced her abated to a small
degree, Belinda breathed a sigh of relief. In hopes of maintaining this conciliatory behavior, Belinda began to answer
Katy's penetrating questions instead of ignoring them.

So when her precocious student once again broached the
topic of Kerry's reasons for wishing her to know the ways of
his world, Belinda did not brush the question aside, but
hesitated, debating the depth of her answer.

"Katy, I would answer you honestly, if I could, but it
would be based primarily on conjecture. Kerry has not, in so
many words, specified his reasoning."

Lord Kerry's covered carriage rolled sedately through midnight streets, carrying them from the world of society to
Katy's modest abode. The incongruity of the sparkling world
she had just left and the shadowed, narrow side street
where she lived struck her forcibly each time they traversed
them, but tonight Katy had the need to know some answers.
Once again, Lord Kerry had not appeared, and she had felt
the flow of whispers and knowing smirks around her more
forcefully than before.

"But his actions have some meaning to you that they do
not to me. I would know your opinion, Belinda," Katy
replied quietly, watching her teacher's shadowed face in the
silent shroud of the carriage's darkness.

"You may not like it, Katherine. You are young and
innocent yet. It may well be best to wait upon his lordship to
explain."

"I am not so innocent as you would believe, Belinda. Lord
Kerry has been more than kind to me and I cannot believe he
would harm me or go against my wishes. I only wish to know

what is expected of me, so I might have some better understanding of how to behave. The position I am in is most
awkward, neither betwixt nor between.''

Belinda nodded thoughtfully, understanding what the girl
meant. It did not mean she would take her explanations any
easier.

''I know nothing of what was between you and Kerry
before I came, so perhaps what I am about to say is nothing
new to you. It is only my supposition, based on Lord Kerry's
instructions for your tutoring.''

Katy waited for Belinda to continue, her gloved fingers
entwining themselves tightly with each other.

''There is a custom on the Continent, though not quite so
prevalent here, for gentlemen to provide for the support of
young, personable girls like yourself.''

Katy heard the hesitation in her teacher's voice and did not
flinch beneath Belinda's inquiring look, waiting for the words
she feared would follow next.

When Katy said nothing, Belinda continued. ''Rather than
let the girls live a life of poverty or be wasted on the streets, a
gentleman might make some payment toward the girl's upbringing or purchase her outright from her parents. He sees
that she is suitably trained and cared for and kept protected . . .''

''And?'' Katy prompted, waiting for the words to confirm
her fears.

Belinda sighed and borrowed Katy's Gallic shrug. ''And
when the girl becomes a young lady of suitable presence, she
pays for her care by becoming the gentleman's mistress.''

Urged on by Katy's dangerous silence, Belinda hastened to
add, ''Lord Kerry is a man of the world. He knows he must
marry a woman with breeding and wealth and he has found
that woman, as I have tried to make you see. At the same time,
he is much too accustomed to enjoying the pleasures of
charming women to be satisfied with that icicle he has settled
upon. He can be assured she will not make a cuckold of him;
I suppose that is important to a man, but of a certainty, she
will raise a hideous scandal if he attempts to carry on as he
has in the past. The only logical solution would be a single
mistress whose company he enjoys and can keep well hidden.

That is what is being said behind your back, and you confirm it by your singular behavior.''

Katy digested this information slowly. Kerry had undeniably purchased her and was providing for her well-being. And even she had come to the same conclusions as Belinda about his lordship's intended, only her thoughts had never followed so far as Belinda's logical conclusion.

Not formally, anyway. Remembering her fears and unease beneath Lord Kerry's sometimes intense gaze, Katy acknowledged that she had occasionally harbored a similar suspicion. The nobleman had every right to assume she would become his mistress if he so desired. Did the noble Lord Kerry desire a tramp off the street?

As an occasional plaything, perhaps, but not the charming courtesan Belinda described. Lord Kerry would never consider her the equal partner a mistress of that sort must be. She did not have enough vanity even to consider it. Yet, if the impossible ever came true, if Lord Kerry should ever make such a request of her, what would she say?

In her heart, Katy knew there could be only one answer, but her mind rebelled against accepting it. She sank deeper into the velvet cushions and turned to stare upon the cold, deserted streets, refusing to acknowledge Belinda's knowing look.

December 1733–May 1734

BY THE END of the year, Katy had saved nearly every small coin she had earned at the bakery, but the few pounds' total could not begin to repay the enormous debt she owed Lord Kerry. Deciding the money more wisely spent if used for Christmas gifts for the Dublins and Belinda, she spent one cold December morn shopping, denying her unpredictable future by surrendering merrily to the spirit of the present.

Lord Kerry's gift had already been decided upon. She could afford to buy nothing for which he could have any use, so she had chosen to put her talents to work. Working secretly in the evenings, she had produced watercolor miniatures of herself and Lord Kerry, the only two people she knew well enough in his world to draw.

But she would need ribbons to wrap the packages in. With this in mind, she stopped at a local street vendor on the way home. This corner was crowded with a motley assortment of people vending their wares, and she greeted them cheerfully.

They returned her greetings warily, uncertain of her place in the scheme of things. She did not speak like a bakery clerk, even if she lived as one. And no bakery clerk had a

tutor and chaperon or dressed in elegant gowns once a week
to ride off in a nobleman's carriage. But her ready smiles and
warm greetings made her a favored customer, despite their
doubts.

As Katy chose from the colorful assortment of ribbons
produced by the old woman behind the counter, a shadow
darkened the box and a large hand slipped easily about her
slender waist. Startled, Katy dropped the ribbons and stepped
away to regard this brash intruder. To her horror, her gaze
was met by an icy gray stare. A small smile flickered about
the tight corners of Joshua Halberstam's mouth.

"Good morning, Miss Devereaux. I was told I might find
you hereabouts." With a proprietary air, his hand once more
went about her waist, inexorably leading her from the safety
of the shop.

Katy flashed a glance of terror at the old woman, but her
look was returned by a blank expression. Her struggle to free
herself from the man's grasp brought no discernible reaction.
Young gentlemen did not normally frequent this part of town,
and this one obviously knew the pretty girl. What reason was
there for interfering?

Seeing the futility of this avenue of escape, Katy sought
another, coming to a halt in the middle of the narrow street.
"Who sent you? What do you want?" she demanded, grasping her small bundle of packages to her chest.

The smile played about Halberstam's lips again as he
removed the packages from her hands. That taunting look of
appraisal once more raked over her, and the fears of past
nightmares flashed back, clutching painfully at Katy's heart.
She knew what it meant when men looked at her like that, and
panic sent her mind spinning.

"I just thought you and I should get to know each other a
little better. I've learned a lot about you since last we met."

The menace in his voice was unmistakable and Katy attempted to free his hold, but his grip bit cruelly into her side.

"I'd suggest you walk properly by my side without creating a scene, Miss Devereaux. A scene would be most unpleasant to all concerned, don't you agree?" Halberstam's
forceful hold pulled her intimately against his side as he
guided her along the unpaved path, past the shop displays.

With dismay, Katy watched as the grocer's son turned away from his window as they passed by, totally ignoring the plea in her eyes. She was being kidnapped right here in the middle of a busy street, and no one cared! Anguish battled terror for a place in her heart. What would he do should she scream? And would any come to her aid if she did?

At her seeming compliance, Halberstam grinned approvingly. "I see Southerland has trained you well. Excellent. We would want no hint of scandal to risk his lordship's marriage plans, would we now? Just keep that thought in mind and we should get along swimmingly."

Abruptly the menacing young rake jerked her through a narrow gateway. Startled, Katy glanced around hurriedly, finding herself in a small church courtyard, a high brick wall concealing it easily from the street and watchful eyes. Halberstam's large figure seemingly filled the small enclosure, and she felt the heat of his breath against her cold cheek as he towered over her. Nameless fears once more made a quivering mass of her nerves, and she huddled fearfully against the hard wall, remembering a night of horror when others had stared at her like this. His words made little sense to her paralyzed mind.

Halberstam's manicured fingers reached to loose a golden curl as his lips turned up in an amused sneer. "Presenting his mistress to society as his ward was a daring but foolish piece of business, even for Southerland. What amazes me is how he persuaded that toplofty brother of his to go along with it. No matter, your secret will be well kept if you obey my wishes. For once, I intend to win this one." As he spoke, his fingers wandered farther, caressing the curve of a porcelain cheek, smoothing the curls about the graceful bend of Katy's throat, lingering intimately at the fastening of her cloak. With his final words, nimble fingers undid the ties and the cloak slid silently to the ground.

This last action brought Katy to her senses, his words finally taking on some meaning, and her terror became more specific. Remembering Belinda's words of the competition between this man and Lord Kerry, she could assume he meant only one thing by "winning."

"You are mad, sir! Take your hands off me. I am Lord

Kerry's ward and nothing more. If you touch me, he will kill you!'' Her words rang out bravely in the chilly air, but her shivers belied their courage.

Halberstam laughed as his hands found the lacing of her bodice and parted the linen fichu concealing the curve of her breasts. ''No whore from Saffron Hill would be ward to the high-and-mighty Southerlands. I told you I have learned much about you.''

Cold hands slid beneath the covering of her bodice, and as icy fingers caressed warm flesh and his horrifying words scorched her brain, Katy screamed. Halberstam cursed and hard fingers bit painfully into tender breasts, but she continued screaming, striking out in any manner available, fists flailing against his impervious chest, lightly shod toes connecting with stockinged shins. She struggled furiously, trying to prevent further invasion of prying fingers, fighting for her sanity. Once before she had been touched like this. Never again. Her screams bounced against brick walls and echoed hysterically out into the street as he fought to keep his hold on her.

A silver blade gleamed brightly in the sunlight, then flashed as it severed the golden buttons of Halberstam's coat. Halberstam fell back, his hands releasing Katy's bodice, and she hastened to cover herself before looking up to her rescuer. With a cry of relief she recognized fiery emerald eyes, and she flew to Lord Kerry's side. His grim glare never swerved from his unarmed opponent.

''I'll send a man to your apartments to make arrangements. You've gone too far this time, Halberstam.''

Behind him, in the gateway, a crowd had begun to form, and in it Katy spied the grocer's son. Their glances met as Lord Kerry's arm went protectively about Katy's back; then the boy turned and left. He had done his duty in bringing his lordship; there would be no reward. Blindly Katy buried her face against Lord Kerry's side, his angry challenge burning against her ears. Everything was all wrong and nothing would make it better! Sobs tore at her throat.

Katy could not remember their return journey, remembered only shocked faces as she was hustled into the front parlor, and an unheard-of fire flickering in the grate as hands pressed

a cup of hot tea between her palms. Then they were left alone
and Kerry paced the floor in front of her.

"Dammit, Katy, quit looking at me like that! What would
you have me do after what he attempted?!" Kerry met her
blank gaze with anguish.

"May I suggest returning to the lovely Lady Elizabeth and
forgetting I ever existed? I am scarce worth the blood or the
scandal." Katy's hands trembled as she sipped the hot liquid.
How had it come to the point where a duke's son would be
fighting a duel over the bookseller's daughter while his ad-
vantageous marriage teetered on the brink of scandal? She
scarce dared look him in the eye.

"You are worth a dozen of Halberstam!" Lord Kerry
bellowed belligerently. "And I will damn well do as I please
and the Lady Elizabeth has nothing to do with it!"

His roar caused Katy to gape at him in wonder. Emerald
eyes glittered with ferocity and the stubborn jut of Kerry's
jaw spoke of his determination, but his anger seemed direc-
tionless. In bewilderment she sat back and waited for him to
come to his senses.

When no response came from Katy, he swung to face her.
Silvered curls fell dishevelledly about a face pale with fright;
enormous violet eyes stared back at him with anxiety. Kerry's
gaze fell to the disarray of her bodice and his blood boiled
once again. Following his gaze, she blushed and tried to
straighten the confining material.

"I am sorry, kitten. Perhaps I should send you to your
room and come back another day."

Katy looked up at that, "if there is another day . . ."
written plainly in her eyes, but Lord Kerry smiled and gestured carelessly.

"Do not worry yourself about the morrow. Much as I
would enjoy skewering the bastard, his cowardice will save
me the trouble. I wager my man will never find him this day
or the next. You will be safe from his scurrilous behavior for
so long as he dares not show his face in London again."

Relief surged through her veins and Katy buried her face in
her hands. Not until now had she realized how terrified she
had been at the thought of a duel. Great shudders shook her
shoulders.

"Now, stop that before I have to send you to your room without saying the farewells I came to say." Gently Kerry took the girl's shoulders and brought her to her feet. It occurred to him that Halberstam's mistake had been in treating her as a woman when she was no more than a frightened child. He stroked her hair comfortingly until the shudders ceased.

"Farewells?" Katy finally muttered tearfully, accepting his handkerchief as she dried her eyes.

"I am off to Southerland House for the holidays. The Lady Elizabeth's family is expected to join us there. Both families seem to think there may be some cause for celebration."

Green eyes peered at her quizzically as she studied his face. She saw no love, no hope, no happiness there, only that slight flicker of amusement she knew so well. "And is there?" she asked cautiously.

Kerry shrugged laconically. "A matter of opinion entirely. Would my favorite sorceress care to add hers?"

Katy wilted. She had been half-afraid he would someday ask that question, knowing she would be condemned no matter what answer she might make. And today was not a day for coherent thoughts. "I am sure the Lady Elizabeth has been brought up to be a fine baroness, or anything else she might be," she replied halfheartedly, avoiding his eyes.

"As in 'duchess,' are you suggesting? It is true my brother has no heir, but she would have to rid herself of both the duke and the marquis before she could hope to gain that title. Do you think she is a witch also and sees into the future?" Kerry spoke teasingly, not paying much attention to his nonsense, but a certain tension in Katy's shoulders caused him to watch her more closely.

Katy shook her head warily. "She is not that kind of witch, but she will not be content with one title if she can have others. She will not make you happy." She had not intended to say that; it was none of her business. It sounded jealous and self-serving and he had not asked for her opinion on that. She regretted the words instantly.

Instead of chastising her for her impetuousity, Kerry stared at his ward thoughtfully for a full minute before replying. "From anyone else I would consider that an example of feminine cattiness, but you are not prone to that particular malady. The lady is sole heir to her father's estates, has an impressive lineage, and is beautiful enough to make begetting sons by her an easy task. Would you have me marry for love?''

"Judging by your past, you would not marry at all, then." Nervously Katy shrugged off his confining hands and strolled toward the fireplace. "But I am curious to know what you intend to do with yourself once you acquire wife and family and all your estates are tied up until somebody conveniently dies. If your wife will not make you happy and your present idle pursuits do not make you happy, what will?''

Kerry stared at that proud, slender back thoughtfully. He had avoided this topic until the last minute, knowing full well she would see through him immediately. That did not relieve the pain of her words. "May I give you my answer to that after the holidays?''

"You need not give me any answer at all, it is an answer you must find for yourself,'' Katy whispered to the fire.

But Kerry wasn't listening. Coming up behind her, he turned her around and pulled her into his arms. Startled, she came reluctantly, but the touch of his lips against hers sent a tingling sensation through her middle that made separation impossible.

Only the swinging open of the parlor door saved them. Belinda's outraged "Katy!" broke the spell, and Kerry came up grinning.

"What's the matter, Belinda? Can't a man steal a kiss from a pretty girl before marriage puts a ring through his nose?'' And with a jaunty swagger, he bussed his cousin heartily and left the room.

As Kerry predicted, no more was heard from Halberstam, but there was no means of halting the rumor of Kerry's challenge from circling town once his man spent a day scouring the haunts of the baronet's elusive son. Rumor had it that Sir Halberstam had found his only son a political appointment to remove further scandal.

It did not take long for Katy's name to be connected with this particular scandal, and she asked no questions when Belinda halted their weekly excursion to the opera. Kerry's family would no longer be interested in sponsoring her now. She felt little sorrow at this development, her thoughts only of Lord Kerry and his haughty lady. Even the fact that the neighbors now conspicuously avoided her was of little importance in comparison to the drama now being enacted at Southerland House, and Katy wished desperately for some word of the outcome.

Betts arrived on Boxing Day with gifts from Lord Kerry. Belinda and Mrs. Dublin watched impatiently as Katy's trembling fingers fumbled with the enormous box addressed to her, and sighed audibly at the contents. Thick folds of heavy blue velvet unfurled as Katy lifted the hooded fur-lined cape from the box, uncovering a matching fur muff. Amidst the excitement, a letter fluttered to the floor, and Betts hastened to retrieve it, handing it with care to Katy.

Lord Kerry wrote as he spoke, and Katy could hear his voice as she read his hasty handwriting telling how the furs had been captured in the colonies and sewn in France, that they were only in style with royalty at the moment but he could foresee the future as well as she and they would soon be popular everywhere. But it was the final paragraph that brought tears to her eyes and caused her to hastily shove the letter into her muff. In it he wrote he had made his decision and his fate now lay in the hands of others; he prayed she wished him well on the outcome.

Silently Katy handed her small package to Betts. "You will see that Lord Kerry gets this from me? I do not have a letter for him, but I will write soon."

"Of course, miss. Is all well?" With concern the old man caught the unmistakable gleam of tears, knowing that his lordship would expect a full report on the receipt of his lavish gift.

Katy produced a teary smile and hugged the cape close to her. "It is the most beautiful thing I have ever known, but tell Lord Kerry if I am to dress as royalty, I will act like royalty and command his presence as soon as possible in order to show off my new attire."

Belinda emitted a shrill "Katy!" and Mrs. Dublin looked astounded, but Betts grinned and bowed. "I will convey your message, miss," he replied calmly. If his lordship was in need of amusement, his report of the ladies' reactions should provide it. It would be one glimmer of humor in the otherwise black mood his employer had been in lately.

Katy's letter of thanks and wishes for his lordship's happiness went out the next day, but Kerry's reply did not come for many weeks. A lengthy letter to make up for his dalliance, it lacked Kerry's usual good spirits. Still, there were paragraphs Katy read and reread with pleasure.

"I did not mean to make you cry with my gift, kitten," he wrote, "but you see, I am taking my guardianship seriously. Just as I would take care of any precious possession, I must take care of you. Explain that to Belinda and Mary when they complain I compromise you."

About the miniatures he added: "I have shown your paintings to my family, and they all agree you show exceptional talent and that I should encourage you. My sister claims you have made me far too handsome and that if your portrait is truthful, I have misled them entirely concerning your beauty, but I have assured her that you have been too modest in both our portrayals." She could see his ironic grin as he wrote that and giggled. "My mother has attempted to persuade me to part with the picture of myself, but the Lady Elizabeth scorns to look at it. Therefore, in retaliation I have had both miniatures framed and they now sit together on my bedside table where she will never see them."

It was impossible to believe that Lady Elizabeth would reject Lord Kerry's proposals—she had assumed them to be agreed in every way but the formalities—but Katy could not interpret that last line in any other way. She cast aside a sudden flare of hope and continued on to the line stating he would obey her command upon return. Perhaps she would learn then what had happened.

He returned one spectacular morning after an ice storm turned the world into a glistening sheen of glass, rooftops and overhangs dripping with festive embellishments of sparkling icicles. The icicles quickly became coated with soot and the pavements became a muddy slush, but for a short while the dreary London street held a magical quality. Lord Kerry's bays snorted smoky protests into the air as they pranced over the icy fragments and Katy curled up inside the warmth of her new cape and stared out into a world transformed.

The park had become a crystal wonderland overnight, the bare branches of trees and bushes bowed down in fantastic castles coated with layers of glittering ice, sending shimmers of rainbow colors dancing in the sunlight. Katy gazed at it with awe.

Hair streaming in golden ringlets from her hood, cheeks cherried by the cold, eyes bright with the stinging wind, Katy was also like one transformed. She was growing up quickly, too quickly, and he would need to see her provided for before carrying out his own plans. The easy solution of marrying her off somehow failed to appeal.

"The ice fascinates you, doesn't it? Glittering and exciting, like a new world." Kerry let the horses make their own pace as he watched the small face beside him turn serious.

Not surprised by his ability to read her thoughts, Katy nodded. "It is beautiful while it lasts."

"Is that how you look at the society I have introduced to you? Does it appear to be a fairy-tale world after the one you grew up in?"

"It is like the ice, glittering and beautiful when new, but cold and hard with slush underneath. I do not know how you have skated on such thin ice for so long." Blue eyes darkened to violet as she looked up at him, all her childish excitement vanished. He deliberately led this discussion somewhere, and she feared to discover the destination.

"I have sunk beneath it more times than I care to count, kitten. The night we met was one such time, Lady Elizabeth another. I intend to skate toward safer shores from now on." He had not intended to direct the conversation this way, but in the brilliant light of this new day and year, Kerry felt he owed some explanation for what he knew would follow.

"I am afraid I do not understand, milord."

"It does not matter. I simply wished to be assured you understood what you were seeing in the glittering company of my friends. If you wish to see more of it, I have only to instruct Belinda accordingly." He spoke stiffly, no longer looking at her rapt expression.

Katy clenched her hands inside her muff. She did not know

what the alternative would be to this suggestion, but it was obvious he was beginning to wonder what to do with her. It did not sound as if he were considering Belinda's proposal.

"Thank you for the offer, your lordship," she replied hesitantly, phrasing her reply with caution. "But I do not belong in that society. I have no wish to be a further burden to you. I must work for my living."

"At the moment, you cost me less than these animals of mine. If you wish to see society, say so, and do not quibble about it." Kerry spoke almost harshly, with no trace of his familiar grin.

"I am not quibbling. I am trying my best to be polite. If you wish my answer in more precise terms: I have no wish to make my living in bed, as you once so crudely put it. That is all society has to offer me. I think I should like to work with children. Perhaps someday I could become a governess."

Katy had spoken as harshly as he and was startled at his sudden grin.

"There may be hope for the world yet if there are any more like you out there, Katy Devereaux. Society be damned, then. Halberstam's tongue will have wagged for naught, though it is a pity he ran before I had time to cut it out." At Katy's look of alarm, he patted her hand. "His tale went no farther than my family, so your reputation is still substantially safe, though mine does it no good. We will have to remedy that situation if you are to be governess or companion. And you will have to learn to curb your tongue somewhat if you wish to keep any such position you may find."

Katy stared up at him in confusion. "You mean you will let me seek such a position?"

Kerry's grin grew broad. "Did you have some other in mind?" And his laughter rang merrily as she buried her blushing face in her muff.

In the ensuing months, Katy kept this memory of his laughter as a steadfast flame within her, fueling her energy when Belinda's criticisms became too cross to bear or her loneliness threatened a return of depression. Lord Kerry had forwarded his request that Katy be trained for the life of governess, and although Belinda found it extremely odd, she carried the task out well, taking full credit for Katy's newly subdued demeanor.

It was Belinda who carried the reports of Kerry's broken engagement, though none had yet ascertained the reasons. No longer appearing in society, Katy heard rumors only through her governess, and she was certain these were screened carefully for her ears. The whispers of scandal over herself and Kerry's challenge to Halberstam, Belinda did not report, but the whispers of neighbors were sufficient to keep Katy's mind on her goal. She must make a living of her own, and soon.

She did not see Kerry again until May, when he obtained Belinda's permission to escort Katy to the theater for her seventeenth birthday.

Katy found the performance of *Taming of the Shrew* an enlightening experience, but Kerry's aloof and somewhat somber mood distracted her. Afterward they sat silent and untouching while the driver urged the horses through the jostling crowd.

Bubbling over with the excitement of the play, Katy could not understand her companion's mood, but she politely held her tongue until she thought she would surely burst from the need to talk about what she had just seen. When he did speak, she nearly sighed with relief.

"Now that you have seen the play performed, what do you think of Katharina and Petruchio?" Kerry's voice was faceless in the dark.

Disregarding his lack of expression, Katy loosed the torrent she had held in check. "It was a love story! I did not know that before. They both behaved despicably, but underneath they were really . . ." She hesitated, not knowing how to phrase it delicately.

"Attracted," he suggested.

"Attracted to each other," she agreed, after considering it a moment. It was something stronger than "attracted," but that would have to suffice. The play had been performed to titillate as well as amuse, and Katy was well aware of the suggestiveness of the performance. "Why didn't the Lady Elizabeth like it? Once Katharina learned to respect the rights of others, and to give a little, Petruchio was free to love her as she wished. Surely love was worth swallowing her pride a little.''

Lord Kerry grimaced wryly to himself. "Perceptive" wasn't the word for her; the child was undoubtedly a witch. Out loud he admitted, ''The lady did not see things quite that way; she accused me of calling her a shrew, among some other impolite comments.''

Timidly Katy touched the hand lying on the seat between them, sensing his need for comfort of some sort. "If she could not learn to love, you are better off without her, milord.''

Startled from his reverie, Kerry took the hand offered and returned his attention to the topic needing discussing. "The lady ceased to be a problem some time ago, kitten. I have other things on my mind now, and I am afraid they will occupy most of my time for some months. Will you be content with the Dublins and Belinda until I can see about some other situation for you?''

This was an unexpected turn to the evening, but Katy had learned to accept his disappearances philosophically, knowing it was only a matter of time before they became permanent. ''The Dublins have been very kind and I treasure Belinda's friendship, but I really should be out looking for a situation for myself. I should not be imposing upon you further.''

"You are in no position to find suitable situations, and I will not have you in some household where you could come to harm. Be patient and I will find something, but do not be disappointed if it takes me a while. Promise me you will wait.'' Lord Kerry's hand clasped hers tighter as they pulled into the lane, and he bent to see her face in the dimness of the lamplight.

"I promise,'' she murmured, uneasily aware of the strange sensation he had stirred in her earlier.

He tilted her chin up with his finger as he had done once before, and her heart stopped beating.

"Kiss me, Kate,'' he whispered teasingly.

And she did.

November–December 1734

GAZING IN AWE at the vast expanses of unblemished sandy beaches and acres of unbroken grasslands and forest as the ship sailed up the coast of the Carolinas, Katy felt a sudden sense of desolation. What madness had made her accept Lord Kerry's insane proposal to journey to the New World?

To be fair, he had warned her she would be separated from all she knew and loved, he had even offered to find another position for her if she did not wish to accept this one, but Katy's decision had been made from the first moment he spoke of it.

She hastened over the memory of that last happy night of her birthday when the touch of Lord Kerry's lips on hers produced a more exhilarating sensation than the first ones. She had made her decision on a much more rational basis than that. Sir Charles Stockbridge was a well-liked, respectable baronet, and his shy nine-year-old daughter Anna would be an ideal student for her first position as governess. The fact that they proposed to start a new life in the colonies did not deter Katy for a moment, though her reasoning here grew more muddled. Though Lord Kerry had pointedly made no mention of the fact, she had heard not only of Lady Elizabeth's engagement to a more eligible viscount, but of Kerry's sudden purchase of the shares of a discontented proprietor in the Carolinas, she surmised that he too for whatever reasons, had determined to make a new life for himself. And whither he went, she resolved to follow.

But as she stared out at the vast open spaces of uninhabited coastline, city-bred Katy knew the misery of doubt. She had discovered, too late, that Lord Kerry had not sailed with this ship of passengers answering the colony's call for new townships, though his name was on everyone's lips. Even Sir Charles spoke of the young lord's persuasion that had made him decide to buy his brother's already established business in a small town upriver from Charleston. But at no time did anyone mention the expectation of meeting the nobleman in the Americas. And in all that land out there, how could she ever hope to see him again, even supposing he had come?

A work-roughened hand grasped Katy's and squeezed reassuringly. With a grateful smile she gazed up into the soft brown eyes of the dark-haired young sailor who had befriended her. Hiding his anguish, Jake Horne returned the smile. Six weeks in the close confines of a small ship had taught him much of all the passengers, but he had learned more of Katy and her precocious young charge than he had ever anticipated.

As the ship slowly made its way up the channel to Charleston, Katy searched the docks anxiously, while her hand compulsively wrung the callused one holding hers. She was scarcely aware of the young sailor beside her, but as Jake's gaze followed hers, his gentle eyes hardened with resolve.

With the eyes of love, he had seen what Katy had yet to guess, and the knowledge tore at his soul. He knew he could never compete with the grandeur of her noble Lord Kerry or replace him in her heart, but he was young and had a lifetime yet to earn his ambitions. When the time came, he felt he would be prepared to offer her what the nobleman could not.

As their destination slowly rose into view, two pairs of eyes watched eagerly from two very different perspectives.

*   *   *

By 1734, Charleston had been part of a crown colony for only five years—the proprietors having given up any hope of making any profit out of their quarrelsome tenants—but already it was the center of all business and social activity in the colonies south of Jamestown. Situated at the confluence of the Ashley and Cooper rivers in a natural harbor, it was the center of trade for shipping to and from northern colonies, the West Indies, and England, despite (and in some cases because of) the latest shipping restraints.

As befitted such an active port, it was a growing, prosperous town with well-laid streets (unpaved as yet except for the occasional brick sidewalk), several churches (although the colonists had consistently refused to establish a state church despite the fact the tax money had already been raised), and a thriving number of inns and taverns (most of dubious nature).

Many of the buildings were of cypress and yellow pine still, but recent fires had brought talk of ordinances to make all new buildings of brick. There were already many fine brick residences with glazed windows, a luxury yet for most colonists, their owners mostly wealthy plantation dwellers who kept them for wives and daughters to visit during the busy summer social season when they escaped the miasmas of the rivers for the windswept salt air of town. This flourishing plantation society had already produced a concert hall that was frequently better attended than the churches. Perhaps not yet as large as its northern neighbors, Charleston was still a small, if imperfect, jewel of a city.

Impervious to this history, Lord Kerry stood on the docks directing the unloading of freight and cargo from one ship while keeping a close eye on the arrival of the second. Checking bills of lading and cargo manifests, he was constantly interrupted by demands from every quarter of the hectic activity surrounding him. His attention divided among a dozen different areas, Kerry muttered mighty oaths at each new interruption, but stripped of coat and waistcoat, his open linen shirt billowing in the breeze, he moved jauntily among the crates, his eyes flashing their singular green. With neither the trappings of a rich man nor the extraordinary physique to distinguish him from the more bulky seamen, his lithe form with its wide shoulders and narrow hips moved with an

assurance and command setting him off from the common
crowd as he navigated the crowded docks.

But even as he marked his lists and directed the removal of
freight, his eye followed the ship newly anchored at the dock.
Carrying mostly passengers, it was too large to be of further
use to him, and he hoped to sell it at a fair profit. With the
price of the ship and the cargo now being unloaded, he would
be able to pay off his debt to the Southerland estate and be
financially on his own again. A grin of satisfaction flitted
across his handsome face.

Considering his interest in the shipping business, perhaps
Sir Charles could be talked into purchasing a share of the
vessel. And the thought of Sir Charles triggered another thought
as Kerry's eyes narrowed, searching the deck of the large
ship more carefully. There, near the bow, that bright head
caught by a golden shaft of sunlight could be only one
person. Damn, but the pitiful little kitten he had found had
turned into a beauty, and threatened to be a real heartbreaker
once she had a few more years of experience. Those damned
bewitching eyes of hers could steal a man's soul if he let
them, but Kerry had no intention of losing his. He hadn't
saved the girl from the life of a public whore to make her a
private one, no matter how beautiful she turned out. He had
some few scruples left, no matter what people said. She
would make a good governess, and, smiling, he shaded his
eyes against the sun to better observe her small figure.

Even when dressed as an ordinary workingman, Lord Kerry
stood out in the crowd, Katy thought as she spied him, her
heart leaping with excitement at his discovery. The telltale
copper glint of his hair in the sun pinpointed him immediately. She watched as he glanced idly up at the ship and then
returned to his work, willing him to look up again. And as if
their thoughts collided, he did, and for a moment they stared
smilingly into each other's eyes. Then Kerry's smile faded
and he brought his hand down to finish his checklist.

A tall young sailor had been standing possessively beside
her, holding her hand, and Kerry frowned at his thoughts,
unable to limit them to cargo manifests. Talking to the boy
when he had hired him, Kerry had decided he was a decent
lad with a fair amount of intelligence, if somewhat lacking in

ambition, but a seaman's wife was not what he intended for
Katy. Glancing up again, he saw his young ward give the
embarrassed youth an exuberant hug and kiss, and he felt a
wrench of pain. He would have to talk to the lass and sound
her out; perhaps he could see the boy got a better position—
preferably on the other side of the world, he grumbled irritably to himself, and attacked the list once more.

By the time the passengers had cleared the decks, Lord
Kerry had overcome his irritation, and he scanned the dock
for some sign of the Stockbridges, coming upon them easily.

Sir Charles's barrel-chested figure rolled toward him, trailing his nervous and chattering wife, their wide-eyed daughter, and Katy. A man of keen intelligence and subtle humor,
Sir Charles had been a lifelong friend of Kerry's and the
perfect employer for Katy. Kerry restrained his expression of
self-satisfaction as his ward's perspicacious violet eyes fell on
him.

After patiently listening to Anna's excited prattle and Lady
Stockbridge's ingratiating overflow of greetings, Lord Kerry
turned to Sir Charles. "Have you accommodations in Georgetown yet?"

"Bought my brother's house. His letters said someone has
been taking care of it for him, so it should still be habitable."

"Will he be down here to meet you, or have you made
other arrangements?"

"No, he's got a lumber mill out in the hills somewhere, so
he won't bother himself with coming in. Thought we'd find
an inn here in Charleston for the night until we could find the
best way up to Georgetown."

Lord Kerry frowned thoughtfully. "Don't know that there's
an inn I'd recommend for the ladies overnight. Your best bet
would be to go on up the river today. It's early yet and the
river ride is supposed to be a relatively easy one. They say
the road is pretty rough. I've hired a sloop to haul some of
my things up to the plantation. Why don't you join me? You
can find a wagon to carry your belongings. . . . Why don't
you take the ladies to an inn for a few hours while you find
someone to do your hauling, and by that time I'll be done
here and we can go out after luncheon? Would that agree with
you?"

Lady Stockbridge was thrilled at the chance to arrive in her new home in the company of so grand a personage as Lord Kerry Southerland. Sir Charles admitted to a desire to spend the night in a bed of his own. And Katy and Anna were quite content at any opportunity of extending their visit with his lordship. So the decision was made.

Lord Kerry found himself as eager as the rest to finish the journey, and he hastened through the remainder of his lists with renewed vigor. He had spent the last few nights at inns in Charleston waiting for the arrival of the last ship, and now he was eager to move on and assess the needs of the plantation he had purchased sight unseen. His brother could have the venerable estates in England; Kerry preferred to start his own.

The sloop slipped past dark pine forests and newly cleared land as well as the already harvested fields of older plantations. The day had grown overcast and the air chilly as they made their way upriver, and the Stockbridges elected to stay below out of the wind. Anxious to see everything there was to be seen in their new home, Katy and Anna stayed topside, occasionally consulting Katy's pamphlets for names of the stranger sights greeting them.

"Mistress Anna, if you will run down to your parents, I believe you will find they have a cup of hot chocolate waiting for you." Lord Kerry came up behind them silently, his words startling them from their studies.

"And what about Katy? Doesn't she get some?" Childish blue eyes looked up demandingly, ready to defend the rights of her newfound friend.

"Of course she does, you silly goose. We will be down in just a moment to join you. You will catch your death of cold if you stay out here too long. Now, run on before the chocolate is no longer hot." The firmness of Lord Kerry's tone convinced the child, and Anna did as she was told without a further look back.

Lord Kerry leaned over the railing beside his ward. Katy had succeeded in tidying her hair into a respectable cap, and combined with her prim gray traveling gown and mantle, she should have appeared every inch the respectable governess, but the dancing blue lights of her eyes could not be hidden behind gown or cap, and the bowed curve of her lips held too much promise to be prim.

"Are there any regrets yet about making this journey?" Once more wearing a well-tailored coat and immaculate fawn breeches, Lord Kerry stared out over the open terrain.

"No, your lordship, not one. Anna is a lovely child and the Stockbridges extremely pleasant people. I shall enjoy working for them." Katy slipped her pamphlets into her apron pocket and leaned back against the railing, facing in the opposite direction.

"You did not seem surprised to see me. I had hoped to keep my journey from you in order to avoid influencing your decision. I would not have your unhappiness on my conscience if you did not like life here." Kerry spoke slowly, carefully phrasing his words.

Katy sensed his caution and refrained from answering impulsively, but there were certain things that had to be said and she would have them done with now.

"I would not have come if I had not wanted to be here. For me it is a perfect solution, a new beginning, and I will be forever grateful to you for giving me the opportunity. But yes, I did hear the rumors you would be traveling to the colonies, and yes, it did influence my decision. You cannot expect it to be otherwise for me."

At Kerry's inquiring look, Katy strove desperately to explain. "I owe you a debt I cannot repay, milord. You once purchased me, not just with money, but with kindness, and now I am yours to do with as you wish. If you wish nothing of me, then I will do whatever is necessary to be of use to you. It is easier to carry out these goals if I am where you are and not separated by thousands of miles of ocean. I know I am being presumptuous, and I will not mention the subject again, but I wished to be totally honest with you." Tense, Katy gripped the rails behind her and did not turn to see his face.

Lord Kerry continued to stare out over the water. It was a terrible obligation to play with the lives of other people; he had not meant to get this involved with what had started out to be a good deed to erase the foul taste in his mouth created by the life he had been living. But he had come to enjoy his indulgence in this particular piece of humanitarianism. He felt already well rewarded for what little bit he had done to help her find her way out of a dreadful situation. But he had to admit, just as she thought of him as her owner, he thought of her as his possession. All his ridiculous efforts at letting her lead her own life were just a sham, and if he needed any proof, his irritation at her taking up with that seaman was ample evidence. Gad, it was going to take some doing to unravel this tangled web.

"All right, Katy, I think I understand what you are saying, but I would much rather you led your own life without thought to mine. What of this young sailor, Jake Horne? Are you telling me you would choose my interests over his, or over those of any other man in your life?"

"Jake is just a friend and nothing more. I cannot deny that someday I would like to have a family of my own, but since I cannot foresee the future, I cannot clarify my position any better than that. I think it is based primarily on the assumption you would never ask anything of me that I could not give or that you did not need. But since that sounds so ephemeral, perhaps I'd better just save my salary and salve part of my conscience by paying you back on more realistic terms." Katy had released the railing and now stood quietly beside his taller figure, waiting for him to look up.

He did. Finding her eyes upon him, Kerry straightened, and with legs spread apart as if to combat a rolling ocean, he looked down into violet pools, unthinkingly reaching out to touch her cheek. "You know the few coins of your salary mean a great deal to you and very little to me. It would be a pointless gesture to attempt it. Right now I have need of a sensible friend with a good sense of humor to keep my feet on the ground and my nose pointed in the right direction. If you can do that for me, you will be well on your way to repaying your imaginary debts." His hand lingered a moment longer, tracing the line of her cheek down to the soft underside of her chin before parting.

It was as if the sun had broken through the clouds as the smile broke across her face. "You have placed me even more greatly in your debt if you allow me that honor; I fear I shall be your slave forever." The warmth of his touch was reflected in her tone, but she did not move to return the familiarity.

Kerry smiled. "You are a fool, Katy Devereaux, but I will suffer you gladly. Come below, out of this wind, or the others will think we have blown overboard and mourn our loss by drinking our chocolate." Good humor finally restored, he took her arm and gaily guided her out of the wind's way, confident he had the situation well in hand once more. Little did he know how far out of hand it could become within less than a year's time.

The six weeks following their landing was a time of settling in for the new arrivals in Georgetown. Sir Charles's brother had been one of the first settlers in the area. A man who preferred the wildness of the frontier, he moved on as soon as civilization encroached. He left behind a thriving shipyard and shipping business and the town's only two-story building—a verandaed brick house with glazed windows and enough rooms to satisfy the soul of society-starved Elizabeth Stockbridge.

Being the wife of the settlement's only titled resident, she considered herself the peak of the town's hierarchy, not including the elusive Lord Kerry, who lived farther up the river. For this reason alone she had agreed to her husband's whims of settling a new land. Tired of being looked down upon by the better-titled nobility in Sussex, she felt she would receive the degree of respect she deserved here, though she would have been incapable of putting these feelings into words.

The lovely two-story home suited her taste for grandeur in an area where log cabins had only recently been boarded and two-room houses were just receiving their first additions. With a grand staircase in the hallway leading to a well-appointed second floor with five bedrooms surrounding the landing, a large salon and study flanking either side of the downstairs hallway, and a public room of satisfactory proportions for dining and entertaining, it contained everything Elizabeth's heart could desire. The back rooms consisted of servant's quarters, and the kitchens and slave quarters were located out past the breezeway.

Slavery was an issue Sir Charles had not yet come to terms with, but the lack of sufficient servants and their exorbitant salary compared to the relative cheapness of a single purchase price for a slave soon convinced him to make the investment. Feeding a slave wasn't any more expensive than the thieving servants he had left behind, and all in all, he was satisfied with the investment, although a niggling conscience made him see that the slaves were better fed and clothed than the servants he had seldom thought twice about in England.

Katy did not come under the rank of servant, and she was housed in the upper bedrooms with the family, in a small room next to Anna's that made her old room at the Dublins' look like a closet. The spaciousness of the new country seemed to have affected the house's architects, and her first few weeks were spent in rapture at the sun-washed space she could call her own.

Anna's lessons began almost immediately upon arrival, and by prior agreement with Sir Charles, Katy began to look for other students to fill her little schoolroom. It wasn't uncommon for tutors to supplement their salary by taking in additional students, and in Anna's case it was preferable. She had been too much in the company of adults all her life and needed the association with other children to learn to deal with others her age.

Katy did not need to search far. Elizabeth Stockbridge's eager tongue soon impressed the town with the knowledge that her governess was ward to the illustrious Lord Kerry, and students with their eager mamas were soon lined up outside the door. Fathers who had never dreamed their daughters needed an education soon found it a social necessity for their children to be enrolled in Katy's class.

The daily antics of Katy's students soon developed an orderly pattern that delighted her as they finally began showing some sign of progress. The fact that she had had no word from Lord Kerry since they docked bothered her not in the least. She was growing accustomed to his departures, and although a day did not go by that she did not think of him, she took his absences for granted, content to know he was nearby.

Not so was Elizabeth Stockbridge. Kerry's continuing absence from all social life frustrated her enthusiastic plans of entertaining on the level to which she would like to be accustomed. It was all very well to have the minister and his wife, and the town's leading merchant, and a traveling judge to dinner, but she needed the *pièce de résistance* to establish her superiority over the wives of the plantation owners. Lord Kerry would be that pièce.

Unable to contain her impatience any longer, she brought the topic to the dinner table.

"Christmas is only two weeks away, and I really think it is our place to provide a Christmas dinner, don't you agree, dear?" Elizabeth appealed to her abstracted husband, who spent most of his time at the dinner meal perusing whatever periodicals he could lay hands on in lieu of the dire dearth of intelligent conversation provided by his beloved wife.

Looking up from his paper, his mind obviously not totally following the question but gathering the gist of it, Sir Charles agreed. "Of course, my dear. I am sure there are many poor unfortunates in the area who would go without, otherwise. A creditable idea, Elizabeth." He was not given time to wander back to his paper, his wife's indignant shriek forcing him to abandon his pursuit.

"I am not talking about poor unfortunates! I understand the custom here is to provide boxes for the poor at Christmas. That is not what I meant. I wish to have a dinner for all our new friends here and I really think we ought to include Lord Kerry among them. He will be far from home and has no family here. I think it is our place to entertain him. And surely he will wish to see Katy; he must be concerned with her welfare in this strange place. I think you ought to write him a note, dear"—she turned to Katy as the flow of words went on. "Tell him how you're faring and mention my dinner and tell him he is welcome anytime. I am certain he would love to come." Wisps of curls bounced from beneath her cap about her pretty face as she babbled animatedly.

"I think if you wish to invite Lord Kerry, you had best send the invitation yourself and not by way of Katy. You are putting her in a rather awkward position in asking her to write

first," Sir Charles commented dryly, noticing sympathetically the slight flush in the governess's cheeks.

"Nonsense. It is perfectly proper for his ward to write and
inform him of her well-being. It is only natural for her to
express gratitude." Elizabeth Stockbridge was a woman of
few ideas and what ones she had were apt to be hopelessly
muddled, but once she did grasp one, she held on to it
tenaciously.

Katy smoothed the napkin in her lap. It was thoughtful of
Sir Charles to defend her modesty, but he did not know that
in her case the point was not worth defending. Lord Kerry
had little reason to expect proper etiquette from her. And
Lady Stockbridge obviously had her mind set on the matter.
To resolve any family battle over her, Katy intruded into the
conversation.

"I am sure Lord Kerry would welcome the invitation. I
will write to him at once, if you wish."

Sir Charles frowned and shook his head in disapproval, but
knowing when he was overruled, he returned to his paper.

Her mistress would have been somewhat dismayed at the
actual rendition of the polite note she had envisioned, but
Katy entrusted it directly to Sir Charles to find a messenger
upriver. As Katy had expected, he made no inquiry into its
contents. In her own succinct terms, she had described the
dinner-table conversation resulting in her writing, having no
intention of putting Lord Kerry in the position of social prize
without his consent. She also included a few lines of her
success in obtaining students and a rather malicious sketch of
kittens representing her older students learning to dance,
which she signed "Catty." If that didn't bring him out of
hiding, nothing would.

She was right in her assumption. Within a few days a
downriver boat left a message with Sir Charles containing
Lord Kerry's acceptance of the invitation to dinner and including a small note for Katy. Sir Charles handed it to her in
his study and impassively returned to his paperwork while she
read it.

It was a perfectly innocuous note indicating he would enjoy
seeing her at Christmas for a change and asking if she had
any more sketches she could spare, stating that the walls of

his cabin were bare and needing something to liven them. The note was written as if it were intended for other eyes, and Katy returned it to Sir Charles for his inspection.

He read it quickly and glanced up at Katy. "I have heard tales of your talents but have yet to admire your work. Do you have a portfolio I could see?"

Caught unaware by this unexpected inquiry, Katy admitted, "I have done a few things since I have been here, but they are all very informal. I draw them mostly to amuse myself or the students."

Fire flickered in the fireplace, sending shadows dancing into the corners. Sir Charles admired the play of it against the golden lights in the girl's loosened hair as it fell about her shoulders. Caught up in the establishment of a new business, he had little time to get to know the girl, but what he had seen had impressed him. Overheard tidbits of conversation revealed a remarkably sensible head sat on those pretty shoulders. He wondered how long it would be before he lost her to one of the overwhelmingly large majority of males in the territory, and found himself envying whoever the lucky fellow might be.

"Run get the sketches and let me have a look before you give them all away," he ordered.

Surprised, Katy did as she was told, coming back with a small folder of assorted kitten sketches and caricatures.

Thumbing through the drawings, he sorted them into various piles according to his own system. "Ummm, I see what you mean by amusing yourself. You have an aptitude for capturing the personal, but you're not a very serious artist, are you?" Without his powdered wig, Sir Charles looked years younger, his brown hair speckled with gray only on top, a heavier streak on the sides giving a distinguished appearance to its rough cut. The lines about his face relaxed as he enjoyed the humor of the sketches before him.

"No, sir. It is nothing more than a knack I have acquired. I do not have the patience to work at anything requiring a good deal of application." Unused to anyone taking her work seriously, Katy twisted her fingers nervously at her employer's evident absorption.

"It is a God-given talent, and I encourage you to continue

as long as you get enjoyment from it. Would you mind my
keeping this one of my wife? It is so like her." He grinned at
the caricature of his wife spinning through the house, leaving
a trail of words behind, her hair flying out around her delight-
fully innocent, cheery face. At Katy's gesture of approval, he
set it aside and pulled out another stack. "These might make
an interesting collage of sketches for Lord Kerry. If I found
you a rather large paper to put them on, with a tinge of
watercolors to brighten them, it should make an acceptable
gift. If you could complete it in time, I would have it framed
for you."

Katy had been complimented on her work before, but Sir
Charles's knowledgeable praise was not flattery. He liked
her work well enough to consider it worth framing. Beaming
with joyful disbelief, Katy took the stack he indicated and
glanced through it. He had chosen all kitten sketches of
recognizable local topics, many of them herself or Anna in
improbable situations. "Do you really think Lord Kerry would
want such childish drawings?"

"I can assure you, they are not childish. It takes consider-
able maturity to make fun of oneself and others with loving
humor and not maliciousness. He will enjoy them." Sir
Charles watched as her eyes darkened to violet in thoughtful
concentration, evidently trying to picture the final results as a
whole.

Lost in the arrangement of sketches forming in her mind,
Katy failed to acknowledge the warmth of her employer's
words or notice his scrutiny. "If you think it will please him,
I will do as you say. It will not be too much trouble to locate
paper large enough?" Clouded with a hundred far-off thoughts,
her eyes saw nothing but the genial older man she called her
employer as she looked up from the drawings.

Smiling sadly at the selfishness of youth, Sir Charles
brusquely dismissed the topic. "It will be no trouble. I will
bring it tomorrow."

Katy spent every spare moment on the drawings, adding a
few that were not included in the sketches, leaving out many
of those that included herself and Anna, as the framework of
an idea worked within her. Only Anna had full access to the
work, and she chortled with glee every time a new portion

was added, gloating over this shared secret, and arousing her parents' curiosity. It added a new suspense to the usual Christmas spirit, although Elizabeth claimed to have no time for such nonsense, being too immersed in the planning of her triumphant dinner.

The dinner became the event of the season outside Charleston. After discovering even the mysterious Lord Kerry would be attending, the plantation owners with eligible daughters consented to their invitations, and after that, anyone who had not yet received an invitation vied for one or pretended other business for that day. Elizabeth had finally accomplished her goal, and in less time than she could have ever dreamed. She was ecstatic.

Christmas fell on Friday that year. Katy finished the sketches on Tuesday evening and unveiled them anxiously in Sir Charles's study after dinner. Laying the large matted paper out on the desk, he studied it carefully, a small smile twitching the corners of his mouth as he recognized the incidents portrayed and understood what she had done.

In the upper corner of the paper a lithe tomcat wearing a feathered tricorne and a wicked grin lay across a conspicuously familiar ebony walking stick, looking down upon a series of unrelated incidents, their underlying thread being only that they had occurred in Georgetown since the arrival of Lord Kerry's ships. There were no people anywhere in the tableau, but the kittens were easily recognizable by various traits and foibles and included not only Katy and Anna but also Sir Charles and Elizabeth, the new pastor and his wife, and several other familar local figures. If Lord Kerry did not know the people of Georgetown before, he would know them at once upon matching them to the sketches. It was a charming conceit and one that could be enjoyed indefinitely. Sir Charles finally allowed his chuckle to escape.

"You have carried the idea much further than I imagined. It is too good for Lord Kerry to hide away in his backwoods lodging. I wish I had asked for one myself."

Tongue-tied for the first time in her life, Katy said nothing, and Sir Charles shook his head in amusement at her bashfulness. "Your modesty becomes you, but I will see to it you

get the recognition you deserve. I will take it in to be framed
tomorrow.''

Warm blue eyes appraised the young girl. If his own
daughter could grow up to be like this one, he would be a
wealthy man. He rolled the paper up carefully as the girl
departed in a graceful swirl of skirts.

Christmas 1734

N E R V O U S at attending the same dinner with Lord Kerry, an attainment of equality she had never dared imagine, Katy hurried toward the stairway and the party below, petticoats rustling satisfyingly behind her.

At the sound of her approach, the men waiting in the hall glanced up and quieted, watching her descent. A piece of blue heaven floated down to join them, golden halos illuminating her angelic face as she smiled in greeting, the smile becoming a look of pure joy when she recognized the faces staring up at her.

Each man betrayed a different reaction at the sight. Jake Horne swallowed visibly at the transformation of the girl governess into this unfamiliar lady, and he glanced nervously at the ill-fitting borrowed coat he wore, feeling totally out of place in this elegant company.

Lord Kerry thought of nothing as he stared into violet eyes, the last two months of loneliness welling up inside him, becoming an unbearable ache as he watched the slender figure glide to within his reach. Unable to tear his eyes away from hers, he captured delicate fingers with his hand and guided them to his lips, kissing them lightly.

Sir Charles nodded his appreciation as the girl descended, noticing the girl's fixed gaze and turning to find its object. At the sight of Lord Kerry's glazed expression, Stockbridge pursed his lips in a silent whistle and his blue eyes contemplated the young lord thoughtfully. He still did not believe the rumors he had ignored in London about these two, but he began to understand what kept them going. The tension between them was almost palpable, yet they seemed to be totally oblivious of it. Fools that they were.

The group drifted naturally into the study while explanations of Jake's appearance floated about. Sensing his nervousness, Katy took the young man's hand and curled her fingers about it as he explained his errand from the ship's captain to Lord Kerry. Jake looked down at her gratefully, not yet accustomed to thinking of this bare-shouldered goddess as the windswept girl from the ship. Kerry poured himself another drink and watched the pair suspiciously, leaving Sir Charles to explain the sale of shares in the larger ship that had finally been completed, making him one of Jake's new employers. Then Katy spied her drawing on the study wall and tensions fled the room as everyone crowded around it, laughing and talking at the same time.

Embarrassed by this public display of a private gift, Katy attempted to persuade Sir Charles to remove it. "If you leave it there, all your guests will be able to see it and no one will ever speak to me again. I beg of you, please, hide it before another soul walks through that door."

"Nonsense. Would you deny an old man his amusements? What do you think, Southerland, will the drawing offend?"

"Personally, I find myself totally offended that she thinks of me as an elegant but decidedly wicked tomcat, but then, everyone else appears to me as totally amusing. I vote it stays." Lord Kerry quirked his eyebrow in the same manner as the maligned tomcat and glanced quizzically at his ward, whose cheeks were rapidly growing pink.

"You deny the connotation, then, milord?" she murmured softly, eyes dancing beneath lowered lashes.

He tweaked a golden curl and grinned. "Cat-egorically, my friend."

The ensuing groans were interrupted by the arrival of more guests and the entrance of Elizabeth, and soon both study and drawing room milled with people. Quickly appropriated by the ladies, Lord Kerry found himself the center of attention in the salon, while in the study his Christmas gift became the topic of conversation.

At dinner, Jake and Katy found themselves isolated at the far end of the room, where Elizabeth had hastily found places for them. Knowing they would never be part of the glittering panoply compounding the remainder of the company, they were content to amuse themselves with tales of their last months apart.

Along with the Stockbridges, Lord Kerry graced the front of the room. Having kept himself aloof from his neighbors for so long, he was now the object of everyone's interest, and he dominated the conversation whether he spoke or not. Still, his eye wandered occasionally to the end of the room and the laughing pair so obviously engrossed in their own *tête-à-tête*.

Watching Katy, he realized her naturally affectionate nature was flowering under the congenial circumstances she found herself in. Perhaps it was her Gallic heritage, but she hugged and kissed easily and naturally, reaching out to touch those close to her as he had seen her do with Anna and Jake. Yet she refrained from touching him unless he instigated it.

Kerry's mind wandered, puzzling over this new discovery. There could be only one reason for her reserve with him, and that was her awe of his title and position. Not yet ready to accept that there might be more elemental reasons for her timidity, he vowed to break through the shell of her resistance. Green eyes flashed determinedly as another burst of laughter drifted up from the far end of the room, and he deliberately turned to stare at the daring décolletage of the woman beside him.

Katy was not totally unaware of Lord Kerry's presence. Without looking at him, she could see the glittering gold braid of his tan superfine coat, the immaculate white fall of linen at neck and sleeves, and the burnished copper of unpowdered hair. But it was impossible to see his articulate, ever-changing features in her mind's eye without looking directly at him, and this she refused to do. She did not need the reminder of the length of that candlelit room and its crowd of powdered and bewigged ladies with their glittering diamonds and jewels to remind her of the distance between them; it was a basic part of her nature. To be forced to visibly see what she already knew existed was too painful, and she refused to look up the formidable length of table separating them.

After dinner, Katy retired to a quiet corner of the salon, much to Elizabeth's relief. But to Katy's surprise, she was soon joined by the older sister of one of her students.

Katy felt an instant antagonism for this self-confident plantation belle, but hid it behind a demure expression as she studied Miss Amanda Lyttle. A buxom beauty with flashing dark eyes and glossy black hair, her companion was all that Katy was not. Well aware her vivacious coloring would contrast favorably against Katy's small frame and colorless complexion when the other guests entered, she placed herself accordingly.

As the large double doors to the salon swung open, Katy felt the girl beside her tense as her eyes eagerly swept the crowd. But Katy had no need to search for Lord Kerry, drawn to those intense green eyes like a magnet as soon as he fastened them on her. A slow smile crossed his lips as he met her gaze, but there was yet a room full of panting ladies and talkative men to traverse before he could reach her. With deliberation he started making a direct path to his goal, stopping to bow over hands and accept introductions as briefly as possible while always heading in the one direction. He would have his pleasure out of this evening if he had to ride roughshod over everyone in the room to do it.

At last Lord Kerry walked up confidently to the settee, bowing gallantly to the two girls and acknowledging Jake with a nod.

"I trust you took good care of my ward during dinner, Mr. Horne. You will not mind if I borrow her for a few moments, will you?"

There was no reply the boy could make to this request, and Kerry turned expectantly to Katy.

"Your lordship, I would like to introduce a sister of a student of mine, Miss Amanda Lyttle. She is eager to make your acquaintance." Katy felt suddenly ill-at-ease, realizing all eyes in the room were upon them. A private conversation with Lord Kerry would be impossible under these conditions, but the glitter in his eye told her he was not particularly concerned. It was easy for him to flout society, but she was forced to walk a thin line if she wished to remain his friend and maintain her own reputation.

Kerry took the offered hand, taking keen note of heaving bosom and eager eyes, concluding there was little virtue to be tested in the soul of Miss Amanda Lyttle. "I am honored, Miss Lyttle. Such loveliness does not often come my way."

Katy's lips tightened at this absurdity, but the fool beside her lapped it up eagerly. "Thank you, your lordship. I had no notion a person of your eminent bearing would take any notice of my humble presence." Long lashes fluttered demurely against rosy cheeks, calling attention to voluptuous ruby lips.

Raising one eyebrow, Kerry looked from this tasty morsel to his ward's scornful expression and smiled inwardly. She had a lot yet to learn about hiding her emotions. "Miss Lyttle, it has been a pleasure, but if you will excuse us, I would like to have a few words with my ward. Katy, if you would fetch a shawl, I'd like to go out on the veranda for a few moments. You look as if you might need some fresh air."

Trembling at her temerity, Katy ignored his extended hand. "No, milord, I believe I'd best stay here. There are other guests waiting to speak with you, and I cannot be so selfish as to occupy your time."

She knew she was right in refusing him. Lady Stockbridge would be furious if she left the room with him, tongues would wag all over town for a fortnight at such behavior, but most of all, she did not trust the look in his lordship's eye right now. He had had something on his mind from the moment he walked in that door after dinner, and she was not yet ready to find out what.

Jaw tightening at this refusal, Kerry could only attribute it to the young seaman at Katy's side, and the anger that had been brewing all evening began to surface. Fully aware of the irrationality of his anger, the knowledge only infuriating him more, Kerry turned to the black-haired wench at Katy's side. "Miss Lyttle, would you care to be selfish enough to accompany me to the veranda? I suddenly find the room quite stifling."

Thrilled that the little governess's stupidity had given her such an opportunity, Amanda quickly grabbed at the chance, taking his arm with simpering theatricality, flashing velvet-warm eyes at him. A cynical smile tilted Kerry's lips at her blatancy, but without a backward glance he spirited the excited Miss Lyttle into the darkness outside the French doors.

Baffled by the entire performance, Jake looked down on his gentle Katy to see tears sparkling in her eyes before she moved to conceal them. Perplexed, he muttered, "I don't understand."

Katy could only reply, "Neither do I," and turn her head away. And she didn't understand. Why, after two years of trusting him implicitly, should she suddenly refuse Lord Kerry? She might as well have stabbed a dagger into her own heart as to send him off to make love to that brazen hussy. No explanation existed for her fear.

The couple did not return immediately and time became a meaningless blur. Jake stayed by her side, having nowhere else to go or place to be. She vaguely remembered Mr. Stone and his wife stopping to talk, pleased to see Jake once again, and the knowing glances between the pastor and his wife seemed to assume a romance in her life. It took all Katy's willpower to avoid staring at the doors and willing Lord Kerry to appear again.

Amanda's mother returned to the drawing room, looking for her daughter, but Katy only mentioned that she had last seen her with Lord Kerry. Shaking her head, Mrs. Lyttle wandered off in search of her hostess. Within minutes, Lady Stockbridge caught Katy's eye, and Katy excused herself to find out what was needed, dreading the question she knew would be asked.

"Katherine, you must go rescue Lord Kerry from that dreadful girl, I have guests here impatient to meet him. It was extremely rude of her to carry him off like that. Why ever did you permit it?"

The monologue threatened to continue, but Katy nodded acquiescence and scurried off before her employer began demanding answers to her inane questions. Angry at herself, angry at Lord Kerry, she raced up the stairs and grabbed a shawl. If she had to go out there and make a fool of herself, at least she would be warm. And maybe by the time she got back down, the aggravating couple would have had the sense to come in.

One glance around the drawing room when she returned told her nothing had changed. She waved at Jake, who stared morosely at the doorway she had departed by; then she slipped back down the hallway before he could follow. If she were going to make a fool of herself, it would be privately. She slipped into the empty dining room, where no one could notice her rescue attempt.

For late December, the air was unexpectedly warm, but this climate was much warmer than the one to which she was accustomed. There wasn't time for her eyes to adjust to the darkness; surely they would see her outlined in the lighted doorway.

"Amanda!" she called lightly, not wishing to attract the attention of anyone near the other doors. The darkness remained silent, only the murmurs from inside breaking the quiet. Moonlight made patches of light through the vine-covered latticework and as Katy's eyes adjusted to the change, she could decipher the shadows creating intertwined figures against the vines. "Amanda!" she cried more insistently, anger boiling to the surface at this unavoidable substantiation of what had been only conjecture before.

The figures parted with a rustle of skirts and a low voice; then the disheveled shape of Amanda stepped forward. "What are you doing out here, spying on us?" Amanda hissed, dark eyes snapping with anger as she brushed her hair back into place and adjusted her bodice.

"Your mother is looking for you. Should I have sent her out here to find you?" Irate at the unjust accusation, Katy wished she had done just that and saved herself the trouble of protecting the girl's behavior. A low chuckle from the darkened corner told her Lord Kerry listened, and her fury grew.

A quick intake of breath was all the reply Amanda made as

she flounced past Katy to the drawing room doors, unaccompanied. When she disappeared, Katy turned to the unseen figure she knew lurked nearby.

"I don't suppose you have cooled off any," she said scathingly, "but Lady Stockbridge is about to have a nervous fit over your absence. If you would deign to put in an appearance sometime before the evening is over, it will be greatly appreciated." Swirling around, she reached for the door, but a strong hand grasped her shoulder and pulled her back around.

"I knew if I waited long enough, faithful Katy would come to my rescue. Now that you're here, stay awhile." A scent of whiskey and muted cologne wafted around her as Kerry's arm covered her shoulders, firmly guiding her away from the safety of the lighted doorway into the vine-covered darkness.

Eyes adjusting to the dimness, she could see the pale outline of Kerry's face next to hers, and shivered lightly. He pulled the shawl tighter around her but the shivering did not cease.

"What do you want of me that you could not say in there? Why bring me out here like this? Put me in this embarrassing position? What is wrong with you?!" Katy whispered furiously, unable to control her shaking. He would not release her; she could feel the pressure of his fingers through the thin shawl, sense the masculine nearness that so terrified her. The rough weave of his coat brushed against her bare arm, and she jerked away.

"At last, my little kitten bares her claws. The lass is not all sweetness and light after all," Kerry teased liltingly, his soothing voice coaxing her gently as he stroked her arm, calming her jitters. "I merely wished to thank you for your handsome gift—is that not enough excuse to see you?"

The hypnotic spell of his voice held her as she looked up into emerald lanterns, her shivers ceasing in the fires she found there. His closeness was warm against the cool night air, and she felt herself drawn to him, the distance between them now measured in inches.

"The idea was Sir Charles's. I do not see you thanking him." Her words were brave but quietly spoken. She could not move from his hold.

"I doubt that much of it belongs to Sir Charles. A tomcat, Katy? Is that how you see me?"

A finger stroked a thick golden loop of hair. His arm dropped to her fragile waist, and heart pounding frantically against the bars of her rib cage, Katy wished she could read his expression in the darkness.

"And did you not prove it tonight with that alley cat? What else would you have me think of you?" Strange, but she could not summon the anger to give her words force. The broad hand at the small of her back brought her closer and now the rough shoulder of his coat brushed her cheek.

"The alley cat needed her whiskers clipped. I prefer kittens, myself." There, now he had her. There was nothing else she could do but step into his arms. And Kerry closed them around her, feeling slender arms slide around his neck as he folded her against his chest, feeling young breasts crushed gently against him as he bent his head toward the heavenly aroma of soft lips.

Katy clung to him, feeling herself pulled up into his powerful arms as their lips meshed and melted together and parted with his persistence. Then she was entrapped in the warmth of his mouth, his tongue darting like a rapier to pierce her resistance, and she succumbed willingly to this devastating intrusion, a strange warmth flooding through her, demanding more, demanding to be touched, held, demanding things she could not put a name to.

Then he was releasing her, returning her to her feet, his lips brushing her hair as his hands caressed bare shoulders before covering them once more with the woolen cloth. "My Katy has grown up," Kerry whispered huskily, a lump in his throat interfering with his speech as he held her shoulders, reluctant to let her go entirely. He had wanted only a casual kiss, a poultice to heal the wound of resentment, but he had found something more, much more than he intended. And he regretted it instantly.

"Is that so bad?" Katy asked timidly. Never before had she felt these sensations, and she was half-terrified at their compelling nature, half-curious to find out where they led.

"No, growing up is not so bad, it has its advantages, my

love. You just must be careful that you use them wisely, and I fear I did not tonight.''

Kerry's arms fell to his sides as he stared into those fathomless pools, violet-black in the darkness. "You are a woman now, Katherine. I will have to start treating you as one.''

She had need of the support of his arms around her while she tried to contain the raging emotions he had stirred inside her, but instead, he was pulling away. She punished him for his desertion by retaliating bitterly, "I don't know that I wish you to treat me as a woman. You seem to have a singular disrespect for the gender.''

"No more so than the fools of either sex." Kerry's eyes were feverishly bright as he stared down at the golden head betrayed by a moonbeam, knowing the time for intimate caresses had ended. Now that she responded to him as a woman, he could no longer play his uncle-like role, and admittedly, his thoughts were decidedly un-uncle-like. "I will not treat you so disrespectfully again, Katherine, if you will excuse my momentary aberration and allow me to remain your friend.''

Katy moved from the moonbeam into a darkened corner of the porch. She knew better than he how impossible it was to think of him as only a friend, but her only other alternative meant ruination, and he would most certainly think her a fool if she chose that course.

"I am in no position to excuse a member of the nobility. As you and I well know, milord, you are free to do with me as you please.''

She spoke softly and tonelessly, ignoring the angry intake of breath behind her. "But if you truly wish to be my friend, you would not harm my reputation by lingering out here longer.''

The cold formality of her words did not belong to the mischievous kitten he knew, but the proper governess Belinda had created, and Kerry bowed to her wishes. "Very well, Katherine, I will return you to Elizabeth's good graces.''

The doors clicked closed behind him as he departed, but a minute later she heard the sound of their reopening and a hesitant step upon the wooden planks. Hoping she remained well hidden by the darkness, Katy chose to ignore the intruder. Not until she recognized his whispered voice did she realize it was Jake.

"Jake?" With a trace of relief Katy turned to face him, clasping the hands he offered her. Feverishly, her mind still awhirl from the passion of a prior encounter, she clutched his hands tighter. "Jake? Will you do me a favor?"

"For you, Katy, anything." Jake spoke lightly, trying to hide his concern. He had seen Amanda's furious arrival sometime earlier, but the controlled look of pain on Lord Kerry's face when he finally rejoined the company sent Jake searching for his recalcitrant Katy. He had not prepared himself for her response.

"Will you kiss me, Jake?" Desperately Katy clung to this one thread of sanity, hoping this burning fever could be satiated with the soothing balm of another kiss, that the memory of Lord Kerry's insistent mouth on hers could be banished by other lips. She moved closer to Jake's ill-dressed lean frame, turning her face up expectantly, eyes wild with a kind of terror.

Heart pounding erratically at this God-sent opportunity, Jake put his hands around her waist and drew her closer, not daring to touch her smooth shoulders with his rough hands. Then her bare arms were wrapped about his neck and his lips hungrily sought the prize he had never expected to achieve.

With disappointment, Katy found no solace in Jake's rough embrace, the warmth of his kiss finding no match in the coolness of hers, and her heart filled with sorrow. She had used Jake, taken advantage of his kindness, and stirred his hopes in much the same manner as Lord Kerry had done her. She was no better than he.

"You deserve better, Jake. Let us go in." Katy slipped from his embrace and turned for the door, but for a second time that night a strong hand prevented it.

"Let me be the judge of that, Katy," Jake pleaded. "I know I can't never be his lordship, but I'll be somebody someday, and I can do more for you than he can." He knew who had inspired Katy's earlier passion; it was a path that led nowhere, and he wished he could prevent her taking it.

Katy bowed her head, sorry that Jake had guessed what she

would have preferred to keep to herself. "It is not like that, Jake. He doesn't know how I feel. He is an honorable man, no matter what anyone says. He will not harm me."

"He's a man, Katy, one used to getting what he wants," Jake said sadly. And any fool could see what Lord Kerry wanted, any but Katy.

She had no wish to think about the implications of Jake's words just yet. "I'm sorry, Jake. Perhaps someday it will be different, but not now."

He nodded miserably and tucked her hand into the crook of his arm, guiding her back to the lighted doorway. He understood, all right, and he would be waiting when it came time to pick up the pieces.

Begging a headache, Katy asked Jake to excuse her. He escorted her to the hallway and stopped her retreat by taking her hand, a familiarity he figured he had earned. "Katy, I'll be going back to the ship in the morning and I don't know when we'll return. I know I ain't got any right to ask you to wait for me, but can I see you when we get back?"

"You are one of my closest friends, Jake Horne. I certainly hope you will wish to see me when you come back. It's a rough life you have chosen—please take care of yourself." She touched his cheek briefly, understanding the mute appeal in his eyes but unable to promise more. If only things could be so simple, she thought sadly, and looked away from the hope she found there.

Then he was gone and Katy turned to the study to find Sir Charles and ask his permission to retire. He had been most kind to her, and she did not wish to seem ungrateful for the exceptional courtesy he had extended; the least she could do was ask if there were any more she could do for him that evening.

She found him momentarily alone, freshening his drink. The study doors had been left open for the benefit of those wishing to escape the crowd, but no effort had been made to illuminate it with the excessive candlelight of the glittering drawing and dining salons. It remained a cool cavern of tranquility amidst the mob.

Sir Charles looked up and motioned with his head as he

poured his drink. "Come in, child. Was that young Jake I heard leaving?"

"Yes. He is returning to his ship in the morning. Is there anything else I might do for you before I retire?" Standing quietly in this haven, Katy felt more relaxed than she had all evening, the strain of Lord Kerry's closeness not extending to this room.

"Giving up the social event of the year so early? I wish I could do the same. I'm just not the society gentleman like your Lord Kerry, I suppose. He seemed quite pleased with your gift, by the way. Said it was too good to waste on the wall of his shack; he's taking it to Charleston with him when he goes in the morning." If Sir Charles noticed the look of shock in the young governess's eyes, he was too polite to mention it. "He's bought himself a town house there and plans to hang it in the place of honor, wherever that might be." He sipped his drink and stared at the fire, allowing the girl to regain her composure.

"I will have to give him the rough sketches, after all, to adorn the walls of his 'shack.' He will be returning there sometime, won't he?" She was breaking all the rules by showing any kind of interest at all, but she could not bear not knowing. Already he was missing the social life. How long would it be before he abandoned the backwoods life of the colonies altogether and returned to England?

"Of course. But a man like that can't be expected to live like a hermit. He'll stay in town long enough to hire some people to work the place and buy supplies and be back by spring, I wager." He would have added that the idiot should have had sense enough to bring a wife if he wished to avoid the loneliness of plantation life, but he sensed Katy was not the one to mention this to.

"Then I shall have time to draw some new sketches before he returns," she said quietly. "If there is nothing else I can do . . ." Eager to take her thoughts to the privacy of her room, she let her words trail off as she moved to leave.

Almost as an afterthought, Sir Charles halted her. "Katy." Staring into the fire, flames highlighting the hills of his craggy face and flickering off the gold buttons of his satin waistcoat, hands jammed in his pockets, pulling the heavy blue coat back from his broad chest, he spoke thoughtfully, without looking up at the wisp of a girl waiting for his words.

"I know you have made friends here, and I hope you are happy with us, but if you ever have the need to talk to someone, I want you to know my door is always open. There are some things that are easier to look upon from the pinnacles of age."

Searching the kindly blue light of his eyes, Katy found nothing there but the best of intentions, and she smiled gently. "I do not think you have quite reached the pinnacles yet, Sir Charles, but I thank you for your offer. It has been too many years since I have confided in anybody, so you will forgive me if I find it difficult to take advantage of your offer?"

"Sometimes I think you are not so young as you appear, Katy, but the offer still stands. Now, go, get your rest before that impish daughter of mine awakes you with her demands for tonight's gory details." A half-smile flickered quickly and disappeared as the girl bobbed a curtsy and left; then he returned to staring morosely at the fire.

Lying awake, staring at the moonlit swatches on her ceiling, Katherine listened to the departing guests, her mind unable to rest easily after the turmoil of the evening. When had her loyalty to the man who had saved her life turned into that consuming need she had felt at his kiss tonight? Was it possible for him to feel the same way too? Or was his passion only the way men felt about women, that drove them to places like Saffron Hill to slake their needs? Remembering the long-ago night she had lain in his bed wondering what the need was between men and women, Katy gently touched her now well-developed breasts through the thin material of her shift.

Earlier, they had ached for the touch of the man who held her, and just the memory of that moment returned the pain. Fondling a distended peak, she tried to imagine what it would be like to have Kerry's hand there, and the ache grew worse. It was exquisite torture and a dangerous path, for she knew now that only Lord Kerry could arouse this feeling in her, and she could never allow him to satisfy it. Sadly she thought of her unresponsive reaction to Jake's passionate caresses, and wondered if it were possible for two people ever to feel the same.

And as she fell into a fitful sleep, heavy footsteps slowed and lingered briefly below her window before moving determinedly off in another direction.

January–June 1735

TALES OF LORD KERRY'S sojourn in Charleston drifted back by way of riverboat, the sloops and rafts connecting the two towns being welcome messengers for those who found themselves isolated from society. The river men eagerly collected the tales to exchange over a tanker of ale or rum at the local inn. As the rumors traipsed from house to house, Katy eventually heard all of them, discredited some, but assumed a grain of most to be true.

Kerry had left for Charleston immediately after the Christmas party. While he had not yet attained the scandalous reputation of his more rakish London days, it did not take much to establish a reputation of any sort in this backwoods society. Obviously the toast of Charleston society, he attended every social function given. That was to be expected, and Georgetown was proud of what it considered to be the success of one of its leading citizens. But as the last months of winter drew on and the rumors of his wild behavior became more descriptive and numerous, his image tarnished rapidly. The nobleman's dissolute behavior might be accepted by the *beau monde* of London, but though the Carolinas had not been settled by Puritans, their morals rivaled those of their country brethren in England and they frowned upon open licentiousness. And Lord Kerry's behavior was rapidly achieving that status.

But the time had to come when Lord Kerry would return to his plantation, and as the first warm days of March brought out the restlessness of spring, Katy's thoughts turned feverishly to his return. He had not written once during the period of his absence, and she wasn't certain he would even wish to see her again, but still she waited with nervous impatience for the sound of his teasing lilt or the sight of a bright copper head.

His disappearances had never affected her like this before, and she blamed Kerry for it entirely. She had been content to be a small niche in his life, someone to turn to when his society friends were of no use, knowing she could be nothing more. But his kiss had destroyed that contentment, and his vow never to repeat it only brought a raging desire for more. Sensibility was not lost, she still knew there could be nothing between them unless she gave up everything she had worked so hard to gain, but it did not prevent her from hearing his bantering laughter in her sleep or seeing him in every jaunty male figure who walked the street.

Sitting in the warmth of mid-March sunlight streaming through the French doors of the salon, working on a long-neglected embroidery, Katy listened with astonishment to the sound of familiar hoofbeats halting in the roadway. Lord Kerry's matched bays had that particular gait, but she could not imagine hearing them so far from the streets of London. Before she had time to investigate, the drawing-room doors flew wide and Lord Kerry filled the entrance, his fitted coat of chocolate brown and tight tan breeches sparkling immaculately in the sunlight, the burnished copper of his hair shining in its knotted queue. Behind him, the black maid stood wide-eyed and clasping her hands, unable to restrain this irrepressible guest.

"Katy! Why aren't you with the myriad of little students I have heard so much about?" As he strode into the room, Kerry's vibrant energy dominated its large proportions and the room consequently seemed to shrink.

"Miz Katy, I couldn't stop him . . ." Apologetically the maid gestured at the stranger's grinning figure.

"That's all right, Tess, wild stallions couldn't stop him." Turning to her grinning guardian, Katy asked, "Shall I have Tess fetch Lady Stockbridge? She's in the kitchens planning dinner."

"For God's sake, no, leave her where she is." He spun his tricorne into a chair seat and sat down uninvited on the settee next to Katy, his polished boots sprawled comfortably out in front of him.

"Don't disturb Lady Stockbridge, Tess, but if Sir Charles should come in, show him in here, please." Dismissing the maid, Katy turned an inquiring eye to her ebullient companion. "Today is Saturday, in case you have lost track of time, and with any luck, my myriad of little students are home writing papers reflecting their present level of development, which means most of them are copying their ABC's. What can you possibly have heard about them?" Despite the coolness of her tone, eager eyes scanned his appearance, finding nothing in the warm light of his eyes or the cynical curve of his lips.

They curved now in a crooked grin. "That's my Katy speaking; the governess would never resort to sarcasm." As he spoke, he watched her appraisingly, noting the new mature assurance gained with the confidence of being secure in her position, but admiring mostly the lively violet eyes. "Your little charges seem to have relatives all over Charleston who delight in pointing up their accomplishments and praising you to the skies. If I did not think they were doing it for my benefit, I would swear it was a conspiracy to prevent my forgetting your existence."

"If I had known that was your wish, I should have stayed in London, but there is little I can do about garrulous relatives at this date. You do realize the grapevine works both ways, and I have been the hapless victim of your exploits ever since you left?" Indignant at his accusations, the violet eyes snapped with anger, and she moved to arise from his nearness.

A hard hand clamped down on hers, holding her pinned to the chair. "I meant that as a jest, kitten. Now sit down and tell me what tales have rubbed your fur the wrong way.

Surely they can be no worse than the ones you have heard in London?'' Long brown fingers circled soft white ones comfortingly.

Tears sprang unbidden to her eyes, and she shook her head and turned away. She should have known better than to believe those wild tales of this man who had shown her only the most extravagant of kindnesses, yet she knew there had to be some germ of truth to these scurrilous rumors. The pressure of his hand increased, and she was drawn to return her gaze to him.

"This is not London and your behavior has shocked everyone! Why didn't you just fight a duel and complete the image? I thought you intended to change when you left London.''

Puzzled by the tears shining in the corners of her eyes, Kerry tipped Katy's chin up and carefully dried the dampness with his handkerchief as he replied. "I did not say I would remain celibate or not enjoy a good wine when offered one. I cannot see where I have done any more than that to offend the dignities of the townspeople.''

"You deny openly keeping a mistress in your town house while sleeping with half the wives of your friends and hosts, not to mention their daughters? And escorting the town's most notorious women to the homes of respectable citizens? The drinking, people seem to understand, but you can never hope to live down the other conduct.''

To Katy's surprise, Kerry's jaw set in grim anger and his eyes flamed with a fire she had seldom encountered in their easygoing nature.

"And you believed all this nonsense? I thought you possessed better sense.'' He released her then and stood up, stalking the room with a complete reversal of the ebullient mood with which he had entered.

"Milord, that is only the smallest portion of the tales told. I discarded the majority of it, but could see no reason for them all to be entirely false. The rumors in London all held some germ of truth,'' Katy protested his anger.

"My God! The bastard must have gone off the deep end, then.'' He swung around and threw himself down beside her once more, his square jaw still set but the fire gone from his eyes. "I'll tell you the germ of truth, kitten. The 'mistress' you speak of is a respectable widowed lady Betts hired to keep house while I am in town. If the truth be known, it is probably Betts who has the attachment for the lady—she is certainly not my type." Staring across the room, he played with Katy's fingers where they rested on the cushion.

"I will admit to one or two liaisons with women I would not like you to meet, but they were discreet, and at no time did I introduce them in public. For God's sake, Katy, I am not totally insane." He turned back to her then, his face frozen in concentration. "The wives and daughters are all nonsense, of course. I have no intentions whatsoever of putting myself into a compromising position that could only result in getting myself called out or trapped into a disastrous marriage. No, Katy, I think I know where these rumors started."

Without even having to search for the name, it came to her tongue. "Joshua Halberstam," she said unhesitatingly. "What would he be doing here?" Alarm tinged her tone and a cloud shadowed her day with the mention of that hated name.

Kerry stared at her with total astonishment. "Katy, I have told you if you keep that up, you will be hung for witchcraft. How in heaven's name did you know who I was talking about?"

Dismally, at the confirmation of her fears, she shook her head, one fine curl coming loose from its pins and falling on her neck. "That is the only man I know who wishes you evil. Have you crossed him again?" she asked worriedly.

"Lass, you are positively uncanny at times. His father had him appointed to the dubious position of lieutenant governor and it seems he was courting the governor's daughter until I came along. The lady, being fond of titles, took an interest in me, and I daresay the vicious rumors being spread started from that time. Mystery solved. Now, my omniscient kitten, what shall I do to convince the good folk of Georgetown I am not a libertine?" He caught the curl and wound it about his finger, studying the intense blue eyes beside him.

"Attend their dinners liberally, charm the ladies as you well know how to do, tell the men a joke or two . . . *Voilà!* Instant success." Nervously attempting to wrest her hair from his captivity, Katy strove to hide her reaction to Halberstam's proximity. No good would come of his presence, she was certain. "Let go before I scream and add proof to your reputation," she demanded a trifle tartly.

"Not to mention adding a little spice to your own." Kerry teased her nose with the curl and was rewarded with a slap that gained him a hand. "Now for a change of subject, where's Anna? I promised to show her my horses as soon as I brought them in." Abruptly rising, he pulled Katy to her feet with him.

"She is with her father at the shipyards. In case you have not noticed, you will seldom find Sir Charles in when his wife is at home." Tugging his hand firmly, she urged him out the door so she might once more make friends with his handsome thoroughbreds.

But the sight of an enormous black man holding the reins stopped Katy before she reached the horses' heads. Standing quite still as a deer does when it tests the wind for unfamiliar scents, Katy took in the immensity of what appeared to be a half-dressed savage, only the wide brow and stern demeanor denoting human intelligence. With questioning eyes she looked up to her companion for explanation.

"That's Mahomet—it's not his name, of course, but it is as close as I can come. Took him away from some fool who imagined he was a new form of mule; figure I'm going to need some help putting the place together, and Mahomet looks to be just the man for the job." Kerry acknowledged the slave with a nod and stroked the rump of a gleaming bay, giving Katy a sidelong glance. She studied the black man with an intensity that was suffered with dignity by the object of her gaze.

Finally she spoke. "Mahomet, it is a privilege to meet you. May I talk to the horses for a moment?" She extended her hand for the reins, and the huge man gravely handed them to her.

Resting an arm against the lead horse to be certain the animals kept their place, Kerry looked at the girl quizzically. "Katherine, are you in the habit of greeting all slaves with the same words used for gentility?"

"Mahomet is a noble, or, more likely, royalty," she re-

plied simply, without further explanation, as the horses nuz-
zled her hands, looking for the treats she normally carried. If
it were obvious to her that this magnificent man with his
stately bearing could have been no less than an African
prince, she assumed everyone could see it.

With a thoughtful stare, Kerry frowned as he tried to
determine who was the primitive in this tableau: the black
slave straight from the jungles of Africa, the barely tamed
high-spirited thoroughbreds, or the prescient twig of a girl
who communicated without need of speech. Or perhaps it
was himself, civilized to a degree that lacked the understanding drawing the other three together. He supposed it mattered
little, but his gaze continued to rest on the golden head barely
visible between the arched necks of his horses.

In the months following, Kerry frequently took advantage
of the Stockbridges' open invitation to visit. As Katy had
predicted, he soon regained the grace of the townspeople and
became a regular visitor to the dinner tables of Georgetown,
but through one excuse or another, he always came in early
or stayed a day late, spending the extra time with the
Stockbridge family. Because he and Sir Charles shared in
joint business ventures, no comment was made on this practice, and he easily charmed his way into the family circle.

Lacking accommodations to house his own slaves, Kerry
hired those of neighboring plantations to work his fields
during the day, and in the lengthening evenings he and
Mahomet repaired and improved the sturdy cabin left by
previous owners. The newly restored barn began to fill with
other livestock besides his prize bays, and paddocks and
fences grew under their tireless hands.

But by week's end, Kerry looked forward to his trip to
town, not so much for the elaborate dinners and entertain-
ments his unflagging hostesses provided, but for the chance
to relax in the comfort of the Stockbridge home, where he
could be himself and not the eligible bachelor of society. If
he were feeling surly and cynical, no one upbraided him, but
by the end of the evening a secretive gamin grin and bubbling
violet eyes would have him laughing at his own outrageous-

ness, and his mood for the remainder of the visit would return
to its normal affable state.

In this manner, the Stockbridges came to know much more
of Lord Kerry's private life than did all the eager young
things he courted. He regaled them with tales of his family
and news from home, but mostly his interest lay in the new
land around them. Katy listened avidly as he described Twin
Oaks and the grassy knoll topped by the two spreading trees
that gave the place its name. His problems with the hired
help, his latest livestock acquisition, even the wild animals
that came to call became part of his lore, and Katy stored the
anecdotes for further perusal, bringing them out later in the
lonely darkness of her room to add to the growing portrait in
her head of this man who dominated her life.

Shortly after his first return to Georgetown, Kerry came to
call with a tale of a wild Indian he and Mahomet had discovered in the woods at the rear of the estate. Not totally wild,
the Indian spoke some English and was in no position to harm
anyone, having been severely gored by a wild boar while
hunting alone.

Kerry and Mahomet carried the savage back to the cabin,
and Mahomet displayed his knowledge of jungle medicine by
treating the wound with herbs found in the forest. Through
the remaining cold months of winter and on into spring, the
Indian lay recuperating from his injuries, gravely silent at
first, until, learning there was no harm in the giant black man
or his master, he allowed them to attempt communication. At
the end of every week, Kerry reported back to the Stockbridges
and Katy on the Indian's progress and his own efforts to learn
the Indian's dialect, until the week in May when the savage
walked into the woods and never returned.

After that incident, Katy worried about Kerry's safety, but
he assured her the tribes in this area were friendly to the
settlers, fighting for the British in their occasional skirmishes
with the French and Spanish who occupied much of the
surrounding territories, in return for British support against
more warlike tribes. Katy remained dubious, but there were
no reports of Indian troubles that summer and she gradually
pushed the subject to the back of her mind, along with the

worrisome Joshua Halberstam, as more immediate problems took their place.

With the hot months of spring and summer came the first reports of the fever sickness inhabiting the low-lying areas. Isolated on some of the smaller plantations in the lowlands at first, it caused no immediate concern in Georgetown, but as the heat continued and the river level sank lower, more cases began appearing in the area surrounding the dock. Although none of the victims belonged to his Anglican church, as the only minister in town Mr. Stone felt called upon to visit the sick. Within a week he too was a casualty of the disease and was confined to bed.

Still, the seriousness of the malady did not become evident until the three younger children of one of the dockworkers died of it within the space of one week. Parents grew panicky and several removed their daughters from Katy's school, hoping to keep them home and away from harm. When the pastor's wife succumbed to the fever also, and several more children and a few of the elderly died of it, Katy took her worries to Sir Charles.

He knew as soon as she entered what bothered her and that he could give no easy solution, but he motioned her to a seat. Katy declined, pacing restlessly before his desk as she spoke.

"Sir Charles, I am worried that I am exposing Anna to this disease by allowing my school to continue, but so many of them have family ill at home, I hate to add to their burdens by telling them to keep their children away. What should I do? Is there any way, anything I can do, to protect Anna? Is it the river that causes this fever? Are we far enough from it?"

She stopped to lean against his desk, violet eyes pleading for understanding. She had come to love the hoydenish daughter of this quiet man, but she felt an obligation to the entire community as well as to the Stockbridges. The death of one of her youngest students had precipitated this crisis.

"Katy, I cannot reassure you on any of your questions. If people are the carriers, my going down to the docks every day will expose Anna as much as your students will. You cannot take the entire world on your shoulders, Katy, you can only do your part, and you are doing it well."

Sir Charles studied the girl's dissatisfied frown, knowing youth's restless eagerness to aid the world, but it was bad enough his wife traipsed about town with her remedies; he would not have this chit of a girl exposed also.

But his concerns went unheeded, and his decision for naught. Before the week ended, Sir Charles fell victim to the epidemic, and Katy emptied her classroom. While the remainder of the household moped in dismal fear of this ill omen, Katy sent her young charge to the schoolroom with a list of assignments and joined Lady Stockbridge in nursing the delirious Sir Charles.

Night and day they worked, taking turns applying cool compresses and spooning liquids into his fever-racked body, nursing him with all the household remedies that ever worked for anyone else. In despair Katy watched as two of the people she loved grew old before her eyes: Sir Charles's healthy body growing weak and emaciated, yellowing with fever, and Elizabeth's pretty face growing tired and lined from worry as her husband daily wasted away. The fingers of death tightened around the household, and the servants hid in the back rooms for fear of its touch.

July 1735

THE IDLE GOSSIP of a traveling salesman first warned Kerry of the rapidly spreading epidemic downriver and sent him dashing for his horses. Hitching them to the carriage with dangerous haste, he hollered for Mahomet. With a few terse words of explanation to the frowning black man, Kerry whipped the horses out of the yard, leaving a cloud of dust to settle slowly behind him.

His reckless speed threatened to throw a wheel as the carriage jolted across corrugated dirt roads. He forced his thoughts to stay with his racing horses, but by the time he reached town, the news of fever in the Stockbridge household had his mind in a frenzy to match the state of his horses.

When no one answered his urgent pounding at the Stockbridge door, he let himself in.

Heart pounding frantically in the ensuing silence, Kerry forced himself to stand still in the murky hallway, letting his eyes focus in the dust-moted dimness before calling out. His voice echoed through empty passageways. Panic-stricken as he envisioned a row of coffins similar to those he had passed in the crepe-draped streets, he flung open the drawing-room doors, half-expecting to find the caskets there. But the sun-filled beauty of the room was marred only by a week's accumulation of dust and the unaired, stifling heat of July.

Half in anger at the terrified imaginings of his mind, unable to suppress the vision of pale gold hair rippling across the inexplicably blue velvet lining of a crude coffin, Kerry returned to the hallway, staring up the darkened stairway to the rooms above, fighting the urge to leap the steps and throw open all the doors until his fears were confirmed or disproved. Vowing to do just that if no one answered soon, he began bellowing "Katy!" at the top of his lungs, shaking loose the cobwebs from the ceiling.

A small figure crept to the railing above and looked down, her pale face framed by loose brown hair. "Lord Kerry, hush! My papa's sick and Katy's caring for him," the gremlin whispered loudly.

Before Kerry could reply, another apparition formed in the upstairs hallway, its pale slightness floating with ghostly gracefulness to the side of the stooped figure at the railing. "Go back to your room, Anna, Lord Kerry will be quiet now," she ordered softly, waiting until the child disappeared behind closed doors before looking down at the irate man below, his auburn hair blown to disorder by the wild ride, coat discarded in the summer heat, muscled arms akimbo as he stared upward.

"Where the hell are Elizabeth and all the servants? Why are you the one tending to Sir Charles? Dammit, Katy, I won't have this!" Anger boiling over into concern at her drawn face, Kerry searched violet eyes anxiously for signs of fever, knowing his faithful ward to be capable of working until she dropped, but he found only a tired coolness.

"Lady Stockbridge was up all night; she is resting now, or was until you raised such an unholy rumpus. The servants are terrified of the fever and are hiding out somewhere in back. You did not pick an auspicious occasion for a visit." Katy made no move to descend the stairs, keeping to the shadows above as if to take flight at the slightest disturbance.

"The hell I did," Kerry muttered angrily, temper rising again at her calm coolness after his terrified visions. Raising his voice with determination, he replied, "Go pack your bags

and Anna's. I'll go put the fear of the devil in those women
and have them out of here before you are done.'' Without
waiting for argument, he started down the hall.

"Milord!'' Katy called after the striding figure. When he
halted and looked back questioningly, she caught her lip
between her teeth at his fierce expression, but stumbled on
anxiously, "Where are we going? I can't leave Sir Charles
like this—''

"The maids and Elizabeth can look after Sir Charles. Your
responsibility is to Anna alone, as I have reminded you
before. Now, get those bags packed or I'll carry you out
without anything.'' Turning on his heel, he strode off, the
white linen of his shirt fading into the dimness of the long
hall.

Bewildered, Katy went to rouse her weary mistress, hoping
she might make some sense of Kerry's erratic orders but
knowing in advance she would not. But Sir Charles was in no
condition to countermand his young friend's commands, and
there was no one else to turn to for authority. Elizabeth
looked at her sleepily as Katy made her explanations, then
drew on a robe and wandered dazedly into the hallway,
coming face to face with one of the errant maids followed
close behind by Lord Kerry.

"Tess! Where have you been? And, Lord Kerry, what are
you doing here?'' Puzzled, she tried to focus her attention on
what was happening.

Impatient to carry out his mission, Kerry waved the frightened maid into the sickroom and confronted Sir Charles's
disorganized wife. "I am taking Katy and Anna out to my
plantation until the epidemic is over. They will be safer out
there away from the town and people.''

Nodding her head in confusion, Elizabeth looked from the
implacable lord to his astonished ward. "Yes, of course,
nothing must happen to Anna. Charles would never forgive
me if anything happened to Anna, and the children go so
quickly. Katy, see that her things are packed. Tess will help
me now with Charles.'' And she wandered after Tess.

"Milord, I cannot go with you, you know I cannot,'' Katy
hissed in hushed tones. "Take Anna, if you must, but I have
to stay here. You see how things are. I cannot leave, and I

most certainly cannot go to stay with you.'' Fists clenched
together against the pale folds of her skirt, she stared at her
guardian with awe, wondering if he had gone quite mad.

"I cannot take care of a young child—that is your job. And
your life is more important than your reputation. Go pack
your bags or I will carry out my threat,'' Kerry answered
firmly, then left her standing there as he joined Elizabeth in
the sickroom, with little hope of finding his old friend sensible.

Not fully understanding his urgency, Katy rushed to do as
she was bid. As she hurriedly packed clothes and gathered
books and papers, her anger began to mount at his precipitate
behavior. By the time the three of them were packed into the
carriage, the tension had grown to cataclysmic proportions.
Unable to conceal her anger and confusion, Katy chose to
remain silent, waiting for an explanation that did not come.
Anna looked from one to the other, and with a child's ability
to test the atmosphere of the adults around her, held her
tongue.

Kerry's temper finally exploded the lengthening silence.

"Dammit, Katy! How do I convince you it is better to be
alive and well and a victim of slanderous tongues than lying
in a cold coffin?''

Katy stared out over the rapidly changing landscape. Flap-
ping tongues were the least of her concerns, though they
meant ruination to all her hopes and ambitions if this tale
spread. What she really feared was the truth behind the
rumors, but how could she tell him that?

Bowing her head in acceptance of the path fate had given her,
Katy responded quietly. "For Anna's sake, I will call a truce,
but do not think you're doing me any favors with this
foolishness.''

Kerry gave her a sharp glance and wisely remained silent.

Looking out over the forest of odd-shaped evergreens inter-
spersed with an abundance of hardwoods, Katy marveled at
the lavishness of nature in this new land. So many trees in
one place was a generosity unheard of to one who had known
only the parks of London. She did not wonder at Kerry's love
for this land, if his plantation in any way matched the vast-
ness surrounding them.

Uncertain of the bounds of familiarity and propriety under

these exceptional circumstances, Katy searched for a safe topic of conversation. "Will we see Indians out here?"

Kerry gave a short laugh at her attempt to appear unconcerned. "Your scalp is quite safe, my dear. Any Indians out here are more interested in trading with the white man than scalping him. They kill each other rather frequently and have adopted the bad habit of making slaves of their weaker enemies, but they consider us as powerful allies."

Katy's eyes widened with interest. "But I have heard such stories . . ."

He grimaced expressively. "Many of them true, I don't doubt, but not here, not now. Some of the traders enjoy telling tall tales to frighten the unsuspecting. It's probably why they get along so famously with the Indians. They both lie through their teeth to keep from injuring each other's pride."

"Then what are they really like?"

Kerry shrugged. "It's difficult to tell. Each tribe is different, yet overall, they have much in common, as I understand it. The Cherokee around here farm and trade and go to war in cycles as natural as the seasons. They're part of nature, even their legends say so. Natural forces such as the sun are familiar gods to them. Don't cross them, and you have no reason to fear them."

Katy nodded slowly, tucking this information away for further inspection at a later date. "How long will it be before we reach your lands?"

"We have been on them these last few miles."

Katy looked at him in amazement, momentarily forgetting her worries. "But where are your fields? Should you not have crops and barns and things?"

"Most of the fields are in the lower-lying river areas. This road runs along a ridge on higher ground, where the house and barns are. We should be seeing them in a few minutes."

As the carriage rattled around the bend, the woods opened into a clearing and the grassy knoll with its twin oaks came into view. Behind the trees, farther up the slope, lay a doll-like log cabin overlooking a spreading vista encompassing fields and barns and, in the distance, a curve of the river. Coming upon this sun-drenched hillside after the level, shady path of the road produced an almost awe-inspiring view, and Katy's artistic nature drank it in lovingly; the blend of dark and light and shades of green produced a longing for paints and brush that actually made her hand ache.

Kerry watched her with satisfaction. If he had been worried at all about bringing this city-bred child out here to the wilderness, the thought vanished, replaced by the anticipation of showing her the modest improvements he had already made and the major ones he planned. This venture might not be so bad, after all, and he urged on horses which had no need of urging, sensing the nearness of home and feed.

Mahomet held the steeds in check as Kerry helped the girls from the carriage, the black man's brow drawing into a frown at this feminine invasion. Intent on getting over the painful ordeal of the cabin's limited accommodations, Kerry ignored the slave's disapproval and Anna's clamor to see the pony. His gaze focused on the slender figure moving slowly toward the mud-packed low log building. Considering it only temporary quarters, he had wasted little time on improving it, and now he wished there had been time to add a few finishing touches.

"It is not the kind of habitation I would see you in, but for a few weeks . . ." He caught up with Katy and took her hand, studying her face before allowing her to enter.

With surprise, she glanced up at him, violet eyes mirroring his image. "It is larger than some of the places I have stayed, and, I venture to guess, cleaner. You forget I am a child of the streets and know far worse than this."

And he was a son of wealth and knew far, far better. Katy found it difficult to imagine the immaculate, fashionable Lord Kerry living in this hovel, but the lean, tough man existing beneath that thin surface elegance might. Gazing up into the angular strength of the familiar face beside her, she saw that man now, and longed to reach out and caress the worried muscle of his jaw.

Firmly tucking her small hand into the crook of his arm, Kerry led her through the doorway, ducking slightly to avoid the low clearance as they entered. Standing in the middle of the small front room, he seemed to fill the limited space as he waved his arm in a welcoming gesture. "My home, my dear."

Katy glanced quickly around, eyes blinking in the dim light of the papered windows. In one corner stood a makeshift table and two incredibly spindly chairs held together by wires and twine. Behind the table stood a bookshelf filled to over-flowing with leather volumes and papers. Across the room, the brick hearth held a flickering fire and a bubbling black kettle whose aroma filled the room with scents of meats and herbs. Except for assorted shelves and sundries, the room was vacant of all other furniture.

"Someone has already started dinner," she said thought-fully, leaving Kerry's side to stir the pot with a long wooden ladle. To say more would be embarrassing to both of them.

"Mahomet. We take turns burning whatever is available." Kerry took the spoon from her hand and tasted the brew. "Aagh. If you can make any reparations to this vile brew, you have the position of cook for the duration of your stay. Now let it be, and let me show you your luxurious accom-modations."

The back room contained only a washstand with the neces-sities, an old wardrobe, and a large bed rigged of leather thongs and feather mattress. Kerry stood in the doorway watching as Katy slowly moved around the room, touching these items she knew to be his.

"And you, milord? If we put you out of your room, where will you sleep?" She was not worried about his intentions, only concerned for his comfort, and a mildly inquiring light shone in her eyes as she looked to him to supply the answer.

Kerry crossed his arms, the bulge of work-hardened mus-cles visible even through the loose-sleeved shirt. "I have a choice, kitten. I can sleep down in the barn with Mahomet, or if you have no strong objections, I can rig up a pallet in the corner of the front room. It is up to you, but I would feel better if you two were not alone in this cabin at night."

"So would I. We are putting you out of your bed, we will not put you out of your house too." Katy moved past his lounging figure in the doorway, almost glad of the hardship of his accommodations and the amount of work they would require of her. Work would keep her from dwelling on his constant proximity for days and nights untold. "Now, if you will tell me where to find the salt and if you have a bottle of wine I might use . . ."

The stew was not a culinary masterpiece, but with Katy's repairs, it was edible, and the pan-fried bread disappeared with gratifying rapidity. Mahomet, being Kerry's constant companion during many long months, remained so now, only removing himself to a corner to eat while Anna and Katy occupied the two chairs and Kerry built himself a stack of crates for a seat. They ate mostly in silence, only Anna's excited chatter keeping the conversation going as Katy's eyes threatened to close wearily after the long week of exhausting hours, and Kerry held his tongue. Noticing again how drained her face was of color, he prayed he had not been too late in rescuing her from the disease-ridden town and that a long night's rest would effect a cure. Once the meal ended, he assumed the chore of cleaning up and sent Katy off to prepare Anna for bed.

It was totally dark outside before Katy returned to the front room to find Kerry seated cross-legged before the glowing embers of the dying fire. At her entrance, he jumped up to move a chair to the fireside, but she shook her head wearily.

"No, milord, I think I will retire also. Anna is in a strange bed and a strange place; she will need my company."

"Don't look so grim, Katherine, you will turn into a Belinda yet. I meant you no harm in bringing you here. Do you not trust me any longer?" He pulled a pipe from his coat pocket and tamped down the tobacco, watching the girl closely as he carried out the procedure.

Katherine stared at her nail-bitten hands as he spoke. She trusted him, but she could no longer trust herself, yet she could not tell him this. He would only laugh at her naiveté. It was only too evident Kerry took his role of guardian seriously and thought of her as he did Anna; if he realized at all how she felt, he would never have brought her here.

Sadly she replied, "How will Sir Charles feel about me when he finds I allowed you to carry us off like this? All the rumors I have worked so hard to bury will be uncovered again."

"The one thing Sir Charles cares most about in this world

is Anna, and if you should risk your reputation to save her
health, I daresay he will find it in his heart to forgive you.''
Kerry puffed the pipe into flame, then removed it from his
lips to give her his crooked grin. ''And if anyone dare malign
your reputation, I am not above creating a cook and maid and
guesthouse to preserve the proprieties. Will that satisfy you?''

''You would not say such things to Sir Charles?'' Katy
asked, aghast.

''No, of course not. My mother long since despaired of my
incorrigible tale-telling, but I employ it only with those who
have no business in the matter. I would not lie to Sir Charles
about something that affects him so closely as his daughter,
nor would I ever lie to you, kitten. My scruples may be
limited, but they do exist.'' Smiling inscrutably, Kerry returned to pulling on his pipe.

He was impossible. Just when she should be angriest with
him, or at least suitably dismayed at his lack of morals, she
found herself joining in his laughter. The months of holding
herself aloof from his friendship, simply because of the emotions aroused by one kiss, dissolved in an instant under the
nobleman's open frankness.

''Remind me to send your mother a note of sympathy; a
son such as you must be a heavy burden to bear.'' A small
smile lit her face as she returned his gaze, admiring the red
highlights of his hair caught in the fading firelight.

''I can well imagine the duchess receiving such a letter and
deciding the writer to be of such sensibility as to deserve her
trust and joining you in conspiracy against me. No, thank
you, Katy, reserve your condolences. And if our differences
are settled, I think you'd best go on to bed before you
become overly tired.'' Kerry refrained from telling her that
while her pale face and glittering eyes enhanced her beauty,
they increased his concern, and he hid his protective attitude
behind words of humor.

With a smile of gratitude, Katy moved swiftly from the
room before he could see how difficult it was for her to do.

Summer 1735

THE FIRST DAY set the pattern for the following weeks. Katy rose in the early-morning darkness, and while Kerry washed and shaved outside, she prepared batter-fried cakes or biscuits baked in an old Dutch oven over the fire. Along with slices of cured pork, freshly laid eggs, and generous portions of molasses and honey, breakfast was ready to be served by the time Kerry came in, freshly scrubbed, in clean linen, sniffing the aromas avidly.

Sipping hot coffee with exaggerated grimaces of pleasure, Kerry reached out to tweak a golden curl when Katy laid the table. "I regret not kidnapping you sooner. Continue treating me like this and I will not let you go."

Neatly evading his questing fingers, Katy hastened to return to the fire. "Then I shall serve nothing but ashes from now on, to avoid such a fate."

"Such a fate! Will you listen to the twit? Faith, and I should have you over my knee for such perversity. Do you have any idea of the number of colleens who would be down on their knees for just such an opportunity?" Irish eyes laughed merrily as he dipped a biscuit in honey and observed her pained expression at his outrageous brogue.

"The Irish always were bloody fools, if you'll pardon my English," she responded sweetly, followed by tersely muttered French to the effect that she would do many things for him, but going down on her knees was not among them.

Welcoming a sleepy Anna with a hug and swinging her into a seat, Kerry replied in kind, revealing a thorough knowledge of the language by assuring her in a most insinuating accent it was not in her knees that he was interested. Then, taking Katy by the shoulders, he pushed her into the remaining seat before appropriating the crates for himself.

"Now that we have sharpened our wits on each other in two languages this morning, shall we eat in peace? What are you two lovely ladies planning to do with this day?"

As Anna quickly sketched a multitude of things, beginning and ending with the pony Mahomet had taken her to see the previous evening, Katy surreptitiously studied her guardian. He ate the meal she provided with evident enjoyment, shared equally with his pleasure at her company. The uncommunicative Mahomet provided little outlet for Kerry's natural expansiveness, and Katy could understand the loneliness he must endure throughout the week with no one to share his meals or thoughts. But he seemed quite content with listening to a child's chatter and occasionally teasing Katy into joining the conversation.

Breakfast ended amicably, and when the two men departed for the fields, Katy and Anna were left to their own devices. Deciding a small vacation from schoolwork was called for, they spent the morning visiting the horses and other livestock, gathering berries for a pie, and preparing a noontime dinner.

When the men returned, hot, sweaty, and ravenous from their labors, they were met at the door with warm water and clean towels and the odor of roasting meat and yams. Incredulous at this bounty after so many cold meals of dried meat and stale bread, Kerry quickly washed and dried himself. Pulling on the linen shirt he had stripped off as soon as he left the house that morning, he strode into the cabin, hair still damp from washing and shirt half-unfastened in his haste.

Inside, flushed with the morning's sun and heat of the fire,

Katy presided like a golden-haloed angel floating from hearth
to table with the results of a morning's work. Tousled and
tied loosely at her neck, her hair fell in fine wisps around her
face, violet eyes sparkling as they encountered his surprise.
In the corner, Anna scrubbed at a bowl.

"Look at me, Lord Kerry! Katy's teaching me to cook. We
made a pie out of berries I picked!" She scrambled hurriedly
down from her stool to throw small wet hands about his neck
as he stooped to pick her up.

Eyes shining with the warmth of his welcome, Kerry looked
over the child's head to the slender figure beyond, her smile
lighting her face and stirring his blood. Radiant with happiness
at finally being useful to him, Katy's eyes met his gaze
boldly, and the exchange made all his senses tingle.

They arranged themselves at the table as before, even
Mahomet giving a smile of pleasure at the feast awaiting
them. To find herself a source of pleasure in any way to Lord
Kerry was a joy to Katy, and all the thanks she needed, and
she blossomed under the warmth of his attentions, bringing a
liveliness to the table that had been missing before.

Kerry marveled over the change from the pale, drawn,
nearly listless girl of the day before, but failed to discover the
source of the change. He simply enjoyed the difference a
woman could make in his dull routine and wished Sir Charles
a long recovery, before willingly succumbing to the gaiety. It
took all his willpower and the knowledge of work left to be
done to drag him away once the meal was over.

Stripped to the waist, the curve of muscled shoulders rippling beneath skin bronzed by long exposure to the summer
sun, Kerry strode back to the cabin in the late-afternoon light.
Mahomet had taken the shotgun and gone to find fresh game
while his master hurried with undisguised eagerness toward
home. As he came over the top of the hill, the cabin and its
split-rail fences lay just below him, and a flying figure leapt
from the nearby hedgerow into his arms, scattering flowers
about the ground in her exuberance.

"Whoa there! And it's wild Indians that be attackin' me!"
Kerry swung the childish form onto his shoulder and looked

around, to be quickly rewarded by another slender figure slipping through the bushes, her hands filled with bouquets of wildflowers.

"You are early, milord. I did not expect you until dark." A wide fringe of dark lashes swept upward as Katy regarded Anna's throne and gently admonished her, "You have lost all your flowers, Anna, and somehow that position does not seem quite ladylike." The twinkle of violet eyes belied the words and Anna serenely made herself more comfortable.

"I knew this little hooligan was eager to begin her riding lessons. Did you and the mare have a nice visit today?" Holding the child steady, Kerry moved slowly toward the cabin, admiring the play of sunlight on Katy's hair, nearly white blond in the brilliance of summer sun.

Uncomfortably aware of the bronzed musculature evidenced by the half-naked man at her side, Katy had difficulty remaining casual under his regard, but kept her eyes demurely to the ground. "We did, and she is very lovely, your lordship. I think Broom to be quite an appropriate name for her, better than Brunhilda at any rate."

"By Gad! And I suppose she told you that was her previous name?" Startled at this new example of her prescience, Kerry could only stare at the suspicious grin flirting about her lips.

"And be hung for a witch? I will tell you no such thing. It just so happens I know her previous owner," she replied with a veiled smile that left room for doubt.

Still suspicious, Kerry gave his protégée a dubious frown before lowering Anna to the ground and propelling her in the direction of the cabin. "Off with you, imp, or I'll be thinkin' the place inhabited by leprechauns." Seeing Anna safely off, Kerry turned to study the pink cheeks and sparkling blue eyes of his remaining faerie. "Confess, Miss, you were waiting for me as surely as yon scamp."

Eyes uplifted, brazenly taking in the nobleman's rather awesome state of undress, Katy indulged herself with a wicked smile at his conceit. "And if I were?" she asked suggestively.

Delighted at her impromptu change from demure governess to temptress, Kerry momentarily abandoned himself to the game, catching her by the waist and swinging her around in a wide arc as he would Anna. "Then I shall condemn you to learning to ride along with Anna this evening."

Both exhilarated by the unexpected contact, they parted reluctantly, Katy leaning into Kerry's embrace as he set her down again, his hand lingering at the small of her back as they descended into the cabin yard.

"I have no riding habit and you have no sidesaddle; you will have to find a more suitable punishment." Katy tarried at his side, not protesting the familiarity of the strong hand at her waist, but reveling in this closeness.

The sun burned warm on their backs and a slight sheen of moisture glistened on Kerry's brawny shoulders as they dallied in the yard, not yet ready to enter the cool darkness of the cabin and surrender this freedom they were experiencing. Katy clung to her bouquet as she gazed up into the cool depths of green eyes, barely conscious of his words as he spoke, only the strong hand at her back and the dancing eyes above forming any reality.

"Nonsense. No self-respecting sorceress rides sidesaddle. You may hitch up your skirts and ride astride; there is no one to know but thee and me, and I will not tell."

"I am no sorceress and I will not be setting a good example for Anna. I cannot." Her tone lacked resolution. She would dearly love to ride the beautiful animal she had seen in the stable, and at the moment, she was having great difficulty denying her arrogant lord anything.

"You will. Anna will have to do the same so there is no example to be set. Besides, I do not believe you are not a sorceress. You cast a spell on me the first night we met and have not broken the enchantment yet. Now we had better go in and see what there is left to eat. I don't suppose any of the pie remains?" Steering her toward the doorway, Kerry broke his own charm by returning to the commonplace, not wishing to let this romantic woman-child understand more than was meant.

The charm safely dispelled, each took up their separate tasks, but the memory of sun-drenched happiness lingered on through the evening. The meal was prepared and eaten quickly with little ado in order to make the most of the remaining daylight. Leaving the dishes to be washed later, they followed the leaping figure of Anna to the stables and paddock.

Kerry watched with amused interest as Katy turned her back on him to tuck up her skirts, admiring the display of trim ankles and the beginning of a comely curve of calf before she turned back to face him. Handing the pony's reins to the waiting slave, Kerry captured Katy's tiny waist in his competent hands and with a reassuring smile to surprised eyes, swung her up on her mount in much the same manner as he had Anna.

"Milord, I cannot believe that is the proper way to mount a horse," she reprimanded him, unable to avoid the green laughter of his eyes setting sparks in her own.

"Perhaps not, but it is a good deal more fun," he replied infuriatingly.

On that note the lesson was conducted. Mahomet gravely put the pony through its paces while Kerry took every opportunity to correct Katy's seating on the horse, relying on his hands and not his words to show her the proper posture. When scolded for his familiarities, he merely replied it was the best way to learn and maddeningly increased his efforts.

When all hope of the last rays of light died, Mahomet helped Anna from her perch and Kerry confidently swung Katy from hers, hands lingering at her waist in the gathering darkness as he whispered, "You will make a fine horse-woman yet, my kitten. Do you regret my offer now?"

Feeling the pressure of his hands beneath her breasts, Katy found herself nearly breathless and helpless to remove herself from his hold. Words were her only salvation, for her body had turned traitor. "Milord, I am regretting everything right now. Please let me go. I must see Anna to bed."

"Everything, Katy?" He released her then, taking her hand in trade as they walked back to the cabin. "I cannot believe you mean that."

"I am regretting letting you talk me into coming here." I am regretting your hold on me, and regretting my falling in love with you, were her thoughts, but they could never be uttered.

"No, you're not. You're enjoying yourself but have grown too prudish to admit it. I will not give up until I have driven away every trace of Belinda's prim governess.'' Kerry kept her from entering the doorway a moment longer, attempting to reach the ghostly shape of her pale face in the darkness but not succeeding. It would have been easy to kiss her, just a brotherly peck on the forehead perhaps, but he felt her shy away nervously and released her.

"You are playing God with people's lives again. I wish you would not interfere; let me do as I think proper,'' Katy pleaded fervently. Then, before he could answer, she ran inside.

When Katy had seen Anna to bed and returned to the front room, she found Kerry waiting for her. Pulling her down before the small fire, he sat beside her, holding her hand. Katy glanced at him with curiosity when he remained silent, but the firm jaw and stubborn set to his mouth told her nothing.

He sat quietly a while longer, feeling his tensions fade away in the presence of the small warmth beside him before venturing on to forbidden territory. Running his thumb across the delicate structure held, he asked, "Do you mind my holding your hand?"

Hesitating, Katy replied honestly, "No, milord.''

Nodding approval, Kerry clasped it more firmly. "Good, because I would do so anyway. You are eighteen and almost a woman now, but you're still the same child I held in my arms like a lost puppy that night we met. You can't deny that.''

"I can't deny that once I was that child, but I am no longer. You cannot continue to treat me as you do Anna.''

"I know the difference between eight and eighteen and have no desire to treat you as Anna, but you have not been completely honest with me lately, Katy. Don't you think I can tell when you're hiding behind that prim-governess act? There for a while today I thought I had you back, but I guess I was mistaken. I'm not giving up, though.''

It was Katy's turn to stare silently into the fire. To deny his words would be a lie; to admit them would be to leave herself open for explanations, and she could not do that. She had given him the only response she could make—let her alone—

but he had evidently chosen to ignore this advice. The silence grew longer.

Golden curls caught up in a cap, fine silver-gold threads escaped about Katy's face and sparkled in the firelight. Kerry longed to set them free and shimmering, but cloudy violet eyes held him back. She was right, he was playing God with her life, and his reasons for doing so were murky even to him, but he felt compelled to hold on to the lively spirit he had been given to protect. He would find the reason for her prim reticence and tease it away if he had to hold her captive until the lighthearted Katy he knew returned.

"I have watched you with Anna; you love her, don't you?" He broke the silence, freeing her from the responsibility of answering his earlier accusations.

"I have grown very fond of her, yes," Katy replied, relieved at her reprieve and not judging its direction.

"You should have children of your own. Anna cannot always be a substitute." Kerry knew he had struck a nerve when she flinched visibly and attempted to withdraw her hand. He held it even tighter.

"For that, one generally needs a husband, and I am not yet ready for marriage," she finally answered, rationalizing the lie with thoughts of the impossibility of marriage to the one she loved.

"A girl as beautiful and intelligent as you cannot expect to remain unmarried long. Perhaps it would be better if I arranged a suitable match." Kerry leaned back on his elbows to watch her reaction, his recumbent figure pointing toward the fire, his hand still firmly clasped around hers.

Horrified that he—of all people—should think of such a thing, Katy retreated into her impassive role. "I have told you I am quite content as I am. Do you think me incapable of arranging my own affairs?"

Laughing at her choice of words and relieved at her reply, Kerry turned on his side and began pulling the pins from her hair, teasing her with them by holding them out of reach. "With that cold demeanor, I have nothing to fear. It is your kittenish nature I worry about. I would see you married to a man who can provide you with a stable and all the horses you would like, and not some poor wandering stranger for whom you have felt pity.'' Holding the pins on his far side so she would have to climb over him to reach them, Kerry looked upon the dazzling cascade of white-gold curls with satisfaction.

"No wealthy man will consider a nameless, penniless governess for wife. I would do better with the wandering stranger if he be young and ambitious. Together we could work to earn our own wealth.'' Katy eyed him warily, aware of his fascination with her loosed hair but unwilling to risk retrieving the pins. The gleam in his eyes was as dangerous as the topic he had chosen.

"An older man who has already made his wealth would be more than willing to settle for youth and beauty. Surely you must know my own father married for wealth and title the first time, for love and beauty the second. My mother's barren estates and empty title were of no use to a younger man; my father married her for herself, and they seem quite happy. With the dearth of females in this fair land, it would not be difficult to find the right man.''

Surely he was jesting. Totally petrified, Katy did not have the strength to turn and see. Staring into the cold fire, she asked in her chilliest voice, "Is that your wish?'' while her mind raced over the meaning of his words. She knew many nobles preferred their mistresses to be married. Not only did a married woman enjoy more freedom, but it eliminated the bastardy problem, and should he ever tire of her, she was already well provided for. Surely he could not think she would ever be party to such a charade? A cold chill clutched at her heart.

"It is my wish to see you happy, and I fear being a governess is not the life you would choose if you had a choice.'' Gravity replaced his earlier laughter as Kerry returned the pins to her lap, and propping his head on one hand, played with her hair with the other.

Relaxing somewhat at this statement, Katy made no effort to return her hair to its cap, but still did not dare turn to look at him. The telltale moisture in her eyes would only bring on more questions. "I cannot think of any way I could be happier than I am now. If the time should come when I am no longer satisfied, I am quite capable of finding my own way out.''

"I tend to forget you are your own woman now. I still think of you as mine," he said softly, willing that proud head to turn so he could see the violet of her eyes.

Relieved at his admission and softened by his tone, Katy turned her head, touching a finger to her lips, then touching his cheek. It was all she dared do, but the swiftness of Kerry's reaction startled her.

Catching her hand on his cheek, he pressed it tighter against the warmth of his skin. Then, moving her palm to his lips, he kissed it gently. Holding both her hands imprisoned, he sat up once again, forcing Katy to face him.

"That is the first time you have ever voluntarily showed any sign of affection for me. Am I such an ogre that you shower hugs and kisses on children and seamen but cannot offer so simple a gesture to me?"

Caught totally by surprise at this unexpected tack, Katy found herself captured and held by the fiery depths of emerald eyes, unable to pull away. Heart pounding rapidly, she answered stiffly, "Milord, you forget my station. Would you allow the chambermaid such familiarity?"

"You little fool. If you are forward enough to kiss young Jacob, whom you scarcely know, surely you can afford a peck on the cheek upon occasion for an old friend? You know my title is meaningless and an artificial barrier between us at best."

"I know no such thing, milord. You are heir to a barony and the younger son of a duke, and I am a bookseller's daughter who should not even be sitting at the same table with you. Old friend or not, I would be as likely to kiss Sir Charles as I would you."

There it was, the cursed barrier that would always lie between them. It did not bother his Drury Lane actresses, but Katy could never attain their worldliness, and he had no wish for her to do so. But still, it would not harm to lower the barrier just a notch.

"Sir Charles would probably appreciate an occasional buss as much as I; he speaks very fondly of you. We are people, too, you know, and an occasional expression of affection would be taken kindly. Would you care to practice before I send you off to bed?" Looking down into her upturned face,

the pink fullness of her lips beckoning invitingly, Kerry
wished for a good deal more than he was asking, but the clear
trusting innocence of violet eyes prevented his taking it.

Mesmerized by the light in his eyes, unable to avoid the
hard warmth of his hands, Katy leaned slowly forward until
her lips brushed the rough, taut skin of his cheek, pulling
back as soon as they made contact to avoid the weakness of
falling into his arms. Lowering her lashes, she tried to pull
away from his grasp, but he held on to help her to her feet.

Standing there, not a foot apart, holding hands, the temptation to pull her closer was overwhelming, but Kerry fought it
with a caressing brush of his hand, pushing the hair back
from her face before releasing her hands. "Good night, Katy."

"Good night, milord."

He watched her disappear into the cavernous darkness of
the back room, then throwing himself down on the lonely
pallet he had made for his bed, he clasped his hands behind
his head and stared into the patch of starlit sky framed by the
front window. Another man, with fewer scruples than he,
would have put the child out here while he lay in the comforts
of the wide bed and warm arms that lay waiting in the back
room.

He savored that thought for a while, imagining the golden
curls spread across his shoulder while she lay snuggled against
his side, her breasts pressing warm against his ribs. It took no
stretch of the imagination to follow that thought to its logical
conclusion, but Kerry put a halt to it by conjuring up the
wide-eyed innocence of Katy's trusting face and the chaste
kiss he still felt upon his cheek. If he were to keep his
promise to see that she came to no harm, he must continue
with his brotherly role, but it was damned hard to discuss
giving her up to another man's bed when rightly she belonged
in his. It was with this thought that he fell into exhausted
slumber, only to be haunted with dreams of dancing blue eyes
and streaming sun-blonde hair flying in the wind, always one
step ahead of him and out of reach.

Late July 1735

WHEN BREAKFAST was cleared away the next morning and Kerry prepared to depart, Katy stopped him at the doorway with one slender hand upon his sleeve. Automatically his arm came up to protect her back, and he smiled down at rosy cheeks flushed with the heat of the fire. Before he realized her intent, she was on her toes and kissing his cheek lightly, backing out of his reach quickly before he could recover from his surprise.

"Come back quickly, milord," she murmured shyly, not all the color in her cheeks from the fire any longer.

"If you promise to repeat that, I will be back sooner than you think." And whistling merrily, Kerry let himself out the door, well pleased with the day's beginning.

To Katy it was a revelation that the nobleman would welcome her kisses, and it gave her a sense of unexpected freedom. His talk of marriage had frightened her, but now she assumed it to be an aspect of his more practical nature and dismissed it from her thoughts. She was growing fond of this role of playing housewife, and now that she had been given the right to carry the act out a little further, she

126

delighted in doing so. This chance might never come again and she was determined to make the most of it, treasuring every minute for the time when she would be left to her lonely room and the knowledge of his absence.

The days settled into this pattern, one passing much the same as another. Lord Kerry found the days passed more swiftly and the toil came easier by indulging in pleasant thoughts of the homecoming awaiting him or reliving the warm intimacy of the previous evening. Vivid pictures of a golden-haired druid formed easily in his mind as he worked the forest, the image changing to a sylphlike water sprite when the river came in sight. There were other, less virtuous thoughts too, but these he confined to the long nights after Katy retired to her bed and he could still feel the soft warmth of her breath on his cheek and the pliant grip of her fingers in his hand.

For the wealthy son of one of the loftiest aristocratic houses of England to spend his time in daydreams of a child from the filthy back streets of London was a highly unlikely occurrence, but Kerry had none of his brother's fondness for the proprieties and all of his mother's love for independence, and found nothing unnatural in his behavior. Katy was in a class of her own, independent of all others, and if he chose to enjoy their interlude together, so be it.

But the time came when Kerry knew he could no longer be satisfied with pleasant fantasies, that his obsession with his young protégée would have to be brought to fruition, and his imaginary possession become real. All his idle daydreams were shattered, to be replaced by firm determination.

It started innocently enough when he came home late one evening to find Katy had dragged in the battered tub he had brought from Charleston and filled it with water. Looking from Katy's laughing eyes to the tub, he inquired skeptically, "Is this a hint, or have you been reading my mind again?"

"No, milord. After the work you have done today, I feared you would be sore in the morning if you did not soak away the aches. Anna and I do not wish to totally disrupt your privacy, so we thought we'd leave you to yourself for a while."

"Privacy is something I have had more than enough of. I

would be happy to have you stay and wash my back." He scratched ruefully at that sunburned portion of his anatomy, but the humor in his leer was unmistakable.

"No, thank you, milord, my services do not extend that far." Her smile hid no hint of shyness. In the last week of constant proximity she had grown accustomed to the presence of his masculinity, accepting the sight of his bare sweat-soaked torso as a fact of life, and enjoying the virile strength with which he touched her. But there were limits to which she could be pushed, and bathing was decidedly one of them.

By the time Katy and Anna returned to the house, it was almost dark, and Lord Kerry waited for them. Dressed in a white satin waistcoat and a tan tailored superfine coat over well-fitted white breeches instead of his usual casual attire of loose-sleeved linen shirt and baggy broadcloth breeches, his still damp hair carefully tied back in a queue, he greeted them with polished aplomb.

"Ladies, I most readily accept your gracious invitation to dinner. To feast on such loveliness as I see before me is all that I ask. Won't you have a seat, milady?" And he handed the giggling Anna into her chair at the already set table while Katy hurried to bring the meal to table.

He continued his parody of elegant dining throughout the meal, igniting gales of laughter as he addressed one imaginary dinner partner after another, staring lewdly into overample bosoms and suavely insulting pretentious countesses.

When the meal was finally cleared from the table, he bowed elegantly over Katy's hand and said, "Now, if milady will allow, I have a small gift for my gracious hostesses."

Producing a bar of scented soap and gesturing toward the water warming over the fire, he continued, "The gift of privacy, milady. Unless, of course, you wish your back washed. In which case I will be more than willing to offer my services, more than many are willing to do." He lifted one eyebrow pointedly.

Katy accepted the soap and curtsied deeply. "You are so very kind, sir, but you have been more than generous in our service, we cannot allow you to stay longer." And she hurried him from the house laughingly.

Drawing the muslin curtains she and Anna had made as a

lesson in sewing, Katy swiftly filled the tub again and soon
had Anna scrubbed pink and ready for bed. Once Anna was
safely tucked beneath the covers, Katy added more hot water
to the tub, and divesting herself of all her cumbersome garments, stepped into the luxury of a full bath. It was an
opportunity not often offered to her, and she reveled in the
sensual sensation of water lapping at her breasts and soaking
untouched white skin.

Outside, Lord Kerry leaned against a fencepost, puffing on
his pipe while watching the candlelit silhouette against the
thin muslin curtains. While she bathed, there was no shadowed image to enjoy, but the shape of firm, uptilted breasts
and reedlike waist swelling into tempting curves below lingered in his memory. Telling himself his fixation was due to
his five-month abstinence since leaving Charleston, Kerry
indulged himself in imagining the contours of soft flesh now
reposing in his old tub, the image so vivid his body ached to
sample the reality.

There was no longer any use in denying his desire for the
violet-eyed sprite who haunted his dreams. She had always
been there in the back of his mind, a refreshing interlude in a
jaded world, but now it had become more than that. Now she
was a woman instead of a child, and every part of him that
was man demanded he treat her as such.

Cautiously Kerry played with the thought. He was not in
the habit of seducing maidens, but with Katy it could never
be just a passing seduction. It would be a commitment and
one he felt fully ready to make. The idea of returning home
every evening to such charming loveliness pleased him; they
were well suited to keep each other company, and to be the
one to teach her the art of love made any commitment
worthwhile.

Yet he had made no definite decision to pursue the matter
until the front door opened, outlining Katy's graceful silhouette in the doorway. After her bath, she had obviously donned
only a thin muslin summer gown, without benefit of undergarments. Without shift or neckerchief to cover the creamy
expanse from throat to shoulders, he could easily detect the
rising curve of full young breasts beneath her bodice, and
even the firm roundness of bare arms beneath turned-back

sleeves had the power to excite him. Kerry crossed the yard
in a few swift strides, catching the door and closing it behind
him as his quarry retreated warily into the room.

The glittering light in his eyes first warned Katy that all
was not as expected, and she backed away, moving closer to
the fireplace and farther from the door where Kerry stood
with hands on hips, a dazed look upon his face. But trapped
between tub and wall, she could not escape when he advanced.

Reaching out a gentle hand to touch still-damp ringlets
clinging to bare throat and shoulders, Kerry let the curls slide
through his fingers as he spoke. "Whatever happened to my
scrawny spaniel, Katy?"

Unnerved by the brush of his fingers against exposed skin,
regretting the mood that had balked at returning to the confinement of hot and heavy shifts and chemises, Katy responded hesitantly. "She is still here, milord, only a little
older."

"What a difference a few years can make, then, Katy. You
have grown into a beautiful and desirable woman—you know
that, don't you?" Unable to tear his eyes from the soft flesh
rising above the neckline of her gown, Kerry halted any
chance of further retreat by placing both hands on her shoulders. The contact was electrifying, and at the same time, he
knew he had made a mistake. Whereas before she had been
standing docile beneath his touch, now she actively resisted
him.

"Milord, it is late, and you must be tired. I think I had
better retire to my room now." She pulled from his grasp and
started around him, her eyes fastened on the darkened doorway and safety beyond.

"Katherine!" The tone of Kerry's voice halted her progress and she turned to look at him. "Are you still afraid of
me?"

Still dressed in his fashionable coat, his auburn hair gleaming in the firelight, he was the image of the distant nobleman
who had befriended her so long ago, and not the rugged
farmer she had come to know this past week, and she shivered beneath his stare.

The magnetism of his touch had frightened her. It would be
so easy, in a moment of defenselessness, to fall into his arms

as if he were truly the young farmer he pretended to be. But
he was not and never would be, and she must be constantly
on guard lest she convince herself otherwise.

"No, milord. But it is late and I am not dressed properly.
It would be better if I went to my room."

Kerry stared into terrified dark eyes and knew he had
frightened her in some way, whatever her words. He had
moved too fast and without enough warning. It would be
possible to have her this night if he wished, but he was not
totally insensible to her feelings. Their surroundings were
scarcely conducive to seduction, but he knew Katy well
enough to believe that would not matter to her once she made
up her mind to give herself. It was to this decision he must
devote himself, courting her as any proper suitor would. She
was entitled to that much, even if he could not provide all the
appropriate trappings of seduction or offer the benefits of
marriage. Admiring ivory shoulders glowing in the firelight,
he admitted he would enjoy the game as well as she; she was
well worth the wait.

"Do I not, at least, rate a good-night kiss?"

Tilting her head quizzically, Katy gave his roguish expression a cursory perusal and shook her head. "I think not,
milord. Good night."

After she was gone, Kerry shrugged off coat and waistcoat,
preserving the modesty of his guests by sleeping fully dressed
in breeches and shirt. Lying down on his roughly constructed
pallet, he clasped his hands behind his head as he had many
nights before, but this time his thoughts were far less virtuous. It was long into the early-morning hours before his need
for sleep overcame his need for a woman's body beneath
him.

True to his vow, Kerry set about his campaign of seduction
with his first waking hours. Unaware of his intentions, Katy
accepted his courteous attentions as an apology for the previous night's behavior, and received them with gentle admonitions. But when her parting peck on his cheek was returned
with a full kiss to her brow, she stared thoughtfully after his
bronzed back as he strode jauntily away.

Kerry's attentions did not cease with the morning meal. He
returned at noon with a bouquet of flowers to adorn the table,

and in the evening, a rose to pin in her hair. Riding lessons
provided ample opportunities for lingering caresses. No longer
in need of his hands to guide her posture, Kerry still managed
to encircle small ankles with his fingers while giving instructions, his hands lingering overlong at her waist as he persisted
in aiding her mounting and dismounting. After Anna's re-
tirement to the bedroom, he lounged casually beside Katy's
erect figure at the hearth, teasing her hair lightly and massag-
ing her fingers with his own. No opportunity for compliments
missed his notice; he bestowed them discreetly but generously.

Kerry's efforts escalated with each passing day, and Katy
found herself helpless in her attempt to repulse them. His
engaging grin offered no harm, and his witty flattery left her
laughing more often than not. She was too quickly receptive
to his teasing, striking back in kind until they were both lost
in laughter, and she discovered herself in his arms.

The elusive Lord Kerry opened up and began to talk of his
plans for the future, of the house he planned to build on the
plantation, of the horses he wished to raise. Occasionally his
words wandered off into talk of his family in England, of his
younger sister, who—already in her early twenties—refused
to marry because she enjoyed her independence too much, of
his older half-brother, who had made an arranged marriage to
beget heirs and whose wife had yet to have a child come to
full term. And while he talked, he played aimlessly with
Katy's hand or stroked her hair, his arm resting lightly about
her shoulders while he wound the long coils around his
fingers, until Katy became accustomed to his touch and learned
to look forward to this pleasant interlude.

Katy was not insensible to the emotions raised by their new
intimacy, but not once had their lips met, and she began to
long for the touch of his mouth on hers, naively believing the
searing passion she had felt at their last encounter would end
the growing ache these moments induced in her. As she lay in
bed at night, her merciless logic told her the time would come
when he would no longer be satisfied with holding hands. But
her trust in him was implicit, and she fully believed he would
do nothing against her will. She had only to decide at what
point to put a halt to his lovemaking, and he would honor her
request, but she was not yet ready to put an end to this

performance. The chance to be courted by the noble Lord Kerry might never come again, and she wished to savor every moment of it for a while longer. Innocent of man's baser nature, it never occurred to her that once they reached a certain threshold, there would be no turning back.

While Katy lay in her virtuous bed considering kisses yet to come, Lord Kerry lay awake remembering the fresh scent of sun-kissed hair and the soft pliancy of young shoulders. His need for a woman had become a need for one woman alone, and he lay contemplating the pleasure that would soon be his in introducing an untouched maiden to the art of love, particularly this gentle maid who had so successfully bewitched him for so long.

A week from the day of his vow, Kerry took the afternoon off from his chores to show Katy and Anna the entire plantation, riding the horses from their nearby field for the first time. Figuring on a slow pace to accommodate Anna and the pony, they took a picnic meal with them, enjoying it along the banks of the river on their return trip home. Maintaining his informal attitude, Kerry made no improper overtures, and Katy felt relaxed and confident when they reached the stables in the late-evening light.

While Kerry and Mahomet brushed the horses down, Katy and Anna returned to the cabin to discover that Mahomet, acting on his master's orders, had prepared the bath for them. Delighted by the luxury of having her wishes anticipated, Katy hurriedly saw to Anna's ablutions and sent her to bed before sinking her own aching body gratefully into the liquid warmth. Muscles unaccustomed to long riding were soothed and comforted by the heat, and it took a tremendous effort of will not to fall asleep while soaking.

Purposely donning only the muslin gown as she had before, Katy dried and combed her hair thoroughly before opening the front door on the late-evening darkness. Silhouetted in the moonlight, Kerry waited at the fence, setting aside his pipe as she stepped out of the safety of the lighted cabin into the cool darkness.

Taking in the streaming silver-gold strands, the thin gown clinging to rounded breasts and tempting thighs, and the soft glow of violet eyes, Kerry knew he had won, and his heart pounded fiercely at the beauty of his prize.

Curbing his impatience, he waited for her to come to him. Then, wordlessly enfolding her in his embrace, Kerry clasped her small body as close as possible to his for fear she would dissipate as in a dream. Not until he felt the firmness of her breasts pressed against his light shirt, the slender arms sliding about his neck, was he reassured of her reality, and then he buried his face in thick tresses and squeezed tighter, groaning out loud with sheer pleasure at attaining the unobtainable.

"Katherine, my love, I have waited too long for this moment to not savor every moment of it." Kerry's lips found her throat beneath the mass of hair and he fervently applied them in a path of burning kisses that reached the hollow between her breasts.

Katy clung desperately to his broad shoulders, nearly swooning at the passion of his embrace, her breasts tingling with the need for his touch as the heat rose between her thighs, inundating her senses. This wasn't the controlled kiss she had anticipated, and desperately she fought against the tide of passion threatening to sweep her away.

"Milord, please." Weakly Katy struggled to disentangle herself from the trap of his embrace, but Kerry had discovered the delights of her supple curves and refused to yield this pleasure, his strong fingers tracing sensuous paths beneath her breasts.

"Milord does please," Kerry replied inanely, kissing the delicate outline of her cheek. "It is not every day he captures a will-o'-the-wisp, a faerie spirit of such surpassing loveliness. I have you now and won't let go until you agree to be mine."

"Do I have a choice in the matter?" she gasped as an inquiring hand cupped a thinly clad buttock and pressed her closer until she could feel the pressure of his hard thighs and rising manhood and her hips moved naturally to meet his, the ache developing in her midsection telling her more of the need between man and woman than she wished to know. Things were well out of hand now; even her own body betrayed her.

"Choice, kitten? What choice is there? I have ignored for

too long what I should have seen long ago. You are mine, you cannot deny it—I see it in your eyes, feel it in the way you mold yourself to me, and if I were to taste your lips, the answer would be there waiting for me. You are mine, Katy, there never has been any choice.'' And he pressed his mouth firmly to hers.

Even as Katy shrank from the contact, her lips involuntarily responded to his pressure, opening under his insistence, allowing him to penetrate the moist sweetness as he soon would the untouched recesses of her body, and achingly she melted into his arms.

Shivering as his heated blood seemed to surge through her own veins, tears rolling down her cheeks, Katy collapsed against his chest when he released her. With care, Kerry showered her face and eyes with soft kisses, tasting the salt of her tears and feeling the tension of her fear, knowing she had more cause than most to fear this next step. With words and caresses he sought to reassure her.

"Kitten, there is naught to fear. I will take care of you as I have before, only this time it will be better. When Anna returns home, you will stay here with me. When the crops are harvested, I will take you to Charleston and dress you in the lovely gowns that you deserve, put diamonds on your tiny ears." Kissing her earlobe, Kerry allowed his hands to stray down the rigid path of her spine, willing her to relax. "I will be the envy of every man in town, and you will be the most beautiful woman. Together we'll make plans for a house to sit on the hill, and perhaps by the time the house is complete, we'll have an occupant for the nursery."

The words he had hoped would most soothe her had wrung a cry of anguish instead, and Katy almost escaped the confinement of his arms before he recovered from his surprise and pulled her back. It had been a mistake to go into such detail before he had made his possession complete, but his own excitement had carried him away, and he could only believe she would feel the same. Apparently he was wrong.

"Katy, I know you feel the same as I, your lips do not lie. I have known too many cold ones to mistake the warmth of yours. You belong to me, and I do not easily give up what is rightfully mine." Kerry made no further attempt to kiss her, but held her close until her sobs subsided, carefully drying her eyes with the sleeve of his shirt.

"Milord, you know me too well for me to deny anything you have said, and I have told you I am willing to do anything you ask of me, but I never thought you would ask me to do anything with which I disagree. Perhaps I am naive, but I believed you when you said you wished only what was good for me." Katy again tried to pull away, but she was held by a grip fiercer than iron.

"You are naive, my Katy, but not for the reason stated." Kerry's voice was harsh, hiding the hurt. "I would not ask if you did not wish it yourself, but you have just admitted you do. So stop the charades, Katy, you are above that. You know I can never marry you, but I will see you better taken care of than most wives. What more can you ask?"

"It is no game!" she cried, pounding small fists against his chest, more in frustration than anger that he could not see her side. "If you were anyone but a lord, a baron, the son of a duke, it would not matter to me if we married or not. People would see us as a couple, and if they respected us, they would respect our decision not to marry. But there can be no respect for a lowborn mistress of a noble—she is little more than a whore. You are asking me to give up my friends, my profession, a name for my children, my future, everything I have, for the brief time we share together. And it will be brief—you know that as well as I. Soon you must marry, and I will not add adultery to my list of lacking morals. Then what is left for me and any children we may have? Your money cannot buy us a new life."

This time when she pulled from his arms, Kerry let her go, his arms dropping loosely to his side.

"You are wrong, Katy. You have painted the bleakest possible picture; no one knows what the future holds in store for us. You are asking us to give up what could be years of happiness for a nonexistent future, as evidenced by the Lady Elizabeth. Did I ever tell you what happened to the Lady Elizabeth?" Kerry's tone was scathing and his eyes hardened at the memory as he looked down on Katy for some reply. At her inquiring glance, he continued. "When I made it clear that our engagement was dependent upon her accompanying me to the colonies, she refused the so-called honor of my hand in preference for a life of ease with a lesser-titled suitor.''

Kerry's eyes held hers with their anger. "How many others would you think I must ask before finding that wife you speak of? Would you have me live a life of chastity until I should find her? Or one of open licentiousness, for which you have chastised me before? Even if I should be forced to marry to produce the necessary heirs, it must be a marriage of convenience, established only long enough to beget the necessary offspring. There are few ladies of noble birth willing to live with me here, and here is where I plan to stay. Is that the existence you would wish on me?''

"You are exaggerating, milord. You have but to look among the plain and less wealthy to find a wide variety of ladies eager to accompany you, any one of whom will make a more suitable companion than I. I repeat, I will do anything you ask of me, but once you marry, I will consider my debt paid and the affair over.''

Standing alone, Katy shivered, though the night was not cold. She was ripping her heart out and handing it to him on a platter, to smash or return as he saw fit. That he spoke no words of love, she understood. If he had truly loved her, he would never have asked what he did. Despite his fine words, she would simply be a temporary fulfillment of a need, to be discarded when no longer necessary. She had no doubt he would take care of her, but she no longer needed that kind of help. She could support herself, and it was only out of love for him that she offered herself now.

"That is not the answer I wished to hear. If I cannot have all of you, I will have none of you.'' Kerry's tone was dull and flat as he drew away from her. "Tomorrow I will watch the river for news of Georgetown. If the fever still prevails, I will take you and Anna to Charleston. Betts can bring in the widow, and I am sure she will take good care of you. You have made your choice. I will honor it.''

"Thank you, milord,'' Katy replied quietly, turning to leave, all hope dead and scattered like ashes.

"Katherine.'' The word was spoken softly but firmly, causing her to glance back at the wiry figure leaning against the fencepost. "I am not giving up. You are mine, and I will have you sooner or later. When you are ready, I will be waiting."

Katherine stared at his shadowy figure a moment, almost feeling the weight of green eyes upon her, and the urge to return to his arms was strong, but resisting, she murmured "Good night" and entered the cabin.

Lying in bed next to the sleeping Anna, Katy muffled her sobs against the mattress while she listened for Kerry in the other room. It was late before she heard his boots on the wooden floor and later still before she heard the thump they made as he pried them off and let them fall. She tried to picture him lying in his own bed, hands behind his head as she had seen him do before the fire at night, and as she lay there, tears rolling down her cheeks, forming puddles of wetness against the sheets, she felt him calling her, felt his need begging her on, and the tears fell faster. She knew she had only to rise and go to him and all would be well, he would make it so, but she could not. His family and his titles would always stand between them, a source of anguish that could only turn to hate, and she loved him too much to allow that to happen. As long as he felt no love for her, the decision and the pain remained with her.

August 1, 1735

THEY ROSE LATE the next day, Katy's red-rimmed eyes and Kerry's unshaven face and uncombed hair speaking wordlessly of a sleepless night. Little was said over breakfast as each carefully avoided contact with the other, and he left with shotgun and fishing gear, without a parting word. Anna seemed oblivious of this rift in the adult world, and she rushed after Kerry for a good-bye hug, returning to the house with a flower he had given her tucked in her hair.

The day grew steaming hot and endless. With no sign of the men at noon, Katy set dinner aside for evening and racked her brains for some method of baking a cake for Anna's birthday on the morrow, the crude facilities not providing much chance of success. Resorting to a method similar to one she had seen in the Dublin kitchen, she fried batter cakes and layered them with jam and icing, hiding it while Anna lay in the back room napping.

The afternoon grew hotter and longer, the open door letting in lethargically buzzing flies but no breeze. Divesting themselves of heavy petticoats and stockings, Katy and Anna wandered barefoot into the nearby grove of trees, savoring the coolness of the shade while searching for late crops of berries. The sun was going down before they ventured out into the light again, and still they saw no sign of the men.

Frowning at this delay, Katy stirred the well-cooked remains of dinner and offered a portion to Anna. She had no appetite for food as she wandered restlessly about the cabin, smoothing the tablecloth she had embroidered with her own hands, straightening the curtains she and Anna had spent so many afternoons sewing. Even the overcrowded bookcase had received the benefit of her cleaning and sat neat and orderly, the framed portrait she had once sketched of herself and Lord Kerry gracing the top of the shelf. Copper pots gleamed on the walls and pewter dishes sparkled along the shelves, all the result of her homemaking, but this would never be her home. She had been foolish to pretend otherwise.

When the room grew dark and the men still had not returned, Katy's misery turned to worry, and as she sent Anna off to bed, the little girl's face reflected some of her own concern. The thought of spending the night alone in the cabin was frightening, although she had never had a moment's fear while she knew Lord Kerry to be on the other side of the wall. But the thought of what could have caused this delay terrified her, and her mind worked overtime at imagining the possible reasons. None of them were pleasant.

She remembered the tales of Kerry's Indian and other, more horrifying tales. Kerry had praised his Indian visitor as a noble savage with a better understanding of nature than any man he knew, but he had also carried tales of the drunken savages and lying thieves he had met among members of that same race. The various tribes had different habits, but unpredictability seemed to be a common trait. Where was Kerry now?

Long after sunset the sound of horses whickering brought Katy to the open door. In the first silver strands of moonlight she made out the outline of two silent figures, the smaller leaning heavily against his massive companion. With a small cry, Katy was out and running up the moonlit path, her heart pounding heavily in her throat as she approached and spied the blood-soaked shirt and waxen face of Lord Kerry.

Grinning feebly, he tried to salute the look of anguish in

her eyes, but the effort caused too much pain, and he contented himself with watching her face, its ivory luminescence marred with anxiety.

"If a little blood is what it takes to make you look at me like that, I'll come home like this more often. Go on back to the cabin and stir up the fire and get some water boiling—we're going to have to try a little minor surgery." He tried to chase her off, but his arm would not obey.

Wide-eyed, Katy stared speechlessly at him for a moment, then spun around and, fleet of foot, regained the cabin. She had water starting to boil and strips torn for bandages by the time Mahomet nearly carried his owner over the portal. Gently depositing him on the pallet on the floor, Mahomet began carefully to remove the blood-soaked linen covering Kerry's shoulder.

Katy knelt beside him and helped the tedious task by sponging away as much of the torn material and blood as she could, visibly wincing each time Kerry flinched.

"Milord, what happened? Was there an accident?" The shirt free now, she flung it aside and began to clean the wound, examining the extent of damage with horror. A gaping hole had torn through his left shoulder muscle, and even inexperienced as she was, she recognized it as a gunshot wound.

"You might say that." Kerry grimaced as she scrubbed too close to the injury. "Mahomet, take that knife of yours and stick it in the fire a minute. Katy, there's a bottle of whiskey on that top shelf over there, or what's left of it after last night." He made a wry face at her shocked expression, but this was no time to discuss last night's fiasco. "Go get it and use it to clean the opening Mahomet's going to make to get that ball out of there, or I'll not be able to use this shoulder again." Not to mention the lead poisoning he would probably contract, but he saw no need to mention that. "Let me have whatever of that drink is left after you've done, or you may have a hard time holding me down. I can think of better ways to test my courage."

Hurrying to comply with his orders, they soon had him propped against a pillow and finishing off the spirits while Mahomet made the first insertion of the sterilized knife. As the knife probed more deeply, Kerry's face drained of color and his facial muscles tightened, but he made no other sign of pain. Katy watched helplessly, tears rolling freely down her cheeks while she wrung her hands uselessly.

With a forced grin, Kerry held out his right hand to her, motioning for her to take it. "Before this bastard butchers me further, hold me down. I'll not be complainin' if I'm holdin' you in my arms."

Katy crept onto the pallet beside him, lying down on his right side so he could put his free arm beneath her. "Arm, singular. You are not so dangerous this way, perhaps Mahomet will be so good as to remove the other permanently." The jest was a feeble one and in poor taste, but she was too frightened to notice, and Kerry too far gone in pain and liquor.

Kerry's arm tightened around her, and he emitted a low groan through clenched teeth as the knife touched the lead ball embedded against bone. Leaning full against his side, her breasts crushed against his ribs, Katy covered his unshaven cheek with kisses, but pain proved greater than pleasure and Kerry soon lapsed into unconsciousness. With a satisfied grunt, the black man pried loose the ball and removed it with his fingers.

Blood gushed from the wound, and Katy hastened to stanch it, using the dregs of the whiskey bottle to clean it out again.

Mahomet rose to his feet and dried his hands on a rag, muttering, "Get medicine," before lurching toward the door.

"Mahomet, wait!" Kneeling beside her unconscious patient, Katy panicked. She still had no idea what had caused this "accident," but she was alarmed at being left alone to tend to it. "We must have a doctor. There is one in town; can we not get him?"

"No. Mahomet make medicine, make better. Wait here."

This was the longest speech she had ever heard from the African prince, and Katy nodded obediently. Kerry had once told her the black man understood everything said, but preferred the role of mute as protection. Kerry theorized that having come from Africa to a land where he understood none of the inhabitants, Mahomet had learned to keep quiet and listen carefully. Assuming a mute to be deaf and presumably without intelligence, despite the fact he responded when spoken to, men came to ignore the black man's presence as if he did not exist. It was a convenient role, and one the African continued with few exceptions: as the man who saved his life, Kerry became one of them; Katy, unaccountably, another.

Now all she could do was sit and wait for the slave to return. Packing the wound to stop the excessive bleeding, Katy held the cloth in place to prevent Kerry's restless tossing from displacing it. He remained mercifully unconscious, only his occasional moans disturbing the silence. Katy stroked his fevered brow and prayed.

Mahomet returned with a variety of wild herbs, many of which Katy recognized for their medicinal qualities, some she had never seen before. She had learned some of the art of herbs from the same old woman who had taught her to read tea leaves, but she had little chance to practice it. Now she watched carefully as Mahomet concocted a poultice of the weeds to draw infection.

As the night grew longer, Katy doubted the success of the medicine, for Kerry's fever seemed to increase, and he drifted into a deeper stupor. While the giant black man dozed at the fire, Katy curled up on the floor next to her guardian, listening for the slightest sound indicating he might need her.

By morning, there was still no change. Heavy-eyed after two nights without sleep, Katy prepared a hasty breakfast, answering Anna's puzzled questions as best she could with the nonexistent information she possessed. Mahomet would not offer further explanation of the "accident" and Kerry could not, and she resigned herself to waiting for an answer, not willing to consider the possibility of never knowing, should Kerry not recover. A world without Kerry's charming grin or laughing eyes could not exist, and Katy devoted the day to applying cool compresses to his fevered brow and cleaning the wound while Mahomet repoulticed it, hoping in some way to bring him back.

Anna's birthday dinner was a dismal affair, the carefully tiered cake creating only a subdued reaction against the backdrop of Kerry's still form. Reassuring Anna that everything

would be all right, Katy tucked the child in early, and exhausted, fell asleep on the floor by her patient.

The soft caress of fingers tugging at her hair brought her
slowly from a nightmarish sleep. Knowing the touch, she
swept sleep from her eyes and knelt eagerly beside the low
pallet.

Dim gray light filtered through the papered windows, darkening the lines of pain around Kerry's mouth, making his
unhealthy pallor paler. His beard created a dark stubble along
his well-shaped jaw, and his hair lay matted and uncombed,
but his eyes had lost none of their brilliance as they gazed up
into the angelic face above him.

"Katy? Why haven't you gone? I told Mahomet to get you
and Anna out of here." Puzzled, he stroked the long, near-
silver curls hanging over her shoulder, eagerly taking in every
inch of that beautiful face hovering anxiously above him.

"I would not leave even if Mahomet told me to, and he
didn't. Does this have something to do with your accident, or
are you still eager to be rid of me?" Katy stroked his brow,
and finding it cool, gave fervent thanks to heaven.

"If I recall, you were the one eager to leave, but now it is
a necessity that you do. Blast that man, anyway, it's already
daylight. You should have been out of here hours ago." He
frowned at the innocent window as if it were to blame for the
lack of darkness.

"You have been in a fever for the last day and a half.
Without Mahomet's knowledge, you might not have lived.
You should be thanking him, not cursing him," she admonished, trying to keep a worried frown from her face. She was
certain the wound was no accident, which meant some danger
lurked out there somewhere. She thought of Anna, innocently
sleeping in the back room, and thought guiltily of how she
had spent all her concern on Lord Kerry without thinking of
what she might be exposing the child to.

Kerry's anguished groan confirmed her fears. "Gad! A
whole day lost." Gingerly swinging his feet over the side of
the low bed, he attempted to rise, but fever and loss of blood
had left him too weak to fight the pain.

Putting a small hand on his good shoulder, Katy halted his
progress. "If you insist on moving about, I will have to tie up

that arm to keep the wound from reopening. Lie back and let me find a neckerchief.''

Back in moments with a makeshift sling of fine linen, she perched beside him, leaning over to tie it behind his neck. Her breath came with difficulty at this intimate contact with masculine, unshirted muscularity, and with good reason. Once the knot was secured, Kerry used his good arm to pin her in place, brushing a light kiss across her forehead as her breasts pressed into his side. Katy's heart skipped a beat, and she made no attempt to struggle free from his grasp.

Kerry grinned wryly at this sudden quiescence. "Do you figure me helpless or are you conscientiously keeping me from harming myself?''

"Both, milord,'' and she kissed his cheek in the manner he had grown accustomed to over the last weeks. "Now, will you tell me your hurry to see us gone?''

Kerry's crooked grin died and he let her go, struggling once more to gain his feet. "Damn, help me up, kitten.'' His head spun from the exertion, and he wished nothing more than to lie back down again, but it was imperative he reach the window.

Scanning the pained lines of her guardian's scowling face, Katy refused assistance. "No, you're not ready to be up. Tell me what you want, and I'll go get it.'' She still sat beside him, anxious eyes watching his every move.

Not yet ready to tell her of his fears, Kerry scowled even blacker. "Not bloody likely unless you wish to become more familiar with male needs than befits a maiden.''

Blushing deeply, Katy rose and returned his glare. "There's no need to be crude or to swear at me. I will fetch Mahomet.'' Unable to resist one parting shot before she woke the slave, she added, "And you might care to notice you no longer wear your breeches.''

When he returned from outside, Kerry looked somewhat relieved but it was not due to any physical release. Eyeing his remarkable ward warily, he motioned for Mahomet to help him back to bed and lay back against the pillows gratefully before summoning Katy to his side.

"Don't light the fire today, and don't leave the house. To all practical purposes, this place is to look abandoned. Mahomet tells me the horses have been given a supply of feed and water. They will have to make do for themselves awhile. Keep away from the windows and keep Anna quiet. Can you do all that?''

The anxiety behind his curt tone was evident and Katy's heart hammered faster. "Yes, milord, of course. But why? What is wrong? Do not leave it to my imagination.''

"Which is too active for its own good, I have reason to know,'' he said dryly. "Which is why I'd rather not tell you, but it is not to be avoided. Katy, this wound came from an Indian with a musket. The tribes around here do not normally carry guns. They make war among themselves with knives and arrows and occasionally indulge in a drunken brawl with traders, but for the most part, the Cherokee are our allies. This could be a lone renegade, or another tribe I do not know about, but in any case, we may be in for some trouble. I see no sign of them out there now, but there could be more in the woods and I would never see them. We are a clear target every time we set foot out the door.''

Katy sank to the floor beside him, her eyes darting from one silent man to the other as they gauged her reactions. Indians! All the horrifying incidents she had avoided thinking about flooded back to mind: massacres, rapes, women taken prisoner, and children brutally murdered, while their men lay scalped and senseless. Yet Kerry had had one of those savages in this very house not so long ago and claimed he was quite safe. She did not understand.

Her bewilderment must have betrayed itself, for Kerry attempted to explain. "Like I said, Katy, I may have just frightened one lone Indian, but that gun worries me. You should have left here the first night; we are totally without protection this far from town. Tonight, when it is too dark for us to make easy targets, we will have to find our way out of here.'' If the Indians didn't find their way in before that, Kerry added grimly to himself.

"But, milord, you cannot even stand by yourself. How will we ever get all the way back to town? Even a horse or carriage is likely to rip that shoulder open again, and you will certainly bleed to death this time.'' Katy's eyes widened as she read the answer in his emerald glare and her chin set defiantly.

Kerry had hoped not to tackle that subject until the time came to avoid a day-long argument, but his perspicacious ward had not only thought of it but also, from the grim set of her fine lips, divined the answer. He greeted her answering silence with relief. Horses and carriages were out of the question—they provided too noisy a target. They couldn't risk reaching the river from this distance; their only means of travel would be by foot, and he could never make it without endangering the others.

The subject was not mentioned again throughout the day. When Anna woke, she was given a cold breakfast without explanation, and her bewilderment became part of the tension that worsened as the day grew longer. They went about their tasks with grim, set faces, taking turns watching from the window for any stray movement. Muskets were taken down and cleaned, ball and gunpowder supplies counted and checked, bundles of food wrapped and packed tightly to fit in hastily constructed rucksacks. Anna watched these preparations with growing alarm, but Katy's calm replies kept panic in abeyance, and she obediently retreated with a book to a far corner.

Unable to lend much of a hand to the preparations, Kerry slept sporadically throughout the day, blissfully unaware of Katy's intentions. Never far from his side, she kept an eye out for any sign of the return of his fever or reopening of his wound, but he seemed well on the road to recovery, and with a few days' rest . . . And her jaw would tighten imperceptibly again as she tied the string around another package of food.

The day was muggy and heavy, a gray pallor settling over the river valley, not even a leaf rippling to life in the breathless air. Eyes grew weary watching the unending stillness, and no movement broke the still-life tableau of field and forest. The day drew on in rigid tension, until the last rays of sun faded behind the ridge of trees, and the sky grew black.

Mahomet strapped the rucksack to his shoulders, black eyes watching the silent interchange between master and mistress, for so he thought of them. The recumbent figure on the pallet lay motionless, green eyes focused on the frail form seemingly radiating belligerent energy in the center of the room. Violet eyes darkened rebelliously as Kerry gestured for her to approach, and she did not budge.

"You are going with us, are you not, milord?" Her words reflected a heavy trace of French accent, and a touch of Gallic scorn, since she knew the answer in advance.

"No, *ma chérie*, you know I cannot. You must move silently and swiftly to escape detection. I can do neither. Besides, if there is no one out there, I will have lost a lot of blood for nothing. Go without me, take Anna to safety, warn Sir Charles and the others, and then send someone back for me. I will go willingly by then." Kerry spoke casually so as not to alarm the child, but Anna watched with wide-eyed terror. Inwardly cursing his weakness, Kerry continued to stare at the luminous vision whose eyes had so effectively ensnared him.

"So will I, then. Mahomet will move much quicker and quieter if he carries Anna and has no one to hamper his movements. I will stay here with you." Acting on her words, she took Anna's hand and gave it to the black giant, then seated herself complacently at Kerry's side.

Silence settled in the room. Mahomet towered over the scene, his thick features impassive, showing no sign of surprise as he awaited further orders. Frightened, Anna clung to the giant's huge hand, trusting this massive man who used his hands with gentleness and skill as he taught her to sit a horse, but terrified at the thought of leaving her beloved friends behind to an unknown danger. Katy and Kerry took no notice of either of them, lost in a battle of wills as they stared, with words unspoken, into each other's eyes. Time passed and the struggle was resolved, but Kerry would not end it without offering another chance for escape.

"Mahomet will have difficulty finding anyone to listen to him, and as an unaccompanied slave, he is liable to danger on the open road." Green eyes searched Katy's placid expression, but she showed no sign of swerving from her decision.

Producing a folded paper from her apron Katy handed it to Mahomet. "I have already thought of that." Tearing her gaze from those magnetic eyes, she turned to the slave. "Mahomet, these papers explain your mission and give you permission to travel unaccompanied. One of them I made to look as official as possible in case you come across someone who can't read. The other is a letter to Sir Charles or whomever you talk to, explaining what has happened. Either Sir Charles or Mr. Stone will believe you and will know what to do; the letter is just additional proof.''

The black man took the folded papers from her outstretched hands and placed them carefully inside his shirt. Still he waited.

Kerry tried one last argument. Speaking quietly, in a voice only Katy could hear, he entreated her urgently. "Katy, go with them. If there are Indians out there, they can do little to me and I am not afraid of dying if it comes to that. But what they can do to you terrifies me, kitten, and I am in no condition to protect you. Go, leave me here and save me that agony.'' He could not even reach out to touch her, but his eyes pleaded his case eloquently.

The reference to his pain should she come to harm made Katy hesitate for the first time, but so certain was she that she could come to no harm while he lived, that she refused to consider it. Shaking her head negatively, she remained adamant. "I have encountered worse savages than Indians and survived. I will do so again. There is no possible way you can persuade me to leave you. Now, order them to go, please, so I can be assured of Anna's safety.''

Kerry nodded. He had known the argument to be already won and accepted the decision; his words were only a formality. The only way of removing his indomitable Katy would be to carry her out kicking and screaming, and there was no sense in that. Their fates had been inextricably bound since first they met, and he was willing to take the chance of keeping it that way.

"Anna, you are to go with Mahomet and do as he tells you. Katy and I will follow later when I feel a little better. Give your father a big hello for us.'' Speaking with reassurance, reminding the child of what waited ahead for her, he succeeded in erasing the look of fear from the child's face, and at his imperceptible nod, Mahomet wrapped a dark cloak about the small figure and hefted her into his arms.

With a cry, Katy rushed to give her charge one last kiss,

and they were gone. The silence filling the cabin at the closing of the door was greater than the one that had gone before. Turning slowly to find Kerry's sympathetic eyes on her, Katy fell to her knees beside him, burying her face in the covers. Desolate, she now knew how it felt to burn all her bridges behind her.

But there were many more bridges yet to be conquered. A quiet voice penetrated her fears, soothing tightly stretched nerves, its familiar cadence lightening the burden.

"Come up here beside me, kitten, where I can reach you."

Warm eyes met hers as she raised her head, and she followed their command obediently, crawling in beside him so he could tuck her head on his good shoulder and stroke her hair with his free hand, bringing comfort to the emptiness gaping before them.

"I hope the step you've just taken is not worse than the one you made that night I first met you," Kerry whispered thoughtfully. Her slender body lay curled beside his, and he remembered gratefully the night Mahomet had carried him home and she had held him like this, and he hugged her closer.

She kissed his cheek lightly and replied, "I would not have met you if it were not for that first step; it could not have been all wrong."

He grinned and returned the kiss to her nose. "The other night I would have sworn you wished me to the devil. Are you changing your mind, or do you think me too weak to take advantage of you now?"

Katy curled more comfortably into his embrace and familiarized herself with a dark curl on his chest, totally aware of the warmth of bronzed skin enveloping her. She was acting brazenly, but naturally; the circumstances called for no less. "The devil may have you later. I have no wish to meet Indians on my own. And yes, I think you're too weak to do anything I do not wish." With malicious glee, she wrapped her finger tighter in the curl and tugged gently.

"Damned little tigress is what you are. I pity the Indians." Instead of removing her hand, Kerry allowed his own to roam more freely. What he lacked in strength he made up for in desire, and he had lain too many nights in this bed imagining her here beside him to let the opportunity go now. "So you think you will take advantage of me in my weakened condition?"

Feeling the surety of the hand boldly caressing the curve of her bodice, Katy was not so certain of his weakness. Yet she felt no desire to spend this night on the floor alone. Releasing the curl, she leaned back against his shoulder and smiled disarmingly. "You need a shave and your hair is all tangled" —she ran her fingers through it, catching them in the knots to prove her point—"and if you attempt anything strenuous, you will bleed like a stuck pig. Is that the romantic way you intend to introduce me to the ways of love?" Fingers trailing down his stubbly jaw, she kissed him again, tenderly.

The vivid image she evoked brought a pained grin to Kerry's face. "Touché, my dear. You have been waiting a long time to get even with me for my spaniel remark, and you have certainly found an appropriate time to do so. My ardor is thoroughly dampened."

Reluctantly his hand returned to a less tempting repose, resting lightly on her arm as he searched the darkening violet of her eyes. His ardor had been dampened not so much by her words as by the memory of her innocence and how hard he had worked to preserve it. To take it now, under such circumstances, after denying himself so long, would be an act of insanity. If they lived to see the end of this siege, he would find more appropriate surroundings for putting an end to her virginity. With a smile of pleasure at this thought, Kerry planted a brotherly kiss on her brow and asked, "Do you always sleep in gown and petticoats or are you prepared in anticipation of our visitors? They are not likely to arrive until morning, and I should think you would sleep a little easier if you were not so closely wrapped."

Katy eyed him suspiciously. "Do you wish me to stay here with you or go back to my room and undress?"

Green eyes flickered mischievously as his hand found the tie to her bodice. "I wish you to both stay here *and* undress. I have already told you I have no wish to molest you while—in your vividly descriptive words—bleeding like a stuck pig, so you have nothing to worry about from me. So why not take the opportunity to make yourself more comfortable? I can see

no reason why I am the only one to go about half dressed."
The lacing undone, her bodice fell open, exposing the lace
and lawn of her shift, freeing her corsetless figure. Expertly
removing the gown from fair shoulders, Kerry gently ran his
fingers along the creamy expanse exposed by the low neckline of her shift.

Catching her breath, certain that he must feel the pounding
of her heart beneath his questing fingers, Katy lay motionless, her eyes searching his face for some sign of his intentions. But Kerry's gaze was almost reverent as he traced the
outline of her shift where it crossed her breasts, and it was
her reaction to this intimate touch that was less than virtuous.
She longed for his fingers to explore deeper, to find the
hardening tips aching to be touched, but though he could not
fail to know her need, he went no farther. Silently, he helped
divest her of gown and petticoats, then pulled her thinly clad
figure to his side.

With the fire cold and the one candle guttering to an end,
Kerry had to rely on the fleeting moonlight to drink in with
hungered eyes the lovely curves exposed to his gaze. She
wore nothing beneath the lawn shift and even in the dim light
it was easy to appreciate such beauty. Lying on her side, the
swell of her hip dipped dangerously to a tiny waistline, while
firm, full breasts pressed generously against his ribs. Beneath
the shift he could see the long line of well-shaped legs, and
he moved to pull the blanket up to cover her before he began
tormenting himself with the image of what lay between them.
She felt so much better than he had imagined, and he could
smell the fresh scent of her hair and the light sachet clinging
to her clothes, making it extremely difficult to keep his
promise while all his senses filled with the heavenly presence
in his arms. There was no denying the stirring in his loins,
and Kerry adjusted the blanket to cover himself.

Katy lay as still as possible, trying to absorb the delicious
sensation of the long, hard line of his masculine body pressed
against hers. Nearly giddy with the desire to know more of
this sensation, she had to restrain herself from allowing her
hand to rove as his had done, knowing instinctively there
would be no turning back once begun. Instead, she tried to
satisfy herself with the knowledge that his desire must be as

great as her own. Her bare leg entwined with his stockinged one and she rested her head comfortably on his shoulder.

"I will not ask if you are satisfied now," she murmured wickedly, feeling the stir of his manhood against her leg. She was behaving monstrously, she knew, but if tomorrow they died, she would be happy knowing she had spent this last night in his bed. On the other hand, if they were rescued, she could return to the role of governess with little remorse for what they had done.

"Personally, I find you better suited for the role of mistress than governess. Are you sure you will not change your mind?" Kerry whispered, the throbbing in his loins equalling that of his wounded shoulder, and his hand slipped experimentally under her arm to knead a rounded breast.

The sensations aroused by that strong hand were tempting, and against her will, Katy found herself being drawn to him, her lips brushing against his hard-muscled shoulder and her fingers entwining themselves in the mat of hair on his chest. When his lips closed possessively across hers, she surrendered gladly, and a shudder rippled throughout her body as she met his passionate demand with a burning need of her own.

But then Kerry freed her breast and caught a handful of golden curls in his fist, pulling her head back until their eyes met.

"And what of the bastards we breed, Katy? Have you forgotten your concern for them?" His eyes hardened when she jerked away as if he had dashed cold water in her face. It was a poor return for the care she had showered upon him, but after discovering her passion to be as great as his own—sweeping away all rational thought and beliefs—Kerry knew he would not be satisfied with just one night. And she would be unhappy if he asked more.

"You play with me, sir," Katy spat out with a blend of anger and disgust, pushing herself from his side with a show of revulsion, but his entangled hand prevented her from going far. That he could betray her like that was unthinkable. That she could forget herself so, even worse.

Kerry pulled her head back against his shoulder but allowed her to keep a space between them. They would sleep easier like that.

"No, my dear, I have only tested your coldness and found it wanting. Your grim portrayal of Belinda is only skin deep, thank heavens, but if your convictions are more solidly based, we had better spend the night in more virtuous pastimes." Feeling some of the tension leave her frail shoulders, Kerry stroked her hair and added softly, "And if you should ever find your convictions to be based on shifting sands, I will be waiting for you with open arms."

Her body still aching from his touch, heart bruised by his words, Katy could only wipe a tear from her eye and shake her head sadly. A future could not be built on passion alone and that was all he offered. For this one night she would give herself willingly, just to be able to hold it in her memory and know that it was he who had introduced her to full womanhood, but he had already made it clear one night was not enough. She brushed a stray lock of hair from his chiseled face and smiled wanly.

"When the sands shift, you will know it, for I will fall into your arms quite abruptly. Will you be able to sleep?"

"I won't be awake waiting for you to fall, if that's what you mean," he grinned half-heartedly.

Katy pulled a face and turned her back on him, curling up like a kitten in the shadow of his embrace. "You are not worth worrying over, milord. I bid you good-night."

"Good-night, sweet Katy," he whispered, and with the golden flow of curls across his chest, Kerry slept.

August 1735

THE FIRST GLOW of dawn had not yet touched the windows when Kerry woke again, instantly aware of two contradictory perceptions: the throbbing pain in his shoulder and the pleasant pressure of a woman at his side. Concentrating his thoughts on the pleasant, he sank back against the pillow and enjoyed the sensual contact of long bare limbs entwined about his thighs and a slender waist beneath his hand. Looking down, he could see the thick curve of dark lashes across her pale cheeks, rosebud lips moist and lightly parted, a dream of childish innocence imprinted on her features, and he had to remember last night's passionate responses to remind himself that this was no child he held. To improve his memory, his hand slipped softly from waist to thinly covered breast, cupping its small weight in his large palm. His smile of satisfaction was met by a violet dark gaze.

"Milord?" Katy felt his hand tighten about her breast, playing with the rising tip as he stared down into her eyes. She lay relaxed and content, one hand curled on the hard drum of his chest, contemplating the strong angle of his jaw and debating whether to touch it.

"Good morning, love. Did anyone ever tell you how beautiful you are when you sleep?"

A faint blush of pink stained her cheeks, and she buried her face in his shoulder, luxuriating in the powerful strength holding her to his side. "No, milord. There was never anyone to see me asleep before."

"I did once," he replied softly, playing with a brilliant curl, "and never forgot the sight. Now that you have spent the night in my bed, Katy, could you not call me something less formal than 'milord'?"

Touching the hand bound up in a sling, Katy allowed her fingers to be captured and returned his light squeeze. "Such as?" she inquired mildly, keeping her attention on the intertwining of their fingers and not the hunger in his gaze.

"Kerry would do to start; anything more affectionate could not be expected from a cold-blooded governess the likes of you," and smiling, he kissed her brow.

"Kerry?" She sampled the sound, letting her tongue roll it around in her mouth, enjoying the sensation and his willingness to part with this barrier, before turning grave and shaking her head in refusal. "No, milord, that would make it too easy to forget who you are and what I am. Sometimes, I need all the reminding I can get."

"Remind me then to turn you over my knee and paddle some sense into you when I regain the use of my arm. You are a woman and I am a man and sooner or later I will make you forget everything else. And unless you wish it to be much sooner than you expected, you had better stop that and get up to find us some breakfast."

Katy had been examining the bandage on his other shoulder, forgetting his vantage point in her present state of undress until his words caused her to follow his gaze. Hastily clasping her hand over the gaping shift providing a full view of the glory lying beneath, she retreated to the far side of the small bed, scrambling toward the foot to make her escape.

Watching with amusement, Kerry let her go with some regret. He might never be offered such a tempting opportunity again, but it was too late now to take any more advantage of it than he already had. Pulling himself painfully from the bed, he recounted happily all the advantages he had taken and declared it a good night's work under the circumstances.

Returning to the front room, Katy found her guardian standing in the dark, gazing out the blackened window, the injured arm tied to his chest giving his silhouette an unbalanced appearance. Quietly, she set about fixing a cold meal. How long would it take before help arrived? She calculated the minutes as she worked, uneasily aware of the stiff figure keeping watch at his post.

As she approached him with a platter of sliced meat and bread, he turned and gestured silently toward a shirt he had thrown across his chair. Understanding, Katy set the platter down and helped him to painfully don the garment, carefully fastening it over the bandages and readjusting the sling. Kerry had never sat at the table without a shirt before and pride would not let him now.

Both now fully dressed, they set up a temporary table near the window so Kerry could continue his vigil while they ate. Convinced somewhere out there in the darkness, the Indians waited, too, he cast up a silent prayer that Mahomet had safely maneuvered his precious cargo past them.

Katy's thoughts had turned in the same direction. Safely diverted by Kerry's antics the night before, her fears for Anna's safety resumed their importance with waking awareness and she found herself incapable of thinking of anything else. Anna could be lying dead and mutilated in some cold ditch right now and nothing could be done about it. Tears formed in the corners of her eyes, and she shoved away her untouched food.

Kerry turned away from his watch to shove the plate back at her. "Eat it. If anything should happen, you will need your strength."

His words were as cold as their meal, and startled, Katy stared back at him. "For what, milord? To spit in their eyes?" she asked scornfully.

"The tribes around here generally make slaves of their captives if they are not goaded into killing them first. Now eat, it will do no good to worry."

His harshness was with himself and not with her, but he had not the patience for explanations. With Anna and Mahomet

already on his conscience, he had to face Katy's fair innocence and imagine the filthy hands of some savage taking
her, and his expression hardened. He would kill her first
before he would allow that to happen.

Muttering oaths, he kicked back his chair and strode across
the room, retrieving a hard object from one of the shelves
before returning to the table and throwing it down in front of
his bewildered companion. "Hide that on you somewhere. If
anything should happen to me, it is your only way out. You
will have only one chance, use it wisely."

Gingerly, Katy lifted the shiny poniard by its ivory handle, and looked up into the fierce emerald fires above her.
Reading the deep lines etched on either side of his mouth, she
understood what he said and she shivered inwardly. To turn
this against herself was a physical impossibility. Hadn't she
proved her cowardice when she had sold herself to him?

Her irresolution would have been obvious to Kerry at any
other time, but the barbarous images projected by his imagination prevented his seeing anything else. He watched as she
lifted her skirts and unwillingly thrust the knife into her
garter, wincing as the cold metal stung her flesh. The sight of
the shapely leg that half an hour ago had lain across his
brought Kerry abruptly to his senses, and he caught her up in
his one good arm, crushing her breathlessly against him for a
moment.

"Damn everything and everybody, but no one is laying a
hand on you unless it is myself, if I must rise from the dead
to do it. Now, sit and eat, kitten, the sun will be up soon."
As he spoke the words, he had no idea how strangely pro-
phetic they would be.

A hysterical giggle rose in Katy's throat as she imagined a
dead Lord Kerry rising from the grave to claim her. If anyone
could, it would be he, and she concentrated on this ridiculous
thought as she returned to her seat and felt the pressure of the
cold blade against her flesh. The warmth of his masculine
hardness still with her, it was easy to imagine his possession
of her body, only the technicalities remaining vague in her mind,
and she allowed herself the pleasure of toying with these
unmaidenly thoughts while she ate. It was better than imagining the alternatives.

The stiffening of Kerry's spine as he stood at the window warned Katy before a word was said. Rising slowly to stand by his side, she could see nothing in the dim gray morning mist, but the tightening of Kerry's fist around the useless musket confirmed her suspicion that something lingered out there. Two pairs of eyes searched the fog for movement from stealthy shapes, separating the dark forms of trees and fenceposts from those meaning danger. It seemed impossible to sort them out as one shadow flitted into another, but gradually the steady movement worked its way into their awareness.

There was no telling their numbers. Kerry set the butt of his gun against the floor and put his arm around Katy's slender waist. With two loaded muskets he might conceivably bring down two of their attackers, but with one useless arm he could not reload fast enough or even aim with any degree of accuracy to ensure their safety from the remainder.

" 'Tis a pity my fine sword does not stand a chance against their arrows, me darlin'," he said sadly, brushing a kiss across her hair.

His lilting accent brought a small smile to Katy's face as she remembered all the times he had used it to tease her, and she rose to her toes to kiss him full on the mouth, feeling his arm tighten about her as their lips met. If they must die, it would be better this way, and their bodies melded together for one last moment's passion.

A low whistle followed by a solid thump put an end to their embrace as they stared wordlessly into each other's eyes before looking once more to the window. Another whistle accompanied by a bright flash of smoking light in the gray mist hit the roof and Kerry uttered a string of curses that even Katy's London-bred ears flinched to hear.

"They're using fire arrows on the roof, they plan to smoke us out." His explanation finally emerged amid the oaths as a third flaming arrow hit the mark. The roof was well tarred and shingled against the blazing summer sun, but already the smell of burning creosote filtered into the room.

Kerry cursed again, wishing he could separate at least one target from the several ghostly shadows creeping along just out of his line of vision. If he had any assurance that their

surrender would not be met with violence, he would give up
their burning fortress without a shot fired. But if he were to
kill even one of them, their own deaths would be assured,
and he wasn't yet convinced that might not be the best policy.
Instant death might be preferable to having Katy torn from
him and subjected to the humiliation of an Indian slave, but
where there was life, there remained the possibility of escape.

While he debated alternatives, the sun broke through the
rising patches of mist, illuminating the one brave who had
placed himself within Kerry's line of fire. Raising the musket
to take aim, Kerry suddenly dropped the firearm to the floor
and muttered a word sounding much like ''Tonga!''

Katy watched with amazement as Kerry ripped aside the
remaining paper on the window and began shouting phrases
foreign to her ear. To her increasing surprise, the Indian
seemed to respond, and within minutes the fiery arrows ceased
as the shadows stood silent and waiting.

Dropping his weapon to the floor, Kerry encircled Katy's
waist with his arm and implanted one last kiss on her brow
while the rafter in the back room burned through and collapsed, sending swirling clouds of smoke up and around
them.

''Katy, this is our only chance, and I'm going to take it.
To fight back would be suicide. That Indian you see out there
is the one Mahomet saved from almost certain death. He has
promised us no harm if we surrender as his prisoners; I can
see no other way out.'' Eyes burning with a passion Katy
could do naught but accept, Kerry pulled her closer for a
moment, then took one last look around his doomed home.
His gaze falling on the bookshelf, he released Katy and
crossed the room to grab one last memento, stuffing it inside
his shirt as he returned to Katy's side.

A quick glance told her the top shelf where the framed
miniatures had rested was now empty, and she searched his
face for explanations, but his thoughts were on the ordeal
ahead and all she could read in the strong planes of his
well-sculptured face was grim determination. Leaning into his
comforting embrace, she allowed him to lead her from the
flaming building into the grasp of the unknown.

The fresh, chill air forced the smoke from their lungs, and

they came out coughing, gasping to refill their lungs with the smoke-tainted morning air. When they recovered some of their composure, it was to find themselves surrounded by a half-dozen nearly naked red men, lurid smears of paint turning their savage faces into masks of horror. Katy shrank back against Kerry's side as one of their taller captors reached out to touch her hair, its sun-bleached lightness gleaming gold and silver in the Indian's hand when hit by the first rays of dawn. Startled exclamations greeted this phenomenon, and the others crowded closer, the stench of animal grease and unwashed bodies bringing her closer to asphyxiation than the smoke.

An angry guttural order put an end to the nightmare and the savages slipped back into the shadows, leaving only the one stiffly erect brave to confront them. "Where's black medicine man?" Eyeing Kerry's sling-supported arm dubiously, Tonga addressed them imperiously.

Knowing the Indian's respect for Mahomet, Kerry explained—half in Cherokee, half in English—how the medicine man had given his powers to this woman, who had already nearly healed the wound made by the brave man's shooting stick. This explanation was greeted by several muttered grunts, presumably from the culprit who had done the shooting, but Tonga remained silent as he poked curiously at the injured shoulder.

Too many Indians had experienced the deadly poison of the white man's gun to believe that any man could survive it. Satisfied that the wound was real and indeed healing, the Indian looked at Katy with new respect and some admiration. Captives as powerful as this would make him a wealthy man. Well content with the morning's work, he signaled for the others to follow and the Indians fell in line around them, guiding them surely and silently into the woods from whence they had come.

Katy threw one backward glance over her shoulder at the clearing where she had spent the happiest weeks of her life. All her attempts at homemaking were going up in a thick tower of black smoke, soon to be burned-out cinders for others to stumble upon and wonder over. Would Sir Charles and their rescuers give them up for dead when they saw the smoldering remains? Tears filled her eyes as she stumbled over a fallen tree limb and was forced to turn back to the trail, and even Kerry's sympathetic hug failed to help.

The Indians moved quickly and expertly down invisible trails. Their captives, one hampered by yards of excess clothing and the other weakened from wounds, made a more difficult progress. Soon they were bringing up the rear with only one surly savage prodding them on, and his guttural oaths had little effect on the weary pair. As the sun rose higher in the sky, the heat invaded the virgin forest, and Kerry's arm grew heavier about Katy's shoulders.

Watching her guardian with growing alarm, Katy tried to support him with an arm about his waist as she had seen Mahomet do, but her slight weight provided little support. Soon she too felt the drag of weariness slowing her steps. Branches tore at her hair and brambles caught in her skirts as she trod blindly on, guided only by the impatient expletives of their captors, Kerry's heavy weight growing heavier by the minute.

Evidently intending to put as much distance between themselves and any pursuers as it was possible to make in one day, the Indians did not stop to rest. They allowed their prisoners to refresh themselves momentarily in a clear stream, then pressed on, deaf to all pleas for respite. Without even the breath to curse, Kerry remained silent, but Katy had no such pride. As the blood began to seep through the bandage and stain Kerry's shirt, she upbraided their captors fiercely and fervently, not caring whether they understood or not. It was inhuman to expect them to carry on this way, and if they did not stop soon, she was terrified she would be forced to watch the man she loved bleed to death in her arms. Terror urged her on.

Finally succumbing to the small one's angry cries, Tonga worked his way to the rear of the procession and inspected the condition of his prisoners. Understanding more of Katy's pleas than the others, he frowned at the growing stain on Kerry's shirt and transferred his angry look to Katy. Too terrified to be frightened more, Katy condemned him for bringing death to a man who had saved his life. The Indian grew grimmer at this insolence from a female, but his orders sent two braves off to look for a place to make camp for the night.

The sun had gone down and they were walking in total darkness before they came to the stream-broken clearing designated as their campsite. Ignored by the Indians, the weary prisoners settled on the bank of the stream while Katy tore off a piece of linen from her petticoat to cleanse Kerry's wound. She worked silently, not wishing to call any further attention to herself, and Kerry accepted her ministrations gratefully.

After the wound was clean and rebandaged, they bathed their sweat-soaked faces in the cool water, then removed their blistered feet from hot leather and soaked swollen ankles in the rushing water. Carrying the half-cooked rabbit his braves had caught for their meal, Tonga found his prisoners in that position when he approached them later.

Refreshed to some extent by their brief rest, Kerry had strength enough to demand explanations from his Indian "friend." Lost in the convoluted maze of mixed Indian phrases and rough sign language, Katy let her mind wander, blanking out the aches and pains of her body as the wash of words swept around her.

The Indian departed shortly thereafter, coming back a moment later with a blanket he had garnered from somewhere, and motioned them back in the direction of the campfire light. Wearily accepting the blanket, Kerry helped his young ward to her feet and found a place for them on the outskirts of the camp, out of range of the firelight where they could rest their backs against an upturned rock and be virtually unnoticed.

He did not like the way the savages kept glancing at Katy's hair; more than once during their journey he had seen them reach out to touch it. Lost in other concerns, Katy had scarce paid them heed, but Kerry understood too well the muttered grunts accompanying her attempts to brush away inquisitive fingers. His brief talk with Tonga had not lessened his worries.

As Katy nibbled distastefully at the bloody piece of meat that formed her share of the night's repast, she observed the angrily clenched jaw of her usually genial companion and decided he could not look any less like the noble lord and gentleman she had known in London than he did now. Stripped of his elegant clothes, his once immaculate linen stained and sweaty, auburn hair tangled and matted, the handsome cut of his jaw shadowed by several days' growth of beard, Kerry was no longer the young blood of London society, but the man she had given her heart to. And when he turned turbulent green eyes down upon her, he was caught by surprise at the dazzling smile greeting him.

"Your thoughts?" Kerry inquired mildly, with a quirk of one eyebrow, as if they were dining in the Stockbridge home and he had no fears to hide.

"What would the Lady Elizabeth think of you now?" Katy asked impishly, aware of his tension but seeking to release it. Discussing their possible fate was not a topic conducive to pleasant discourse.

"The Lady Elizabeth?" Puzzled by this strange tangent while his thoughts were entangled in a more immediate situation, he took a moment to switch to another place and time. Remembering the ice maiden he had almost made his wife, Kerry gave the small sprite beside him a contemplative look. "And what brought her to mind at this particular moment?"

Blushing, and hating herself for it, Katy shrugged and wiped her fingers on a green leaf. "If you must answer questions with questions, what were you and that savage talking about a minute ago?"

"If we continue making such conversational leaps and bounds, there will not be a topic untouched by morning. I was just beginning to get interested in the Lady Elizabeth. Let's return to her. Do you think she would not approve of me now? Do you?" Ruefully Kerry ran a hand over his rough beard.

"The Lady Elizabeth never approved of you. My approval, you never sought, so there is no reason to give it. I was simply making a comment on the different worlds you inhabit. Now, will you answer my more pertinent question?"

"As far as I can see, your questions are generally most impertinent. I am not done with the Lady Elizabeth. Do I now detect a note of jealousy of the Lady Elizabeth, or are you sharing her disapproval?"

"Milord, this is neither the time nor the place—" A spate of angry words erupted around the campfire, and Katy hurried to cover them up. "I never said I disapprove of you, milord."

But Kerry was listening with a worried frown to the argument erupting among the Indians. Several of the younger braves were casting glances in their direction and the phrases he recognized did not sound promising. When Tonga arose to quell the argument, Kerry turned back to Katy's inquiring eyes.

"This is a scouting party, kitten, for a much larger gathering that is determined to declare war on the English. I have not got all of it, but someone has been trading guns and liquor to our friends here but delivering only half or a quarter of the quantities paid for, and of poor quality at that. Coupled with the usual complaints of land-grabbing, poor hunting, and woman-molesting—all of which I can't deny have happened—it has triggered a small-scale war that may soon endanger the plantations and maybe Georgetown. The younger braves seem to be feeling particularly frisky now that they've got some guns. It was one of them who nicked me and started things off a little in advance of their plans. Now they've got to make tracks back to camp and see things started."

The argument grew louder and Katy recognized the Indian who had first terrified her by grabbing her hair. His violent gesticulations seemed to encompass them, and she shrank back against Kerry as the savage's black eyes pierced the darkness to find her. The one called Tonga argued him down, but she noticed Kerry's growing uneasiness.

"What are they saying?" she whispered, as their captors' voices lowered to angry mutters.

"Tonga has told them you have the powers of a medicine man, that we are his property, and that he has given his word we will come to no harm. The others are evidently of a different mind." He did not mention of what mind they were, but it was as he had feared, and it would take quick thinking on his part and Tonga's if Katy were to escape unscathed. Himself, they had little interest in, other than recommending he be permanently discarded if he continued to slow them down.

At that point Tonga arose from his place at the fire and stalked through the surrounding darkness to the place where his captives waited. Without a glance at Katy, he addressed Kerry in sonorous tones, adding emphatic gestures when

Kerry failed to understand the corresponding Indian phrase. A single word seemed to crop up frequently. Katy picked it out when Kerry demanded an explanation of it twice, and received it in rather graphic terms. Some words were universal in every language and she had little difficulty defining it, as neither did Kerry. He responded vehemently, once assured he was interpreting it correctly. Katy felt herself grow numb as she realized she was the object under discussion, and she shrank further behind her protector and away from the ring of staring black eyes.

When Tonga finally retreated, Kerry turned his back on hostile eyes and pulled the quivering figure of his young protégée into his lap, cursing his own stupidity for bringing her into this and raving at himself for not having stripped her innocence away long before. In a world of corruption, innocence was a handicap, and her virginity was quickly becoming a peril to them both. If he hadn't been so fastidious about forcing the issue, she would be much better prepared for what he feared would happen next.

Pulling Katy's golden head down against his uninjured shoulder, Kerry began to play with the linen neckerchief covering her breasts, loosening it until his fingers found the sensitive skin beneath. Ignoring her sharp inhalation at this contact, he methodically began to arouse her desires and his own while shielding her from the view of the savages around the campfire.

"Milord, what are you doing? What is happening?" Katy whispered huskily, the words sounding strange to her ears as ripples of pleasure coursed through her at his experienced fondling. A familiar ache took up residence in the center of her being and began to spread rapidly through her as his hands cupped her breasts and caressed their peaks to quivering hardness.

For what was about to happen, Kerry had to offer some explanation. If Tonga's arguments were unsuccessful . . . He refused to consider that possibility. "Katy, do you still have that knife I gave you?" There would be only one way out in that case.

"Yes, milord. Shall I give it to you?" Trusting as ever, Katy surreptitiously removed the small weapon from her garter at his nod.

Carefully considering dark-rimmed violet eyes, Kerry held
the sharp point under her breast where one swift upward
move could puncture both heart and lungs. Years of military
training and swordsmanship had taught him few skills, but
rapid death was one of them. She suspected nothing as he
commanded, "Keep an eye over my shoulder. Tell me if
anyone but Tonga approaches." That would be the only
signal he had, and Kerry prayed for the courage to follow
through. Visions of the alternative kept his hand hot and
sweaty and determined on the handle of the deadly dagger.

Understanding only that some peril awaited them, Katy
nodded her agreement, waiting for further explanation. Why
would he choose a moment like this to make love to her if
they were truly in danger? And what did he hope to do with
one knife against all those Indians? Her eyes begged for
enlightenment.

Still fondling one soft breast with his injured hand, Kerry
attempted to explain without revealing his fears. "This tribe
has an ancient legend about a sun spirit with magical powers.
Tonga has boasted of your powers to heal, and coupled with
their fascination at the color of your hair, the young bucks
have taken it into their heads that you may just be what they
are looking for." In truth, Kerry sensed much of the legend
had been manufactured by the wily savages to save face while
violating their promise of safety, but the details mattered little
against their intent.

As the voluptuous pleasure of Kerry's touch radiated to all
her senses, Katy tried to puzzle out his words while keeping
one eye on the activity at the campfire. It made for difficult
concentration; perhaps that was his intention. "I don't understand, milord. Isn't that good?"

Stalling for time, Kerry nibbled at the nape of her neck,
regretting the necessity of using lovemaking as a distraction
until their fates were decided, but she still had the right to
know what would be expected of her.

"No, my love, not necessarily," he whispered hoarsely as
he kissed her forehead, eyes, ears. "It seems this particular
spirit is a generous one—she shares her powers with her
favors—and those young bucks are eager to sample both."
There, he had said it, and by the tightening of her shoulders,

he judged she was beginning to comprehend the situation. Would she then, too, understand the knife at her side? That under no circumstances would he stand by helplessly and watch one filthy savage after another invade her innocent body? God, if only Tonga could persuade them . . . Sweat poured freely from Kerry's brow as he held her slight figure close and awaited their decision.

Katy had ceased to think. She drifted into a state somewhere between awareness and unconsciousness, unwilling to imagine the horror of those unwashed bodies touching hers, and not daring to contemplate Kerry's revenge. She clung to him, allowing his hand to rove where it would, but no longer conscious of the sensations he aroused as her eyes fixed unthinkingly on the figures at the fire.

At last one dark silhouette separated itself from the others, and as it approached, she shuddered violently. Kerry clutched her urgently, and when she didn't respond, he chanced turning his head to see what had made her tremble so. Letting out a small sigh of relief, he relaxed his knife hand. It was Tonga.

The older Indian squatted down beside the young couple and muttered a few low phrases, and once again Katy heard the word he had repeated so frequently earlier. Kerry frowned fiercely and shook his head, gesticulating emphatically in his attempt to make himself clear with the unfamiliar words. But the Indian continued to shake his head solemnly and indicate the burning fire. An impasse had been reached, and with his knife buried in the folds of Katy's gown, Kerry bent his head in reluctant acceptance of the terms laid down.

As the Indian returned to his companions, Kerry slid the knife into his boot and removed the sling from his neck, casting it aside so he could move his arm more freely. Katy watched these preparations with apprehension. She had no wish to die, but she suddenly realized she much preferred it to the alternative, and she watched Kerry's apparent resignation with growing horror.

"Milord, tell me what is happening, for God's sake! What are they going to do to me?"

"With luck, they will do nothing." Using his good arm to help her to her feet and his injured one to invade her bodice, producing a firm breast with its swollen crown, Kerry bent to kiss the tender tip before replying further to her urgent inquiries, his eyes hooded as he explained.

"Tonga has succeeded in persuading them that the goddess chooses only one man, and you have made your choice already. Unfortunately, they are skeptics and cannot believe you would settle for such a poor specimen as I, when all their talents eagerly await you. They demand proof of your decision, and because they are heathen savages, they demand a public display of your affection."

While these words burned their way into Katy's consciousness, Kerry led her toward the firelight, arranging the blanket on the ground while the Indians drew closer, pointing greasy fingers at various parts of her anatomy and snickering grossly among themselves. Still not quite comprehending, she allowed Kerry to lower her to the blanket, all the time keenly aware of the ring of eyes staring avidly at her.

But when Kerry began to speak, kneeling over her and whispering low in her ear, Katy turned panic-stricken eyes to his familiar face and found it contorted with the grim pain of what was to come. She followed his words with difficulty as he laid her back against the hard ground, firelight dancing about their shadows.

"Whatever you do, my love, do not make a sound and do not fight me. Close your eyes—it will make this easier. I'll be as gentle as I can, but I intend to be quick, so it will hurt. Try to relax, please, kitten . . ." Kerry's words continued soothingly, urgently, warning her of what to expect, consoling her, promising haste as he unfastened his breeches and raised her skirts, throwing them back and covering her protectively with his own body as he lowered himself over her.

Reality finally struck as, incredulously, Katy felt the firmness of Kerry's hands separating her bare thighs, his fingers brushing the hidden recesses so long denied him. A scream caught in her throat as his mouth roughly covered hers, stifling her outcry while his stiffening manhood pushed at the entrance to her body.

Her eyelids closed tightly in terror, and the flames from the fire blazed patterns across them. A dozen eyes burned her exposed flesh as she dug her fingers hysterically into Kerry's back. This couldn't be happening, not now, not in this way. . . .

With one sharp movement he sundered the membrane of her innocence, and Katy froze instinctively against his painful invasion, denying him easy access to her body. Nearly insane with fear and shame, all desire dead, Katy fought back, making his penetration a dry and agonizing ordeal. Firm hands held her still as she felt her insides as well as her pride being ripped asunder with his relentless battering. Blood trickled, salty and warm, into her mouth when she bit her lip to keep from crying out.

Tortured by thoughts of that ring of prying eyes, exclamatory grunts reminding her all too frequently of their avid audience, Katy felt sanity being ripped from its fragile threads with each punishing blow of Kerry's maleness. She tried to deny the body joined obscenely and painfully with hers, and her mind grabbed frantically for reason. To be subjected to this humiliation after waiting so long . . . Had he planned it that way? Had Kerry and his Indian friend dreamed up this torment to punish her for her refusal?

No matter how hard she shut her eyes and willed unconsciousness, she could not rid herself of the heaving body above her, and her fingernails dug deeper into his flesh with each lunging thrust. Eternity stretched before her as she waited for that final excruciating pain that would put an end to torment, but Kerry kept his promise. He came quickly, months of abstinence and weeks of desire abetting his need, and his final shudders brought grunts of satisfaction from their audience.

With a quick movement Kerry wrapped his ravished ward in the blanket, and heedless of his injured shoulder, swept Katy's slight form up in his arms, carrying her out of the firelight, back to the privacy of their dark haven. Laying her carefully on the hard ground, he attempted to pull her into his comforting arms, but Katy twisted away, turning her back on him.

There were no sobs, no tears, only stony silence, and he respected her anguish by moving away, leaning his back against the hard rock while he tried to stanch the renewed flow of blood from his shoulder. To have protected her all those years, carefully erasing the painful memory of her first encounter with men, building up her trust, and then to demolish it all with a rape like this . . . Staring grimly at the huddled figure beside him, Kerry swore mighty oaths, and he rested little that night as the ache in his body coupled with the pain in his mind to torment his sleep.

Mid-August 1735

KATY AWOKE to the movement of silent gray figures about a cold campfire and quickly closed her eyes again. The stickiness of dried blood on her thighs and the sore, throbbing ache between told her there had been no nightmare, and a cold chill settled in her soul. Just the thought that she had once desired this invasion of her body made her shudder; if she had only known what it would be like, she would have starved that long-ago night rather than submit to a lifetime of such humiliation. Tears stung her cheeks again as the horrifying images of last night's firelit rape filtered through her memory, and she felt nothing but revulsion for the man she had thought she loved. Her stomach heaved, but she choked back the bitter gall rather than expose herself to further embarrassment.

Turning away from the scene of last night's desecration, she discovered Lord Kerry still propped against the protective outcropping of rock, a waxy pallor replacing his normal color and the side of his shirt blood-caked and plastered to his skin. There was no sign of consciousness in his awkward position, and for a moment Katy panicked. Without him, she would be at the mercy of all those savages. Whatever her emotions might be, she still needed him, and she breathed with relief as she noticed the faint rise and fall of his chest. He lived.

Carefully removing another strip of linen petticoat, Katy rose awkwardly and slipped back to the creekside, soaking the rag and returning to sponge loose the ruined shirt from Kerry's shoulder. Peeling the cloth from the wound, she felt his eyes on her, but she continued working silently, cleaning the wound and rebandaging it as best she was able. There would be no wandering the woods for herb poultices today; she could only hope it stayed clean. Taking his soiled shirt back to the creek, she rinsed it in the stream, scrubbing it against rocks in an attempt to make it usable again. It would be the only clothing he possessed until a miracle returned them to civilization.

By the time she finished, the Indians had eliminated all trace of the campsite, and Tonga presented them with some dried meat for their empty stomachs. Katy ignored her share, but Kerry tucked it away inside his damp shirt in the event she should change her mind.

Allowing her to retie the sling about his neck, Kerry ventured to break the silence between them, finding his usual facile tongue strangely tied. "Katy, can we not speak of this?"

"There is nothing to be said, milord." Tightening the knot, she moved painfully away from him, following the impatient gesture of their guard.

As he watched her hobbling movement, Kerry's heart twisted in its cavity, and he hurried to catch up with her. She rejected his offered arm, but he kept in step beside her. "On the contrary, there is everything to be said."

Coldly moving ahead of him, Katy ignored his plea, and for the moment Kerry respected her privacy. She needed time to understand what had happened, and why, and to recover from the awful humiliation she had been subjected to, if that were possible. Time would heal some of the pain, but unless the deeper wound were treated soon, she would suffer from it forever. Even if she must hate him for the rest of her life, he would see that wound cured.

The day grew steamier than the one before. Flies swarmed

and bit at their sweat-soaked faces, brambles and branches slapped at legs and arms, leaving painful welts across every bare expanse of skin. Though Kerry felt weaker than the day before, he stood on his own, slowing the pace but unwilling to impose his weight on his faltering, weary companion. As the day grew longer and Katy repeatedly stumbled, Kerry once again offered his arm, and this time found it accepted. More or less supporting each other, they trudged on, oblivious of the irritation of their captors, only thankful that the sun goddess's prowess was apparently not expected to extend to day-long hiking.

They entered the Indian war camp shortly after sunset, the fading red light illuminating a small clearing obviously once made by white settlers. Two small log huts sat at either end of the open space and Tonga hustled them toward one of these.

Finding the hut empty and apparently intended for a prison, Kerry refused to enter, exchanging a few sharp words with his captor while Katy drooped wearily against the log wall. She could not understand the argument, finding the privacy of an enclosed cabin immensely preferable to another night under the open stars and an entire camp full of staring eyes.

Grudgingly the Indian submitted to his recalcitrant prisoner's whim, guiding them outside the boundaries of camp into a line of bushes flanking the stream that supplied the site's water. Making an irritated gesture and barking a warning, the Indian turned his back on his prisoners.

Responding to the question in Katy's smudged eyes, Kerry said, "If you are quick, there is time for a bath in that pool over there. Don't be long—he has little patience with such foolishness." When she still did not move, he made a disgusted gesture and turned his back on her. "I will not intrude on your privacy, you are safe from me, but I have given Tonga my word we will not attempt to escape. The Indians could find us faster than we could walk, so do not get any foolish notions."

Moving behind a bush, Katy quickly stripped off her soiled and ragged clothes and slipped into the quiet pool of rippling water. She couldn't swim, but the water was not deep. Locating a mossy rock, she sank gratefully up to her neck in the

soothing coolness. The water lapped over her bruised and
battered body, washing away aches and irritations along with
the uncomfortable reminders of last night. If only it could
wash away the memories, she might truly feel refreshed, but
inside she still felt as dirty and soiled as her clothes.

Throwing a wary glance over her shoulder to check the
bank, she was startled to discover the clothes gone, but hasty
inspection revealed the noble Lord Kerry farther down the
creek bank, cleaning her linen in the running water as she had
done his that morning. Looking up at that moment, their eyes
met over the blood-speckled residue of last night's ravish-
ment, and Katy quickly glanced away, not just in embarrassment, but because of the depth of emotion in those clear
green eyes. It had been foolish to think he would intentionally
harm her. He had risked his own life to save her from the
hands of those savages, and she had treated him cruelly in
return, but she still could not forgive him for committing such
a disgusting, degrading act. Men might receive some satisfaction from such an animalistic performance, but how could he
have wished to submit her to such degradation? Her cheeks
burned at the thought of how close they had come to it
without being forced, when she had once actually desired it.
Never again, she vowed silently.

Becoming aware of Lord Kerry standing on the creek bank
above her, Katy hastily sank deeper into the water.

"There isn't time for your gown to dry, so I did not wash
it. I thought it wise not to parade you through the camp in
wet clothes." He spread the damp petticoats and shift across
the bushes and remained standing, holding the bramble-torn
and dusty remains of her gown over his arm.

Katy blushed and looked away, his frank stare telling more
than his words. "It was not necessary for you to do that,
milord. I could have done it myself." To have a man washing her linen, particularly this man, spoke of an intimacy she
was not ready to accept.

"I thought if I did it for you, there might be time for me to
wash while you dressed. Besides, I had no wish for these
savages to see the signs of your virginity. Our story would
lose its credibility."

Must he remind her with every word of what she would

rather forget? Was there no escape, no place to hide from the knowledge in his eyes? Dully Katy replied, "If you would turn your back, I will come out."

Obediently he turned around, and she scurried to pick up her gown and still-damp shift. The petticoats would be too wet and heavy to wear. Slipping into the protection of the bushes, she donned the shift, listening to Kerry's one-handed struggles to undress. Remembering the abashed look on his face as he washed the proofs of innocence from her clothes, she felt a sudden surge of compassion for his plight. Deeming decency to be a moot point after the last few nights, Katy hastened to his aid, unaware the wet fabric of her shift clung in a display more unseemly than her actual nakedness.

Prying boots off swollen feet, Kerry was unaware of her approach until she knelt before him, grasping the heel and pulling the loosened boot until she nearly fell backward at its release. Biting his tongue, he made no comment on her appearance but accepted her help perfunctorily. When his boots were off and he stood to strip off his shirt, she had to press against him to release the sling and Kerry's resistance wore thin.

"Me darlin' water sprite, if you do not remove yourself, I will be attackin' you again, and more willingly than last time."

He didn't touch her, but Katy reacted as if he had, starting back as if struck. "Damn you to bloody hell," she choked out, before spinning around and dashing back to the bushes.

"If swearing at me helps, you have my permission," Kerry called after her, grinning despite himself at the thought of his demure governess using such language.

A barrage of oaths followed his remark. He recognized most as coming from himself originally, but as she developed the knack of it, more ringing epithets struck his ears, vaguely reminiscent of the streets of London from whence she came. As her repertoire ran thin, the curses became mere mutters, and as he sank himself into the cool waters, giggles greeted him from behind the bush. Kerry smiled to himself. If she could still laugh there was hope. She was young and would recover quickly if proper care were taken, and he intended to administer that care.

Lord Kerry carrying boots and shirt, and Katy her petticoats, they emerged from their bath nearly as naked as their
captors, but there were few eyes in the darkness to notice. A
bonfire at the far end of camp provided reason for the absence
of curious onlookers, and Tonga escorted them back to their
prison without incident. As the heavy door closed behind
them, leaving them in nearly total darkness, Kerry heard
guards being ordered for the door, and then there was silence.

The single small rear window provided the only source of
light, and that only a small patch of moonlight. While his
eyes adjusted to the blackness, Kerry groped about until his
fingers encountered Katy's hair. Stroking it gently, he drew
closer to her trembling figure.

"Katy, my love, don't be frightened. You must know by
now that I would never willingly hurt you."

"Don't touch me," she whispered hysterically, not moving
from beneath his hand, but cringing nervously at his touch.

"Do you blame me, then, for what happened?" Kerry
asked softly, wishing to draw her into his arms but knowing it
would be folly to attempt it.

Yes, she blamed him, knowing it was not rational to do so.
The pain in his shoulder must have been excruciating, and he
risked bleeding to death in the process of saving her from the
multiple rape that would surely have been her fate, but it was
his body that had invaded her, leaving her with this disgust
that would not scrub off. She could not help loathing his
every touch, just as she could not help loathing the feel of her
own body.

When she said nothing, Kerry replied somewhat stiffly, "I
will not apologize. I had reason to believe you would prefer
me to any of those savages, and I had hoped you would not
find it a fate worse than death, but if my judgment was
wrong—"

A sob echoed through the cabin, interrupting his words,
followed by another, and another, until a torrent of pent-up
anguish broke through her defenses and Katy finally gave in
to tears. No longer able to hold himself aloof, Kerry crushed
her quivering body to his chest, lowering them to the floor,
cuddling her protectively in his lap as the painful sobs ripped
through her.

The interruption of an Indian with their meal had the effect of calming Katy's sobs to some extent, but she could not be persuaded to touch the food. Using his fingers, Kerry sampled a bit, then placed the next piece between Katy's lips.

"It is not gourmet dining, but it is better than some of Mahomet's attempts." he declared, forcing her to accept the food.

Too exhausted to protest, Katy chewed slowly, taking the next piece when offered, and swallowing it. But by the time her bowl was half-empty, she had regained sufficient strength to refuse the rest, revulsion once more forming at the back of her throat and threatening to spew out if anything more was forced upon her. Calmed by Kerry's patience, she no longer feared his touch, but moved to take herself from his proximity.

Anticipating her action, Kerry had already set the bowls aside, and now used his good arm to hold her in place. "No, kitten, we have some unfinished business to conduct." And lowering his mouth to hers, he pressed against her lips with undemanding tenderness.

Gripped by an indefinable terror, Katy struggled against his hold as she jerked her head away. "No, please, no, milord," she cried, trying wildly to tear herself from his embrace.

Anger and pain ripped at the seams of Kerry's heart at this rejection, but he had not come this far to give up easily. Last night's possession made her irrevocably his, and he would not be satisfied until he repaired the damage done, restoring her to the gentle, loving Katy he knew. Gently but firmly he kept his grip, reducing her helpless struggles to feeble ones with his greater strength.

"Katy, I cannot go on letting you feel this way. I am not blind or insensitive to your disgust, but there is only one way to cure it. If you fall from a horse, you must get right back on or you will never ride again. The same thing applies here, if my comparison is not too offensive. What happened last night was not lovemaking, and you got hurt; I promise it will not be that way again. With time, we can erase the worst of those memories, but you must trust me now, kitten. Later will be too late."

Horrified at the meaning of his words, Katy renewed her struggles, silent tears streaking down her cheeks. Never again would she be subjected to that humiliation. Never again would she allow him to woo her into complacency, allow him to put his arms around her, to kiss her until the moon stood still and her body cried out to meet his . . . But already she had fallen into the trap of his comforting embrace, and his kisses covered her face, warm and inviting and not in the least terrifying.

Stifling her sobs, she ceased her struggles and buried her head against his shoulder. "No, milord, please. I can't . . ." she whispered, praying for his understanding. Her body still ached from last night's invasion; there could be no physical desire for a repetition of the act.

Holding her close, stroking her hair reassuringly, Kerry murmured against her ear, "Yes, you can, Katy. All you have to do is want to." Pulling her hair back so that she was forced to look up at him, her eyes a dark glow in the blurred pallor of her face, Kerry pursued his argument. "I could have had you anytime I wanted these last few years, Katherine, but I would do nothing you did not wish, as you so rightly surmised. Now I'm not asking. When we escape here—for I have no intention of becoming an Indian slave—you can pretend nothing happened, if you like. I will not force myself upon you against your will. But right now, while we are here, I intend to teach you what it is past time you learned. It would be criminal for me to allow you to go on thinking what happened last night had any relation to lovemaking at all." Releasing her hair, he buried his face in those soft tresses and pleaded fervently, "For God's sake, Katy, if you feel anything for me at all, trust me in this."

And she did. Despite all the raging horrors of her mind, her body was already reaching out to his for comfort, the habit of trust too hard to break, the solace of his arms too strong to evade. Desire did not exist in her childish urge to be loved and held, but she knew it lingered still in some quiet harbor of her soul, and she was frightened of what would happen should his passion release it. Already his kisses blazed scorching trails across her skin, and Katy could summon no strength to stop them.

Timidly her arms slipped of their own accord about his neck, and she heard Kerry's faint sigh of relief as he crushed

her to his chest. His familiar masculine scent made it easier to
remember pleasant times and to follow the pattern set then,
offering a shy peck to the rough stubble of his cheek and
sensing, rather than seeing, his familiar grin.

"That's a fair start, me kitten, but not nearly enough to
satisfy. I have seen you kiss young Jake with more eagerness
than that."

Startled by this unexpected reference, Katy momentarily
forgot her fears. "When?" Guiltily remembering a long-ago
night on a veranda, she did not think of her farewell kiss at
the docks, and could not imagine how he could have seen.

"See? You admit it. Pretend I am Jake, if you must, but do
a little better this time. I have received better kisses from my
dog."

"The spaniel, I suppose?" Half-angered at his mocking
words, understanding his purpose, she couldn't help but rise
to the bait. Finding Kerry's lips close to hers, she tasted their
hardness, only to find them melting beneath her touch, drawing her down into their vortex, drowning her in the whirlpool
of her senses.

Dizzied by this headlong plunge and frightened by her
inability to control these emotions, Katy tore her mouth away
from the terrifying abyss of his, but once unleashed, the flood
of desire could not be halted. Guiding her gently, letting her
come to him first, Kerry set about seduction with the skill of
an experienced lover. Figuratively she was still an untried
virgin, one needing more reassurance than most, and he
applied all his skills to encouraging the small seedling of
desire growing within her. Last night's fiasco had nearly
obliterated it, seriously stunting its growth, but Kerry knew it
was there, buried beneath layers of fear and ignorance.

As light kisses rained down upon her face and throat,
offering nothing more threatening than the pleasure of his
touch, Katy once again tried to respond, daringly exploring
Kerry's unshirted back with timid fingers, feeling sinewy
muscles tighten at her touch, making her aware of the tactile
sensations of his nakedness. He held her close, so that her
breast crushed against his chest, and she longed for that last
shred of thin material to be gone from between them, but she
was as incapable of unfastening her bodice at this moment as

she was of preventing his hands from doing so. Feeling the laces loosen and fall free, Katy sought to stave off what was bound to come next, and she threw her arms tighter about his neck, seeking his mouth once more in a frenzy of fear.

Rejoicing at this more natural reaction, Kerry let her set the pace, not invading the sweet recess of her mouth until her lips parted invitingly, his fingers satisfied with tracing the soft skin beneath the loosened neckline of her gown until she pressed up against him of her own accord. Freeing his arm from its sling, he gently pushed back the shoulders of her gown and lowered his kisses to the bare expanse exposed there. With patience, he worked the bodice of gown and shift over her arms until, with a shrug of irritation, she lifted them free, and for the first time he could feel the warmth of her skin pressed against his, her small nipples searing the skin of his chest.

Keeping a tight curb on his rising need to sample every nuance of that slender body she was giving up to his enjoyment, Kerry encouraged her to explore his own, to discover he was flesh and blood and not mythical beast. Laying her gently against their one blanket, the hard earth floor making their bed, he kissed the swollen crown of each breast as he had done the night before and felt with satisfaction the deep shudder quaking her body at his touch.

"My lovely Katy . . ." he whispered, caressing the soft mound of flesh she offered to him in her nakedness, pressing kisses against fine gold hair between his words. "If I could do this properly, you would be dressed in silks and lace, and I would be laying you back against satin sheets, offering you sips of champagne to calm your fears, before making love to you on a bed of the softest down. Can you pretend we have put down the champagne while I remove the last of your silks and laces?"

Kerry's strong hand moved down her fragile rib cage, encountering the curve of slender waistline, and with the slight arch of her back at this intimate touch, it traveled on to her hip, pushing the tattered gown and shift aside as his experienced fingers coursed over rounded buttocks and firm thighs. A whisper of a sigh escaped her as the last of her clothing fell free, and she lay totally exposed and quivering to his touch.

Softly inquiring as he lay down beside her, Katy wrapped her fingers in the rough mat of hair on his hard brown chest. "Milord . . . ?"

"Yes, love?" He drew her up so she lay half-covering him, golden curls spilling recklessly across both their shoulders.

"Does this mean I may run my fingers through your hair too?" Shedding the daze of fear holding her, coming alive to his touch, every inch of her skin tingling from the contact with air and expanding at the points brushing him, Katy gave in to the flood of desires so long inhibited, and with her physical inhibitions went all others, too.

Kerry laughed, a deep throaty laugh rumbling up from his chest, where Katy could feel the vibrations.

"Anytime you wish, my dear," and because he had gone too long desiring this child-woman's body, he pulled her down to him so she might reach his hair while his mouth hungrily devoured hers, and there was nothing left to disguise his excitement, and no reason any longer to hide it.

In those few minutes, Katy learned the ferocity of need, and understood the reason why, through all the ages, women willingly gave up their bodies to the possession of men. The memory of last night's pain and humiliation was obliterated by the passionate ache to be joined with this man as one. Even after he had stripped off his breeches and she could feel the weapon that had so agonizingly impaled her before, she had only the one urge to open up and let him enter.

But knowing how quickly that eagerness could be dispelled, Kerry did not lay her back and immediately pierce her as he had done before. Instead, he pulled her on top of him until her slight form wrapped enticingly around him, and again he let her set the pace.

"It is your move now, my love. 'Twill save your patching me together again, and you may go as slowly as you wish. Just do not dally too long or I will regret my generosity." Pulling a lock of hair back from her face, Kerry nibbled an earlobe while his other hand urged her on.

"I do not believe your champagne has made me that giddy,

milord,'' Katy murmured, feeling the need to do his bidding but lacking the courage to do so on her own.

"Then I will make you even giddier,'' and Kerry placed both hands on her hips, guiding her downward into position, until violet eyes opened wide and startled at this first voluntary contact with his masculinity, and he chuckled lightly. This casual manipulation was not what he would have wished had he been given a choice of circumstances, but for now it would serve his purpose. He could only hope it would pave the way for a more exciting future.

To Katy, this eminently desirable joining of their bodies was a moment of piquant torture. The past weeks, the past years, had prepared her for it, but now that the time had come, her body was too hurt and torn to fully appreciate it. But her mind had successfully wiped out all thought of a possibly nonexistent future, and Kerry's hands were efficiently erasing all memory of the past, and now only the present slowly blossomed to reveal its treasures. And she gladly gave herself up to this play of their desires.

If this second consummation of their desires was not entirely satisfactory, it bore no resemblance whatsoever to the first, and for this, Katy was immeasurably grateful. As Kerry took over her inadequate motions, Katy felt the pleasure of being desired and possessed, and from this man, that was enough for now.

Riding high on the tide of his pleasure, Katy nearly cried at the agonized shudder of his release, collapsing willingly into his waiting arms when the explosion ended.

August 1735

THE ROSY glow of morning filtered through their tiny window, casting silver-blond hair into sparkling rivulets and giving Katy's fair skin a blushing hue. Kerry moved her into a more comfortable position against his shoulder, admiring the thick lashes that gave her sleep a look of childish innocence. Small and light in his hands, she could easily be the fifteen-year-old he first knew, but he felt no guilt in removing the last vestige of her childhood. Confident of his own powers and Tonga's debt to him, he had no doubt they would soon be free, and then he could show this perverse little sprite the world she had first refused.

Waking to Kerry's gentle fondling, Katy snuggled drowsily closer to his warmth, allowing his admiring touches to wake her more fully as his sensual nature eagerly took advantage of her quiescence. With the dawn light striking against copper highlights, throwing broad shoulders into dark relief, Katy became aware of the awesome strength in his masculinity, more so since he withheld it to ply her with only the tenderest of caresses, acquainting her with the delights of her own body while giving her time to overcome any fear of his.

When she was relaxed and ready, violet eyes wide and eager as they met his, Kerry moved carefully over her, capturing her lips with his kiss as he entered her. They made gentle love, savoring the delights of this gift of their bodies, avoiding the more harmful violence of passion. For Kerry it was enough to bring Katy to the brink of ecstasy, to see the startled, sparkling light in her dark eyes as she gave in to his urgings and felt the first small stirrings of satisfaction as he exploded with the propulsion of his own. He would generate the need in her for further experimentation when next he touched her body. And smiling with this thought, Kerry rolled over and pulled her back into his arms.

"You learn quickly, my love."

Stretching languidly beside Kerry's masculine form, one bare limb sliding teasingly across his muscular thighs, Katy luxuriated in this intimacy, treasuring the endearments he showered upon her, knowing they meant nothing to him, but pleased at his choice of words and praise.

"I have an excellent teacher, milord."

"Do you not think we could dispense with the formalities now, my love? I should think we are well enough acquainted after this for you to call me by name."

"I suppose, while we are here, there is no reason to remember my place. One slave is as good as another." A dancing smile lit Katy's eyes as she leaned over him, and taking advantage of her new equality, kissed him directly on the mouth.

Rolling her back to the blanket, Kerry held her pinned as his cool glance covered her from violet eyes to bare toes. "I believe I have created a monster."

Wriggling under his careful scrutiny, more aware of her nakedness now than earlier, Katy struggled to free herself. "It is only your champagne quite gone to my head, sir, and you may as well know, your satin sheets are abominably cold."

"Are they now, by Gad? Well, let's see if you like these, then." And roughly pulling the edge of the blanket on which she lay, he tumbled her over on top of him, tightly binding her to him in a cocoon of woven wool.

Gasping with giggles at this outrageous maneuver, Katy

found one hand caught beneath his armpit and began tickling this sensitive area, and soon they were rolling on the floor in a tussle of sheer exuberant animal spirits, their gales of laughter resounding outside the cramped cabin, bringing looks of consternation to those Indian captors awake enough to hear. If they associated the behavior of their sun goddess and her paramour with the rising of the sun, they were not far wrong.

After another successful bout of lovemaking, they reluctantly dressed, unwillingly admitting by their actions that this was not the Garden of Eden and at any moment they could expect an end to their idyll. Already they could hear the first sounds of the camp stirring, and began to dread what the day might bring.

Examining Kerry's shoulder before helping him on with his shirt, Katy bit her lip and broached a subject that had not once left her mind, no matter how much she tried to suppress it. "Kerry . . ." The name felt strange to her tongue, and stranger to her ears, but seemed appropriate to this wifely action. "Did this Indian friend of yours say anything about Mahomet? Do you think he and Anna escaped safely?"

"Mahomet saved his life as much as I did. Tonga would never harm him unless provoked. And if one of his braves did, he would have told me. No, I'm certain they are safe; you have no need to worry on that account." Taking her fair head into his hands, Kerry tilted her face up to meet his gaze. "Do you regret not going with them now? I blame myself for not ordering you out of the house at the time."

"I would not have gone and left you alone. So there is no blame or regret to be applied," she stated firmly.

"But there was a time yesterday when you blamed me for what happened the other night. What changed your mind?" Green eyes searched her face intently.

The memory of this large, virile man, one of the noble lords of England, down on his knees scrubbing her petticoats, brought a smile to her eyes as she replied quite frankly, "It is hard to imagine a rapist willing to clean his victim's linen. It was foolish of me even to consider it." Her arms went naturally about his neck with a freedom she delighted in.

But Kerry's demeanor remained serious. "There is nothing

foolish about it. I have taken something precious from you that can never be given back. Perhaps I should have done it long ago—Lord knows, I thought about it enough—but the fact remains that what should have been an important occasion became a degrading spectacle, and I am not proud of the part I played in it.''

But the episode was too recent and painful to consider, and Katy blanked it out, dwelling instead on his admission that he had thought often of taking her to his bed. And she had thought him barely aware of her existence!

''I would rather not speak of it, please. We are alive and well and you have done nothing you did not have a right to do,'' she replied guardedly.

''A right?'' Kerry cried, outraged at her choice of words. ''Then do you think you were bought and paid for like some whore to be taken at my convenience? What other right have I?''

''You know full well that is just what you have done, and I have never denied that you had the right to exercise that privilege at your will.''

Wonderingly Kerry stared down into fathomless blue and felt himself diving deeper than he wished to go. ''No, I suppose you have not. It was only my foolish talk of houses and children that frightened you, though I felt sure they were the surest way to win you. I cannot believe you prefer to be thought of as a whore.''

Back stiff, hands resting lightly against his chest, requiring no support from him, Katy spoke cautiously. ''That is not what I wish to be, but it is what I am. 'Lord Kerry's whore' is how I was known to half of London; if we should survive this debacle, all of the Carolinas will know what I am.''

Kerry's hands gripped her shoulders so tightly his fingers left bruises on her fine skin. ''You would have me give you up now that I finally have you? You are mine, Katy. I will not see you in the arms of any other. My generosity has found its limits,'' he said harshly.

Bowing her head in acknowledgment of his ability to do as he claimed, Katy answered softly, ''I am yours to do with as you will, milord. I am not ungrateful for what you have done for me.''

His string of violent curses was interrupted by the arrival of their guard bearing food, and shortly thereafter, Tonga. While Kerry and their captor worked their way around the difficulties of the language barrier, Katy retired to a corner of the room to collect her thoughts. They had been speaking with the assurance of the inevitability of their escape, but the bilingual argument going on in the middle of the room did not bear out this assurance. Kerry's possession of her was of a nebulous nature for as long as they were in the power of the Indians, and for that reason, their argument was senseless. Yet Katy could not help but contemplate what the future held in store if they should be set free, and the picture was not the one she would have wished.

The argument came to a crashing halt with the Indian stalking rapidly from the room, leaving Kerry to pace the hard earth floor angrily. With his arm once more resting in its sling, it produced an unevenness to his stride that seemed to throw him off balance, and he soon gave it up, throwing himself down on the blanket beside Katy and leaning, disgruntled, against the wall.

"You had best rest and eat well while you can, for one way or another, we are leaving here tomorrow night." Kerry patted his pocket as if looking for his pipe, and upon not finding it, cursed mildly and reached for Katy instead, cradling her head against his shoulder.

"Why can we not leave tonight?" she asked reasonably.

"We would leave today if Tonga had his wishes, but I will tell you now that I have refused his offer of safety. He feels he has done all he can to help us by offering to have us escorted back to his camp as his slaves. That is our only guarantee of safety in the war he claims will be declared tomorrow night." He paused, gathering his thoughts, and Katy waited patiently for some explanation of his reasoning.

Kerry cast a quick glance at his seemingly docile companion. Her unemotional description of herself as a whore earlier had unsettled him, her mechanical acceptance of his decisions struck him as unnatural, but there was no specific complaint he could put a finger on. His own volatile nature demanded expressing, but Katy kept her emotions bottled up behind her cool demeanor, and his attempts to release them met with little success. Perhaps her rationality was an asset at a time like this; hysterics would be of little purpose.

"I questioned Tonga, and his camp lies two days west of here—that would be four days' hard walking to return home. Neither of us is in any condition for that kind of trek if we should escape, and weaponless, we could not expect to survive long. I prefer to take my chances on escaping here, nearer to home and civilization."

"But why tomorrow? If there is some way of getting past our guard, why could we not go tonight?" The thought of wandering lost and defenseless through miles of unfriendly forest terrified her, but the prospect of being helpless in the hands of these savages was no better.

"Because they would have time to track us tomorrow. If we go in the confusion of their all-night war council, they will not notice our absence until dawn, when they are ready to set out for their camps."

Kerry's face looked lined and weary as he spoke these grim words. His audacious plan might possibly work, but he had not revealed the full extent of danger represented by this coming together of various Indian tribes. Armed by some treacherous segment of the white settlers, the Indians were more powerful than ever before in their pitiable rebellions. Just a few random renegades could destroy entire plantations. With one or two good leaders and an arsenal, they could eliminate most of the frontier settlements. Escaping now meant little, if it resulted in certain death further down the road.

Katy digested this information silently, comprehending more than his words revealed and realizing they were not the only ones endangered. "If we escape, will there be time to warn the others?"

Kerry gave her a quick look. She had followed his thoughts and jumped on ahead to his conclusions with amazing perceptiveness; he was still not certain she did not have the power to read minds. "Let's take one step at a time. We might wander for days out there without meeting another soul." He sank back against the wall in black thought.

"And the guard? How will we dispose of him?"

Startled out of his reverie, Kerry looked at her blankly at

first, then glanced significantly at the boot hiding their one
weapon. "You are better off not knowing. Why don't you lie
down and rest awhile? There is little else we can do until the
time comes."

Their captors walked in and out, unannounced, throughout
the day, bringing them food and water, allowing them brief
forays into the bushes behind the cabin. With nothing to do
but lie in the semidarkness, they rested and talked desultorily
while waiting for the next interruption. Occasionally Kerry
grew restless and paced the floor, putting his head outside the
unbolted door and irritating the surprised guard with outrageous requests. If he had a reason for his madness, he made
no mention of it. His animal energy permeated the room, and
Katy knew that with nightfall, it would soon shift to her. He
needed some outlet for his frustration, and she was closest.
There would be no love to their lovemaking this time.

On one of their brief forays into the bushes, Katy persuaded one of the young guards to strip the bottom boughs off
a few pines. Kerry noted with sardonic humor that she needed
no translator to put her point across; the young brave even
helped to carry the branches back to the cabin, filling the
stuffy air with the fresh scent of pine. Katy covered the stack
with their sole blanket. Their bed now had a soft foundation
and considerably fewer insects.

Eventually, darkness eclipsed the room, the last meal of
the day was presented and removed, the guard saw them out
and in again, and closed the door for the final time that night.
As the door slammed shut, Kerry placed himself against it,
standing with arms crossed over his chest while his eyes, like
a cat's, pierced the gloom.

"Katherine?" Demanding, not questioning, he searched
the room for some trace of a shadow.

A slight rustle, a movement, and she appeared as a flickering outline against the faint glow of the rear window, her face
a ghostly image in the darkness.

"My God," he stated flatly, his hand reaching out of its own
accord to test what his vision obscured, coming in contact
with a bare shoulder, dipping down to caress an unclothed
breast.

Katy moved closer, sensing the wary tightening of his

self-control as his hand gripped her arm. Ignoring the tension between them, eluding his grip, she raised her arms to circle Kerry's neck and felt with satisfaction his muffled gasp as he relaxed his guard and crushed her to his chest. That she was giving what he had been prepared to take, Katy knew. Anticipating the violence of his passion, she met it halfway with her own, doubling the intensity in proportion.

Lips fastening hungrily, they strained to consume each other, and when that was not enough, they found their way to the pine-scented pallet where Kerry's hard body pinned her helplessly. The gentle tenderness and playful frivolity of their previous lovemaking were only a preliminary to this violent coupling, their need for each other so complete they needed no other words or touches to ignite it. In what seemed like moments of eternity, Kerry brought her to the brink of that abyss she had only glimpsed before, and with a violent thrust plunged them over the precipice, hurtling rapidly to the bottom, where the explosion of impact quaked their bodies, melding them into one, leaving them gasping and shuddering in each other's arms.

It wasn't enough, could never be enough, and even as the last convulsive shivers took them, they were tasting the sweet juices rolling freely from their bodies, savoring the sensual delights they had forgone in their earlier urgency. But as the ecstasy of the moment faded, reality raised its ugly head, and Kerry fell victim first to its bite.

Favoring his aching shoulder, leaning heavily on his right one, Kerry traced a path from throat to waist, lingering at the bridge of Katy's breastbone. "You play the part of whore well, Katy, but I'd rather be assured you will share your favors with no other man. Are you ready to give your consent to be mine?"

Katy looked up, imagining she could see the twin emerald fires she knew burned above her, feeling their intensity as she hesitated in giving her answer. The argument was a futile one under the circumstances: even if they had a future, she had little choice but to submit to his wishes, but some small part of her withheld agreement. Tonight could be the last night they ever spent together. For that reason, she had wanted to make it perfect, so that whatever happened in the future—or their lack of it—she would be content with this moment of happiness. To agree now would be to extend this happiness, but it wasn't in Katy's nature to lie.

"Would it not be better to wait until we and the others are safe from danger before worrying about such things?"

Stifling a curse, Kerry replied grudgingly, "A simple 'yes' would have sufficed, but not for my contrary Katy."

Lying down beside her, he gave vent to a few choice expletives before concluding, "Dammit all to hell, Katherine! Why is it that I can have any woman I want, and more that I do not want, but the one woman I have every right to expect to be mine is such a wanton harlot she cannot wait to jump from my arms into any stranger's that comes along? Is this your method of meting out justice?" Trying to hide his bewilderment, Kerry attempted to temper anger with humor, meaning little of what he said.

Katy sighed. It was futile to tell him this argument was irrelevant if they were to die tomorrow or the next day; he was too confident of his own prowess to doubt the future held a place for him. And for the first time since their abduction, she was forced to think ahead to what would happen should they escape unharmed.

"You are being deliberately cruel, mi . . . Kerry." There was no point in angering him further, but she deliberately placed his title before his name whenever she thought of him. "If you have given any thought to the matter, you will know I am totally at your mercy. Sir Charles cannot possibly be expected to take me back after this, and without references, I have nowhere else to go. I am yours to do with as you will."

"Fine. It is no harlot but a martyr I have on my hands now. Lord Kerry, the Great Despoiler, toys with young virgins to see them cast out upon the streets disgraced." Dramatic irony threatened to turn to fury until he finished flatly, "I should shake you until your teeth rattle."

"Does it matter so much how you gain me so long as you know I will always remain true? You will have other women, a wife, but unless I become the harlot you claim, once I appear in public with you I will have no other man. What more can you ask of me?"

"That you come willingly," Kerry answered promptly.

"To take you against your will would make a mockery of everything I have done for you, although there are times I am willing to settle for that. Am I so offensive that you cannot tolerate a life with me?"

Violet eyes grew moist, but in the darkness he could not see the tears rolling down velvet cheeks, yet he heard them in her voice as she spoke.

"You have heard my arguments and know that, if offered a choice, I cannot choose you, that the gap between us is too great for me to bridge. But since there is not likely to be any choice should we return, I shall endeavor to be the best mistress you have ever had. But I am trusting you, in return for whatever years I give you, to provide me with the means to leave here when you tire of me or wed. Is that too much to ask?" Her voice nearly broke as she reached the end of her speech, but she contained it with the help of years of practice.

Kerry scarcely heard the latter part of her speech. Something in her wording, her inflections, had triggered a key in his mind, and a long-locked door flew open on a revelation of far-reaching proportions. He had been a damned blind dunce of monstrous stupidity not to have seen it before. The gap between them was greater than he thought; she was right. It served him right for becoming involved with romantic young virgins instead of staying with his sophisticated ladies and courtesans. What had he expected to happen when he plucked her from the garbage heap and planted her in rich soil, showering her with attentions and gifts that were meaningless to him but must have seemed enormous to one who had so little? He had quite expertly and without a thought in the world made her love him.

And he had wooed and seduced her like any of a dozen less virtuous maids. Not one of the women he had courted and taken to his bed had professed love with any degree of sincerity; he had no experience with the emotion himself, having long since decided it was not in the cards for one who must marry wealth and title. But to be so blind as not to see it when offered was bordering on the scandalous. He had thought himself to possess a little more integrity than to deliberately entice a lovesick child to his bed. What had made him so blind?

Brushing a stray tear from Katy's cheek, Kerry pulled her closer. "You may be right, my lovely Katherine. Perhaps we should save this argument until we see what awaits us when we reach civilization. I would hate to give up the best mistress I ever had, but I do not wish to send away my best friend, either." His grin was mechanical but his kiss was not. If he had to do the honorable thing and give up all this loveliness once they arrived home, he would certainly not let a minute of their time together now escape.

Katy's relief was evident in the manner in which she surrendered herself to Kerry's caresses. With the tension gone, she could delight in the sensations he aroused in her and learn the art of pleasing him in return. Delighted by her efforts, Kerry encouraged her further, wishing only that he could have the comforts of bed and candle to make the scene complete. And an operable shoulder. He chuckled grimly to himself as he once again found himself in a position limiting his movement.

Dozing half-asleep and content some time later, they were startled into wakefulness by a hard thud in the boards overhead. Holding Katy down against the makeshift mattress, Kerry glanced around quickly, not immediately finding the cause of their alarm. But then the moon shifted from behind a cloud and a small pale square of light grew on the cabin wall, illuminating a shining object that hadn't been there before. Drawing a quick breath of recognition, Kerry stealthily put a hand to the object and with a violent jerk removed it from its berth.

"Mahomet!" he breathed quietly in explanation, showing her the saberlike knife the giant favored. "Don your clothes quickly, kitten. We're escaping sooner than planned." Tearing another tatter from the remainder of Katy's petticoat, he waved it briefly in the tiny window, then began to dress himself. "When we are safely back in Charleston, I will have to see that your valuable petticoat is replaced, my love. I do not know what we would do without it."

Heart pounding erratically in her fear, Katy dressed silently, then turned to lend a hand to Kerry. It was one thing to talk about escape and freedom, quite another to do it. How would they pass the guard?

As if answering her thoughts, Kerry adjusted his boots, and standing up, motioned Katy to be silent. Then, as he had a dozen times that day, he threw open the door, but this time with a difference. When the guard turned to see what annoyance was to be perpetrated now, Kerry swung as hard as he could with his good right arm, catching the wiry Indian off balance and knocking him to the ground before he could make a sound. In total silence, a black shadow slipped out of the darkness, and together with Kerry, rapidly trussed and gagged their captor.

It was over in minutes. With knife tucked in waistband and miniatures safely hidden again in his shirt, Kerry led Katy from the cabin and back into the shadows that had produced the black giant. The noise of their departure was hidden beneath the rhythmic pounding of drums and monotonous hum of voices at the other end of the camp. They wouldn't be missed until daybreak.

In the first stand of trees they were joined by another shadow, tall and thin, his gangling posture immediately recognizable as Kerry grasped him by the shoulder and shook his hand. They retreated silently into deeper darkness, following Mahomet through grasping brambles and tree branches until they reached a relatively moonlit clearing and the African called a halt to their procession.

At the sight of Jake in this unspeakable habitat, Katy felt the urge to run and hug him and share her joy in this reunion, but Kerry held a protective arm to her waist and she dared not break his hold. She was his possession now, no longer free to act indiscriminately.

The intimacy of Kerry's gesture did not escape Jake, and his normally open expression went blank. Katy could do no more than send him an imploring look as explanations flew back and forth above her head. She was truly Kerry's woman now, and nothing could be done to change it.

As their conversation gradually seeped into her awareness, Katy began to listen more intently, an array of emotions sliding rapidly across her face: relief that Anna and Mahomet were safe and Sir Charles recuperating from his fever, dismay and sorrow upon learning that Lady Stockbridge had died within two days of contracting the disease, surprise that

Mahomet was acting as guide for a band of militia commissioned to wipe out the Indian uprising before it started, and horror that Kerry intended to join them. This last brought Katy completely from her trance.

"Milord, your arm! What you need is rest, not war. You cannot possibly be of any use in your condition." Even as she said it, she could see the grin creeping up the corners of his mouth. He had just spent two days and nights making vigorous love and laid an Indian flat on his back with only one hand; his condition was good for something. Katy felt her cheeks redden under Kerry's ironic gaze.

"Be that as it may, my love, my place is with the soldiers. An Indian war can only cause more deaths than we can afford. Perhaps I can find some way to circumvent it. I have to try. I'll bring young Jake here along to keep an eye on me, if he doesn't murder me first. You, my dear, must go back to Sir Charles and Anna—they will be needing you more than ever at a time like this."

Katy's eyes flew from Jake to Kerry and back again. She had missed some vital part of this conversation.

Keeping his expression guarded, Jake kept his eyes on Katy while he spoke. "When the captain heard about Lord Kerry bein' kidnapped, he thought mebbe I should go with the militia, bein' as how I had messages for both his lordship and Sir Charles. When we got to Georgetown to find Sir Charles, he and Anna were 'most besides themselves, what with Lady Stockbridge bein' gone and all, and you up and disappeared. He made me come along to find you, said bring you back—no matter what." The last words hung ominously in the air after he said them, and Jake hurried to cover them up. "He said for Anna's sake you got to come back."

Katy looked up and found blazing green eyes fastened on her. The strong arm around her waist tightened possessively one last time, then fell free, releasing her completely.

"Sir Charles will look after you, kitten, until I return. We can have our discussion then, can't we?" Emerald eyes held her motionless for a minute; then, tilting her chin up, Kerry kissed her slowly and thoroughly.

In disgust, Jake turned his back on the scene and stalked into the bushes, presumably in the direction of the waiting militia camp. Mahomet stood stoically by, arms crossed, legs apart, waiting for further orders.

Gazing into violet eyes brimming with tears, Kerry wondered how long he could keep his resolution to allow her to return to respectability. If he stayed away long enough, perhaps time and distance would put things in proper perspective. Pinching her chin, his eyes not straying from Katy's face, Kerry gave Mahomet his orders.

"See that she is returned to Sir Charles as swiftly as possible. Take good care of her, my friend, for she is more precious to me than anything else I own." His mischievous grin did not reach his eyes and he turned away abruptly, striding after Jake without looking back.

Katy watched him go, eyes swimming with tears. If he would only turn back just once, show some need of her, she knew nothing could keep her from him, she would give it all up: Anna, Jake, any chance of respectability, just to be by his side. And she watched his back longingly for some reprieve as he disappeared into the darkness of their forest surroundings. As the last hope of his turning back slipped away without having any idea when she would see him again, the tears broke loose and flooded her cheeks. He was gone, out of her life as she had asked. What had made him change his mind?

She turned away and allowed Mahomet to lead her into the bushes where the horses were hidden. His silence matched her mood, and she followed his lead without further discussion, giving her horse its head to follow the intricate path through the darkness behind the bay Mahomet had chosen. At least the animals had survived the Indian raid intact, and she stroked Broom's neck lovingly, the mare's answering whicker sending Katy's mind racing back to days past.

Her thoughts stayed in the past, reliving the last few weeks, every look, every word, every touch of her time with Kerry as the journey took them farther into the night. Taking his master's words literally, Mahomet seldom stopped to rest, and then only long enough to water and feed the horses while parceling out their limited rations. Katy had no idea of the time they left the Indian camp, but it was late afternoon of the next day before they reached country even remotely familiar to her, the river being her first sight of home territory.

Their route differed from the one the Indians took, bearing farther east and avoiding the burned-out cabin and plantation, moving more directly toward town. Despite their nonstop traveling, their weary horses did not tread the dusty streets of Georgetown until well after sundown, after most of the windows had already grown dark.

But a candle still burned in the study window of the Stockbridge home and when Katy knocked at the crepe-draped door, it flew open almost instantaneously, revealing a haggard Sir Charles in the dim light of one candle.

"Katy, thank God, you're alive." His words held a weary tonelessness, but his relief was evident as he welcomed her in.

"Mahomet, take the horses around back. They will do well enough there for the evening. Bertha is waiting for you in the kitchen, she'll find you a place to sleep. Have her send up some tea and a cold platter for Katy." He gave his instructions to the slave before closing the door and turning back to usher Katy into the study. He found her a seat before retreating to stir up the small fire that provided the room's main light.

Katy sank gratefully into the soft chair that neither bumped nor jarred her grievously sore buttocks. Her limited riding experience had not prepared her for such a ride as they had just undertaken, and she was just beginning to realize the full extent of the damage. Every bone and muscle in her body ached and tore, and the immensity of her exhaustion threatened to overwhelm her as she sat there. She knew there were a dozen things she should be saying, but her tongue refused to function.

Sir Charles watched sympathetically as the young governess's head fell forward tiredly, violet eyes hidden by thin blue-veined lids, hands, cut and bruised by brambles, twitching slightly with nervous exhaustion. There were explanations to be made, apologies to be exchanged, but eager as he was to hear her tale, he could see it would be unforgivable to ask for it tonight.

"Katy," he said softly, watching her head snap up with a

jerk. "I'll send Bertha with your tea to your room. Have her bring you up a few pitchers of warm water so you may soak the dust off and get a good night's sleep. We can talk in the morning."

Panic leapt to her eyes. There were so many things to be said—he must understand what she had done and why, she had to know if she were still welcome here—but the crepe-draped door stood in the way. How could she explain deserting them in their hour of need? If she had stayed, perhaps Lady Stockbridge would still be alive. . . .

"Sir Charles, I am so sorry . . . I do not know what to say. You have been so kind and I have been so . . ." She was too tired to cry, but there were tears in her voice as she strove to find the words that would make everything better.

"Katherine, take my advice and go to your room now. There is nothing to be said that cannot wait . . ." He hesitated a moment as a thought occurred to him, not for the first time that evening or for every hour since he had heard of the abduction, but for the first time since she had walked through the door. "Unless you would like me to call a physician or someone to come and have a look at you. You have been through an excruciating experience, there might be something they can do for you . . ." His voice trailed off anxiously as she shook her head.

"No, no, I will be fine. If I could just wash a little . . ." She longed for Kerry's tub, but tubs were not common and the Stockbridges had never thought to possess one. She would have to content herself with warm cloths and plenty of soap.

Frowning slightly, not certain if he should dismiss the subject yet, Sir Charles missed his wife's feminine presence more than ever. She would know what to do for the child, but he could only take the girl's word for it. Raising his head at the rapid knock announcing the cook's arrival, Sir Charles turned the problem over to the bulky black woman who entered.

"Bertha, take Miss Katherine to her room and give her her tea there. See that she has enough water to wash." His tone of voice pleaded: Take care of her—but the words were never mentioned as the cook took in the frail figure with one look and understood the unspoken statement.

When they reached Katy's room, Bertha bustled around, stirring the embers of the fire, setting out the tea tray, disappearing for a few minutes to produce warm water and towels. Before Katy was well aware of what was happening, the efficient woman had stripped off the tattered remnants of her clothing and tossed the filthy rags onto the fire while muttering dire imprecations in a foreign tongue. Never having had a maid of any sort to assist her in dressing, Katy raised a protest, but she was too tired to resist the woman's deft refusal. As the last of Katy's clothes disappeared into the now blazing fire, Bertha soaked a cloth in water and began the process of scrubbing mud-caked cuts and bruises, but at this imposition, Katy remained adamant, wrestling the cloth away and applying it more gently to her sore and aching body.

Bertha shrugged and grinned. "Dat black man downstairs say you one tough woman, but I no believin' it. You gwanna show me wrong."

The first small smile of the day crept across Katy's face as she dismissed the woman to return to her kitchen. Mahomet had obviously made a conquest in the Stockbridge household in less time than it had taken his master.

Thoughts of Kerry chased away the weariness as Katy rubbed the soap and water across the tender parts of her body. Remembrances of how he had touched her sent warm shivers tingling down her spine and she hurried to finish. If just his memory could stir her like this, how would she ever refuse him if he should come back for her again? Sliding between the cool sheets of her bed, Katy remembered Kerry's wish for satin ones, and she snuggled deeper into the down. Despite her weariness, it was a long time before she gave herself up to the bliss of sleep.

Fall 1735

THE MORNING SUN had left her windows by the time Katy woke the next day, and she hurriedly threw back the covers to sit up, a paroxysm of pain making her groan and move more gingerly in climbing from the bed. Every bone in her body felt shattered from the long, hard ride, but she stubbornly made the attempt to dress, pulling the last lace closed when a pert brown head peered around the bedroom door.

"Katy?" she whispered, and before an answer could be made, a small figure flew through the crack and darted into Katy's arms, brown hair unbraided and flying around her shoulders.

"Anna!" With tears of delight, Katy caught the little girl in her arms and hugged her tight. If she could not have Kerry's love, at least she would have the pleasure of a child's. It was no substitute, but for one hungry for love in any form, it would suffice.

"Katy, Papa said you came back, but I had to see. Katy, Momma went away to heaven and isn't coming back, and I thought maybe you weren't coming back either." The burst of words bubbled out before the peaked little face that had once glowed with ruddy health buried itself in Katy's shoulder.

And as tears gave way to sobs, Katy rocked the little girl in her arms, praying for words of comfort. What could she say to a child who had trustingly left home and family and come back to find half her world disappeared? It would be a long time before Anna would willingly let any of her loved ones out of sight again, and Katy knew her place was here. If only she could have the strength to say so.

Hesitantly, hovering outside the open study door, not wishing to wake Sir Charles if he were truly sleeping, but needing to discuss her position here, Katy apparently made some movement that caught Sir Charles's ear, and he swung around in his chair, motioning her to come in.

"If you don't mind, Katherine, would you shut the door behind you? I would rather talk in private."

Last night he had called her Katy, but now he had returned to more formal address, as if he meant to reprove her. Obediently she shut the door and prayed a chastisement was all he intended, for if he were to put her out without references, her cause was certainly lost. Anxiously she watched as her employer clasped his hands together on the desk. His dark hair seemed to have grown more streaks of gray since last she had seen him, and his face had grown leaner and more lined. The stalwart, healthy country squire she had known had acquired a patina not unbecoming to his age and position, and Katy realized how much she had come to rely on his esteem. The thought that she had probably lost it depressed her further.

Sir Charles motioned for her to take a seat, but Katy remained standing, nervously clutching and unclutching her hands.

"Sir, I do not know where to begin. A mere apology is not—"

"Apology?" His dark eyebrows lifted as he looked at her closely for the first time since she had entered. "It is I who should be apologizing, but I can find no way to frame it. Anna is my only child, and I adore her more than is good for her nature, but for you to risk everything to save her, not once, but twice, is more than even I would ask of you. You know I would have prevented you from going with Lord

Kerry if I could have done so.'' Perceptive blue eyes stared out from behind the desk at the small figure quaking in front of it like a pupil before a stern master. He had wished to offer her comfort, but instead, had only succeeded in frightening her.

''I know, sir, but his lordship was insistent that we leave, and I knew it was the best thing for Anna. There didn't seem to be much choice.'' Especially after Lady Stockbridge gave her permission, but Katy did not add that, out of respect for her memory. She had meant well, even if her intentions were a little confused.

But Sir Charles knew his wife too well, and the omitted fact did not escape him. Lord Kerry would never have kidnapped his daughter without some species of permission, and Sir Charles could well imagine who gave it. ''I am not criticizing your decision, Katherine—it probably saved my daughter's life. I would have been truly bereft if I had lost both wife and daughter to a fever I so foolishly brought into the house by insisting on returning to the docks every day. But I am afraid your decision may have irreparably harmed your reputation. The fact that you and Lord Kerry have lived unchaperoned in the same house for two weeks has already spread through the community. The Indian abduction only served to do further damage. I intend to do everything in my power to make amends, but I fear there are some things even I cannot do.''

''Sir Charles, I cannot pretend that I do not care what people say of me, for I have grown to enjoy their respect, but more than anything, I am concerned for Anna. If you feel my influence would be harmful, I will leave at once.'' Katy spoke firmly, her delicate jaw set with resolution, but tears lurked close to the surface of dark-lashed violet pools.

''My God, what kind of monster do you think I am? Of course you will stay here, unless you prefer otherwise. Anna needs you, and I will beg you to stay if necessary. I will increase your salary to cover the loss of your additional students and do everything within my power to squelch the rumors. I have no idea what you have suffered at the hands of those savages . . .'' His last words were tortured, his face twisted with pain until he slammed his hands down on the desk. "Katy, I have worried myself ill over you! Would you please sit down and tell me what happened?"

Startled at his sudden vehemence, Katy hastily pulled up a chair and searched for reassuring words. It was not in her nature to lie as easily as Kerry seemed able to do, but there was no way in which she could tell this sympathtic man the true horrors of her tale, not any more than she could tell him of what so naturally followed. Haltingly she gave a brief account of the past week, hoping Sir Charles would understand the pain with which she told it and not require further details. If she were questioned, the gaping holes in her tale would surely be revealed, and she was not prepared to explain them.

With nearly three times the age and wisdom of the young governess, Sir Charles could sense the whole tale was not spun, but he did not press for more. Her normally delicate skin seemed stretched to the breaking point over cheekbones suddenly too large for her small face, and dark shadows smudged the thin skin beneath her eyes. If there were more to be told, she would tell it in her own time and in her own way. He could not expect more of her now.

Rising and coming around the desk, Sir Charles gave Katy his hand and helped her to her feet. "You look exhausted still, you poor child. I will take a horsewhip to your guardian for endangering you in such a manner, but you, I will send to bed. Go back and rest for a day or a week or whatever it will take to bring the color back to your cheeks."

Katy refused to be rushed. "Sir Charles, I am so sorry—" Meaning to express her sympathy for the loss of his wife, she found herself at a loss for words.

Sir Charles interrupted before she could continue. "Do not be, Katherine. Elizabeth was the mother of my child and a faithful wife. She probably saved my life by nursing me through an illness that cost her her own, but there is nothing anyone could have done to save her. She was a good woman and is probably happy wherever she is now. I only wish I could have loved her while she was here." And with that cryptic remark he turned his back on Katy and stood staring out the window to the street below, effectively dismissing Katy from his thoughts.

Instead of resting, Katy returned to the schoolroom to tell children's tales of Indians and Indian princesses to Anna, to relieve the child's fears. She could not replace the child's mother, but she could distract her from her grief and earn some of the trust Sir Charles had placed in her.

At the dinner table that evening, Sir Charles announced he had hired a housekeeper to supervise the running of the household. An older widowed woman whose children had long since grown and gone, she would move into one of the spare upstairs bedrooms, an unusual honor for a servant, but Katy understood. This was now a bachelor household, and to protect both their reputations, a chaperon would be needed. Bitterly she wondered if it would have been necessary had she maintained her so-called "respectability," but she did not put this question to words. A housekeeper was needed, and where she slept was of no consequence to Katy.

Other than the loss of her students, Katy felt little of the effect of her social ostracism through the week. It was a house of mourning and no entertainment was expected; dinner included only the three of them, the housekeeper having excluded herself from this honor. With Sir Charles returned to work and no lady of the house present, they had no social callers; there was no one to convey gossip or turn a cold shoulder to the governess of loose morals.

But Sunday morning brought the full extent of her isolation home to her. She sat in the Stockbridge pew with Anna and Sir Charles as always, but the whispers behind her back had the power of gale-force wind, and Katy felt as if their stares would bore holes through her skull. After services, she was left to herself as Anna ran to play with friends and Sir Charles stopped to speak with neighbors. The mothers who had once come up to discuss their daughters' progress, the older girls who had used to congregate to discuss the latest gossip, even the younger children—held back by tight-lipped parents—all deserted her, leaving Katy to stand alone on the church steps.

The minister's wife broke the invisible barrier. Not wanting to pry into her young friend's recent experiences, Emma Stone simply asked permission to call later in the week, and stood valiantly by Katy's side discussing the latest local happenings until Sir Charles discovered their plight and hurried over. Gratefully Katy took leave of her one friend, and walked bravely through the crowded churchyard, head held high, on the arm of her employer.

But it was harder to be brave through the long hours at home without companionship. Anna was a model student, needing little instruction to complete her lessons, and the long empty hours Katy had used for other students stretched before her like an eternal path, with no break in the monotony in sight. At times like these Katy was forced to wonder how it could be worse to actually be Kerry's mistress than merely to be branded so. As his mistress, she would at least have Lord Kerry to turn to for comfort, and the lonely nights would be spent by his side instead of in long bouts of weeping. It grew difficult to remember her reasons for rejecting his offer, and if he had stopped by during one of these depressions and repeated it, he might have been surprised at her response.

Sir Charles was well aware of Katy's red-rimmed eyes in the mornings and sought to make amends by bringing home what tidbits of information he could garner as to Lord Kerry's latest exploits. The militia had evidently staved off any united Indian warfare, but there were still disgruntled tribes to be pacified and the question of selling arms to the Indians to be looked into. Katy accepted the information dispassionately, knowing Kerry seldom thought of her unless in her presence, and expecting his continued absence.

Instead, she tried to divert her thoughts and repay Sir Charles's kindness by listening intently to the other news of current affairs he brought home with him. To her surprise, she began to enjoy these discussions and looked forward eagerly to their evening exchanges. But after dinner, he disappeared into his study, and once Anna was put to bed, the long evening hours stretched out endlessly.

Alone at night in her room, Katy gave way to all her pent-up misery and loneliness, and it was late into the night before her tears slowed and she slept. In the mornings she grew increasingly reluctant to leave her bed, lying lethargically beneath the covers and staring blankly at the ceiling. As the weeks wore on and the tension of Kerry's absence combined with the anguish of her banishment from society, she began to lose weight and grow listless, the pallor of her fine skin becoming nearly translucent. She became nauseous at the mere thought of rising to meet another day and took to missing breakfast when she could. A numbness in her soul was rapidly paralyzing her body; torn between her physical desire for Kerry and her emotional need to be loved—and knowing that she could not have both—she could do nothing.

Emma Stone kept her word and came to call whenever she could, but Katy could not confide her lethargy to this friend who was fighting valiantly on her side. Aware of the trouble she was causing the minister and his wife, Katy could only show her appreciation without complaint, and when they were gone, wonder what they would think if Lord Kerry came back to carry her off.

Sir Charles used his influence to prevent any direct snubs when Katy went to town, and as time wore on, Katy's own demure behavior lent credence to the story Sir Charles and the Stones spread of her innocence, and she found more of the shopkeepers willing to exchange a few words with her. But her depression lingered, and each day of Kerry's absence, she grew increasingly more ill.

The nightly disappearance of Sir Charles into his study was not a result of his need to overwork himself or to avoid the boredom of female company. On the contrary, he spent the evenings pacing the room or staring blankly at the pages of a book much as Katy did her ceilings. He had always considered himself a respectable, sedate family man with little inclination to wander from the small pleasures of his life, but a golden-haloed head and violet eyes were intruding more frequently upon his thoughts, and he was having difficulty banishing them. Instead, he chose to tread the path of virtue by absenting himself from temptation.

Unaware of her employer's mixed emotions, Katy sank silently into a world of her own making, coming alive temporarily when drawn out at the dinner table, but retreating rapidly when left alone. In bed at night, she imagined Lord Kerry beside her, ready to draw her into his arms if she should just turn to him. Her nights grew restless, sleepless with this new torment, and she wished desperately for some word or sign that he would return to her, but weeks, and then months, passed without a word.

Katy thought little of it when she had been home several weeks without any recurrence of her monthly "female troubles." She had always been irregular and the trauma her body had suffered was more than enough to disrupt everything. But when she lay in bed one night counting the days since she had last seen Kerry, she suddenly realized another month had slipped away without this normal function. Anxiously Katy tried to recollect the whispers, gossip, and taunts that had been the major part of her worldly education, and every small remembrance confirmed what she had now begun to suspect. Horror gripped her with tentacles of steel, and she nearly cried out with the pain of sudden knowledge. What she had struggled so long to avoid suddenly became stark reality: she was bearing Lord Kerry's bastard!

And the crack in the foundation of her independence began to widen, the newly laid mortar to crumble, and she wept herself to sleep.

The possibility of pregnancy jolted Katy abruptly from self-pitying depression. It no longer mattered what the neighbors thought of her; they would condemn her—rightly—soon enough. In the meantime, she had to count the days and pray anxiously that she was mistaken, while making plans for the time when she discovered for a certainty she was not.

There seemed little choice but to go to Lord Kerry's town house in Charleston and await his arrival, but the ordeal of telling Sir Charles his trust had been misplaced and the resultant permanent separation from Anna burned at Katy's heart. She had wanted nothing more than to support herself in a respectable occupation until she could find a suitable man to marry and have children of her own, and now all hopes of any of this were dashed, along with all the friendships she had so carefully nurtured. Even Jake would despise her when he learned the truth. Lord Kerry was her only alternative, and though no longer certain he still wanted her, she felt confident he would at least support her until the baby came.

In mid-October a package bearing her name arrived from Charleston. Katy carried it carefully to her room as if it might explode en route, avoiding the curious questions from housekeeper and Anna alike. With her heart in her throat, she gingerly unwrapped the gift, more interested in finding any note enclosed than in the contents of the box. Disappointed, she found only Kerry's hasty scrawl indicating the present was to replace the ones destroyed in good cause. Dully she withdrew the cotton gown and elaborate lace-trimmed petticoats, admiring the workmanship but too upset at the lack of reassuring words to appreciate it.

The main sustenance she received from this gift was the fact that Lord Kerry must now be in Charleston instead of lost in the woods combating Indians somewhere. There would be someone there to welcome her when she arrived, as soon as she gathered the strength to break the news to Anna and Sir Charles. After all his support and kindness, she could not imagine how to tell Sir Charles she was leaving, without telling him why she must desert him now.

Trying on the gown, realizing the tightness of the waist was not due to poor judgment on Lord Kerry's part but to the thickening of her waistline, Katy knew she would have to make the break soon, before her pregnancy became obvious to all. With no maid to spy on her, her morning sickness had gone unobserved, but the slight rounding of her stomach and the growing firmness of her breasts could not be laced in forever.

But two more weeks went by before she gathered the nerve to confront Sir Charles in his study. He had been unusually attentive lately, to both herself and Anna, and she felt he would understand rather than condemn her plight, but bringing herself to speak of it was something she had not yet been able to do with anyone.

Sir Charles had retired to his study as usual after dinner, but passing through the hallway on her way up the stairs, Katy noticed the study door had been left open for a change, and taking pride in hand, she dared to stop in the doorway, willing her employer to turn around and notice her.

He was standing before the fireplace, sunk in thought. The gauntness of his illness had never quite left him, but Sir Charles was still a strongly built man with no sign of stoop or paunch to mark his age. He held himself erect even in repose, his thick hair caught back in an unpowdered queue, its silvered lines stark against the surrounding blackness. Only the lines on his face and the weary wisdom of his eyes betrayed his age, and Katy noticed neither as he turned to find her standing there. She saw only the sympathetic, kindly man who had befriended her, and she advanced more confidently into the room.

"Katy! I was just thinking of calling you. Come in and sit down." Sir Charles moved toward her welcomingly, extending his hand to clasp hers warmly and guide her to the settee.

Caught by surprise at his words, Katy sat silently watching as he crossed the room to close the door. Only once before had he done that, and she wondered if he had guessed she had come to finish the tale told that day. But when he came back, it was to pace the floor restlessly in front of her like one who has much to say and no words to say it in.

Thinking to put an end to his problem, Katy spoke first. "Sir Charles, I have come to tell you that I must leave." Before she could continue, his muttered exclamation put a halt to her prepared speech.

Standing still now and facing her, he wore an expression that brooked no interruption. "I have seen this coming, Katy, and have looked for ways to forestall it, but none are appropriate. I beg you to reconsider, but if I give you my reasons, I am afraid it would only confirm your decision. I know you have not been happy here lately, but things will improve with time. Can you not give us a little longer?" His last question was almost wistful as he contemplated the pale face before him. The roses had never returned to her cheeks and her violet eyes were nearly black with some emotion, but she held herself straight and looked directly at him as she replied.

"No, sir, I am afraid not. That is what I have come to tell you. It is not that I wish to leave you and Anna—you are almost like family to me and have always been more than kind—but I feel that . . ."

Sir Charles held a hand up to halt the flow of words. "Your words encourage me to go on, Katy. It is as family that I would like to think of you." Nervously pacing again, he stopped before the window with his back turned toward her as he went on. "My wife left us only three months ago, so this is still a house of mourning, and I in no way wish to demean her memory, but if expressing my intentions can in any way delay your leaving . . ."

Aghast at the import of his words, Katy cried out in alarm, "Please, sir, do not say any more, I beg of you! Hear me out before you continue."

Smiling, he turned around to look at her and shook his head. "No Katy. It is one of the advantages of age that we are free to make an occasional fool of ourselves to get what we want. I have had many years to learn what I want, and if I must make a fool of myself to get it, so be it. Let me say what I have to." He returned to pacing, stopping to prod the fire in counterpoint to his words. "I thought I had done with this nonsense twenty years ago, and I fear I am severely out of practice. If I am a bit rusty, I beg you to bear with me. I had meant to wait until an acceptable period of time passed and you had grown more accustomed to my company before presenting my proposal, but I will plunge in now and take my chances." No longer smiling, he set aside the poker and faced Katy. Her already pale face was now drained of all color and there was definitely pain in her eyes as she sat clenching her hands in her lap and biting her lower lip. Refusing to accept defeat in advance, he plunged on.

"You and Anna have grown very fond of each other, have you not?" At her silent nod, Sir Charles continued. "As I have grown very fond of you, Katy. More than fond, if that is acceptable from an old man such as I. That is why I would like you to stay, Katy, as my wife and Anna's mother."

Sir Charles had not had time to rehearse his words, but he had given much thought to the subject, and particularly to her reaction to such a proposal. Never had he imagined this hysterical burst of tears from the normally calm young governess. She wept thoroughly and unashamedly, covering her face with both hands until he offered his handkerchief. As her sobs quieted, he sat down beside her and took up her hand, not daring to do more.

"Forgive me for surprising you like that, Katherine, but since you already planned to leave, I felt I had nothing to lose by asking, and everything to gain. If you would just give it time, there is no hurry in a matter such as this. I know to you I must seem very old, but I can offer you other advantages a younger man may not, and I can promise no one would ever take care of you better than I. Is it too much for me to ask

that you stay long enough to consider my proposal?'' He took
the handkerchief from her hand and began drying the tears
from her face.

"Please, Sir Charles, you are making it that much harder
on me.'' Katy withdrew her hand and brushed away the
remaining tears. It had taken every bit of strength she possessed to confront him, and now he had totally shattered that
brave front with one blow. She floundered about, searching
for words to explain.

"I should think if we are familiar enough for me to pro-
pose marriage, you might call me Charles. Now, what is it
you wish to tell me?''

Katy turned away, no longer able to meet his eyes. "Your
proposal is an honor I am ill-prepared to match. Please do not
think me ungrateful if I repay all your kindnesses with honesty; it is all I have to offer, though it be crueler than deceit.''

"Your honesty is one of your many virtues, Katherine, and
one of the other advantages of old age is that there is very
little that can shock me. I cannot believe I am such a
poor judge of character that you can tell me anything that will
change my mind.''

"I am carrying Lord Kerry's child—is that not enough to
change it?'' Contained under pressure too long, the bitter
words burst out angrily of their own accord, spilling over
with tears.

"I see,'' he said thoughtfully, taking up her hand and
patting it absently. If he had not been so blind with his own
thoughts, he would have seen earlier: the depression, the
sickness, the easy tears. He should have investigated the
change in her much earlier. "Well, I admit that surprises me,
although it should not. Young Southerland did not spend all
those weeks coming here just for the pleasure of my company, and once he had you alone . . . Even your character
could not be that strong.''

"Oh, no, sir! Don't think that,'' Katy protested. "Kerry
would never do anything against my will, and I could not
. . .'' But she had, eventually, and would again if he would
have her. There was no other choice. Still, she could not bear
this honorable man to think so poorly of her. He deserved
some explanation, and hesitantly, groping for the least painful

phrases, she unfolded the remainder of her tale. The torment of describing her deflowering was difficult enough; she did not bother to explain the nights that followed.

When she finished, Sir Charles rose and stood before the window unable to watch the pain in her face any longer. "My God, Katy, why did you not tell me this sooner? To suffer that and keep silent . . ." He shook his head in disbelief, then abruptly changed the subject. "You love him, don't you?"

Forgetting he could not see her, Katy nodded her head miserably.

Turning quizzically to catch her answer, Sir Charles saw the brief nod and took a deep breath. "I would think less of you if you did not, under the circumstances, but you know he is in no position to marry you, don't you?"

"I would refuse him even if he should feel compelled to offer. But you can see, I am no longer able to work here, and once word gets out . . . I am fairly certain Lord Kerry will at least support me until I am able to go elsewhere for employment." Katy stared at her hands, unwilling to watch the figure at the window, knowing full well the employment Kerry would offer.

Hands behind his back, eyebrows pulled down in a contemplative frown, Sir Charles gazed at her bowed head a moment before continuing. "Tell me, Katy, what answer would you have given my proposal if circumstances had been otherwise?"

Startled, Katy looked up at him, unable to read his face in the flickering shadow of firelight. She considered the question before replying. "I would have said I was greatly honored that you could think of me in that way, and if at the end of your year of mourning you still felt the same, I would need my guardian's approval before accepting. I do not think I could find a finer or more understanding husband anywhere." And without having considered it before, she knew she spoke the truth. If circumstances had been otherwise . . .

"Well, obviously we will have to skip the year of mourning, but I believe there is time yet to obtain your guardian's approval. Do you wish to write to him or shall I? I would do it normally, but the news you have to impart is of such a personal nature . . ." A small smile formed on his lips as Sir Charles looked into the shocked face of the wide-eyed girl before him. "I do not mean to rush you, but according to my calculations, we are already going to have difficulty pretending prematurity. I think a prolonged wedding trip to visit my brother will solve that problem, but we had better get Kerry's approval soon. Banns need to be posted three weeks in advance, and I mean to see the first one called a week from now. That will give you an entire month to become accustomed to the idea."

"You will marry me carrying another man's child?" Katy was aghast, unable to believe she heard aright. Her whole world had suddenly turned upside down, and everything looked different from this new viewpoint. To be respectably married to Sir Charles, never parted from Anna, and her child to have a name—it was more than she could comprehend at once.

"If you can marry a man who already has a daughter, I think I can accept your child, too."

He stood before her, waiting for an answer, but she still could not believe it. "What if it should be a boy?" Her eyes pleaded with him for understanding. It was too sudden to change her thinking; too many lives were involved. Would Lord Kerry approve of another man raising his child? Would he allow her to marry at all?

"Then I will at long last have a son to inherit my title. I could not have asked for one of more noble breeding than the Southerlands." Taking her hands, Sir Charles sat down beside her. "I can answer every objection you make, and you have an entire month to make them. I will argue Kerry out of every complaint he may have. I have decided I want you and no other for wife. I do not use these words lightly, Katy, they are words that have had no meaning to me for some time, but I love you, and with time, perhaps you can learn to love me a little in return. Will you marry me?"

The magic words every girl longs to hear. If it be the wrong man, it mattered little. Her child would have a name and she would have a home and Lord Kerry would be far out of the reach of temptation. Sir Charles was opening up a whole new world for her; it was impossible to refuse. "Yes,

Charles, if you will have me," she murmured, and with those words, Katy sealed her future.

He kissed her as a gentleman would a lady upon plighting their troth, and with none of the tempestuousness that governed even the most innocent of Kerry's kisses. But there was pleasure in his respect, and even if she would have preferred the strength of one of Kerry's bone-crushing embraces, she imagined Sir Charles would not lack for strength or passion when the time came. For now, it was good to be loved for a change, instead of giving love without hope of return. It would not be difficult to learn to love this man who would accept her child as his own, although it might be a different kind of love, a more sensible, mature kind of love than the emotional turmoil stirred by Lord Kerry. That was much, much more than she had come to expect, or even deserve.

As their lips parted, Katy laughed nervously and held onto his hand. "You will forgive me if I do not know the proper procedure, but I have never been engaged before. What do we do now?"

Looking down fondly at her golden head, Charles realized the responsibility he was undertaking. At times, it might be more like having three children in the house, but he was confident she would soon grow into her position. He had already seen sufficient evidence of her maturity; the child should speed the process even more. There was time for everything in its turn.

"The first thing you do is write a letter to Lord Kerry so we may send it off in the morning. I expect to see him on the doorstep the following evening with murder in his eyes, but even Kerry must learn to listen to reason upon occasion." He smoothed away her worried frown with a smile and his hand. "Then you must go directly to bed and stay there until you are feeling well in the morning. I will send up a maid with a choice of things for you to breakfast upon, and you must promise to eat some of them. It will not do to starve yourself and the child."

Overwhelmed by the unusual luxury of surrendering herself to the care of another, Katy felt her eyes mist with tears. She had been carrying a heavy burden for three long months and suddenly realized what a relief it was to share it. Now, perhaps, she would be given the chance to relax and enjoy the prospect of having a child of her own. If only it were not for this wish that Lord Kerry be the one she share it with. . . .

Katy shook that thought from her mind. The privacy of their cabin life was gone, burned by the Indians, and she would not live the public life of mistress in Charleston. She had had enough humiliation in her short life, and the scars still ran deep; she would suffer no more. With that resolve, she clung firmly to the hand of Sir Charles as he helped her to her feet.

"What of Anna, sir? I cannot replace her mother. Will she accept me as your wife?"

"We will tell her in the morning. I see no reason why it should change the friendship you share. You have a way of correcting her extravagances without seeming to do so that no mother could ever achieve. Do not think I have not noticed how well you have handled my child this last year; I always know what my employees are doing." He smiled gently, teasingly.

It had not occurred to her before that the busy, preoccupied man she had seen so often at the dinner table had actually been paying close attention to what she was doing. Yet he knew enough of her to want her for his wife, and she did not think he was one to make such a decision blindly. There was much she had to learn about this stranger she had agreed to marry, but instinct told her she would find nothing unpleasant.

Pink lips blossomed into a smile. "I see now what you are doing. By marrying me, you will save both the expense of governess and housekeeper. You are truly a wise man."

"Not if my demure little governess takes advantage of her new position to turn into a little tease. I will most likely lose what few wits I still possess. Now, to your room with you, you have a letter to write," he admonished gently, an indulgent smile lighting his lined face.

The letter was the most difficult one she had ever written, and several times Katy almost swore off, to ask permission of Sir Charles to go to Charleston to tell Kerry in person. Only the certainty that, once confronted with Kerry's presence, she would weaken and be unable to return kept her pinned to the task. If Kerry should answer in person, Sir Charles would give her the strength and the arguments to resist.

The final draft was stilted and artificial, but little could be done about it. She would not conceal Kerry's child from him even if she could, but asking him to surrender his rights to it to another man was a painful task. Only she knew how much he longed for a wife and children, even to the point of asking her to be temporary substitute, for that was what his offer had been. Now she was the one denying him even that solace. If she had thought there was any possibility of love behind his offer, she would never have been able to write the letter, but as it was, it seemed the best thing for everyone.

But when she went to sleep that night and dreamed of lying in her husband's arms, the eyes staring back at her were green, not blue.

November 1735

LEAVING Anna stirring a chocolate cake in the kitchen with Bertha, Katy and Sir Charles strolled through town together to the docks. Not trusting the fledgling, haphazard mail service, Sir Charles had hired one of his riverboat captains to personally deliver the letter, and had asked Katy to accompany him while he handed the letter over. For November, the weather was warm and sunny, and Katy was delighted with any excuse to leave the house.

The fact that they were together without Anna telegraphed itself through town before they could reach the docks, and on their return trip a number of industrious souls who had suddenly decided to sweep their steps were rewarded with the sight of the unusual couple turning in at the gate of the parsonage. That Katy wore her new beribboned yellow gown from Charleston and not her usual dull-colored habits was enough to put a seal of certification on the occasion, and there was not a surprised look in the church the following Sunday when the banns were read.

But surprised looks abounded in the parsonage when Sir Charles first declared his intentions that morning, and the

Reverend Stone hastily asked his wife to serve Katy tea while he talked alone with the prospective groom. With the wisdom of a well-trained minister's wife, Mrs. Stone interpreted her husband's suggestion correctly, and whisked Katy off to a private conference of their own.

Katy fended off Emma's questions as best she could. She hated lying, but she could not betray Sir Charles if he were to claim the child as his own. She could say nothing that would explain their abrupt decision to marry.

"Believe me, Emma, when I tell you we know what we are doing," she begged. "Sir Charles is an intelligent man. if you think me foolish, then take his word. He would not allow me to do anything that is not in my best interests."

With a sigh of exasperation, Emma threw up her hands. "But what of love, Katy? I have not heard the word mentioned. You are young and beautiful, you may have your choice of men, why do you not wait for one you might love?"

Because I have made my choice and cannot have him, Katy thought, but declined to repeat it out loud. "What choice do I have in my position, Emma? I have no name, no title, no dowry. I am a governess, and if youth and looks are all I have to offer, they are of little consequence once my reputation is questioned, as it is now. I love Anna, and I am sure I can learn to love a man like Sir Charles. Can you name me one other who would be better than he?"

"Young Jake. Where is he? With Lord Kerry? I thought you two had some understanding." On firmer ground now, Emma spoke more positively and was rewarded by Katy's sudden flush.

"He understands that I could never marry him. Emma, you do not fully understand my position." Katy pleaded for that understanding. "I owe Lord Kerry a very large debt of gratitude, and I would do anything to please him. He would not approve of Jake, and nothing Jake can do will change his mind. But Sir Charles is Lord Kerry's friend, he respects him, and although his lordship may not approve at first, Charles will be able to convince him that we are doing the right thing. Do you not see?"

"I see more than I care to," Emma replied tartly, giving

the young girl a sharp look of consideration. "It sounds very much as if the man you marry must be able to stand up to Lord Kerry, and I do not think I wish to know why. Perhaps you do know what you are doing, in which case we had better discuss preparations for the wedding. A much more pleasant subject to enjoy with tea, don't you agree?" And pouring the cooled beverage, she briskly turned the topic to easier matters until the men joined them.

With an air of assurance, Sir Charles crossed the room and appropriated the seat next to Katy, giving her hand a collusive squeeze as he confronted the pastor and his wife. "Well, you two, is it quite settled, then? The banns will be read this Sunday and we will be wed at the end of the month?"

"There *is* one small matter," Emma answered thoughtfully. "It is not very appropriate for the bride and groom to share the same roof before the wedding. Katy, I think it will be best if you stay with us until then. Let Sir Charles call here as any suitor must. You would certainly have no objections to that?"

"No, of course not. You must let me show my appreciation of your kindness to Katy by coming to dinner this evening. Then Katy may accompany you when you leave, without causing too much of a stir. I will have her trunks sent over as soon as they are packed." Sir Charles rose, and the others rose with him. The first obstacle was conquered.

The next obstacle was Lord Kerry, and the shadow of his presence loomed large over their future. Katy lay in her strange bed that night, trying to imagine his face when he read her letter. Would the cynical lift of his eyebrows dive down into a displeased frown? Or would there be a smile of relief on his lips that the problem was so well settled? Or had he already found another mistress to fill his bed, and would unconcern be his only reaction?

Somewhere deep inside she harbored a secret dream of Lord Kerry riding to her side to declare his love and carry her off with him to Twin Oaks, where they would rebuild the cabin and live happily undisturbed, free to make love in their own bed every evening and raise their child without worry of titles or estates. It was a fantasy of impossible proportions, so fantastical that she dared not even believe Lord Kerry would

care at all. That she still saw the twinkling of his eyes above
her, felt the pressure of his hands on her body, tasted the
pleasure of his kiss, did not mean he felt the same. Katy
knew this well, but could not root out the dream.

Even when no word came the following day or the next,
she kept one eye on the window for the prancing thoroughbreds or started at the sound of hoofbeats in the street. He
could be anywhere, could appear anytime, and she grew
nervous in her anticipation. Surely he would not desert her
completely at a time like this?

But Sunday came without a word. Katy walked down the
church aisle on Sir Charles's arm with Anna at her side,
sitting in the first pew as they did every Sunday. Heads
turned as they passed, and only the beginning of the service
prevented the murmur of whispers from rising up behind
them. When the public announcement of their proposed marriage was finally made, a sigh and a stir of collective righteousness rushed through the crowd, and they barely made it
through the church at the end of the service as the crowd of
well-wishers massed around them.

Though many disapproved and had voiced their disapproval loud and long all week, Sir Charles held too important
a position in the town to be ignored, and there were always
those who loved a wedding to assure all who listened that
they had believed the young governess to be a credit to her
station all the time. After all, she was the ward of Lord
Kerry, and though she worked for a living, her family was
rumored to be among the gentry. Where else would she learn
the manners and grace that set her off from the rest, if it were
not good breeding? So the announcement was grudgingly
accepted with the right amount of scandal to titillate back-
door gossip and with a proper show of respect in public.

Now that the announcement was formally made and the
wedding officially in preparation, Katy found her time fully
occupied. Though technically still engaged as Anna's governess, while her young pupil worked her exercises, Katy spent
much of her time sewing and altering a small trousseau to
accompany her on their wedding journey. Old gowns were
modified and retrimmed, new ones were made with ample
room for alteration for her expanding waistline. For her wed-

ding gown, she gratefully accepted the loan of a seed-pearl-studded lace-and-satin ivory bridal gown that had once been Emma's. They spent many evenings lovingly altering the filmy lace into a billowing cloud to float over the rippling satin.

Believing exercise to be the best cure for Katy's illness and the fastest way to bring color back into her cheeks, Sir Charles took time off from the shipyards to take her on long walks into the countryside. They strolled slowly, enjoying the lingering days of sunshine and the opportunity to adjust to their new roles. Any courtship is a period of adjustment before marriage, but the dramatic change from governess to Lady Stockbridge required mental and emotional leaps of some magnitude. Just to address her employer as Charles required concentration, her extreme respect for this older man making it difficult to assume familiarity. Understanding some of this difficulty, Sir Charles made no significant demands of her, biding his time with the patience of one accustomed to waiting. Like newly discovered lovers, they strolled hand in hand, content to be together and nothing more.

It was at night that all Katy's restless yearning erupted, and she held her pillow in tears much like despair. Not unappreciative of the marvelous fate that had brought her so fine a man as Sir Charles who could enjoy with her the pleasure of Lord Kerry's baby, Katy still could not inure herself to the fact that she had been totally abandoned by Lord Kerry. A second letter from Sir Charles had equally been ignored, and she knew now that she must give up her noble guardian and lover in favor of her new husband, but it was not a dream she could easily surrender while her body still cried out for Kerry's caresses and her mind still saw his laughing eyes and heard the teasing lilt of his words. The child within her was sufficient reminder of her love, and she would finally drift off to sleep with her hand covering the place where it rested.

As Sir Charles predicted, Anna accepted Katy as her new mother with equanimity, deciding with gravity that if mothers were a necessary evil, she could not think of another she would rather have. But she, as everyone else, asked what Lord Kerry would do when he heard. Having associated her two favorite people with each other for so long, she had difficulty separating them in her mind, assuming somehow that one would come with the other. The fact that Lord Kerry did not appear remained a mystery to her as well as to others.

After the weeks of tension and anxiety, the wedding itself came as an anticlimax, occurring without incident. Out of respect for Sir Charles's mourning, the service was private and brief, a simple affirmation of vows in the presence of a few witnesses. But as the newly married couple left the church, they were inundated with a crowd of friends and well-wishers who, prepared in advance, led the way to the parsonage and a lavish repast prepared with the compliments of Emma and Bertha.

Expecting at any moment a last-minute interruption by an irate Lord Kerry or at the very least a thundercloud of cataclysmic proportions to strike her down, Katy was left drained and shaken by the emotional tension of the ceremony. When the service ended without incident, she wished only to be taken home in the safety of Sir Charles's protection, and the crowd waiting outside came as an unwelcome surprise.

Standing at her husband's side in the foyer of the parsonage, greeting their guests and accepting congratulations, Katy felt the last of her strength sapping away. Tears formed in her eyes at the thought of one more handshake, and the snickering gibes about the night yet to come and the furtive whispers and elbow prods received by her new husband from the circle of men about him enhanced her nervousness. She was married and would soon be expected to enter the bed of this man who had suddenly become a stranger to her, and her mind fought with this reality. It could not be true. A scream formed in her throat at every question of Kerry's absence, and she clung desperately to her husband's arm for support, praying for quick release from this torment. Until, when someone addressed her as Lady Stockbridge, she could no longer hang on, and turning startled violet eyes up to Sir Charles, she crumpled slowly to the floor.

Panic ensued in the small area where they stood, but Sir Charles quickly took charge, whisking his wife into the privacy of the parsonage's small study, ordering bystanders to fetch Emma. Leaving the Stones to make plausible explanations and express their regrets, Sir Charles worked to revive

Katy's limp form, cursing himself for his blindness in not
seeing her weariness earlier. By the time the crowd dispersed
and the Stones returned to the study, Katy was showing some
signs of coming around, and Sir Charles declared his desire to
return home immediately. The sooner they were away from
prying eyes, the better Katy would feel, he was certain.

When Katy revived enough to stand and take his arm, the
newlyweds expressed their gratitude and stepped out into the
darkness of a starlit night. The air was clear and cold, and
Katy clung closely to Sir Charles's warmth as they traversed
the small stretch of street between the parsonage and the
house they would now share together. Only the immense
expanse of sky above observed their journey.

The normally darkened hall and stairway were lit with the
suffused glow of a dozen candles, and the rustle of the satin
train of Katy's gown was magnified in the silence as they
ascended the stairs to the master bedroom Katy would now
share with Sir Charles. Sensing her nervousness, Sir Charles
gripped his bride's elbow tightly, firmly guiding her into the
well-lit room prepared for them.

Taking pity on Katy's hollowed dark eyes, Charles brushed
a kiss across her forehead and retired to his dressing room,
leaving Katy to modestly prepare herself for bed. Staring
blankly about the room after he had gone, Katy realized the
bedchamber had been redecorated since last she saw it, and
again she recognized her husband's thoughtfulness. Removing her shoes and padding lightly across the uncarpeted floor,
she traced with her fingers the patterns of familiar toilet
articles, lying now next to those of her husband on the
dresser. Most of her clothes had been packed away in trunks
for tomorrow's journey, but her fur-lined cloak hung in the
wardrobe next to a new traveling gown of the softest, finest
wool she had ever touched. Tears sprang to her eyes, and she
turned back to the elongated mirror over the dresser.

Katy had never found her pale coloring and frail features
beautiful in comparison to the voluptuous, more boldly
painted demoiselles of Kerry's world, but tonight, even she
was forced to admit there was an ethereal beauty in the wide
violet eyes staring from the delicately carved ivory image in
the mirror. Carefully removing the pins and lace from her

elaborate coiffure, she allowed the silver-gold cloud of curls
to disperse in a golden nimbus about the reflection, sending
shimmers of light down shoulders and breasts. A small smile
crossed her lips as she remembered Kerry's admiration for
this tangled mass of curls. Tonight she would use it to please
her husband.

Slowly unfastening the tiny buttons of her bodice, allowing
the heavy satin of her gown to fall from her shoulders, she
stood in front of the mirror and critically surveyed what she
had uncovered. The fine lawn of her shift was cut low over
the rounding firmness of her breasts, revealing the deep cleft
between, falling loosely over the small lump of her stomach
where she sensed the first stirring of life, clinging to the
curve of hips and thighs. Her shoulders slumped slightly as
she contemplated the new roundnesses of her usually slender
body. This was the night a girl dreams of all her life, and she
could not present even a semblance of virginity to her new
husband. What else was there for her to give him?

Climbing between the covers of the massive four-poster,
Katy waited quiescently for whatever would follow. Any
excitement or anticipation she might have felt at finally sharing a bed with a man who was her husband had evaporated
with the tensions of the day, and now she lay inert, with no
other thoughts than those of the present.

When Sir Charles entered, stripped of coat and waistcoat,
Katy realized she had never seen him about the house in less
than full dress before, and she watched with stirring interest
as he removed his cravat and gave her one of his rare smiles.
He was larger and more sturdily proportioned than Kerry, but
what he lacked in deftness and dexterity he made up for in the
firm sureness with which he moved.

Charles's eyes roamed eagerly over the creamy expanse of
flesh revealed by Katy's low-cut shift, but the dark shadows
beneath her eyes commanded his attention. While eager to
sample the pleasures of his marital bed, Sir Charles was too
well aware of Katy's delicate condition and the childlike trust
of her open gaze to press for more than she was willing to
give.

Extinguishing the candles but allowing the fire to continue
to flame high, illuminating the room with its glowing shad-

ows, Charles finished undressing, easing in beside his child bride. Wide, dark eyes stared up at him as she clenched the covers to her breast, and he smiled gently, stroking her lovely hair back from her forehead and smoothing it over the pillow.

"Will you faint again if I tell you you make a lovely Lady Stockbridge?"

A tentative smile crossed her lips. "I am dreadfully sorry that I made such a scene. I do not make a habit of it, I assure you."

"Nonsense. It made me feel very manly and competent and reminded me necessarily of the delicacy of your condition. I should have made you retire long before this. It has been some while since Anna's birth, but I remember well that fainting spells and dizziness seemed to be the order of the day more often than not. You have done remarkably well under the circumstances, and you will soon get over it."

"But I don't think I will ever get over being Lady Stockbridge. It is much too magnificent a title for me. I would rather be just plain Katy." These weren't the words she had intended to say, they had just appeared on her lips of their own accord, her mind too weary to stifle them and produce the words of love and praise she wished to use.

"You will never be just plain Katy, you are too beautiful a woman for that. You will never convince me you were not born a Lady Katherine. But whatever the name, you are very tired, and I think it would be better if you went to sleep now." The hand stroking her hair now fell to her cheek, cupping her face in its sturdy width.

Not able to hide the relief in her eyes, she closed them, concentrating on the warmth and masculine scent of this strange body beside her. "I am really quite all right. It was just the long standing that—"

Sir Charles stopped her protests with his kiss, not the light, affectionate pecks of their betrothal but a passionate promise of what is to come. To his surprise, she began to respond to his pressure, returning his promise with a vividness that almost destroyed his good intentions, but as his hand slid from her cheek to her breast, the tensing beneath his touch restored his common sense, and reluctantly leaving that tempting field, he withdrew his hand.

"I will not rush you, Katherine, there is time enough for everything. Go to sleep." Brushing a kiss across her cheek, he turned away.

Lying stiffly beside her new husband, Katy did not fall asleep easily. After many months of lying awake wishing for a man's arms to hold her, to comfort her and ease the aching longing Kerry had left behind, she had withdrawn from the one man to whom she was allowed to give herself. It was going to be more difficult to drive away Kerry's touch than she had expected, but she would do it. She fully intended to be the best wife Sir Charles could ever have, and her duties began right here in bed. And with this resolve, she finally surrendered to sleep.

As the first shaft of icy morning light hit Katy's eyelids, she snuggled deeper into the bed's warmth, shivering in the chill air of the unheated room. But as a hand not her own pulled the covers more tightly about her, her eyes flew open, encountering soft blue ones smiling back at her.

"Good morning, Katy. How are you feeling?" Charles stared down into startled violet pools, amazed as always at their depth and clarity, even at this hour of morning. The shimmering gold strands of her hair caught the first rays of sun, forming an unruly incandescent halo about her face.

Katy's hand automatically flew to her usually queasy stomach, eyes registering surprise when she realized all was momentarily calm. "Fine, I think."

"Good. That, too, will pass in time. It is a good thing, for I am rather fond of mornings." His eyes caressed her delicate beauty as his hand reached out to caress her hair.

Momentary panic crossed Katy's face as she realized his meaning, but she quelled it, forcing herself to lie quietly beneath her husband's touch. Almost reverently he stroked her hair, gathering it up in a sheaf of long, silky curls and pulling it back over her shoulder, laying bare the fine skin of her throat and shoulders. Katy quivered slightly as he traced the curve of her neck with his hand, but the firm assurance of his grip as he pulled her to him let her relax into his control. Charles's kiss was warm and tender, awakening her interest before intensifying into last night's passion and beyond, leaving her nearly breathless when he let go. She stared at him with darkening eyes as his hand slid over her hip and pulled her closer with a power she had no wish to resist.

"I thought last night a fluke, a result of your exhaustion, but there really is some feeling lurking beneath that cool exterior of yours, milady," Charles said contemplatively. Elizabeth had been a faithful wife, and in the first years had tried to match his strong passions, but for the last twenty years he had unleashed his desires on an unresponsive body. Katy's willingness took him completely by surprise. He knew her to be warm and affectionate by nature, but he had never suspected the strong sensual streak his kisses revealed.

He did not attempt to conceal his excitement. "Shall we try that again?" Without waiting for her reply, he kissed her again, and this time he was rewarded with the slight arching of her body into his embrace as his hand roved up and down her spine. Aching to touch the tender flesh beneath the flimsy material of her shift, he tore his lips away. "Shall I go on?" he asked breathlessly.

"Please." Eyes shining with the pleasure she was giving him, Katy touched his cheek timidly. "Teach me to be your wife."

"With pleasure, my dear." Grasping her shoulder, Charles laid her back against the pillows, covering her face and hair with gentle kisses. Pausing to catch the awe in her wide eyes, he smiled and said gently, "Lie still and let me do it; there is nothing to fear."

Pushing down the shoulder of her shift, he released one taut breast, circling it reverently with his hand while he waited for her to relax before tasting the distended pink tip. As his mouth touched her in this way, Katy felt the mounting ache that Kerry had stirred and left unquenched these last months, and she strained eagerly upward, wanting more. Quick to sense her desires, Charles unfastened the bodice and slid it down to her waist, filling his hands with the firm young flesh he had only admired before when covered. Their differences disappeared in timeless sensations, and they were simply man and woman, discovering each other for the first time.

The shift quickly disappeared below her hips, and as warm, thick fingers caressed the tender insides of her thighs, probing the soft moistness between, Katy felt the explosion of long-pent-up desires and threw her arms around her husband's neck, urging him on. That it was the heavier, more awkward body of Sir Charles covering her made no difference as her hips rose expectantly to meet his plunge, and all comparison died as she felt him gain his pleasure. Her body ached for the bruising battle of passions Kerry had taught her, but she was content to have brought her husband joy, and her smile reflected her happiness.

Bracing himself on one elbow to gaze down at the frail figure that had brought him such unexpected pleasure, Charles let a slow smile inch across his dark face at the shining eyes staring back at him. "I do believe you enjoyed that, Lady Katherine!"

Katy lightly traced the path of his smile with her finger. The serious, preoccupied Sir Charles she had known this past year had metamorphosed this last month into a charming lover, and she hoped fate would allow him to stay that way. "Is that wrong?" she asked curiously. She had enjoyed the tenderness of his lovemaking and was beginning to feel the first stirrings of guilt at betraying Lord Kerry. She had allowed another man to possess her when she knew herself to be irrevocably Kerry's, no matter what words the minister muttered over her head, but right now it was more important to belong to her husband, and she shoved Lord Kerry aside as he had done her.

Laughing for the first time in Katy's memory, Charles caught her in his arms and rolled over so that she lay nestled on top of him. "It is the best wedding present a man can receive, my fair innocent. If Lord Kerry knew what a valuable gift he had given me, I do not think he would have parted with you."

She did not dare tell him Lord Kerry knew better than he and had still given her up without a word. It was hard to admit, even to herself, and she unconsciously frowned at the thought.

Charles saw the frown and tipped her chin up so their eyes met. "I know you love the man, Katherine, it is no secret between us. He has done the only honorable thing possible for him under the circumstances, so do not think too harshly

of him. When we return, we may still think of him as friend.
I hope by then to have won enough of your affection and
loyalty to make any other relationship impossible. Do you
understand?''

She understood too well. That he could think her capable
of adultery was evidence of the large gap left in their understanding. ''I would never—'' she started to protest, but he
interrupted.

''I am not insulting you when I say this, Katy. You are a
young and, I suspect, very passionate woman, and I cannot
expect to replace a man like Lord Kerry in your affections.
Human nature being what it is, the temptations will be great,
and I fear neither you nor Lord Kerry has a high moral code
ingrained in you. I may be old, Katy, but I am no fool, nor a
stranger to temptation myself. My only hope is that that
intense loyalty of yours and a modicum of affection will keep
you from harm's way—that and a certain amount of precaution
on my part.'' A wry smile accompanied this last statement as he
kissed away her distressed frown. He had expected a frightened, nearly virgin bride and found one more qualified to be
a courtesan. His conclusion was an accurate one: Lord Kerry
had taken advantage of his opportunities to comfort his de-
filed ward in the best way possible. That he had not returned
her to Charleston as his mistress was a credit Sir Charles was
not certain where to apply and would not question. Whatever
the circumstances, he was convinced he had the better end of
the bargain.

The accuracy of his statements could not be argued in any
way but performance. Returning his kiss more fervently,
Katy replied, ''I respect your judgment more than anyone's I
know, but I fully intend to prove you wrong in this matter,
sir. I have already told you I intend to be the best wife
possible, and that includes faithfulness with whatever moral
code you use. Your precautions will be wasted.''

''I cannot think of a matter I am more willing to be wrong
in, and if you keep that up, I will imagine myself a younger
man and you will find yourself assaulted once more.'' He
captured the lips that had been covering his face with kisses,
and the morning of the first day grew later.

January 1736

CURLED AWKWARDLY in an overlarge chair, Katy graded Anna's latest composition, more absorbed in its contents than in correcting the numerous spelling and grammatical errors. Unlike Katy, Anna had developed a flair for words, and her compositional efforts were rapidly outdistancing Katy's ability to judge them. The last two months had given Katy plenty of opportunity to realize her limitations; there was little else she had been allowed to do.

Sir Charles's communications with his taciturn brother had been such that it was not difficult to write in the same letter of the death of Elizabeth, his remarriage, and his new wife's pregnancy without causing consternation on anyone's part. When he also added he wished to have his second child delivered by the same trusted midwife as the first—his brother's wife—he received an immediate reply in typical form stating they had better make the journey soon, before the winter snows, or they might well find themselves delivering the child in a snowbank come the spring thaws. Katy soon discovered this was as much of a welcome as they would ever receive from this strange pair.

They had been in the Jason Stockbridge household for nearly two months now and so far had exchanged few words with its members that were of anything but a practical nature. Dinner-table conversation consisted of discussions of the various Stockbridge enterprises, and any attempts by Katy to introduce more social topics at other times with Jason's Quaker wife, Martha, were rejected by the good woman's simple process of finding too much to do to make more than the minimally acceptable replies. Katy swiftly learned to keep quiet.

From the beginning, she had offered her services in helping with the household chores, since the rough-hewn house of ample proportions but limited amenities had few servants and many tasks. But in one way or another she found herself unwanted in the kitchen or elsewhere, Martha preferring her accustomed methods to those of an outsider. Katy resigned herself to caring for her immediate family and the rooms they occupied, carving out a niche of her own on which none dared trespass. Still, it was not sufficient to keep her fully occupied, and she spent many hours applying herself to Anna's lessons and wishing for her husband's small library.

Absorbed in her thoughts, Katy failed to hear the bedroom door open and didn't look up until she heard the scraping sound of its closing, finding her husband leaning against the door and staring at her with a peculiar expression. Sir Charles had been more than patient and considerate with her in the two months since their marriage, and Katy had grown to think she knew all his moods, but this one she had never met before.

"Charles? Is something wrong? You look rather disturbed." Actually, "disturbed" wasn't the word: he seemed tense, vaguely displeased, and more than a little worried as he continued to study her with those penetrating blue eyes.

At last he came forward, and tucking a stray strand of hair back into Katy's cap, he commented, "You are supposed to be lying down, resting." He stalled for time. The color had never returned to Katy's cheeks as he had hoped, and her illness continued with lingering persistence, leaving her weak and tired most of the time. Yet she never complained, insisting on doing what she claimed to be her duties, and only his sister-in-law's insistence that she be allowed to continue had prevented his ordering her to bed and making her stay there. Now he wondered what effect his news would have on her already precarious health and contemplated withholding it.

"I am resting, sitting up; it is more comfortable, and you are evading some issue. You had best tell me or I will worry the more." Katy caught his hand and pressed it against her cheek.

"We have a visitor downstairs," he said slowly, watching for her reaction.

"A visitor? In this blizzard? I thought no one could get through for the remainder of the winter." Katy looked up at him questioningly when he did not reply. "Who would be mad enough to go visiting in this weather?" Suddenly she realized there was only one possible answer to that question, and her eyes widened as she stared up at him and found it confirmed in his eyes. "Lord Kerry," she breathed softly.

Charles nodded. "He has been in Virginia. Our letters followed him there and back again; he only just received them upon returning to Charleston less than a month ago. It has taken him this long to find us, since I had not foreseen a need to leave directions." His expression was serious as he clasped her hand and awaited her response.

"Oh, dear." Katy sank back against the chair. As long as Lord Kerry had not answered her letter, her conscience had been clear on her decision. For some reason, it had not occurred to her that he had never received either letter. "How is he taking it?"

Charles sat down on the arm of the chair, still holding his wife's hand. "Putting it mildly, he is furious. Actually, I think he has worked himself into a state near madness. I am afraid I seriously underestimated that young man. If it were not for the weather and your condition, I do believe he would be throwing you on his horse and carrying you off. I am not at all certain that my reasoning is reaching him at all."

"I am sorry, Charles. I had thought it quite settled." Disturbed by the images her husband's words wrought, Katy closed her eyes against the picture of an angry, hurt Lord Kerry. The one thing she could not bear to do was cause him pain, and she knew instantly that her desertion had done just that.

"It is quite settled, so far as I am concerned. You made your choice quite freely and he has no power to change it, but he asks to see you. I have told him you have not been well and are resting, but he insists that I ask. If you wish, I will tell him you are sleeping." The concern in Charles's eyes reflected the depth of his emotion. It had not occurred to him that the noble Lord Kerry, with all his many mistresses, would be so concerned over what had, after all, been an act of fate.

"No, Charles. It was my decision that brought us to this, and I cannot hurt him more by refusing to see him." Katy untangled her skirts and attempted to rise.

Assisting her to stand, Charles held her in place. "Then you do realize how badly he has been hurt?" He studied her face anxiously, wondering how much she was keeping hidden behind the placid curtain of those violet eyes.

"That is why I insisted on his permission to marry. Despite evidence to the contrary, Kerry is very much a family man, and as far as I know, has never fathered a child before. To ask him to give this one up . . ." Katy stopped, wondering at the relief suddenly flickering across her husband's face.

"Of course, that is understandable. But I will insist on waiting outside the door if you need me." If it were just the child and not Katy that had brought Kerry storming up here like a madman, he had little to fear. Uneasily, he hoped he was not underestimating the young lord again.

Katy smiled faintly and accepted her husband's offer of assistance, her mind now with the angry man downstairs more than on their conversation.

She knocked softly on the partially closed parlor door, accepting the grunted reply from within as an admittance, and pushing open the door to enter. Lord Kerry stood in front of the fireplace with his back to her. His wet coat was hanging over a chair, drying in the heat of the roaring blaze as he seemed to study the patterns of the flames. His broad shoulders stretched taut the travel-worn linen shirt, and at the familiar sight, Katy's heart skipped a beat. It was as if it had been five days and not five months since she had seen him last, and all the defenses she had built against his power crumbled. Her only prayer was that he would not realize it. She shut the door behind her.

The sound of the closing door swung Kerry around, and he stared at the figure who entered the room as if she were a figment of his imagination come to life. His gaze quickly took in Katy's thin, pale face, the dark eyes staring out from the pallor like two overlarge saucers. Then his stare traveled to the growing protrusion of her stomach, well hidden among numerous petticoats but obvious to the eyes who knew her slenderness well, and his anger mounted unreasonably.

"Why, Katy?" he demanded suddenly, furiously, green eyes flashing with the heat of his fury and pain. "Do you love him? Tell me you love him and I'll walk out of here without another word." Darkened by exposure to the elements, Kerry's face was drawn and lined, evidence of weeks or months of distress.

Katy countered his fury calmly. "May I sit, milord? I find it difficult to remain long on my feet."

"Oh, for God's sake . . ." Irritated at her return to formality and at his own ill manners, Kerry swung a chair in her direction and indicated that she sit.

"Thank you," she murmured graciously, rearranging her skirts while he stared at her with irritated impatience. "Now, you were asking . . ."

"And you have already answered." He began stalking the room restlessly, jerking at the draperies to stare out frost-covered windows, poking at the roaring fire. "If you loved him, you would have declared it at once without that inane performance." Spinning around to confront her again, he blurted out, "Do you hate me so much that you would rather marry anyone than face living with me?"

Checking all emotions, Katy replied, "I do not hate you, and Sir Charles is not just anyone. I wish you would sit down like a civilized human being instead of pacing the floor like a caged beast. I have done nothing that I have not told you I would do, so I do not understand why you act so surprised. My only regret is that you did not know about the child; you have as much right to decide its future as I do."

"You're damned right I do! So can you tell me why you've gone and tied it all up like this? You knew I would take you in, didn't you?" Kerry's tone was accusatory as he continued stalking the room, refusing to look at her.

"I knew," she answered softly, looking down at her hands. "But I wanted our child to have a name, and you could not give it one."

With a maddened curse Kerry struck the poker against the stone wall of the fireplace. "Dammit, Katy! You have sold yourself for a name! What good is a name? You had no right to sell yourself at all, you are *mine*, and so is the child!"

"If you cannot continue this discussion without yelling and cursing at me, I will get up and leave the room," Katy threatened coldly.

Finally turning to face her, all the anger seemed to drain out of Kerry at once, and his shoulders slumped as he saw the tiny figure straighten itself proudly beneath his tirade, though her face revealed the effort it cost her. She had known she could turn to him, but she had deliberately chosen Sir Charles instead; he had lost, and there was no further reason to argue. Turning back to the window, he stared blindly at the white blur beyond the frosted panes.

"I am sorry, Katherine. When I sent you back to Sir Charles instead of Charleston, I as much as relinquished all rights to you." He did not tell her he had done it deliberately and spent the next five months trying to drive her memory from his soul. He had thought he succeeded, too, until he read that letter and it all came rushing back to him with the impact of a volcanic tidal wave. He had been a bloody fool from the very start, but it was much too late to do anything about it. She had made her choice and was happy with it, as were Sir Charles and Anna, he supposed. He was the only one to suffer, and there was justice in that, since he was the fool who had willingly given her up.

"Sir Charles informs me he has no intention of turning his head and allowing you to become my mistress, as is the practice apparently among some of my peers. Do you know anything of this?" Kerry kept his voice well moderated as he continued staring at the icy panes.

Katy felt the heat rise to her face and was grateful for his back. "He thinks I am weak and seeks your support as the stronger of the two, I assume. I am sorry if I insulted you."

Kerry turned to look at her with curiosity. "Are you? Weak?" If there were also a hint of hope in his question, he strove to conceal it.

"I trust you are gentleman enough not to find out," she said stiffly.

"Right," he replied curtly, turning back to the window. "Are you happy with him, then?"

Relief flooded through her at this more reasonable turn of the conversation and she answered eagerly. "I could not have a better husband. Charles has been more than thoughtful and kind, and exceptionally understanding. I have grown very fond of him, and of course I will not be parted from Anna. It seemed the ideal solution, Kerry, you must see that. Even you recommended that I find an older man looking for a second wife who would take me for myself without need of money or name. That he would also take me carrying another man's child speaks for itself. Please say you approve, I cannot bear to think you would disapprove of the way I have chosen to spend my life after all you have done for me. I would never have done it if I thought you would not approve." Anxiously she awaited his reply.

"I have always thought of Sir Charles as one of the few good men I could rely on, but I never considered him as a husband for you. If you are happy, my approval does not matter." The voice from the window seemed suddenly strained and weary. "He has asked if I would be godfather to the child, said it would give me reason to visit as frequently as I wish without cause for gossip. Do you have any objections?"

"No, of course not. Then you are not angry with me?" she asked joyfully. "You will wish to see the child?"

Kerry finally turned back toward the room, his face softening slightly at the return of Katy's good nature. Studying the face now glowing with happiness, he gave his assent with a silent bow of acknowledgment. "You could not keep me away if you tried. Have you decided on any names yet?"

"Your mother's name is Maureen, is it not?" At his nod, Katy continued, "We thought if it were a girl, she might be called Maureen Elizabeth, or is that too presumptuous?"

"Not at all. I like that, and it would amuse my mother greatly. She has a rare sense of humor. I wish you could know her." Kerry stepped farther into the room, unable to avoid the magnetic pull of violet eyes.

"You would not tell her, would you?" Katy asked, horrified.

A small grin quirked the corner of his handsome mouth. "Why not? It will be my first child, and I am rather proud of the accomplishment. What have you chosen for a boy?"

"I was afraid your father's name would be dreadfully presumptuous and your name too obvious, so we have made no decision." She could not believe he meant to inform his family of his bastard child, and she ignored his silliness.

"It will be Charles's first son. You will have to call him Charles. If you wish to use the name Edward, by all means do so. It is a common enough name and my father can scarcely object. Charles Edward would make a fine name. Your husband does not object to his title going to a child not his own?" He moved nearer, willing his hand not to touch the fair hair now within reach.

"He says it is better than the title being laid to rest as he had come to expect." Not noticing Kerry's reticence, Katy could not contain her joy at his return and reached naturally to take his hand with both of hers, squeezing it excitedly now that she was sharing her dreams with the father of her child. "Will it not be better for your son to be called a baronet than a bastard?"

A weaker man would have fallen to his knees and buried his face in the lap of this ingenuous innocent, but Kerry resisted stoically. "I will just be grateful that he and you do well. I only wish that I could be here with you when the time comes. I have already missed the joy of watching him grow."

Suddenly understanding some of the unnatural strain in his voice, Katy shyly placed his hand on the undulating movement of her abdomen. "The child is already as active and ambitious as his father, and I will allow nothing to happen to him, or her," she said softly.

Feeling the movement of his first child under his hand, tears sprang to Kerry's eyes and he finally bowed before the enormity of the occasion. He knelt before this woman who had taught him the meaning of love, though he would never be able to speak the words that burned in his heart.

Kneeling before her, Kerry grasped her hand tightly. "I apologize for anything I have said today, Katy. All I want is to see you happy, and if this is what it takes, you have my blessing."

Catching her hand in the thick auburn hair she so loved, feeling the warm pressure of his hard body close to hers, Katy was stabbed by the intensity of the longing she had thought satisfied with her marriage. Would there never be an end to the joyous pain of his touch? Tears sprang to her eyes, but she ignored them.

"That is all I need to make me happy, thank you." Wanting to keep him by her side, she continued stroking his hair. "Will you stay awhile? It is no weather for traveling, and I'm sure—"

Kerry shook his head and stood up, bringing her with him. He was not yet ready for the trial of seeing her with her husband. Perhaps by the time they returned to town he would have learned to accept it, but the wound was too deep to test it now. Resting his hand on the bulge of her skirts, he smiled warmly. "Your husband will be glad to see the back of me, and I think I better spend my time finding something to keep me occupied until you come home. It may be time to begin building that house at Twin Oaks. The next time you visit, you will need room for a husband and two children." The smile faded as he added, "I am afraid I have about run out of excuses not to marry. If I should happen to find that cooperative wife you claim exists, I suppose I must have a home to offer her. Take care of yourself, kitten."

Sensing he wished to be left alone, Katy gave the hard hollow of his cheek a familiar peck. "You too, Kerry," she said, before turning her back on the man she loved and opening the door to enter the arms of the man with whom she had chosen to spend her life.

March 1736

THE MOUNTAIN snows did not begin to melt until March, and by the time the first snowdrops appeared, Katy was bedridden with the burden she carried, her strength failing to carry the extra weight. Rallying briefly after Kerry's visit, she had overexerted herself, and the ensuing months of debilitating inactivity left her weak and lifeless. Even Anna's cheerful compositions failed to raise her spirits, and Charles spent many anxious hours at her bedside trying to revive her interest.

By Martha's calculations, the baby wasn't due until the first of May, but the first contraction came in mid-April, gripping Katy with such painful intensity that she let out a startled gasp. Charles immediately appeared at her side, holding her hand while the rolling pain subsided.

"Shall I get Martha?" he asked quietly, masking his anxiety at the sight of his wife's fear-filled eyes.

"No, not yet. It's gone away." Attempting a smile, Katy picked up her sketchbook and resumed her drawing of rampaging kittens, but it seemed only moments later when the next pain attacked, and she dropped her pen, splattering ink across the covers. This time Charles let her clench his hand until the pain dissipated, then firmly insisted on calling for his sister-in-law.

By late evening the pain had intensified and settled into more frequent patterns, and Anna was sent to a neighboring house for the night as Katy's muffled moans threatened to escalate. By the following morning it became apparent to everyone the birth would not be an easy one, and Charles sought oblivion in his brother's hidden whiskey cache while Katy sank into unconsciousness.

Martha did not succeed in turning the babe into position until midafternoon, thereby reviving Katy and her screams. Within the hour, Kerry's daughter was roaring vigorously, and after making certain the infant lived, Katy lapsed once again into oblivion.

This time her senselessness was not to be lifted for weeks. Fever set in several hours after the birth, and while Sir Charles watched helplessly, Katy wasted away in a deep sleep only bordering on consciousness occasionally with unintelligible murmurings and piteous cries for Kerry. They took turns spoon-feeding her liquids continually, but her milk refused to come, and her occasional unconscious cries were punctuated by the nonstop screaming of her starving child. Tension built in the small household while frantic searches for a wet nurse ended unsuccessfully and all other attempts to get milk into the premature babe were limited; it nursed frantically at its mother's unyielding breast, bringing the only sign of sanity back to Katy's lifeless eyes and causing Sir Charles to bury his face in his hands with grief.

But during the first week of May, with the scent of pine needles wafting in on the first warm breezes, the fever abated, and with it went Katy's fevered nightmares, leaving her alert but weak. The first sign of her return to sensibility came with Martha's attempts to force a brewed concoction past her parched lips, and Katy's immediate demand to know what it was before she drank it. Startled by her usually unresisting patient's inquiry, Martha divulged the contents, and to her astonishment, found herself listening to a list of the medicinal properties of several herbs Katy wished added to the ingredients.

Sir Charles was consulted, and with his relieved approval

of all Katy's wishes, the concoction was fortified as instructed and continued to be through the next weeks while the milk began to flow from her breasts and the infant to thrive. Only Katy remained slow recovering; though she insisted on leaving the bed as soon as her legs would hold her, she could not summon the strength to stay up long, and the weight lost during the fever was not easily regained.

As the month of May moved into June, Katy begged to be allowed outside. Believing the warm sun to be beneficial, Charles acquiesced to her request, carrying her down the stairs and giving his arm for support as they walked slowly along the mountain lanes. But though her legs grew quickly stronger, she remained pale and weak, and the sparkle returned to her eyes only when she held the infant Maureen.

With reluctance, Charles began to consider her requests to return home. Katy insisted her enforced idleness caused her lethargy and she needed the stimulation of her own home and kitchens to revive her strength, perhaps even give a class or two for the younger students to relieve her boredom. When she spoke like this, her husband could almost hear the animation in her voice return, and he became increasingly convinced that she was right. In the interest of protecting the infant's parentage, he had intended to stay until autumn, but Katy's health was of more importance and her arguments persuasive, even if, as he suspected, it was Kerry's presence she sought, and not their home. Charles was willing to admit the younger man's importance to her, but prayed it could be overcome with time and the return of her health.

They lay in bed one hot night late in June when the subject arose again. A cool breeze caught the curtains as Charles admitted his eagerness to return to his business before the assistant he left behind ran into difficulties with the summer river trade, but he still retained strong doubts on the matter.

"Katy, there will be no fooling anyone about Maureen's birth if we should return now. Even if we should say she was premature, you would have had to leave childbed to make that trip and return now."

"Charles, once upon a time it mattered to me what people thought, because my entire future was based on their opinions, and if you had a background like mine, that would be important. I was fighting to climb out of a pit whose depth you cannot imagine. But if you do not mind too much being thought a lecherous old man, I do not mind being thought a wanton woman. They have labeled me that before and I have survived. I will survive again. It only matters that they think Maureen your child, and they will. No one would ever believe the truth.'' Katy curled up by his side and rested her head on his shoulder. They had discarded all pretense of sleepwear with the first warm nights, but there had been no bodily contact between them in many months while she recuperated. But as some of her strength returned, so did her needs, and she badly wanted to be held.

It was the first time Katy had voluntarily come to him, and Charles was not certain that she had not done it in all innocence of the effect on him after a five-month abstinence. Trying to concentrate on her words and not the warm pressure of her breasts against his side, he tried to dispute her argument. ''My reputation is of no concern to anyone. I am too old for gossips to be anything but amazed at my virility, and no amount of gossip will harm my businesses. But you were unhappy at being shunned when they thought you Kerry's mistress, and if they should suspect Maureen to be his child, it can only be worse. I don't think you're prepared for the results.''

''I'll keep them talking about your virility—let's make the next one a boy,'' Katy replied teasingly, kissing the lobe of his ear.

''After this last one, I'm not certain there ought to be a next one. I do not know if either of us can go through that again.'' Gently Charles drew her away, even while his body ached to possess her. ''And you have not answered my objections.''

Katy lay still, summoning her thoughts to put them to the best use in the argument she sensed she had already won. ''It is very difficult to be shunned by everyone when you are all alone in the world, as I was then. And it wasn't just the gossip, but the fact that I would have to become Kerry's mistress that made me unhappy. Now I have you and Anna and Maureen and I need no one else. Is that very selfish?''

''Very,'' he agreed, kissing her forehead and waiting for

her to continue. She had apparently thought this out for a long time, and very thoroughly; the least he could do was listen, although his mind was already made up. The fact that she knew Kerry would have had her, but she chose him instead, did not escape Charles.

"Then I will be selfish. I feel I have repaid Lord Kerry whatever debt I owed him, and now I am free to act on my own. I cannot instantly switch my affections from him to you, and I doubt if I will ever stop loving him, if for no other reason than that he is the father of my child, but I want to begin being your wife, and I cannot do that here. I want to learn to love you as you deserve, to be a partner in your life as a wife should be, not just an extra burden for you to care for, as I am now. I want to bear your children, Charles, give you a son, return some of the happiness you have given me. And the sooner I can start, the better I will feel. Let's go home now, please?"

Charles felt the pain in his heart ease and lessen. He had been right to choose her: there was no doubt in his mind that she could do as she said. He squeezed her shoulders. "If that is how you feel, then we will go. The gossips may take care of themselves."

Katy threw her arms around him and began to shower his face with kisses until, laughing, he held her off.

"My dear child, you will leave me no choice but to ravish you here and now if you persist in this display of affection. I am not a weak man, but even the strongest could not resist your charms. You must regain your health first."

"It has been more than two months since Maureen's birth, and I am fine." Katy escaped his hold and pressed eager lips to his, her need expanding at his response. There was no need to imagine Lord Kerry in her husband's place tonight: her body had been too long denied, and the embrace of her husband was more familiar than the long-ago caresses exchanged with a man she had seen but once in almost a year. Tonight, she wished her husband to hold her.

"In that case, I am not one to argue." Laying her gently against the bed, Charles tortured her with his patience, until, when they came together, they exploded quickly with mutual satisfaction. That he had never achieved Katy's satisfaction before made the moment doubly fulfilling.

As they lay wrapped in each other's arms, the supple youth-fulness of Katy's small body pressed warm and soft against his, Charles was not fooled by the moment's ecstasy. He was a man swiftly approaching mid-fifties and she was barely more than a child of nineteen, a loyal, trusting wife by nature, but a woman whose needs were already growing as his diminished. He could only hope that their next few years together would produce the understanding necessary for him to accept gracefully her need for lovers and for Katy to be discreet. His one fear was that Lord Kerry would be that lover, and he would lose her entirely; it was not a subject he lingered on.

They returned to Georgetown in mid-July, after a long, excruciating trip by wagon. Katy immediately proved her husband's concern about gossip ill-founded. She collapsed on the last day of their journey and was carried off to bed, necessitating a call for the doctor, thus convincing all inter-ested parties that she had indeed left childbed too early and that the story of premature birth was a true one. The infant's tiny size was accepted as conclusive evidence, and the fact that the few women close enough to be allowed to see her were childless and knew nothing of newborns went unnoticed.

Katy's collapse was not feigned. The return journey had drained what little strength she had regained, and the doctor ordered complete bedrest and a strengthening diet, threaten-ing her with the possible loss of infant's milk if she did not comply. That he knew the infant to be a good deal older than a newborn did not signify: it was not his business to talk about the town's leading citizen or any other, and the doctor kept his mouth closed.

Kerry had been notified of his daughter's birth, but there had been no further communication between them. Charles considered his wife's health of first importance and made no attempt to contact her guardian after their arrival. Knowing Kerry, he figured he would arrive soon enough.

Charles's calculations were correct. Exactly one week after the Stockbridges' return, the matched bays pranced up to the house and an immaculately dressed Lord Kerry stepped from the cab of his newly acquired barouche and signaled the driver to wait. Sir Charles watched from the window of his study as the younger man eagerly scanned the windows of the house he was about to enter; his step as he approached was that of a man visibly restraining himself. Sir Charles sighed and poured himself a glass of wine, preparing himself for the interview ahead.

Kerry followed quickly on the heels of the servant's introduction, extending his hand and warmly shaking that of his host. "I apologize if I am overhasty, but I could not wait another day longer. Throw me out if I am intruding, but I beg of you, do not do it until you have told me how they are."

Charles could not help liking the young lord. He had often enough wished he could have had a son like this one, and there was no use in denying it now. He motioned Kerry to sit. "I have no intention of throwing you out, Southerland. You're as welcome here as ever. I have rather been expecting you," he admitted wryly, pouring a glass of wine and offering it to his guest.

"I heard of your arrival days ago, but I did not wish to intrude immediately. Only this morning I heard Katy was seriously ill, and I could not wait longer to guess at the truth of rumors. How is she? And the babe?" Kerry did not seem to be aware of the glass in his hand after accepting it, as he intently watched his host's movements.

Charles remained standing, moving idly about the room as he spoke. "I think you ought to know we almost lost both of them at birth. My sister-in-law said that some women seem to worry themselves sick about childbirth until they no longer have the strength to bear the child naturally. She seemed to think Katy one of these, and she did everything in her power to keep Katy healthy, but it almost wasn't enough." He stopped and sipped his wine before continuing, staring out the window and not directly at the man teetering at the edge of his chair. "You and I know that Katy is not the type to worry about something as natural as childbirth, that she was under other, more painful pressures." He paused, waiting for this to sink in.

When Kerry bowed his head, Charles went on. "I had hoped that the security of marriage would relieve her of some of the strain she has been under, and eventually it may, but right now she needs all the reassurance she can get that she has done the right thing. I am not the man to give her that reassurance.'' His voice became stern as he turned and stared directly at Kerry.

"I will support you in whatever way I can," Kerry replied quietly. He had little other choice. This was the man Katy had chosen for husband; to protect her happiness, he would do anything. "She is still ill, then?"

"She contracted a fever after giving birth. It would have killed any normal woman in her weakened condition, but Katy has a tremendous will to live. She has not fully recovered. Today is the first day she has been up since we arrived home." Charles spoke tersely, setting the wineglass down on the tray and seating himself behind the desk.

"Do you wish me to leave, then?" The painful effort it cost him to ask this was apparent on Kerry's face as he waited for a reply.

Sir Charles relaxed. The man was not a fool—he would know what was required of him without being told. "Without seeing your daughter? I am not so cruel as that." The relief on Kerry's face was so evident, he nearly laughed aloud. "Katy is in the nursery with her now. Go on up and get acquainted with your offspring. I will not interfere."

Kerry was on his feet and halfway out the door before the words were out of Charles's mouth. He stopped in the doorway and asked, "I bought a few things in Charleston for everyone. Will it be all right . . . ?"

Charles waved his hand in dismissal. "You have spoiled the women this long, until they have come to expect it. You may as well continue now. I'll call someone to carry them up for you."

Kerry grinned gratefully and bounded up the stairs two at a time.

Katy was rocking the infant Maureen and listening to Anna's vivid rendition of an old fairy tale when Lord Kerry appeared in the doorway. Absorbed in the tranquillity of this occupation, she did not notice him immediately, and he hovered quietly out of sight, taking in every detail of the domestic scene before him.

Anxiously he scanned Katy's pale face. The shadowed darkness beneath her eyes and the new hollows beneath her cheekbones added contrast to her pastel prettiness, but bore the tale of pain and weariness too well. Her gown hung loosely about her already too-slender figure, leaving the impression she was made of ghostly substance and would disappear at the first whisper of breeze. His heart contracted tightly at this image, until he observed the direction of her violet gaze, and he felt the stirrings of new joy at the sight of the child she held so tenderly.

Some movement must have given him away, for Katy and Anna both looked up at the same time, Anna springing to her feet and running to hug him as Katy had once done, while Katy waited with warm happiness for him to come to her. Not taking his eyes off the waiting figure, Kerry caught Anna up in his arms and squeezed her delightedly, then proceeded to carry her across the room to Katy.

"You timed that well, milord. Anna has just finished her story and Maureen is ready to start on hers. She has learned to gurgle most convincingly." The radiant smile she gave him made everything else easy; there were to be no repercussions, no further scenes, just a calm return to their previous friendship.

Kerry set Anna down and whispered loudly in her ear, "If you will run down to my carriage, you may find a thing or two for yourself in it, but don't tell anyone."

Giggling delightedly, Anna ran off, leaving the two adults alone for the first time in six months.

Staring down at mother and daughter, wishing to hold them both but not daring to move for fear of breaking the spell binding them, Kerry left it to Katy to make the first move.

Seeing his longing, she held out the wide-awake infant. "Would you care to hold your daughter, sir? I have been selfish in keeping her to myself these many months."

Awkwardly Kerry accepted the small bundle and tried to position it so all the tiny fingers and toes did not escape. Entranced by this living, breathing embodiment of himself and Katy, he soon lost his awkwardness in the eagerness of his inspection. Katy's fair hair curled enticingly about tiny ears and neck, but the startling green eyes staring back at him held him captivated, their dark lashes forming enormous circles in the small face.

While tiny fingers wrapped themselves around his large one, Kerry commented, "You have named her well. She has her grandmother's eyes."

"Not to mention her father's," Katy replied, smiling. That the child had her mother's hair, everyone noticed, but so far only Charles had commented on the telltale eyes.

Kerry grinned broadly. "Have you begun explaining how two blue-eyed parents produced this green-eyed monster?"

"I am an orphan, remember? Who knows what color the eyes of my parents might have been?" Katy asked half-seriously. She knew she was not a convincing liar, so had concocted this defense as close to the truth as possible.

"I am willing to wager one of them had the most beautiful pair of violet eyes I have ever seen, but then, I am prejudiced." Speaking softly, adoration evident in his eyes, Kerry added, "She is beautiful, Katy. I only wish I could have shared the suffering; it does not seem quite fair that I receive only the pleasure."

"The next time she has a bellyache and screams all night, I will send her to you."

"Send whom to where? Do you mind if I join you? I have never celebrated Christmas in July before." Sir Charles appeared in the doorway, followed by Kerry's driver and a maid, both carrying stacks of packages. Anna burst through them all, carrying her gifts and beaming ecstatically.

"Katy, look what Lord Kerry brought me! I know it is mine because it is too big for Maureen and too little for you." She flaunted a powder-blue riding habit in front of her, the hat tilted precariously on her head. "And there's another one just like it and I bet it's for you. Can we go riding with Lord Kerry now, Papa?" She jumped about excitedly.

Lord Kerry watched with detached amusement. He had seen this scene played too often in the Stockbridge home, and now, holding his daughter, he felt more at home with it than ever. He caught Sir Charles's amused look and returned it, remaining an observer for the moment.

"We will have to wait for Katy to feel better before anyone does any riding. Then you must wait for an invitation from

Lord Kerry. Why don't you go try the habit on to see if it will fit?'' Sir Charles tried to slow down the whirlwind of excitement that was his daughter, but Anna was too thrilled at being once more with one of her favorite people and wouldn't be parted so easily.

"It will fit, I know it will. Lord Kerry always gets the sizes right. Besides, he says Lady Jane is my pony and I can ride her anytime I wish. Can't I? But I will wait until Katy can ride with me,'' she amended her brashness, sitting down beside Katy.

"I will settle the point by hereby offering a standing invitation to Twin Oaks. I wish to make you the first visitors to my new home, though it is not quite livable yet.'' Leaning back to support the wall with his broad shoulders, Kerry made a strange face and moved his daughter a few inches from his good broadcloth coat, revealing a growing dark wet spot where the infant had rested.

Katy began to giggle and Sir Charles actually grinned as his wife rushed to Kerry's rescue, removing the damp infant from his arms. Maureen's delighted gurgles at all the attention she was receiving compounded the merriment and even Kerry had to give in to it. It was a sensation he had not openly enjoyed in months, and it felt good, eliminating any remaining tension he harbored.

While Katy changed the baby and Anna willingly opened the gifts Kerry had brought for his daughter, they talked about the house going up on the plantation and Kerry's new acquisition of slaves to work his fields as well as aid in building. During their absence, he had successfully harvested and sold last year's crops with the aid of a neighboring plantation owner, reinvesting the profits by buying the best workers he had hired the year before. With the help of Mahomet, he had built quarters for his new field hands and their families, and once that was done, they started on the big house. Spring planting had slowed the building's progress considerably, but a few experienced carpenters and plasterers had been hired to do the majority of the work, and it rapidly approached completion. The interior had yet to be finished, glass for windows had to be ordered, and Kerry was still sleeping on a makeshift bed in one of the downstairs rooms, but everything would come with time.

It did not take much persuading to keep Lord Kerry for dinner, and even Katy felt well enough to join them. The topic turned to the success of Sir Charles's business under the management of his assistant, and his desire to spend more time with his family now that there was no need to be constantly working. From there they went on to Kerry's trip to Virginia and the governor's offer to create an Office of Indian Affairs if Kerry would accept the post. Now that the situation had lessened to some extent, Kerry thought the post unnecessary and had declined, but the position remained open for the taking. He made no mention of unscrupulous gun dealers or of Joshua Halberstam, and Katy breathed more easily. Perhaps all would be well now.

They talked late into the evening, catching up on a year's worth of news and information. After securing Kerry's agreement to the christening date two weeks hence, Katy retired and left the men talking as if there had never been any differences between them. That the man she loved and the man she had married could get along so amicably was a constant source of amazement to Katy, but she suffered it gladly, not realizing their love for her was the binding factor in their relationship.

September 1736

BY THE FIRST of September Katy's health had recovered enough for her to be granted permission to make the grand tour of Lord Kerry's newly built home.

As the Stockbridge carriage rolled around the familiar bend to Kerry's homestead, Katy gasped in surprise and awe. Towering between the two mighty oaks that gave the place its name, Twin Oaks gleamed brilliantly in the white glare of the morning sun. The porticoed two-story mansion rose from the top of a knoll, giving a clear view of the river below.

There were no house servants as yet, and Lord Kerry himself advanced down the wide sweep of stairs to greet his first visitors.

As Katy took his hand to descend from the carriage, a familiar tingle coursed through her veins, and Kerry grasped her fingers a little tighter, searching violet eyes for shared memories of this place.

Anna erupted from the carriage, dispelling the moment, insisting on visiting the stables first. Her father made a wry grimace and with an understanding look at the young couple with babe in arms, fell in with his daughter's demands, leaving Katy and Kerry to explore the house alone.

"He knows you well, does he not?" Kerry inquired mildly, looking down into Katy's upturned face.

"Better than most, I imagine." The sun turned gold-tinged highlights of hair into a shimmering halo of curls as she gazed up at him.

"Not better than I, kitten." Hastily stepping over that enigmatic remark, Kerry added, "Let us get our sleepy miss in out of the sun, and I will show you what I have done." Taking the heavy burden of carrying the infant from Katy, he escorted her up the stairs on one arm while holding the sleeping babe in the other, and they entered the heavy front doors as a family returning home.

The empty, wide entrance hall was filled with light from the south-facing entrance windows, but the room to the right captured the eye. Ablaze with morning sunlight, the generously proportioned salon was virtually constructed of windows, eclipsing the sunny Stockbridge drawing room entirely. It had been Katy's fondness for that familiar room which gave Kerry the idea of creating a room made for sunlight, but he had taken it even further with his wall of windows, completely demolishing the usual Georgian style of the architects.

Katy gave one ecstatic gasp, then flew from panel to panel, admiring the myriad views of the plantation as it lay exposed around them. Only the river was out of sight from this vantage point, but rolling acres of pastureland and forest made a verdant backdrop for the glass-enclosed room.

"You need plants in the windows, to bring the outdoors in. Large ones to fill the spaces between panels, and small ones to admire." Not needing to close her eyes to imagine the way the room should look when complete, Katy spun around excitedly, the possibilities for filling such magnificent space brimming over and spilling out without thought.

"No draperies, only swags, and then only in the lightest colors—golds, I think. And the furniture must be light so the sun does not fade it, in greens and golds so it is part of the landscape, too. It is beautiful, Kerry! I could never have dreamed of such a room." Skirts sweeping the floor as she danced about, Katy gave herself up to admiration.

Not the room, but the slender figure flitting from window to window like a caged butterfly held Kerry's admiration. For the first time in months, Katy appeared healthy again, her golden hair glowing with life, cheeks flushed with color, eyes sparkling with excitement. Her figure no longer held the girlish reediness of before, but had rounded beautifully to the womanly perfection her youth had promised. Kerry's fingers ached to span that tiny waistline, but he held tight to his daughter and his inclinations.

"I am glad you like it, kitten, and it is just such suggestions I wish to hear. I know nothing of the fripperies that attend interiors. It needs a woman's touch."

Katy swirled about the room one more time and returned to his side, ideas tumbling about faster than she could hold them, overwhelmed with the prospect of having the chance to decorate such a palace. "You will need paint and paneling and all sorts of things to finish the interior. However will you find all that?" Eyes gleaming with excitement, mind racing ahead of her words, she did not wait for an answer or notice the shadow crossing Kerry's face. "May I see the rest? Please? Is it all so beautiful?"

Relieved that he was not forced to answer her questions as yet, Kerry led the way to the other downstairs rooms. There was a study as well as a library, and a room just for dining that encompassed most of the rear of the building and looked out over another veranda and the river vista. Enchanted by the love and skill that had gone into all she saw, Katy floated from room to room on the wings of awe. She had known Kerry to be an exceptional man, but all the patience and labor that this house represented went deeper than she had ever been allowed to see into him. It was as if he were opening himself up to her for the first time, and her chatter quieted as his tour continued.

When they returned to the polished mahogany railing of the circular staircase at the rear of the entrance hall, they both stopped involuntarily, taking a quick assessment of their emotions before going on. Sir Charles and Anna had not yet returned, and the tension between them had heightened dramatically in the last half-hour, without either one saying a personal word.

"Would you care to wait for Charles before continuing?" Kerry asked politely, watching violet eyes for some clue to her thoughts. She had grown silent in these last minutes, and he wondered uneasily if he had given too much away. He had created this house with Katy in mind in every nook and cranny and cupboard. Knowing her tastes as well as his own, he had heard her voice with every panel laid and molding set, and her words today were only echoes of what he already knew. Was it possible that she could sense this from empty laths and dusty planks?

"He will catch up to us in his own good time. Let us go on." Brushing a stray hair from the face of the sleeping infant, Katy took Kerry's arm and waited for him to lead the way. Convinced nothing more than simple friendship existed between them, she laid the blame for their tension on her excitement and Kerry's eagerness to see his efforts appreciated. Through sheer willpower she laid to rest all else that had been between them except the one fact that could not be denied: they had bred a child together. This fact she simply laid to the hands of fate.

They skirted through the empty upstairs bedrooms, the dust of plaster and wood thicker here and the bare walls looking naked and unadorned. Still, with a little imagination, the rooms were quickly paneled and painted and dressed in suitable style with Katy's vivid descriptions, and even Kerry came to see how they would look once completed.

Before they entered the final wing of the house, they heard Anna's chatter echoing in the hollow rooms below, and they stopped at the head of the stair to call down. The dark heads of Sir Charles and Anna soon appeared below them and a minute later they were all together in the upper hallway, with Anna's excitement filling in all the empty spaces of the adults' conversation. There was a moment's adjustment as the young couple and their child broke apart and reformed again as a different family, and Kerry once more became the gracious host and outsider.

"You have missed the main events of the tour, so there is only my final plea for help left to be seen. I was saving that for last. Come, let me show you my room." Kerry led the way down the hall and through the last doorway.

A large sitting room led into an even larger bedroom whose
north walls were broken by French doors leading out onto a
balcony stretching the length of the rear of the house, giving
an inviting view of the river from every angle of the room.
Katy stopped in the center of the room and stared around her,
finally seeing the farmyard and fields she had grown to love
in the few weeks of her last stay, seeing them as she had that
summer when the elegant gentleman beside her had stridden
through them shirtless and sweating, exulting in his power to
make the land produce, telling his dreams to the young girl
who walked breathlessly beside him.

The memory glimmered in her eyes as she glanced up into
Kerry's open face, and she read it again in his expression.
That summer was gone, but not forgotten, and this would
have been her room now had she wanted, shared with the
man who shared her memories and had built this room in
token of them. Katy's eyes widened at this unbidden thought,
and she quickly shoved it away. It was only Lord Kerry
standing there, staring at her now, and her husband had his
hand on her shoulder while his words flowed on around them.

Kerry's reply to something said by Sir Charles broke Katy's
reverie, and she again returned her attention to the conversation.

"Furnishing it will be a problem, yes. Southerland House
has quite a few pieces I can probably use and they will gladly
relinquish, but this is where I wish to enlist Katy's aid, if
possible." Catching Katy's eye and seeing he had her full
attention, Kerry continued. "I need someone with more decorating skills than I to tell me what paints and paneling the
rooms will need, and what furniture and draperies would be
suitable for each of the rooms. Your suggestions today, Katy,
have already transformed the place for me. If I could only
persuade you to make more complete lists, it will aid my
shopping immensely."

Katy stared at him thoughtfully. There was a tension beneath his casual request that did not match his words. "My
suggestions were only idle dreams, milord; they could not
possibly be fulfilled with the materials available here or in
Charleston." Sensing some return to their past relationship,
she reverted to her former mode of address.

"I realize that, Katy—that is why I am returning to England shortly. With the aid of your lists, I will ask my sister's help in securing all that I need to return again next spring with the makings of a new household.'' Green eyes pleaded for understanding, as if they were the only two in the room.

Anna had disappeared down the hallway, but Charles's hand tightened on his wife's shoulder as he felt her slight figure tense. Kerry's eventual return to England was inevitable; it simply had not occurred to them it would be so soon.

"I am not certain it is my place to take on such a personal task, Kerry." She forced the name between her lips to remind her of the present and not the past, when he had left her so many times before. "Your sister will have a better knowledge of what furnishings will be appropriate, and someday you will have a wife who will wish to decorate the house to suit her tastes. You would be better off waiting for their aid than asking mine."

"I trust your judgment, Katy. My sister has never seen the house, and if someday I should find a wife to live here, she may make whatever changes she wishes. In the meantime, I would like your advice."

They had reached a stalemate. Knowing Katy's desire to put her imagination to work, understanding her reluctance to accept Kerry's request, Charles stepped in to ease the impasse.

"Katy, I can see no harm in your making a few suggestions for Kerry to abide by if he wishes. Lists can be thrown away if they become unnecessary, but you will still have had the pleasure of making them. I find Kerry's request quite reasonable."

Gratefully the younger pair turned to Sir Charles as he spoke, yielding to his wisdom. Katy broke into a smile as he finished, and the tension vanished.

"You are spoiling me, as usual, but I will do it. Halfway across the Atlantic, Kerry may toss the lists to the winds, but in my eyes, the house will always be done as I see it."

With that decision, they made a merry luncheon of Bertha's picnic basket, and after that Katy wandered into a shady grove of trees overlooking the area while the others spread out to enjoy themselves in whatever way took their fancy. With the infant Maureen at her breast, Katy leaned against a tree, the effort of avoiding all thought making her sleepy.

She hadn't realized she slept until she woke with a start and felt eyes upon her. Glancing up quickly, she found Kerry lazily standing with his back against a tree, arms crossed, as he gazed at her with an inscrutable expression.

"Are you happy, Katy?" The question was blurted out, without any attempt to preface it.

Without looking at him, Katy replied musingly, "I am content. That is more than most can say."

"You will let me leave with only that to say? I would like to leave knowing you to be happy and in safe hands." Throwing himself from the tree, Kerry bent down on one knee to better read the violet depths of her eyes.

Riveted by the contact with his gaze, Katy did not answer immediately, and when she did, it was hesitatingly. "I . . . could be in no safer hands."

She stopped. Could she say she was happy? She could, but he would know immediately that she did not tell the entire truth. There were too many sides to happiness to make it an easy state to find. Happiness was the exhilaration of the time he had taken her to the fair and first kissed her, or lying in the darkened hut with nothing between them but their passion, a transitory state at best. Perhaps she had outgrown it. She was content. What more could she say?

"I am not unhappy, if that helps. I will miss you."

"You and Charles seem to be well satisfied with your arrangement; you make . . . an admirable couple." With a bitter grimace, Kerry added, "I could not have found you a better husband."

Holding back the tears stinging her eyes, Katy replied stiffly, "We had best go back down and join the others. They will be looking for us."

Kerry caught her shoulder and held her in place. "I have not said any of the things I came to say; we may not be alone again before I go. You distract me into saying things I do not mean to say."

He touched a finger to the outstretched palm of his daughter and watched tiny fingers curl about it. "I have written my brother of the existence of my offspring and the circumstances surrounding my breach of promise. He has excused my indiscretion and applauds your decision to marry and give the child a name. As a matter of fact, I think he approves of your actions more than of mine, but then, I have never been known for my prudence.''

Kerry shrugged lightly and continued. ''Anyway, he agrees that a trust should be set aside for Maureen's upbringing and dowry so that Sir Charles may leave his estate entirely to his own children. I would not wish to deprive Anna of what is rightfully hers, and I have acted accordingly. Charles knows and protests, but he cannot stop me. So whatever happens in the future, Maureen will always be provided for. I intend to take my share of the responsibility for her.''

The tears spilled over and Katy made no effort to stop them. ''I never doubted your intentions, Kerry, but it is your presence and not your money that I require. It always has been, though you never seemed aware of it. Just a piece of your time now and then is all I ask, if that is not too extravagant a request.''

A smile broke across his face like the sun coming from behind a cloud. ''With an invitation such as that, I will be living on your doorstep. I feared you might find my frequent presence a burdensome interference; you have your own life to live now, and my place in it is small.'' He produced a spotless handkerchief and began to wipe her eyes. ''I did not mean to make you cry, kitten. I only wished to assure you that our daughter's future is safe with me.''

Katy took the handkerchief from his hands and dried her tears. ''If you don't know me better than that by now, you will never learn. Now, help me up from here and let us go back down before you have me crying again. I hate it when you go away.'' She returned the handkerchief and held tightly to the hand clasping hers.

Kerry stood and pulled her to her feet, taking the sleeping infant from her arms. ''I wish I could promise never to go away again, but you know I can't.'' The smile was still there, but his gaze was thoughtful as he studied her averted face. She had never spoken so openly of her feelings before, and he wondered what chord he had touched to produce this effect. Or perhaps she felt safer now that she was married, and the need to conceal her emotions was not so great. A sense of loss filled his chest.

"I don't expect you to. I have always known my place in your life, and I do not expect Maureen's birth to change it. Your family comes first, and that is the way it should be until you have a family of your own over here. You will be happier once you are with them." Katy lifted her skirts and started down the path to the house, not wishing to watch his face.

Kerry resisted the temptation to state he had a family of his own over here. For once she was wrong about something, but it would only frighten her to know how drastically his feelings had changed. He did not think the few months apart would change them—he had already learned that lesson the hard way—but he could not go on living as he had in the past. He must look ahead to the future, and that path lay in the direction of England.

December 1736

KERRY'S leaving left a gaping hole in the fabric of their lives, but with the arrival of the Christmas holidays a southerly breeze blew in Charles's ship, and with it, Jake. Anna danced excitedly at this unexpected arrival and Katy insisted he share the holiday as guest.

With a hesitant glance over Katy's shoulder to her stalwart husband for approval, Jake smiled with relief at his employer's nod of acceptance. When told of Katy's marriage to the older, wealthy Sir Charles, Jake had accepted the news with grace and some relief that she had found someone to take care of her when he could not. Yet he still found it difficult to think of the little governess as Lady Stockbridge.

The discovery of the infant in the nursery, however, was a blow from which he found it difficult to recover. Finding himself gazing down into the same pair of laughing green eyes he had good reason to remember, Jake muttered a dismayed ''Good God!'' and turned a tortured gaze to the violet eyes of his dreams. ''Katy?'' The agonized note of his whisper formed his question without words.

Katy nodded slowly, kissed the child, and offered her to

Jake to hold. "It is a long story, and Charles will tell it better than I. Try not to think less of me until you hear it." Her arms fell to her sides as Jake gingerly took the infant.

"I could kill the bastard," Jake muttered through clenched teeth.

Katy laid a reassuring hand on his rough jacket, wishing there were some easy way to wipe the anguish from his face. "Jake, you have never known how much Lord Kerry has done for me. If it were not for him, I would be working a house in Saffron Hill or walking the streets of London right now. Don't look so shocked, it happens." If it were true you had to be cruel to be kind, she was doing the kindest possible thing for him, but why did it have to hurt so much?

"Talk to Charles and let him explain. You will see that Lord Kerry only did what was necessary, and he is the one who has suffered the most from it. I have Charles and Maureen and Anna to comfort me; he has no one."

Jake looked down at the cherubic spirit in his arms, her joyous expression putting truth to Katy's words, and he fought to hide the despair threatening to engulf him. He had never considered Sir Charles as a challenge to him; Lord Kerry was the opponent he had to fight for Katy's affections. As long as she was married, he had thought her safe, but he could see now that he had lost. Whatever had happened between them in that Indian camp, it had produced this child and sealed Katy's feelings forever. She would never be his now.

With a tearing sense of loss, Jake returned the infant to Katy. "She is beautiful, Katy. She must make you very happy."

At this glimmer of understanding, Katy broke into a joyful smile and kissed his cheek. "Thank you, Jake. You have always been the best of friends. You will not stay away so long this time?"

"I don't know. The sea ain't in my blood, but it's the only thing I know to do. I'll just have to wait and see what happens." He had a standing offer to work for Lord Kerry ever since the Indian escapade, but had been unable to take to the idea of working for a man who would dishonor Katy. Now, more than ever, it seemed impossible to accept. He would make no decision yet, but there seemed little point in continuing a life at sea if the riches he made would not win him Katy.

The holiday was happier for Jake's arrival. Anna clung to him as a special gift sent just for her, and Jake recovered some of his good spirits with the attention he received. Like Katy, he had no family, and to share a holiday with friends in a home, not on a ship, was an exhilarating experience, and he showed his appreciation in any way he could. He even grew fond of the tiny Maureen and carried her about the house like a pet puppy, leaving the maids giggling at the sight of the tall man trailing about the house with two children in tow.

Kerry's gifts came as a bittersweet offering. That he had taken the time to locate the perfect items for everyone in the household, from the cook, Bertha, on up to Sir Charles himself, was a revelation in itself, and Katy marveled at the thought that went into each gift. Perhaps he had been homesick when he chose them.

But as she opened the packages containing the finest paints and brushes available in all London, a copy of *The Taming of the Shrew* by Shakespeare, and a bottle of the light perfume she favored but could not buy in the colonies, tears rolled down her cheeks, and she had to make some excuse to leave the room before someone saw them. All the gifts were perfectly appropriate between guardian and ward, but each one held a meaning closer to her heart than she cared to admit. That night, she lay in her husband's arms and dreamed of the man she could never have.

A few weeks later, Katy had reason to regret her disloyalty to the man who had given her a home when no one else would. Sir Charles had never fully recovered his good health and stamina after the fever that nearly took his life, but the aches and pains he suffered he blamed on age and hid from his young wife. Until a chill from a cold January downpour brought the doctor to the house again, Katy was unaware of his illness. When the chill went into pneumonia, the doctor thought it time that Katy learn the truth.

"It's a type of pleurisy of the lungs, Lady Stockbridge. There isn't any known cure for it, and it usually gets worse instead of better. This chill has aggravated it more than usual. With proper care we might bring him out of it this time, but he will have to be very careful in the future. I do not mean to frighten you, but I must ask for your cooperation in following all my orders as carefully as possible if we are to return him to health at all.''

While they stood in the drawing room discussing the proper procedures in the care of the invalid, Katy ached to be beside her husband. He had always seemed so healthy and full of life, she had never given thought to being parted from him, and she was suddenly filled with terror at the possibility of his death. She felt if she were beside him, holding his hand, talking as they spent so many evenings doing, he could not possibly leave her, and she wished for the doctor to leave so she might start up at once. Tears of frustration filled her eyes, and she hurried the doctor out most improperly, before racing up the stairs to be with Charles.

Sir Charles was confined to his bed for the remainder of the winter, while Katy lived by his side, nursing him through fevers and coughs with remedies from the doctor—and if they were not satisfactory, from potions of her own or Mahomet's.

Whether it was his strong constitution or Katy's nursing or a combination of the two, Charles survived the bout of pneumonia and made it through the winter, though the weakness in his lungs made breathing difficult and recovery slow. Unable to be up and about for long periods of time, he left most of his business to the young assistant he had been grooming these last years, conducting only those affairs that could be handled at home in his study.

If Sir Charles was resentful of his weakness, no complaint passed his lips. Grateful for Katy's loving care when he most needed her, he would not burden her further with his fears and worries. His greatest concern became his inability to satisfy the physical desires he knew his young wife to possess. He had come to enjoy the charms of her responsiveness in bed, and he fondly believed it had brought him closer to winning her heart than anything else he might do. If he had to spend the remainder of his life as a sickly, helpless old man, he loved her too much to saddle her with the entire burden of his care and none of the pleasures she so richly deserved.

Too occupied to be aware of her husband's anxieties, Katy felt none of the consuming need that she had shown in the early months of their marriage. It was as if with Lord Kerry's departure and her husband's ill health, she had lost a part of herself, and she spent no time regaining it. Her hours were filled with the care of her husband, a household, and a mischievous imp now approaching a year of age and already walking. If Katy missed the physical pleasures of marriage, she gave herself no time to think about it.

With the first warm winds of March, her thoughts, instead, flew to Lord Kerry's imminent arrival, adding a small measure of sunshine to the long, dreary days of winter's end. It would be good to see him again, to hear his laughter fill the solemn rooms with lively merriment, to feel the bright twinkle of his eyes as he observed the antics of his small daughter. That chances were good he would return with a wife bothered her not at all, or so Katy told herself. He would be happier if he brought home a wife to grace his mansion, and Katy was certain it would in no way interfere with their friendship. She had gained much confidence in the past year of their strange relationship, and she awaited eagerly the sound of prancing hoofbeats outside the door.

But Kerry gave them no such advance warning. Arriving in Charleston with his shipload of furnishings, he decided to return with them upriver by boat, with the intention of going straight through to Twin Oaks. But the familiar sight of the shipyards at Georgetown struck him with a yearning so deep, he made the boat captain let him off there while the goods went on to the plantation without him.

Telling himself it had been six months since he had seen his daughter, Kerry excused the eagerness he felt as he drew nearer the large house at the edge of town. There had been no sign of the stocky figure of Sir Charles at the shipyards; perhaps he was home for luncheon. If Kerry felt disappointment at this thought, he did not acknowledge it. His eyes were so firmly fixed on the house ahead, he did not see the waves of greeting from passersby.

Katy was sitting, sewing, in the drawing room with Sir Charles. His recumbent figure rested uneasily on a settee not made for lying down, a compromise elicted by his wife when he refused to retire to the bedroom. In this way he received the satisfaction of Katy's company and a chance to be involved in household activities while she guaranteed the rest he needed. Despite the discomfort of his position, they were both satisfied with the arrangement.

Not expecting midday visitors, they met the knock at the door with raised eyebrows and waited with curiosity for the maid to answer the door. Katy knotted the thread in the piece she had finished, breaking it off as the maid came in to announce their visitor, but Kerry had not waited for this formality, following close on the heels of the startled black girl.

Before the maid could utter a word, Katy dropped her sewing, flying across the room with a cry of "Kerry!" in the same manner she had once done when she was younger. Kerry caught her by the waist and swung her around in joyous greeting, forgetting everything but the happiness of sparkling violet eyes and the familiar slender waist in his hands. For a moment they were the only two in the room, until a polite cough drew them back to earth and to the twinkling eyes of Sir Charles.

"Now that the first act of your return has already set the servants gossiping, would you be so kind as to return my wife to her feet and take a seat like the grown man you purport to be?" Charles asked dryly. Sure of Katy's devotion, he wasted no efforts on jealousy, preferring to succumb to the infectiousness of her excitement. She had led a dreary life these last few months, and he would not deny her an innocent moment's pleasure.

Flushed as much from excitement as from embarrassment at her wayward behavior, Katy hastily retreated to her armchair, leaving the floor to a grinning Lord Kerry. As always, he looked tanned and handsome, and she could see little change in the well-loved twinkle of green eyes, but there was a difference somewhere beneath the surface, a new strength of determination she would have to investigate further. That he arrived unannounced and without a wife told her much in itself.

"You have certainly become a gentleman of leisure to lie about at midday like this. Has catering to a houseful of women become too much for you?" Kerry continued his cheery front as he settled into the nearest chair, but he had instantly noted with concern the change in his friend. Hair now almost completely silvered, Charles showed the signs of age in other ways. Illness had shrunk his stocky build to wrinkled flesh, and only the serenity of pale blue eyes remained unchanged in the lined face. For the first time in his life, Sir Charles looked his age or more, and Kerry felt a grinding misery deep in his soul as he switched his gaze from the aging figure on the settee to the youthful loveliness of his nineteen-year-old wife.

"I do not know what I would do without my harem. They wait on me hand and foot, and the youngest has appointed herself court jester; I have been thoroughly spoiled. But I am sure you have not come to discuss my idleness. Katy, why don't you take Kerry to his daughter before his impatience gets the better of him? It will be easier to carry on a sensible conversation when he is able to quit fidgeting and concentrate on the talk." Unwilling to discuss his health with the younger man, Charles dismissed him to let Katy do the explaining.

On the stairway, Katy answered Kerry's questioning look in a hushed voice. "The doctor says it is a pleurisy of the lungs. I do not know what that means, but it leaves him very weak, and he is a long time recuperating from a chill he received this past winter. I am hoping with the return of sun and warmth, he will recover more rapidly."

She did not mention the doctor's admonitions about his health never being fully recovered and possibly worsening with the onset of the next winter. Katy considered these words the pessimism of a cynical man and refused to repeat them. It would be only a matter of time before her husband regained his health again.

"Why didn't you mention this in your letters? I had no inkling of the situation here . . ." Kerry halted in the hallway outside the nursery door and studied more closely the translucent blue skin beneath her eyes. There was no sign of last summer's frail weakness, but it was as if her vitality had been sapped with the passage of time, leaving a ghost of the exuberant spirit he had once known.

"There was nothing you could do, and I had no wish to worry you. Besides, writing cheerful letters made me feel better than self-pitying ones would, and now he is getting

better, I have saved us both a lot of trouble." Katy smiled
brightly at Kerry's dubious frown.

"Let us hope so, kitten. You have had your share of
nursing invalids, and I would not wish you saddled with
another." At the disapproving pucker of Katy's brow, he
smiled and added lightly, "Thank you for the cheerful letters,
though. The sketches of Maureen helped lighten many a
dreary day, though I lost many to my mother when I made
the mistake of showing her her namesake. She was enchanted
with them, if not too pleased with me."

"You didn't!" Katy's hands fled to her cheeks. "Kerry,
how could you tell your mother . . ." Her sentence floundered as she searched for appropriate words.

"That I have fathered a bastard? Very simple, my dear
Katy. I proudly brought out your sketches at what I considered a most opportune time . . ." Kerry stopped and grinned
at the sight of her shoulders shaking with ill-contained laughter.

"And I can well imagine what you considered to be opportune." Katy attempted to speak severely, but the scene was
too clear in her imagination, and she had to check a smile at
the thought of Kerry grandly producing her hasty sketches in
the presence of the duchess. "You were being chastised for
not marrying and producing offspring, and you could not
resist the temptation to show off. You are shameless. And
what must your family think of me?"

"Actually, they quite admire you for withstanding not only
the whims of fate but also my whims. My sister claims it is
about time some woman had the good sense to put me in my
place, and my mother is grateful for your attentions to her
only son in the face of adversity, although she modifies that
by adding I was scarcely worth it. Now that you can see what
sort of family I have, you can understand why I felt no shame
in confessing the existence of my beautiful daughter." He
spoke lightly, teasingly, admiring the return of sparkle to her
violet eyes. She was sadly in need of laughter, and he was
lucky she could not guess how badly he needed the same.

"Yes, well your beautiful daughter is about as shameless
as her father and is no doubt doing anything but napping at
the moment and will charm her way out of a scolding as
usual. Do not spoil her any more than she is, I beg of you."

Suddenly too aware of his proximity, Katy turned to the nursery door and away from his masculine solidity. It had been a year and a half since she had rested in his arms, but the memory burned so indelibly on her skin, it seemed like yesterday, and she could not bear the pain.

They entered the nursery together, and as Katy had predicted, Maureen had toddled from bed to window seat and was busily engaged in decorating the wall with a piece of charcoaled stick. At the sight of her mother, she beamed proudly at the opportunity to show off her handiwork, but the tall stranger next to her caused the toddler to hesitate.

"I see she has inherited more than her beautiful hair from her mother," Kerry commented dryly upon discovering his daughter's artistic display.

Katy scooped her wayward daughter into her arms and hugged her tight. "She has seen me drawing and apparently thought to do the same, but that is no excuse for being out of bed, you naughty thing," she finished with a scolding admonition that was contradicted by the proud gleam in her eyes. Maureen ignored the warning, her green gaze fastening on the man at her mother's side, one finger stuck in her small mouth as she studied him closely.

Kerry gravely took a tiny fist in his large hand and shook it. "It is good to see you again, my little one."

Not removing the finger from her mouth, eyes widened in a gesture reminiscent of her mother, the little girl replied equally gravely, "Da-da." Then, grinning delightedly at this new sound she made, she repeated it, "Da-da." Flinging her arms out to be held, she went eagerly to the now laughing stranger.

"You are raising our precocious daughter to be a terrible flirt, madam," Kerry laughed, his face lost behind a tousled mop of white-gold curls as the little imp attempted to reach his hair ribbon.

"I need teach her nothing, she is her father's child in that," Katy commented, heart swelling with love and joy at the sight of father and daughter together, the small blond head on the shoulder of the tall auburn-haired figure creating an image her fingers itched to duplicate on paper. If she had thought her love for this nobleman to be diminished by her love of Charles, that notion was quickly laid to rest. There would never be another man to replace Lord Kerry in her heart.

Kerry sensed the warmth of her gaze and looked down in time to catch the look of love long lashes hastened to hide, and he rejoiced in the discovery. Since leaving London he had worried at his foolishness in rejecting his family's requests that he marry, in favor of the hope that he might one day yet win Katy back. The possibility she might no longer love him, or that he had been wrong in ever thinking she did, haunted him continually throughout the long return voyage. Now that particular ghost was safely laid to rest.

For years he had avoided marriage in hopes of finding the rare woman he might love, and now that he knew he had found her and could not have her, he was too stubborn to concede defeat. He would rather forsake all others and do without before admitting he would never have the pleasure of Katy's love again. Despite his laughter, Kerry's jaw set with firm resolve.

June 1737

AT THE END OF MAY, Katy's twentieth birthday presented the occasion for the next invitation to Twin Oaks. Most of the rooms had been furnished, and Lord Kerry was eager to exhibit the results. There were other reasons behind his week-long invitation, including the knowledge of two new cases of river fever below Georgetown, signifying an early start to the fever season, but these he did not divulge to his guests.

They crossed the portals of the plantation house for a second time, gravitating naturally to the sun-filled "Jungle Room," as Kerry had come to call it. Following Katy's instructions to the slightest detail, it had indeed been transformed into a veritable jungle, open bamboo blinds blocking the heat of a June afternoon but not reducing the light washing over potted trees and plants, vines trailing from elevated hangers, and sweet-scented gardenias tucked in among the mass of foliage for fragrance. The furnishings were sparse and light, many of the pieces cane and bamboo, stolen from the attics of Southerland House, relics of the duke's connections with the British East India Company. The setting was a tropical paradise, and entranced, Katy strolled dazedly through it, gently touching one plant after another as she absorbed the picture of her imagination come to life.

Kerry surrendered his daughter to a waiting maid who delightedly carried the sleeping toddler off to the carefully prepared nursery. Free to turn his attention to his guests, Kerry watched anxiously as the room's designer inspected this vision of a dream come true. There was only one other room he had spent as much time on as this one, and he did not intend to open it for public inspection. This would have to be his contribution to Katy's talents.

"Does it meet your specifications, kitten?" He had never used his pet name for Katy in another's presence before, but Kerry seemed unaware of anyone's existence but his own and Katy's as he awaited approval of this gift so personal he was not certain even the recipient would appreciate it.

Any doubts he may have retained in that regard were instantly dispelled when Katy swung around, the stars in her eyes evident even from this distance. The room had been furnished with all the attention to personal preference and details only love and a keen memory could create: it was Katy's room, from the herbal scented plants in the window to the pair of watercolor miniatures on the wicker table, and Katy could not fail to understand its significance. That she did not believe the evidence of her own eyes was part of the barrier between them, but for an instant the barrier fell away and Katy saw through the intensity of Kerry's green gaze.

The vision broke open the box in which she had hidden away the tumult of emotions that had precipitated her marriage, and only years of self-control kept them from spilling out. With the clang of an iron will, she locked the box closed and recreated the barrier. For that one instant she had let her imagination carry her away and found all her dreams and wishes come true in Kerry's eyes, but with the return of sensibility she could only see her husband and the young lord who was their closest friend and could never be anything more. The possibility of love between them was unthinkable, and Katy closed her eyes and mind against it.

As Katy returned to the safety of her husband's arm, Charles chuckled and answered for her. "Since this is the first time I have ever known Katy to be speechless, you must have done something right. I do not think you have much to worry about in that regard." If he had seen anything in the look exchanged between wife and friend, he dismissed it upon feeling the pressure of Katy's fingers on his arm. He was certain of her loyalty, and jealousy was an emotion he had never felt.

The laughing look returned to Kerry's eyes, disguising whatever emotion had been there earlier. Once again he became the gallant host, showing his guests his latest acquisitions, leading them through the freshly painted hallway to the remaining rooms.

The nursery he saved for last. When Katy stepped into the room's center, she sank to the floor in utter amazement, her skirts billowing about her as she stared helplessly at the changes wrought in this room. Kerry had paid little attention to her recommendations of neutral colors for walls and surfaces and easily changed bright ones for rugs and curtains, and he had doubled her recommendations for furniture, creating two rooms in one. As Maureen toddled delightedly over to join her mother on the floor, Katy tried to take in the meaning of what he had done.

One side of the room had been done entirely in pink, a lighter shade than the rose of guest room and salon. Cradle and crib of dark-colored hardwood stained to contrast with the light coloring of the plank flooring were frothed entirely in pink lace and ruffles. Scattered rugs of pink and blue dotted the floors, and pink dolls and stuffed toys decorated the chests. Maureen dragged a pull toy behind her and rattled excitedly on about the tiny rockinghorse she had discovered in the corner.

But it was the other side of the room that held Katy's attention. The furniture duplicated the pink side, but instead of the pink froth of frills and lace, it was adorned with a paler shade of blue than the azure of the other rooms. The floor was covered with the same pink-and-blue rugs, but the hand-carved toys marching across dresser and chest were more masculine-inclined and all painted with the identical color of blue. It was a room with a split personality, ideal for an assortment of small children, but curious in a house with no children at all.

Katy anxiously scanned Kerry's noncommittal expression after completing this inspection. "You have gone to a lot of trouble, sir, for a room little used."

Kerry's gaze remained enigmatic. "It should amuse Maureen while she is here, and I have installed a number of books Anna might appreciate. If I do much entertaining, the children of my friends should be as well treated as their parents."

"Of course," Katy replied flatly. Watching Maureen toddle off to continue her explorations, she added, "You do realize little girls will be as much fascinated with the toys on the boy's side of the room as the boys will be with the ones on the other side?"

With a flicker of amusement, Kerry repeated her "Of course" and casually picked up a small blue carriage from the dresser, inspecting it carefully before rolling it across the floor to Maureen. "I figure within a week's time she will have the toys so intermingled they may never be separated again. It should give the maids something to do." He nodded in the direction of the young black girl who had taken charge of his daughter. She seemed as much entranced with the room as Maureen and eagerly brought forward new playthings when the toddler tired of the old.

Katy rose from her sitting position to give her daughter a swift kiss and return to her husband's side. "She will be spoiled beyond all hope of retrieval by the time she leaves here."

"And beg forevermore to come back." Kerry grinned mischievously.

Katy returned the grin and set out in search of Anna, studiously ignoring the final set of doors at the end of the hall she knew led to the master suite, Kerry's private chambers. That was a room she would never enter, and she refused to acknowledge her curiosity about what might lie behind those closed doors.

The two men watched admiringly as she swept away. Sir Charles waited until his wife was out of earshot before speaking. "I am not much of an expert on the decoration of interiors, but it seems to me there is one adornment this establishment sadly lacks.''

Kerry eyed the older man coldly. "That is possible. There is one for which I have searched for many years but' have found unobtainable.''

"Perhaps you have searched in the wrong places." Not disturbed by his young friend's cold tones, Charles continued to watch the fleeting figure of his wife below them.

"That advice comes too late for me, I fear." Now Kerry followed the direction of Charles's eyes, and sadness replaced the cold tones of earlier.

It was not what Charles hoped to hear, but it gave him something to ponder on in the long afternoons as he rested. The young lord was not one to linger in the past; what effect did his words have on the future?

The week passed much too rapidly. Charles watched as life came back into Katy's movements and a healthy glow returned to her face. Hours spent riding, careless of hat or bonnet, left her skin sparkling with color and lightened strands of her hair to near-white. He found her more incredibly attractive than the quiet young governess of seventeen had been.

While Katy and Anna rode the paths of the plantation, Charles rested on the veranda, supervising all that went on in the fields beyond. Serene in the knowledge of his wife's fidelity, he watched as the tiny figures of his wife and daughter stopped to exchange greetings with Kerry or Mahomet in whatever fields they happened to be working that day. Dozing off as the heat of the warm afternoons overtook him, he would know that when his eyes opened again, Katy would be at his side with a cold glass of spring-water tea or lemonade to refresh him. He could learn easily to enjoy this life.

In the mornings, Katy brought Maureen out of the nursery to romp about their feet while they strolled the neatly laid-out grounds to the rose garden Kerry had imported with the furniture. That her husband looked more rested and content than he had all winter, Katy noticed, and was grateful. She almost dreaded the return to Georgetown and the fear of fever which it meant. Another onset of sickness could mean her husband's death while the weakness was still on him, and

Katy was not willing to think what life would be without his warm understanding and protection.

In the evenings, after Katy settled the children into the nursery, she came back downstairs to the coolness of the open solarium where the men sat and talked, sipping their drinks. Perching on the low stool at her husband's feet, she rested her head on his knees and felt the gentle caress of his hand on her hair while the words of business and politics flowed on about her. If this position afforded her the best view of green eyes glowing in the darkness, no one noticed, and she was left to reflect on the evenings she had spent alone by Kerry's side, talking in much the same way as he did with her husband now. She made little effort to enter the conversation, unwilling to bring their attention back to her, content simply to be in Kerry's presence as she had been once before.

On the last day of their visit, Katy and Sir Charles came down to breakfast late, their faces still flushed with pleasure as Katy leaned closer into her husband's embrace. Their self-centered smiles told Kerry immediately the reason for their tardiness, catching him unprepared for the physical stab of pain at the knowledge that Katy was wife in more than name only. He had managed to ignore this aspect of Katy's marriage to a great extent, but faced with the evidence of her satisfaction, he was forced to admit Charles had been too healthy a man to marry simply to give Maureen a name. And Katy too passionate a woman to be satisfied otherwise, he was compelled to add, twisting the knifing pain in his chest further.

If Kerry paled slightly and his knuckles whitened around the dining utensils they gripped, his guests made no notice. With great effort he greeted them with his usual courtesy, but behind the calm facade a resolve was forming. A question he had debated throughout the week now hardened into certainty, and characteristically, he acted upon it immediately.

While Katy chattered of packing trunks, bemoaning the need to return to Georgetown, Kerry impatiently interrupted.

"You do not have to return yet, you know. The fever is still there, and I would worry less if you would remain here awhile."

He could not have caught their attention faster if he had

fired a cannon in their midst. Sir Charles looked up from the slice of ham he was cutting, to meet his young host's gaze. "We could not impose ourselves like that on you, Kerry, as much as we have enjoyed our stay. A short visit is a pleasant break in the routine, but a long one would make nuisances of us."

Katy remained silent, allowing Charles to do what he thought best while she contemplated Kerry's reason for suddenly springing this on them. He was occasionally impulsive, but this was not a matter for impulse. He could have mentioned it any time, given them time to think about it and discuss it, to talk Charles into agreeing. She desperately wished to stay, but it wasn't her place to admit it.

"That is just the point. You would not be a nuisance, but doing me a great favor." Kerry's gaze took in Katy's puzzled expression but he swept over it, concentrating on her husband. "Some of the other land owners around here have asked me to go to Charleston as their representative before the council, believing I might have some influence on their decisions. I've been hesitating over leaving Twin Oaks in the hands of a manager in the middle of my most productive season. He's a good farmer, but no businessman, as you must be aware by now. If I could leave you here in charge of the day-to-day decisions, I would feel more free to go. I've hesitated asking, knowing you have a business of your own to operate, but Katy and the girls seem to be so happy here. I thought I could persuade you to consider it."

He would be leaving them here alone while he went to enjoy the summer season in Charleston. It was not what Katy had had in mind, but she refused to recognize her disappointment. Twin Oaks would be healthier than Georgetown this time of year, and Charles seemed to be benefiting from the relaxation; those were excuses enough to stay. That the distance between Charleston and Twin Oaks was so great that Kerry would probably not return for the remainder of the season was a thought she had no right to entertain.

"I have been meaning to have a word with you about the shipyards before I left. Perhaps if you have a few moments after breakfast we could continue this discussion." Charles remained noncommittal, refusing to make a definite decision on the spur of the moment. Like Katy, he was uncertain of Kerry's motives in making the request, and he would study them further before committing himself. He was not insensitive to the fact that his wife and daughter would prefer to prolong their stay, but he had no desire to be under more obligation than necessary to the young lord. He had always been an independent man and he would not allow ill health to interfere until it was unavoidable. That it might soon be unavoidable was a factor he had come to consider more often than his wife realized.

While the two men wandered off to the study, Katy hastened to the nursery, chafing at the delay in making a simple decision. Both men were acting decidedly oddly this morning, and she could find no logical explanation for their behavior. Giving up any pretense at understanding them, she told Anna to don her riding habit and prepared to take her exercise early. If this were to be their last day here, she would need the afternoon to pack.

By the time she and Anna reached the stables, Kerry was already there and waiting for them.

"I thought I would go along with you, if you do not mind my company. If this is to be the last day shared with you for the summer, I prefer to make the most of it."

Kerry had made no attempt to be alone with her all week, preferring the safety of distance, but now that he had made the decision to extend the distance to totally out of sight, he wished a last minute's indulgence. Smiling calmly at Katy's surprise, he awaited her approval.

"Then you are going to Charleston?" she asked, taking the bridle he offered from his hand.

Assisting Anna into her saddle, Kerry kept his eyes on Katy. "Yes, your husband has agreed it would be best if you remained here until the fever season is over. Would you enjoy that, Anna?"

Listening wide-eyed to the adult conversation, Anna nodded vigorously, afraid any further intrusion might prevent her hearing more.

She was doomed to disappointment for her efforts. Katy simply nodded her head, mounting her horse without assistance, urging the mare into the morning sunlight and down

toward the river path. If there were to be further discussion of
the decision, it would be without little ears around.

They rode for the most part in silence, following Kerry's
lead as he surveyed the progress of his fields one last time
before he left. Occasionally he pointed out a sight or made a
remark of explanation, but too many unanswered questions
lay between them to encourage conversation.

Finally giving up on such dismal company, Anna spied
Mahomet in a bottom field and took off at a canter down the
path, leaving Kerry and Katy to themselves.

Stopping the horses on the crest of a knoll, Kerry glanced
over the fields beyond, then turned to Katy, who sat straight
in her saddle, staring ahead, stray curls dangling softly from
beneath her hat and blowing gently in the slight breeze off the
river.

"You have little to say this morning. I thought you would
be pleased to stay awhile longer."

"I am. I love it out here. And Charles seems so much
better since he came, don't you agree?" Avoiding his eyes,
Katy attempted to retain a formality that forever eluded her in
his presence. She was afraid to be alone with him, even in
full view of the entire plantation; formality was her only
defense.

Kerry replied gravely, not tearing his eyes away from her
slim figure. "He is that." The Irish lilt betrayed his thoughts,
and she threw a swift glance over her shoulder, catching the
twinkle in his eye.

"You are laughing at me again. You are forever laughing
at me. Do I make such a figure of fun that we cannot hold a
sensible conversation together?" Katy protested, refusing to
give in to his amusement and the resultant demolition of her
lovely formality.

"It is either laugh or make love to you, and I rather
thought you might object to the latter. Why don't you get off
your high horse both literally and figuratively, and we will try
a little of your sensible conversation?"

"Is there something we need talk about?" His words struck
a chord that vibrated throughout her being, and Katy hid her
reaction behind a mask of indifference.

"I am sure we will find something," Kerry commented dryly.

This time Katy did not look away as she stared back at him. Levelly, keeping her eyes on him, she nodded. As he dismounted and came forward to help her down, she asked, "Why are you going to Charleston?"

Catching the mare's reins, Kerry took her hand and assisted her to dismount before replying. "See, you have already found a topic. Shall we sit in the shade?"

"You are avoiding the question." Settling her riding skirts on the blanket he threw out for their protection, Katy looked up to watch the expression of his angular face.

"I told you this morning why I am going." Kerry sat on a tree stump at a proper distance; to sit closer would be to invite temptation, and he wished to keep a clear head during the inevitable interrogation he had encouraged by telling her nothing for so long.

"That was an excuse, not a reason. The summer season will just be starting there. Are you hoping to have better luck in finding a wife there than in London? Perhaps you already have someone in mind, such as the governor's daughter who prefers titles?"

Kerry's gaze pierced the pert set of her small chin and violet eyes. "You do believe in being direct, don't you?"

"It is the only way to avoid your nonsense. I expected you to return from England with a wife."

"I do not intend to marry. Is that answer direct enough?"

The royal blue of Kerry's fustian coat nearly matched the shade of sky behind him, making his lean figure a natural part of the setting as he casually lounged against a nearby tree trunk.

It was not the answer Katy had been expecting. Stunned into silence, she stared back at his casual pose, unable to sort through the flurry of responses leaping to mind. How could he not marry? Sunlight crowned the familiar aura of his auburn hair, glinting off the brilliant green of his eyes, and she could not understand why he had not already married instead of proclaiming he never would. In her eyes, there could be no more eligible man in all of Christendom.

"You are quite mad. Too much work has affected your

mind. You must marry—if anything should happen to your brother, you are heir to your father's title and estates. Your brother's marriage has not produced the children your family needs; it is your responsibility now. Surely you do not intend to disappoint them?'' The repercussions of his decision spread out in ever-widening circles like a pond disturbed by a stone. Did his family know? What would become of the Southerland lands and titles, an ancient lineage so carefully preserved? Could he really mean to deliberately destroy it? And why?

Placing his hands behind his head, Kerry replied calmly, ''I do indeed, and have told them so. My life is here and not in England. I have never expected to hold a title any grander than baron and have no use for their estates. My father and brother can manage them quite well without me, and I am sure there are cousins or second cousins somewhere who would have no objections to taking over once they are gone. I see no point in ruining my life for the sake of a piece of property and a title.''

This philosophy was outright heresy to one who had been raised in the poverty of the streets, looking up to the glittering lords and ladies of the land as earthly gods. They had everything Katy could never have—family, name, title, wealth, power, whatever they chose—but even at an early age she understood that all this also carried an overburdening amount of responsibility. Now that she was older she could realize they were all too human, but she could not shake the feeling they represented a more noble race of humans. It was tantamount to rejecting heaven in favor of hell.

''Kerry, you cannot mean that,'' she finally gasped, her face losing some of its color. ''Twin Oaks is no more than a piece of property—it is your family that is important. And you will never be happy until you have children to fill that fancy nursery you have built. Why else would you build it? What happened in London to bring on such a decision?''

Kerry stared at her thoughtfully, wondering what wheels were turning inside her mind to produce such a dramatic effect to a subject that had no bearing on her life. ''Do you really wish to know?''

''Would I ask if I did not? I have better things to do than make idle conversation. Of course I want to know!'' She was furious with him now, sitting there as content as if he had just told her of his decision to buy a new cow and not the earth-shattering remark he had so devastatingly dropped on her. Never marry! She would kill him if he did not explain at once, and to her satisfaction.

"Other people don't, you know." At her bewilderment, Kerry added, "Have better things to do, I mean. You should have attended some of those social affairs to which you were invited in London. It would have opened your eyes to the manner of the society in which I am expected to associate."

"My God, Kerry! Would you please come to the point? Surely there are as many good people in your society as mine?"

"And as many illiterate, lazy, and downright stupid, also, if you must know. In other words, it is as difficult to find a person you are willing to spend your life with in my society as it is in yours. Hear me out." He put up a hand and motioned her to be silent, preventing another outraged outburst. "I went to London with every intention of finding a wife, giving up all romantic notions of love, title, or wealth. If you and Charles are any example of a marriage of convenience, I felt I could endure the same, and with any luck, learn to love my wife as you have learned to love Charles." Kerry studied the slight flush covering her cheeks at his words and wondered how close he had come to the truth, but he could not stop to ask now.

"When I returned to England, my mother—as I anticipated—had a host of young lovelies eager to meet the prodigal son. The duchess is no fool, she had trained her favorites in topics close to my heart, encouraging them to read up on the colonies and to show interest in plantation life. I was flattered as one lovely lady after another listened breathlessly to my tales of life in the Carolinas and I began to think choosing among them would be my most difficult task."

Here Kerry stopped and gave an abrupt snort of laughter at the memory he prepared to relate, his thoughts turned thousands of miles from the woman at his feet.

"Then, one by one, they grew tired of listening, and I encouraged them to speak, thinking if they were truly interested they would have many questions to ask." A bitter smile tugged at his lips as Kerry continued. "One wished to know if the ladies of Charleston were as far behind in fashion as everyone said. The next asked if I knew her cousins in Boston, she had heard it was rapidly becoming the center of aristocracy in the New World. They wanted to know if I went to the theater often, and if there were any respectable mantuamakers in Charleston. All highly intelligent and relevant questions that proved how closely they must have studied the subject." The sarcasm Katy had scarcely heard in his voice since leaving England now found its way back with new venom.

"One evening, after finding myself cornered by one of the dimmer of these dimwits, I could bear no more, and with the gallantry of one drink too many, I began to relate garish tales of cabin life on the frontier and Indian kidnappings. In no time at all the young lovely ran to hide behind her mother's skirts and was seen no more. The scheme worked so well I practiced it on the remainder of my mother's list of hopefuls until within two weeks I found myself blessedly alone again. The duchess did not speak to me for a week."

Kerry's smile was more amused than bitter as he finished his tale and reached to brush a stray curl from Katy's cheek, and he was caught by surprise at the glimmer of tears in her eyes, though her lips hinted of laughter just below the surface. "Katy?"

She shrugged away his hand and bit her lower lip to prevent laughter from bubbling upward. She could well imagine the stylish misses contemplating marriage to the son of the Duke of Exeter, the handsome Lord Kerry, their eagerness to please and their horror at discovering he contemplated living in a cabin among Indians. The absurdity of his tale did not mask the bitter results, however.

"You are as mad as I assumed, milord, telling such horrible stories to poor young girls. It would have been wiser to educate them than to frighten them."

"Poor young girls! Katy, those imbeciles were older than you. My mother knew better than to present impressionable, untried children to the scourge of London. One or two of them had been married before and expressed small objection to my advances until they learned of my supposed living conditions. No, Katy, no amount of educating would have given them wisdom. I swore then and there to have nothing more to do with the lot of them, and I have not regretted my decision once.''

"And what does your family think of it?"

"My father threatened to throw me out of the house until my brother's common sense intervened. When I left, Burlington swore there was time yet for him and his wife to have a dynasty. I do not think he seriously believes my vow. My father was busily scanning the family tree in search of suitable successors.''

"And your mother?"

"She told me the next time I came back to bring Maureen.'' Kerry grinned and straightened up, stretching his long legs before him. "Does that answer your questions?''

"You are lucky to have such a family; I would dearly love to know them. Your brother has always seemed to me to be a man you should listen to more often.''

"So he thinks, too, and he gives his advice freely, which is what it is worth, so do not side with him, my sweet Katy. I am quite content as I am, and no one can change me.''

"You desire no son to fill the other side of that nursery?'' It was a question Katy knew better than to ask, but she still found it hard to believe his decision.

"You and Charles will have to take care of that for me; I could easily look on any son of yours as one of mine. Is there no chance of producing that heir to the title yet?'' Kerry asked teasingly, safely evading the issue at the cost of his own pain.

Katy blushed. It was not a subject she could discuss with ease, let alone admit to the unsatisfactory nature of their recent couplings. With hope, this morning's success might mean a change for the better, but it was too soon to tell.

"Not so soon. Maureen is still a babe yet, and Charles worries about my health.'' She picked at a corner of the blanket and refused to look at him. It was impossible for her to lie convincingly.

The gemlike hardness of Kerry's eyes bored through her, seeing beyond the bent head and nervous fingers. "Katy? You do love him, don't you? I have not forced you into an unfortunate match?'' That he had been responsible for her marriage to a man so much older than she, he had come to understand, but that made it no easier to accept. The horror of another man touching the perfection that had once been his alone lay buried just beneath the surface coating of Kerry's sophistication.

Katy's head rose defiantly at his tone, but the depth of concern in his eyes caused her to soften her reply. ''You have forced me into nothing, Kerry, the choice was made willingly. And, yes, I have come to love him. It was not a difficult thing to do.''

A familiar ache stirred inside him, disturbed by her words. ''As you have come to love Anna and Jake?'' he asked, deceivingly softly.

Unable to retreat before the starvation of his eyes, Katy was snared by his gaze. ''Yes, as I love Anna and Jake,'' she acknowledged weakly, leaving ''not as I love you'' unsaid.

He stared at her thoughtfully for a moment, then moved to rise. ''Perhaps we had best return to riding before Anna leaves us far behind.''

Allowing her hand to be encased in his firm brown one, Katy rose from the blanket and met his gaze. ''You still have not told me why you have suddenly decided to leave for Charleston.''

''Have I not?'' A flash of the familiar twinkle in his eyes dissolved rapidly as he searched for a suitable reply. Playing Katy's game, he gave an answer as close to the truth as possible. ''Perhaps it is because I do not wish you to return to Georgetown and risk the fever there. I feared Charles would not stay unless I gave him a more pressing reason.'' Perhaps he liked to think of Katy living in the rooms he had built for her and did not trust himself to remain so close to her while she did. Or that he could not bear to see her in the arms of her husband any longer. All reasons better left unsaid.

''Perhaps,'' she said mildly, sensing at last that it might be better if she did not know. Their conversation had already left her with more than enough to think about, and she was strangely silent as they returned to the horses. Intuition told her more lay behind his words than Kerry was willing to reveal, but she did not dare trust intuition in a matter so close

to her heart. She cast a quick glance to the square-jawed
visage she knew so well, but he did not intercept the look,
and she remained uncertain, unable to tell if she had imagined
the hunger she had seen in his eyes.

Intending to leave before the others rose, Kerry was up before
dawn, seeing to his horses and leaving last-minute instructions with Mahomet. Returning from the kitchens with a
fresh-baked biscuit in hand, he met Katy waiting in the dining
room.

"You are leaving early, milord."

Joy surged through him at this unanticipated delay in his
departure. To see her standing there, morning sun pouring
over golden hair unpinned in her haste to arise, brought hope
unbidden to his eyes. Cautiously Kerry forced himself to
answer sensibly. "I am taking the horses instead of the river.
If I am to find shelter before nightfall, I must set out early."

"Then I will not keep you. I only came down to thank you
for what you are doing for us. I do not believe I showed my
appreciation properly yesterday." Downcast violet eyes slowly
rose to meet his emerald ones, instantly shattering her composure. The look she had thought she imagined was once again
in Kerry's eyes, drawing her like a magnet against her will.

"You do not need to thank me for anything, Katy. I have
always done as I wished and this time is no different. But if it
is appreciation you wish to show"—he grinned wickedly, the
light in his eyes all too familiar as his polished boots moved
across the wooden floor—"I will willingly accept that."

His biscuit-laden hand swept around Katy's waist, catching
her by surprise as he lifted her from the floor to press a hasty
kiss against her lips. The intoxicating pressure of her warmth
in his arms made him giddy with desire, and Kerry fought the
urge to continue their embrace. He quickly restored her feet
to the floor, dropping his hands abjectly to his side.

Steadily, without reproach, Katy asked, "Do you have any
idea how many times over the years you have said good-bye
to me?"

Gravely contemplating the implications of her coolness,
Kerry replied evenly, "Too many."

A shadow passed across her face and she stepped away, retreating from the intensity of his gaze. "You will write?"

"If you wish."

She nodded briefly, then disappeared down the darkened hallway, the golden glimmer of her hair lingering briefly as an afterimage, leaving him wondering if she had been just an effect of sunlight and his own desires. The light scent of her perfume drifting on the morning air convinced him otherwise, and he went on to his study with a thoughtful frown pressed across his brow.

June–July 1737

AFTER KERRY'S DEPARTURE, their days continued much as before. Charles tended to the plantation's business in the cooler morning hours, occasionally receiving or sending off messages to his own business via the sloops and rafts navigating the river, but showing little concern for his extended absence. Katy knew he had turned over the management of the shipyards to his assistant, but his lack of interest in its fate worried her.

To their mutual disappointment, Charles's continued ill health prevented a repetition of their recent lovemaking. Afraid to allow her disappointment to show, Katy claimed contentment with simply sharing his bed, thankful to have him at her side. Sighing, Charles would take his young bride in his arms and hold her against his chest, grateful for her loyalty but knowing her affectionate nature too well to believe her lies. She needed a whole man, and for the first time in his life, Charles knew the frustration of being less than one.

Resigned to the limited role he must play in Katy's life, whether temporary or not, Charles tried to make it up to her by being an attentive husband and a devoted father to both his

children. He strolled about the gardens with them, listened to
their chatter, discussed the day's events with his wife, giving
of himself what he could and deriving pleasure from it. Still,
he found himself thankful for Katy's insistence that he retire
to their room after lunch to rest and regain his strength, for
this was the only time he could drop the mask of well-being
and come to terms with the pain gnawing at his insides,
eating at the breath of life in his lungs. In the dark coolness
of their tree-shaded bedroom, he lay panting for the breath
needed to sustain him throughout the remainder of the day.

Katy worked out her unease and physical restlessness by
using the afternoons for long walks while Maureen and Charles
slept and Anna kept to the coolness of the veranda with her
books. At first, keeping to the paved walks and neat gardens,
she tended the flowers and herbs and talked to the gardeners
assigned to keeping the grounds well-groomed, but as her
restlessness grew stronger, she took to wandering farther
afield, following the river and circuiting the fields, wearing
herself to exhaustion before returning to the house.

Katy could lie to herself no more easily than she could to
others. It was not just her husband's illness worrying her, but
the look in Kerry's eyes the day he left and her own reaction
to it. For the nearly two years of her marriage she had
worked at convincing herself that what had once been between them was no more: that Kerry's desire for her had been
satisfied with their days and nights at the Indian camp or he
would never have permitted her to return to Georgetown; that
her own love for him was no more than her gratitude for
everything he had done for her. But at night, her dreams
spoke a different tale, and it was Lord Kerry and not her
husband who made love to her in the fantasies of her sleep.
Now the fantasies were spilling over into the daytime, and as
she walked, she had to drive out the images of Kerry walking
beside her, his lilting voice seducing her to the coolness of
the shade, and she walked harder, faster, outdistancing the
look of love and need she had conjured up in his eyes.

By mid-July they had received only one brief, noncommittal letter from Kerry and it grew easier to believe she had
imagined more to his words and actions than was there. He
was a man who enjoyed whatever woman was at hand, and

now that he was in Charleston, there were many more for him to admire than Katy. They lived in two different worlds; while hers was so small Kerry easily became the center of it, she could not expect to be the center of his more cosmopolitan one.

With no thought at all but escape from the tedium of household chores, Katy strode out of the house in the midst of a sultry July heat wave. As she stepped off the shaded veranda into the white-hot glare of the afternoon sun, she almost turned back to the cool cavern of the house, but there were herb transplants in the garden needing watering, and nothing or no one to claim her attention inside. With visible effort, she swam into the humid heat of the garden, filling her watering can at the kitchen pump and waving to the women in the sweltering outside kitchen before moving on to the neatly trimmed garden paths.

Her thin white cotton gown clung limply to her damp skin. In the unaccustomed heat of the Carolina summers, she had taken to wearing as little as possible beneath her lightweight gowns, all thought of stays and petticoats too burdensome to contemplate. Now she even regretted the fine shift sticking to her back like a second skin, and she glanced longingly at the distant river, wishing she had learned to swim.

After watering the herb garden, she ventured onward, inspecting the roses for blooms suitable for cutting later in the evening for a table setting. When she reached the far edge of the garden path, she glanced backward at the house rising up behind her, then forward to the shady grove of trees overlooking the grounds. The trees were farther away, the beginning of Kerry's timbered woodlands, and she seldom set foot in them alone, fears of Indians and other dangers still lingering in her memory.

But without conscious effort, she found her feet moving in that direction, across the sun-beaten grassy lawn to the beckoning dimness of the thick woods. Amazed at her sudden madness in risking heat stroke by strolling unshaded lawns instead of returning to the house, Katy considered turning back, but like an unseen hand, her restlessness guided her forward, drawing her through the sticky air to the cool breeziness of woodland shadows.

The abrupt change from glaring sunlight to cavernous darkness made her giddy, and she closed her eyes to steady herself.

Kerry had watched from a distance as the small white figure glided about his gardens, tenderly nurturing the plants as if they were her own. He knew that was Katy's nature, just as she had taken in Anna and loved her as she did Maureen. It did not mean she had come to think of his home as hers, but his longing for her to belong there made him wish it so. When she reached the edge of the rose garden and turned back toward the house, he willed her onward, his heart skipping a beat when she stepped off the path in the direction of the woods.

With bated breath, Kerry watched her move slowly closer through the shimmering heat, her diminutive figure and white-gold hair floating insubstantially in the humid haze until she drew close enough for him to discern the flushed color of her cheeks and the sparkling blueness of her eyes, and then he was frozen to the spot where he stood, unable to hide himself even as she stopped to close her eyes on the edge of darkness.

Long lashes flickered upward, and for a moment Katy feared she saw a specter, terror gripping her as she imagined the ghostly image of the white-shirted figure of the man she loved haunting this forest. But then a ray of sun crept through the thick canopy of branches, striking burnished copper and glittering against emerald eyes and Kerry stood there, dressed only in linen shirt and white breeches. As his arms stretched out to welcome her, she did not require explanations, but flew into his waiting arms with waking joy.

Holding Katy's fragile figure close, feeling her heart pound frantically through the thin protection of her bodice, her breasts crushed tightly against him, Kerry could no more resist temptation than the seas could resist the pull of the moon. With Katy's arms clenched tightly behind his neck, he lifted her free from the ground, her slenderness seemingly weightless beneath his hands. Her lips turned eagerly to his, giving in swiftly to his pressure, and a sigh much like a moan escaped him as he ravished her mouth as he would her body. His joy ballooned and exploded under her kisses, the aching loneliness of the past months and years dissolving with this renewal of her touch.

But there came a moment when kisses were not enough, when the desire to hold and possess was a longing too fierce to fight, and he had no wish to fight it. Feeling the breathless quivering of Katy's small frame against his chest, Kerry knew there was only one end to this path they were taking, and he had to make certain she understood before it was too late to turn back.

The question burning wordlessly in his eyes, Kerry set her feet gently to the ground, his hand caressing the golden fronds at the nape of her neck as he stared down into dark violet pools. "Katy?"

Without hesitation, Katy responded by pressing urgently against him, no doubts any longer in the depths of her eyes as she murmured, "Yes, Kerry, please," her hands instantly seeking the solidness of his chest beneath the linen shirt. She was back where she belonged, the hows and why of it inconsequential. The sands had shifted, and as she had once predicted, she fell abruptly into his arms.

The pent-up flood of desire inside Kerry burst under her butterfly touch, her words releasing him to the passion he had kept hidden so long. He buried his lips in the hollow of her throat, his words vibrating against the thin, white skin.

"My God, how I love you!" he breathed, folding her into his arms once more. At last, she had come to him, openly and without persuasion. After all these months and years, she was willingly surrendering to him, and she was finally his to love at will.

With prayerful thanks, Kerry's mouth sought the lips that were now his to kiss, and the two white-shrouded figures blended deliberately into one, caught in a golden swirl of sunlight breaking through the towering evergreen cathedral of trees above them. The heavy silence of the forest remained undisturbed by human voice or call of birds.

Later, they found themselves beneath a tent of pines where Kerry had made his bed the night before. Breathless and disheveled, they lay wrapped in each other's arms still partially clothed—the urgency of their needs too demanding for hooks and ties. Rectifying his error, Kerry began slowly to unlace the ties of Katy's bodice, loosening the clinging material until his hand could slip inside and find the softness within, freeing her breasts and exposing them to his gaze as he fondled them lovingly.

"I did not think it possible, but you have grown more beautiful than I remember." Tenderly kissing the distended tips that had fed his daughter, Kerry felt the slender coolness of Katy's fingers in his hair, and he looked up to search the violet pools staring back at him from the puddle of golden hair he had loosed in his haste to possess her.

Katy glowed in the warmth of his gaze. She belonged to Kerry, had never doubted that she was his, and she could feel no guilt at what they had done. The words he had whispered in her ear still flowed through her veins, sending the thrill of love to her very fingertips. He loved her. She had not imagined the look in his eyes; Kerry would never lie to her about something as important as this. She might possess little else, but love was something she could repay in kind and with interest.

Tracing her fingers down the bridge of his nose and across the angle of his cheekbone, Katy whispered the words only her pillow had heard before, "I love you, Kerry," and she rejoiced in the fierce embrace with which he caught her up.

"Damn your prickly little hide for not telling me that before. It might have brought me to my senses sooner." Kerry rolled over and pulled her on top of him, submitting to the unfastening of his shirt with lazy grace. "I have had little experience with love or virgins before. How was I to know you felt any more than all the other leeches who cling to me?"

"You think me a leech?" Katy pummeled his chest with her small fists, succeeding only in tickling him as Kerry crushed her in his arms, totally disarming her. "You know better than that." She bit at his ear and snuggled closer.

"If I had not been so blind, I would have. I should have realized it was not just coincidence that you were the only female of my acquaintance outside my family to whom I could talk with sensibility. But no, you let me make a complete ass of myself, pretending you were no more than a pretty bauble I picked up off the streets and polished. Why didn't you smack my face and scream obscenities when I suggested making you my mistress? That might have woke me up.'' Kerry peered at her with curiosity, trying to see beyond the lovely, fragile prettiness to the character behind it.

''That is what a lady would have done, but you knew I was no lady. It would have been hypocritical to pretend to expect anything else. To you, I was no more than that pretty bauble you spoke of, and I did not expect you to think of me otherwise. It would have solved nothing to know that the bauble loved you.''

''It would have made me treat you with more respect.''

''As you are now?'' Katy lifted her head and grinned at him as the last of her gown fell to the ground under his careful maneuvering.

''Now you are only getting what you deserve for having deceived me for so long.'' Kerry's hands began to move assuredly over her slender body, expertly finding the secret places that made her shiver with excitement. ''I discovered what a fool I'd been when I learned of your marriage, and I have been paying for my stupidity ever since. Have I not suffered enough?''

Suddenly serious, Katy grabbed the hand fondling her breast, holding it still. ''I never meant to make you suffer. If I had known how you felt, I would never have married. I only did what I thought was right and would make you happy.''

''If I had been in full possession of my senses, I would have taken you back to Charleston and married you immediately, instead of abandoning you to your fate. My suffering I brought on myself.'' Gently brushing her face, Kerry tried to brush away the fears he found there.

At the mention of such a marriage, Katy paled. ''You would have had to be insane to consider such a thing. I am no fit wife for you, and I only wish you could find someone who could make you as happy as Charles does me. Why are you not in Charleston as you said?'' The last question was asked hurriedly, staving off the argument she sensed in his frown.

"If you are so happy with Charles, you would not be here with me now. Now that I know what I want, I do not intend to make the same mistake twice. If I cannot have you, I will have nobody. And I am not in Charleston because there is a smallpox epidemic there, and the council has been postponed until it is over." He spoke as if enumerating each answer to her questions. Firmly holding her against his nakedness, Kerry let his reality drive out the fantasies of her romantic notions. He was a man, not a god, and he would have her, whatever the consequences.

Katy was well aware of the hard-muscled body beneath her and needed no reminding of his manliness, but she was a married woman and he a lord of the realm, and there could be no talk of marriage between them. Discarding his foolishness, she fixed on more practical matters.

"Then why have you not come back to Twin Oaks instead of lurking out here in the woods? How long have you been out here?"

"Only since yesterday, when I could bear no longer to be away from you. I had only planned on watching from afar; I never dreamed you would find me so quickly." Knowing she did not understand the firmness of his intentions, Kerry allowed her to dismiss what was for the moment an irrelevant point. What mattered now was that she was here, through whatever prescient miracle had brought it about.

"You were not going to tell us you were here? Are you quite mad? Have we driven you from your home, then?"

"I only wished to talk to Mahomet and see how everyone fared, perhaps catch a glimpse of you and Maureen before paying some calls at some other plantations. If Charles knew of the delay, he would not let you stay here, and I could not allow that."

"And now?" Katy asked quietly, suddenly becoming very still.

Gently Kerry returned her to the blanket, lovingly running his hand the length of her body, his gaze following lingeringly over creamy curves. "I would stay a few days longer if I thought there was any chance of seeing you again." Carefully studying Katy's face, he knew her desire to be as great as his own, but he could not ask her to continue this dalliance. In London, it might be acceptable for a wife to take a lover, but Katy was not one of his London ladies, and the Carolinas were not that cosmopolitan city. It would have to be her decision.

"You know I could not stay away if I knew you were here, but you cannot stay out here in the woods, sleeping with the insects. What would you eat? Have you had anything to eat at all since you arrived?" Swiftly guiding the subject away from her answer, Katy turned her concern to his welfare and away from her adultery.

But Kerry had his answer now and could not be moved from his position. "Mahomet has been keeping me in food, and I am quite content where I am. As you have reason to know, my morals are few, but I still consider myself a gentleman, and I cannot bring myself to betray a friend by sleeping with his wife while we are under the same roof. I know the point is moot, but out here I can pretend we are still with Tonga, that we are a part of nature, with no ties or boundaries to limit us. Bear with me, my lovely Katy, I know it means we are without satin sheets or champagne once again, but it is the only way I can ease my conscience. I had not come here intending to seduce you like this, and I am ill-prepared for the result."

His lips lingered at her throat, working slowly toward her breast while his fingers returned to their exploring. It had been a long time since he had any desire for a woman other than this one, and his passion was not easily quenched. He would have her again before she slipped away from him once more.

"All your arguments are specious, milord, but I cannot resist them when you touch me like that," Katy murmured, her arms finding their way about his neck once more. No man, not even her husband, could arouse her so easily as this one, and she was long starved for physical affection. If there were a need to reconcile her guilt, it would have to be postponed.

Making up for their earlier haste, they gave in to the need to reacquaint themselves with every inch of each other's bodies, savoring the pleasure of all their senses until their delight gave way to their needs, and once more Katy felt the heat of Kerry's passion piercing her, and she welcomed the invasion. They had come a long way from that first horrifying rape, but there was still the stigma of wrong hovering over them, needing to be drowned in the mindlessness of their physical joining.

With quiet reluctance they dressed themselves afterward, Kerry's nimble fingers aiding with laces and fastenings and lingering lovingly on the firm white breasts that were his to touch now. Filled with the thrill of possession, he could not bear the thought of parting with her loveliness so soon after recapturing it. She was his now, and the thought of sharing her drove him to the brink of madness.

"Katy, I do not want to let you go. You realize this will never be enough for me? An afternoon's pleasure was enough with a mistress I knew little about and cared nothing for, but you are different, my love. I have a craving for you that will never be satisfied but grows stronger each time I am with you. Tell me you love me again." He drew her into his arms and held her tightly against his chest, feeling the brush of golden hair against his chin.

Alarmed by his intensity, Katy clung to him in fear and joy. Their lovemaking of this afternoon was an innocent aberration they might get away with, but it could not go on forever. She could never live with him, but how was she ever to live without him again? It was a thought that could not bear inspection. Flinging her arms around his neck one last time, she whispered, "I love you, Kerry," then flew from his arms, dashing down the hill with her sunbonnet trailing from her hands as she ran.

Still glowing with the knowledge of her love, Kerry watched her go, but his eyes grew pensive as she reached the manicured gardens of the house and returned to the world of family and responsibility. His possession of her was an illusion, a mirage conjured up by the heat and their fevered imaginations. He was left with nothing but a memory to cling to.

A few days turned into two weeks before Kerry could gain the courage to tear himself from Katy's side, knowing he might never have the opportunity to share her love again. The longer he stayed, the greater was their risk of discovery, and he could not destroy her marriage so callously.

He waited until she rested in his arms, relaxed and content, still flushed with the exhilaration of their lovemaking, before gently explaining that their idyll was over, that he would be returning to Charleston the next day.

Katy lay tranquilly in his arms, absorbing the sensations of these last moments together to embroider them on her memory forever. The sun could not reach them through the canopy of leaves and evergreen branches, but the heat of it beat down on their skins and a fine film of moisture coated their skins where they clung together. Her breasts crushed against the hardness of his chest where she lay half on top of him, and her legs entwined about the sturdiness of muscular thighs.

As Kerry spoke, she could hear the deepness of his voice against her ear, and his arm tightened possessively about her shoulders. The warmth and his strength felt good while they lasted; only the coldness of her husband's sickbed awaited her when it ended. Tears stung her eyes, but she fought them back.

"You have left me so many times before, I should be accustomed to it by now, but it grows worse each time. I could almost wish you would leave forever and put an end to my torment." Katy buried her face in his shoulder, refusing to meet his stricken glance. She had known this day would come and meant to take it calmly, but now that it had arrived, she could not bear to face his loss.

"You do not mean that, Katherine. You must know by now that even if I cannot be with you in person, my thoughts are always with you, and now that I am certain of your feelings, you will not be rid of me so easily. I made the error of letting you go once before. I will not make the same error again. You are mine, and I will have you one way or the other." Kerry clutched her fiercely to his chest and buried his face in the billow of golden hair covering him.

"You know we cannot risk this again. Charles is not a jealous man by nature, but I am no keeper of secrets, and when he regains his health, he will know if I lie to him. If it were not for . . ." She hesitated, casting about for a fitting phrase. ". . . circumstances," she amended badly, "I would

never have come here at all. I do not think I can do it again."
This Garden of Eden setting they had chosen for their trysts
made their lovemaking seem the natural conclusion of
irresistible forces, but Katy knew once they returned to society, the awful reality of their guilt would prevent her from
repeating their sins. She would not leave Charles's side again.

"I will not ask you to, Katherine," Kerry said gently. "I
will simply be there when you need me until the time comes
to claim you for my own. If I have to wait until I am one
hundred, I will have you, my Katy; do not ever doubt my
intentions."

Kerry smiled patiently at the frown crossing her face. He
would have a difficult time making a believer of this little
skeptic, but time would tell. The fates could not be so cruel
as to deny him his heart's one desire. Little did he know what
the fates had in store.

August–November 1737

AFTER KERRY'S DEPARTURE, the month of August moved interminably. A week of rain at its end swept the river clean, bringing an end to the fever season. Charles's health had not remarkably improved with the days of warmth and rest, but by September he was wishing restlessly to return to his own home. A brief note from Kerry warning of his impending return spurred Charles on, and by September's end, though Kerry had not returned as promised, the Stockbridges departed for Georgetown.

The arduous carriage ride from Twin Oaks to Georgetown sapped Charles's little remaining strength. His labored breathing and pain-creased face prompted Katy to send him directly to bed while one of the servants raced for the doctor. By morning, when the doctor finally arrived, Charles breathed more easily and his color was less ashen, but the physician left the room shaking his head.

Alarmed, Katy ushered him into the downstairs salon and questioned him anxiously, receiving no satisfaction for her trouble.

"There must be something I can do, some medicine he can

take. He seemed so much stronger for a while—perhaps another climate will help? I have heard of hot springs and healthful waters that work miracles. Please, Dr. Jackson, I will do anything . . .'' Katy clasped her hands in the lap of her blue muslin gown, her eyes imploring the physician to give her the miracle she asked.

Finding those magnificent violet eyes out of proportion to the drawn frailty of Katy's face, the doctor searched the translucent skin beneath them and his brow puckered. ''There is nothing you can do, Lady Stockbridge. Travel—to better climates or hot springs or whatever fanciful notions people take—would kill him. You have seen the result of one short day's journey. If it is a miracle you want, you will have to work it here. There is nothing more I can do but recommend the strengthening diet I have given you, and bed rest. And I might recommend the same for you—you do not look at all well.''

Startled, Katy clasped her hands tighter and stared down at them. Except for her guilty secret, she felt fine, but the doctor need not know of her guilt. It was time she confirmed what she had not dared to consider until now.

With eyes downcast, Katy confessed her suspicions, and after a few curt questions and a brief examination, the physician confirmed what she already knew.

''I would say Sir Charles should have his potential heir by mid-April.'' The doctor gave his young patient a covert glance, but she turned her face away from him, lost in her own thoughts. ''Your holiday in the country must have been good for him. I must congratulate you. This child might be the miracle you ask for; stranger things have happened. Have you told him yet?''

''No. No, I wished to be certain before raising his hopes,'' Katy replied vaguely. There were so many things to be considered. Mid-April. Was the doctor right? Would thoughts of ''his'' child keep Charles alive through the winter? She had never deceived him before, not like this, but to tell him she was bearing Kerry's child again would surely kill him, and if to let him think it was his would keep him alive . . . There seemed little choice.

''Lady Stockbridge?''

Katy became aware the doctor had been speaking to her, and startled, she returned her attention to his concerned face. "I am sorry. You were saying?"

Sympathy appeared briefly behind the bespectacled eyes. She was too young to bear the burden of motherhood alone, but that possibility faced her now. His suspicions concerning the real father of her children were irrelevant in the face of those circumstances. He was certain her concern for her husband was real.

"I was saying, due to your history of complications during your last pregnancy, you should show extreme care with this one if you wish to retain your health and your child. I will see that Sir Charles has a suitable nurse if his care grows too difficult for you to manage," he ended on a questioning note.

Katy woke to his words and shook her head emphatically, loosening a flurry of curls as she did. "No, I feel much better this time, and I am the only suitable nurse for Charles. I will not give up on him. He will live to see his child grow and prosper if I have to breathe life into his lungs myself." She stood up, effectively dismissing the physician.

Dr. Jackson gathered up his hat and bag and bowed slightly to the stiff figure of his young patient. "I sincerely believe that if such a thing is possible, you will do it, Lady Stockbridge. Just do not neglect yourself or the child while trying. I will leave you to give the happy news to your husband. Good day."

After seeing the doctor to the door, Katy started slowly up the stairway. That the child was Kerry's, there was no doubt, but if she could convince Charles she was a month further along, he would think it a result of their last lovemaking at Twin Oaks. If ever there were a need for her to lie convincingly, it was now, not for her own sake, but for her husband's. If the thought of a son could bring Charles back to health, she would lie until her dying day about it.

Entering the bedroom they still shared, Katy thought he slept until the gentle closing of the door brought his eyes open. Charles smiled and gestured for her to sit beside him.

"Did you browbeat that damned doctor into letting me out of bed for a while? I will warn you now, I have no intention of spending the rest of my life in here." He squeezed Katy's cold hands as a pang of pain crossed her face. So she knew, too, and his feeble joke fell flat. Charles hid his sorrow and waited for Katy to speak.

Katy lovingly stroked his brow and attempted a smile. "On the contrary, I told him under no condition would I allow you out of this room. I finally have you where I want you, and I intend to keep you there."

"As it is, I am of no possible use to you here. Perhaps you should send me to the shipyards and leave me there," he joked, waiting for the message he read in her eyes. Had the doctor told her something he should know? What did she hold back?

"Would you care to make some small wager on your use in bed?" Katy grinned impishly, tucking her feet up under her skirts and leaning over his pillow-propped figure.

With an inexplicable surge of joy, Charles pulled her down on top of him, mussing her already disarrayed hair. "Did you have something in particular in mind?"

"I was thinking in terms of a son, somewhere about March, perhaps." Katy snuggled closer, irreparably wrinkling her gown as she buried her face in the familiar curve of his neck and shoulder.

Charles held his breath for a moment, easing the torment of breathing as his still-powerful arms tightened about his young wife. Then he lifted her chin until their gazes met. "Is this what your discussion with the doctor was about?" he asked quietly.

Katy nodded her head, eyes shining with joy. She had not given herself time to think of the thrill of carrying a new infant into the world, and her lips turned up at the thought of the small being now forming in her womb. He would be as beautiful as Maureen, and as loved.

Charles exhaled slowly. A child, possibly a son, after all these years. Was it possible? There was no questioning the joy in Katy's eyes, she wanted this child—and so did he, he suddenly realized. "A son, you say. I suppose if it is possible to will yourself pregnant, as I swear you must have done, it is possible to will the child to be a boy. Katy, the most sensible thing I have done in my life was to marry you."

A smile spread across her face. "You are happy, then?"

"Happy? I have never wanted anything more in my entire life. I only wish . . ." His expression changed as he gently brushed a lock of hair from her face. He grew serious, and a worried frown appeared. "Did the doctor think there would be any difficulty this time?"

"Not that he could see, so long as I stay healthy. And in case you have not noticed, I have been very healthy. I have not been sick once; that is how I know it must be a boy."

Her lighthearted words did not ease Charles's concern. "Katy, I am depending on you. If anything should happen to me, you must be both mother and father to our children. They cannot afford to lose you. As much as I have wanted this child, it has come at a most inopportune time."

Katy's lips tightened and her chin went out in stubborn denial. "Nothing shall happen to you. Your son will need the wisdom of his father to guide him, as your daughters need your love."

Charles touched her cheek tenderly. "You have ever been practical, Katy, you must see that try as I might, I cannot hope to live forever. What will you do when I am gone?"

Tears welled up in Katy's eyes. "You cannot ever be entirely gone, for I will always carry a part of you inside me. I love you too much to let you go."

A flicker of happiness replaced his frown. "Do you, Katy? Can you learn to love an old man like me in the brief space of two years?"

She laid her head on his chest and sought comfort in his arms. "You have never been old to me, and there is no difficulty in returning love to a man as generous with love as you."

Charles closed his eyes and clung hopefully to her words. He was not so foolish as to believe she had replaced her love for Kerry with that for him, but perhaps it would give her some protection when he was gone. A young woman like Katy needed a man to hold her, and she would be particularly vulnerable to Kerry's temptations after so many months without the passion she needed. But the combination of his child and her love could provide the fortress she needed until someone else came along. And Charles had no doubt there would be a line of suitors at her door once he was gone. He smiled irreverently and wondered if he should start picking his successor now. Katy would surely kill him for such thoughts. In any case, he did not plan on going anywhere until his son arrived.

When Katy left the room later, Charles had fallen asleep with a smile on his lips, and she rested easier. He believed her completely; Kerry would be another story. They had not heard from him since they left Twin Oaks, and she was mildly puzzled by this lack of communication, but with Charles's illness there had been little time to worry over it. Now that she had something of importance to communicate, she wondered how she would reach him. It did not seem fair to keep him from knowledge of this child, too.

Letters of thanks went out to both Charleston and Twin Oaks, but Kerry acknowledged neither of them. Katy, settling into old routines and turning the house upside down with fall cleaning, thought little of it. Not until Jake showed up late one night several weeks later with lines of worry painted across his brow did Katy become aware of danger, and she sensed it immediately, without a word being said.

"Jake, what has happened?" She tugged him into the house, feeling the coldness of his normally friendly hand. "Is it Lord Kerry? Is he ill? Why aren't you out to sea somewhere?"

"I've been working for Lord Kerry these last months." Jake answered the last question first, uneasily twisting his newly acquired hat in his hands. He had begun to shed the awkwardness of youth, but facing Katy with his news would have reduced the cruelest of men to jelly. Warily he evaded the issue. "I came to see Sir Charles. Betts and I decided he'd know best."

"You and Betts?" Katy sank into the nearest chair at the sound of Kerry's trusted manservant's name. "What is it, Jake? You must tell me; Sir Charles is asleep. Is Kerry ill?"

"Aye, he's that, as any man of Lord Kerry's rank and station should be after six weeks in that stinkhole they call a jail!" Jake's thin veneer of new polish slipped as his anger built. "They finally let me in to see him yesterday, and he's wasting away. That's why me and Betts got kind of panicky and thought we'd best look to someone else besides these goddamn continental lawyers that can't do no better than let a man of Lord Kerry's rank rot with all the other vermin. Katy, you all right?'' Jake hastened to Katy's side as she paled and gripped the arm of the chair as if she would tear it off.

''In jail? Why is he in jail? What happened, Jake?'' Hysteria tinged her voice but she worked to control it, clutching Jake's hand for reassurance.

''I thought you'd know by now, but I suppose they ain't letting it get about much. I'm sorry, Katy, I didn't mean to break it like that.'' He sank down beside her and took her hand, searching for the explanation she demanded. ''Damned if I know what happened. Pardon my language, but I've been all over creation trying to find out, and I'm about as mad as they come. Someone's accusing him of dealing with the Indians and encouraging anarchy, whatever in hell that means. That's what they're saying down at the taverns. And the lawyers tell me they can't get him out because the council's refusing some kind of writ to enemies of the government.''

Jake's voice rose as his anger mounted. He had often considered Lord Kerry an enemy, but that was in a different kind of war, one Jake had lost. As an employer, Lord Kerry was fair and honest, and not only loyalty made him certain Lord Kerry was incapable of any criminal dealings.

''A writ of habeas corpus?'' Katy had heard Sir Charles discussing this newest controversy just the other day and had not understood the complexities. Now it came home to her in basic terms. Kerry could be imprisoned without trial and kept without the chance of proving his innocence.

Jake shrugged. ''Whatever. Nobody can hardly get in to see him and he needs a doctor, he's burnin' up with fever. Can't we wake Sir Charles? There's got to be something we can do.''

Katy shook her head thoughtfully, not meaning it for a negative answer. There had to be a very good reason for the council to accuse someone of such eminence as Lord Kerry of a crime he had once worked to prevent. It made no sense. Who would accuse him of such a thing? And why?

''Charles sleeps badly, I hate to disturb him, and there is little that can be done tonight. Could we not wait until morning, when he is feeling better?''

"Lord Kerry mentioned he'd been ill. Is it that serious?" Jake asked gravely. Sir Charles had been the picture of ruddy health when Jake has last seen him, a man well content with life and his new bride. It was the man in his memory he had come to see, the one he depended on to take care of Katy.

"He has not been able to leave his bed since we returned from Twin Oaks. I had hoped for some small sign of recovery, but I very much fear he is growing weaker. Do not tell anyone that," she added hastily, feeling disloyalty in her pessimism, but when all around seemed dark, it was hard to be joyful.

"I'm sorry, Katy, I didn't realize . . . Perhaps we shouldn't say anything at all, in that case. It will only worry him more." Jake twisted his hat into a formless shape. He had come to rely on Lord Kerry and Sir Charles as guides in his life and Katy's, and suddenly he was without the support of either of them. The opportunity to win Katy's favor lay before him, but he was at a loss as to how to handle it.

Katy's immediate reaction was to go to Charleston herself. Kerry was ill and needed her; she should be with him. But if Jake had difficulty reaching him, they would never allow her in, and the trip would compromise too many lives. As soon as this realization rooted in place, another began to form.

"We must tell Charles. He is the only one we know with any influence with the governor, and he might be able to rally enough of the others to lodge some kind of formal complaint that will at least free Kerry until they hold a trial. But that will take time, and if Kerry is ill, he needs help immediately. Do you know how to reach Twin Oaks?"

"If its up the river, I can just hire a sloop, and they will take me. I ain't made for these damn horses." Alert and questioning, Jake waited for instructions.

"Kerry has a slave there with more knowledge of medicine than most physicians. If I give you a letter to the overseer, I think he will let Mahomet go with you. Do you think you can find a way to get a slave into the jail?"

"If there ain't no other way, I'll have him heave a brick through a window. They're all locked together in one common cage, blacks and whites, men and women, makes you feel like you're back home in Newgate. I do a slow burn every time I think of it. Should I come back here after I fetch this Mahomet?''

"If you can, Charles might need to ask you some questions. Otherwise, we'll just send a letter to Betts. Will that help?''

"I'd best get out and see if I can find a man willing to ship out tonight. If you'll write me that letter, I'll be on my way.'' Anxious to show some initiative, Jake grasped eagerly at any suggestion for action.

The letter was hastily written and sealed with Sir Charles's stamp, giving it some authority. Katy made no effort to delay Jake, her concern for Lord Kerry lying in some filthy cell overriding her worries for Jake's safety. When he was gone, she traced weary footsteps to her marital bed. Charles tossed restlessly in the center of the bed; rather than disturb his precarious sleep, Katy chose to rest on the small cot in their dressing room. It was not the first night she had slept apart there, nor would it be the last.

Morning came early, and unable to sleep, Katy rose with the dawn, seeking out Sir Charles before venturing anywhere. He lay awake and staring thoughtfully at the ceiling, his hands plucking idly at the bedcovers. At Katy's entrance, he glanced up and smiled, but the light failed to reach his eyes. Over the last few weeks of inactivity he had grown listless and depressed, and he rarely laughed or jested anymore.

"Good morning, Katherine. Did I disturb your sleep last night?'' he asked, in pointed reference to the empty bed beside him.

"No, I feared I would disturb yours. We had a late visitor last night and you were quite asleep when I came to bed.'' Katy settled on the covers beside him, taking his cold hand between hers to warm it.

"Surely Kerry would not call at that time of night? He is impetuous, but not that . . .'' At the sight of Katy's darkening eyes, Charles stopped with alarm. "What is wrong, Katherine?''

Disconnectedly, the entire story tumbled from her lips, and the tears she had refused to shed last night fell now that she had a shoulder to cry on. While Charles attempted to make

sense of her tale, he held her limply against his chest, stroking her hair comfortingly.

Once he understood the predicament, he began to take
charge again. Feeling useless and incapable these last weeks,
he knew now that he was still needed and reacted with the
strength and energy of the man he had once been.

"I'll write to the governor immediately, Katy, and try to
persuade others to do the same. If we were in England, the
duke could use his influence, but it would be months before
he could effect any change here."

"But if your letters have no result? What can we do then?
Perhaps we should write to the duke as some kind of insur-
ance against the possibility of their doing nothing?"

Charles considered this audacious proposition and nodded
slowly. "I would hate to disturb a man of his stature with any
triviality, but this matter is serious enough to be recognized
even if it were not his son involved. They are depriving an
Englishman of his basic freedom. I think we could draft a
letter that might capture his attention and bring some response. If Kerry is freed immediately, there will be time to
notify the duke before any drastic action is taken. I can think
of no better second line of defense. It might be best to learn
more from the lawyers, also."

Letters flew back and forth between Georgetown and
Charleston. Jake safely arrived with Mahomet, but they had
difficulty smuggling the black into the jail. Sir Charles's
knowledge of ships and captains saw the letter to the duke off
on the fleetest, most reliable ship in port, but it would be
months before an answer would be forthcoming. Alerted to
their benefactor's danger, all of Georgetown and the surrounding plantations protested Lord Kerry's imprisonment,
to no avail. The council remained mute on the charges and his
incarceration.

Not until the end of October did the Stockbridges hear that
Mahomet had succeeded in reaching Lord Kerry. Jake's ill-
written letter was little better than Mahomet's uncommunicative speech, and they learned little more than that Lord Kerry
suffered from some type of prison fever leaving him wasted
and delirious much of the time. Jake had bribed the guards to

smuggle in food and medicines, but the results of their efforts were unknown.

More than ever, Katy felt the urge to be with Kerry. She could not keep still for the restlessness that said she belonged at his side, that if he were to recover, it would be through her. But even if she were to desert Charles to travel alone to Charleston, they would never allow Lady Stockbridge to enter their filthy dungeons, and the trip would be for naught. She could not risk her husband's health for nothing; there had to be some means of guaranteeing results.

The niggling suspicion that Kerry's imprisonment was somehow related to his weeks spent with her began to grow after Charles received an answer to his letter from the governor.

When she brought the crown-encrested envelope to her husband, Katy sank into a nearby chair and watched anxiously as he read the letter through. When he finished, Charles silently handed the heavy vellum to his wife. She read swiftly, her eyes continually going back to the one name that meant anything to her, and superstitious terror filled her heart.

"Halberstam? Halberstam accuses him? And that is the word they take over Kerry's? How is that possible?" Incredulous, she dropped the letter to her lap and stared blindly at Charles.

"He is lieutenant governor, Katy. Do you know him?" Charles asked curiously. There were many things in his wife's past he did not know and did not care to question, but a knowledge of political appointees did not seem characteristic of what little he had ascertained.

"He is an evil man and hates Lord Kerry," she replied simply, her gaze once more returning to the letter with a look of distaste.

"How do you come to know a man like Halberstam?"

"I met him in London," she said absently, not caring to discuss the circumstances.

"And after one meeting you know he is an evil man? That is not like you, Katy." Charles searched for some clue to this dilemma, but Katy's reactions were purely emotional, and he could find no practical solutions to her replies.

It was no use explaining to a man of logic like Charles that evil is sometimes as visible as the nose on his face; he would

never believe it. Katy shrugged and answered vaguely, "All
of London knows they have hated each other for years. Most
of Kerry's notorious reputation is a direct result of rumors
deliberately spread by Joshua Halberstam. Unless you believe
Kerry guilty, you must see he has deliberately lied to put
Kerry in prison and keep him there."

Those were words Charles could understand and he was
satisfied with the explanation. But to fight the word of the
lieutenant governor from a sickbed was a problem for which
he had no solution. The lawyers had already tried demanding
evidence and had been told it would be forthcoming. Not
soon enough to save Kerry's life, if all reports were correct.
Charles's brow knit in deeper worry than Katy had reason to
understand. He had been counting on Kerry for more than he
would willingly admit, and as Charles gazed at his pregnant
wife's imploring eyes he knew he would have to survive the
pain that was his constant companion until he was assured of
Kerry's freedom.

Despairingly Katy watched as more futile letters went out,
each one a tiny drop in a barren bucket, creating sound but
not a single ripple. Jake's return letters contained few reassur-
ances. Mahomet's medicines were having some effect, but
debilitating conditions and Kerry's depressed state worked
against him.

A letter from Jake in mid-November delivered the first
resounding effect. Katy stood stricken as her gaze flew over
the pen-scratched words searing her soul. A casual comment,
thoughtlessly thrown in as if common knowledge—as it probably was in Charleston, but not in the isolation of the
Stockbridge home—burned in glaring letters in Katy's guilty
eyes.

". . . it's as if he don't care if he lives or not. Arrogant
stubbornness, not saying where he went last summer when
the whole damn town knows he wasn't here them weeks . . ."
Jake's words went on in a tirade about not having the sense to
protect himself, but Katy read no more. It was not himself
Kerry protected, but her. The only alibi he could provide for
those vital days would destroy her reputation and Sir Charles
as well.

Katy tore the letter into shreds and flung it into the fire;

then, lifting her skirts high above her ankles, she raced in a most unladylike manner to her husband's bedside.

"Charles, I have decided to go to Charleston to intercede with the governor on Kerry's part personally. Letters have had no effect and I cannot countenance doing nothing while there is any action left to take." She spoke with firm decision, leaving no room for protests.

Charles stared at Katy's flushed face and darkened eyes and wondered if her delicate condition caused hysteria. Soothingly he gestured for her to sit. "I do not think the doctor would recommend travel in your condition, and who would you find to accompany you at this time of year?" Despite his words, he seriously contemplated her proposal. She would not rest easy until every possible alternative had been explored, and he would not rest at all until the impossible had been accomplished. If a trip to Charleston would ease her mind . . .

"I will send for Mahomet and request the use of Kerry's carriage. I need no one else to accompany me. Betts will allow me to spend the night in Kerry's town house and I will be home the next day. You cannot talk me out of it."

"I see that," Charles mused. "You have thought about this for a while, then?"

"It is something that has to be done. I will go with or without your permission, but I would feel better if you agreed to let me go. I have no wish to aggravate your health at the price of Kerry's."

"I realize you are being torn between two duties, Katy. Go, by all means. I will give you another letter to the governor as your introduction. Perhaps a personal plea will speed up the process. But a word of warning, Katy. If any promises are made, get them in writing. And better yet, be certain one copy comes home with you—tell them I have requested it, and they will not refuse." Charles's hand went up to caress the softness of her cheek. Seeing the confusion of emotions in her eyes, he continued, "But travel wisely, please. I will count the hours until you return."

Torn by the softness of his words, all her angry defenses crumbling, Katy fell to her knees beside the bed, burying her face in the blankets covering him, while sobs racked her body. How he could understand so much and so little would remain a mystery to her; she was only grateful it was so.

November 15, 1737

M A H O M E T arrived within two days in the small, partially covered curricle Kerry kept in Charleston. It provided little protection from the elements but it was twice as fast as the unwieldy barouche and had the advantage of being available while the carriage remained another day away at Twin Oaks. Deciding time was worth the discomfort, they set out early the next morning under chilly, overcast skies. With luck, they would beat the weather to town.

Luck did not accompany them. The chill November breezes turned increasing colder and sharper. The loosening of a carriage wheel necessitated makeshift repairs that delayed their journey longer than anticipated. By the time Mahomet picked up the reins again, a driving rain had begun, the darkened sky promising worse to come. Katy shivered beneath the drenched wool robes, her fur-lined cloak soon plastering itself to her hair and gown. Mahomet drove stoically on, oblivious of cold and rain. There were no stopping places between here and there, and his duty was to get Katy to Charleston as soon as possible, and this he had every intention of doing.

By the time they reached the city of which Katy had heard
so much and seen so little, she was in no condition to take in
its delights. She had only one thought in mind: see the
governor and free Kerry. The rain had turned to a wet snow
and the last light of day was fading when Mahomet drew up
at the governor's residence without consulting Katy on her
destination. Too cold and weary to question his choice, Katy
took the slave's helping hand to step down from the curricle,
then stood facing the palatial mansion holding all her hopes.
Without further thought, she straightened her slender back
and marched up the cut-stone stairway, unaware of dripping
cloak or shivering fingers as she focused on the task before
her.

A servant answered the door, staring forbiddingly at the
small drenched figure darkening the doorway, then hesitating
as his gaze took in the familiar curricle waiting outside. At
Katy's request to see the governor, he again assumed his
haughty air, informing her the governor was not in before
moving to close the massive door.

Hair coated with fine flakes of snow, rivulets of water
dripping from cloak and gown, Katy daringly stepped forward, ruining the parquet flooring. "I must see the governor
at once. If he is not here, you will please inform me where I
might find him." She spoke with all the authority of one
accustomed to obedience, a knack she had learned unconsciously from Lord Kerry and her husband. It stood her in
good stead this time; the butler hesitated long enough for an
older, elegantly dressed woman in towering powdered wig to
enter the hallway.

"What is going on here, James? Who is this young woman?
What does she want?" The lady moved closer, the kindness
of her lined face more reassuring than her sharp words as she
quickly took in Katy's pitiful state, and as the butler had
done, the waiting curricle beyond. "Should I know you?" she
asked Katy directly.

"I am Katherine Stockbridge. I have come to see the
governor. If you will kindly tell me where I might find him, I
will trouble you no more." Shivering violently now, Katy
was impatient to be gone, away from inquiring eyes. She had

only one message to deliver and only one man could hear it; she must conserve her strength until the proper time.

The woman's eyes widened slowly, taking in the richness of the fur-lined cloak and the delicacy of the small, wet figure beneath it. "So you are the fabulous Katy of whom I have heard so much. Come in, child. I cannot send you back out in this weather, you will catch your death of cold. I am the governor's wife, and I have heard of you from Lord Kerry." She took Katy by the arm and urged her in, gesturing for the butler to close the door behind them.

"I cannot impose on you like this. I must see the governor as soon as possible. My carriage is waiting outside and I . . ." Confused by the woman's admission to knowing her, Katy faltered.

"Send the carriage away. You are going no farther on a night like this. The governor should be home anytime now and you may see him as soon as I have you dried out and warmed up."

In the woman's competent hands the cloak was removed and handed to the butler, Mahomet sent on to Lord Kerry's home, and Katy ushered up the stairs to a guest room, where a warm fire already blazed. Shivering and too chilled to protest, Katy gratefully gave herself up to these warmhearted manipulations.

Within half an hour, wrapped in a warm robe, sitting by the fire, balancing a cup of hot chocolate across a small table from the governor's lady, Katy was spilling out the entire story in an effort to enlist the aid of her sympathetic listener. She no longer cared if she was looked on with scorn as an adulteress, if only she could free Lord Kerry with her confession. And this woman's sympathies evidently lay with the imprisoned nobleman.

"And you say you have proof that Lord Kerry was with you at Twin Oaks when young Halberstam claims he was up at Williamsburg with the Indians? What kind of proof?" The older woman set her cup down and eyed her small companion dubiously. She did not doubt the chit's loyalty to Lord Kerry; to make a confession of adultery to see him freed was a grand, if foolish gesture, but the governor was not likely to take the word of this unknown youngster against his appointed lieutenant, no matter how much his wife despised the man,

Katy bowed her head and involuntarily covered her swelling abdomen with one hand. "We have witnesses that will swear to my being at Twin Oaks the entire summer, a slave who will swear to his master's presence during that time, and my word that Kerry is the father of the child I am carrying. Dr. Jackson will confirm the dates and that my husband has been a bedridden invalid for months."

The lined face of the woman across from her softened. She had lost all but one child, a daughter, in infancy, and no longer held any hopes of more. The plight of these young lovers and their unborn child affected her, and she believed Katy's story implicitly. The light in Kerry's eyes as he spoke of his young ward had given him away long ago; she needed no further proof.

"Stand up, child, and let me have a look at you. If you aren't the tiniest thing I've ever seen . . . Kerry was right when he said you were no bigger than a kitten and twice as pretty." If she had needed any further evidence, it was there in the disproportionate curve of that slender body and the swelling breasts. She had been through too many pregnancies of her own not to recognize the signs and guess the timing was right. "I'll have the maid fetch one of my daughter's gowns. She's larger than you, but perhaps one of her older mantuas can be made to fit. We'll see what we can do. You certainly can't address the governor wearing that wet gown of yours." And rising to her feet, she bustled efficiently about the room, ordering maids to clear the tea things and others to search the wardrobes for clothing that would suit their guest.

Nervous and uncertain of her benefactor's reaction to her confession, Katy submitted willingly to the woman's commands, allowing the maids to scent and set her hair in a stylish coiffure, donning the silken gown and petticoats they retrieved from the absent daughter's wardrobe. They were a trifle long, but high-heeled slippers raised her height somewhat, and the tightly laced bodice and flowing mantua concealed her growing waistline. When she was finished and presented with a mirror, Katy barely recognized herself in the elegant lady appearing in the reflection.

Turning to the older woman with questioning eyes, she asked, "Why are you doing this?"

"I am doing it for Lord Kerry. My husband is a reasonable man, and he will listen to your story with an open mind, but you are much more likely to convince him while you are blinding him with your beauty. He is only human, like anyone else. He is downstairs now, warming up before a roaring fire, and sipping his favorite beverage. If you are ready, I think this will be the perfect time to confront him."

Without further ado, Katy was hustled downstairs, letter of introduction in hand, and presented to the governor in his study.

The governor held his position as much out of his stately bearing as for his aptitude for the office. A solidly built, bewigged gentleman of above average height, he rose immediately upon Katy's entrance, raising an eyebrow inquiringly to his wife while taking in the diminutive beauty of her companion.

Introductions were made, the letter from Sir Charles presented, and the governor's wife discreetly departed, leaving Katy to spin her tale and weave her charms while the governor mused, dazzled, over her words. He made no comment over the revelation that the beautiful young woman before him was Lord Kerry's lover, merely nodding his head over the circumstances of their affair, and raising his eyebrows delicately at the mention of her condition as evidence. When Katy finished, he frowned thoughtfully and summoned his wife.

"I take it you have heard Lady Stockbridge's tale?" At his wife's nod, he added, "And you are satisfied that her, ah, 'evidence' is convincing?" He waited again for his wife's nod before returning his attention to Katy.

"The fact that Lord Kerry refuses to give his whereabouts during the period in question seems to verify your story, Lady Stockbridge. He would not risk being hung for anything less than a lady's honor, and I admire your courage in stepping forth to reveal the true facts. I will do everything in my power to keep your secret, but there are a few loose ends that I must tie up before making any decisions. If you will excuse me, I would like to talk to my wife alone for a few minutes."

He stood, and a servant was summoned to return Katy to her room.

Katy's nervousness grew with every passing moment. She walked the bedroom floor, clenching and unclenching her hands as she waited for some word from below. Doors opened and closed, voices drifted up from downstairs, but nothing told Katy what she wanted to know. Shivering again, she poked at the fire, but its heat could not warm her anxiety. Had the governor believed her story? What would he do now? Would he call in Halberstam and, heaven forbid, tell him her tale? This possibility caused Katy's thoughts to revert to Sir Charles, and in a rush of affection she wished she were home with him, wished she had never been so foolish as to betray him, and prayed he would never find out what she had done. Vowing never to be unfaithful again if only she could see Kerry freed without harm to her husband, Katy resumed her anxious pacing. Her head was pounding from the tension of her thoughts and fears by the time the governor's wife reappeared.

And then only to say the governor had gone out and Katy was invited to have dinner. Under the circumstances, she could scarcely refuse, and Katy simply nodded her acceptance, pausing in her pacing only long enough for her hostess to leave again, then resuming her nervous walk to the detriment of the flooring. Images of Kerry lying fevered and wasted in the filth of some cold prison flashed across her mind in increasingly more vivid horror.

A maid came to announce dinner and Katy considered pleading illness, but she could not be so ungracious to her well-meaning hostess. She could eat nothing, but she could at least put in an appearance. Steeling herself for the social formalities she was in no mood to conform to, Katy began her descent to the foyer.

Lost in the blackness of her thoughts, concentrating on the evening ahead, Katy did not notice the dim figures in the half-light below. Not until she heard Kerry's muffled voice calling to her did she look up, startled from her reverie, certain that the sound had been in her head. At the foot of the stairs stood the governor and his wife, and beside them, leaning on the newel post for support, stood a scarecrow figure of unkempt and disheveled appearance, his tangled hair matted and filthy and as indistinguishable in color as his unclipped beard. Only the glittering green of his eyes gave him away, and the whispered voice of astonishment she heard once more, before the room started spinning and her mind went dark and blankness claimed her.

"Katy!" The voice rang stronger, panic-stricken now, reverberating in all the potency of fear against the four walls surrounding him as the scarecrow dashed up the stairway just as the elegantly clad figure lost balance and came down. Where once he had not the strength to stand alone, he discovered the power to catch the tumbling figure before she fell, lowering her gently the few inches remaining to the landing.

"Get a doctor! What in bloody hell is she doing here?" Kerry demanded furiously, muttering curses under his breath as he held Katy's limp form in his arms, stroking her cheeks with his chapped hands, praying for some movement from the long lashes.

"I'm sorry, lad, didn't think what the shock could do to her in her condition. Let me get James and we'll carry her back to the room." The governor turned to his wife, but she was already hurrying down the hall, scattering maids and errand boys in her wake as she sent for butler, doctor, maids, and smelling salts.

Scooping Katy's slight form up in his arms as if she were of no weight at all, Kerry threw the governor a sharp glance before starting up the stairs, but his only comment was a curt demand to be shown the way to Katy's room.

As Kerry arranged the lifeless form on the bed indicated, the governor's wife hurried in with smelling salts, but Kerry ignored her. As he sat on the bed and began unlacing the tight bodice of Katy's gown, he demanded acidly, "What condition were you were referring to, Governor?"

Embarrassed, the man mumbled uneasily and cast a surreptitious glance at his annoyed wife. "Nothing, my boy, nothing, just the heat of the moment, you know. We'll get the doctor here to have a look at her. She's been out all day in this miserable weather and may have caught a chill."

"What is she doing here? Why am I here?" Kerry's tone was curt, unimpressed by the older man's explanation. His fingers shook as he worked the laces, but his mind was steady. Katy's pale face floated insubstantially before his eyes, and he prayed for the strength to keep his grip on reality.

Katy stirred slightly and the governor's wife moved decisively, preempting Kerry's position. "Get out of here now before you shock her again, couple of fools that you are. Carry your argument elsewhere, but make yourself respectable before you come back here. Poor child has had enough for one day without having to smell the likes of you." She wrinkled her nose expressively, eyeing Kerry's tattered garb with distaste. At the first sign of Kerry's protest, she added, "She is fine, the doctor will be here in a moment, and there is nothing else you can do; now, get out."

Obediently Kerry retreated before this onslaught, too conscious of the sight he must present to deny the truth of her words. As Kerry followed the governor out, the doctor entered the downstairs hallway, and he felt relief at leaving Katy in more competent hands than his own. His mind immediately turned to more relevant subjects.

Hair still damp from his bath, Kerry returned to Katy's room some time later with the prison stench removed and his hair restored to its natural color. Wearing his auburn locks pulled back from his face, he exposed the pale gaunt lines of a newly shaved jaw. Clothes hastily sent for hung loosely where once they had fit snugly against his muscular frame, and his eyes still glowed feverishly, but there was no keeping him from Katy's side. He had drawn the entire story from the governor, and there was a wistful look on his face as his hand rested on the knob of the room he was about to enter. Commanding all his poorly practiced capacity for control, Kerry entered the room.

Katy lay sleeping against the pillows, her hair no longer piled in its sophisticated coiffure but streaming across the linen in a fine gold mist. Gone was the borrowed gown; in its stead was an elaborately laced shift that did little more than cover her creamy skin with a translucent haze. Kerry caught his breath, afraid any movement of his would dissolve this hallucination, and he would find himself back in the filthy dungeon once more. So many fevered nights he had dreamed of her by his side; it seemed too incredible to believe this was any more than another trick of his fevered imagination.

Katy stirred restlessly in her sleep, and gradually Kerry exhaled, stepping farther into the room. When dark lashes swung, startled, from violet pools, Kerry was by her side, the first image her gaze fell upon.

"Kerry!" Hungrily she took in the transformed figure at her side. He looked ill, but human, and best of all, free. She held her arms out to him, and he fell into them joyfully, pulling her hard against his chest as he had dreamed of doing for so many lost nights and days, touching her warmth and softness and knowing for certain this time it was real.

"Oh, my God, Katy, it was just the thought of holding you like this one more time that has kept me sane. I am not sure yet I dare believe this is real." Kerry sat at the edge of the bed and smoothed back the cascade of curls falling about Katy's neck and shoulders, admiring every wave and sparkle and absorbing every touch as if he were a blind man just returned to his senses.

"Believe me, I am real." Her hands crept behind his head, pulling him down until their lips touched. The satisfaction of this one forbidden kiss served to ease the pain of all the days and nights of worry, and briefly she gave herself up to its ecstasy.

But remembering her vow of faithfulness, Katy gently extricated herself from his embrace when it ended.

Kerry's eyes darkened sorrowfully. "I am sorry, Katy. I have no right . . . but you are a feast to a starving man. I will try to behave. We may be interrupted at any time, and I must talk to you. The governor and I had a long talk . . . You have done a courageous but foolish thing in coming here." Unable to keep his hands to himself, he pressed them around her small white ones, his eyes greedily devouring all that lay exposed before them.

"It is worth whatever price I must pay to see you free again. We have been frantic with worry: you are the one who has been foolish." The love and pride in Katy's eyes belied her words.

Concern puckered Kerry's brow as he ran a rough hand down her smooth cheek. "The governor has promised to keep our secret; it is not a promise I could have extracted from Halberstam or the council. Still, you risked much in coming here. Is Charles well?"

Sadly Katy shook her head, dark eyes expressive of the suffering she could not describe. "No. He is in great pain much of the time, though he never says a word to me. The doctor has offered him medicine to ease the pain, but it makes him sleep and he wishes to remain alert. It will do him good to see you."

Green eyes glimmered feverishly, and Kerry's hand scorched against her palm. Words spilled from his tongue without control. "Katy . . . the story you told the governor, is it true? You would not lie about such a thing? Am I truly father of your child? Do not lie, Katy, I will know if you do."

Lowering her gaze, Katy pressed his hand and nodded dumbly. She could not keep such a thing secret from him, though it would be better for all concerned if she could.

"You are certain it cannot be Charles's?" Pain and hope twisted alternately within him, and he watched anxiously for the answer.

"I am certain," she replied in a low voice. "Charles has been too ill since you left . . ."

"Oh, my poor Katy," he whispered. Forgetting his promise, Kerry pulled her against him once more, rocking her consolingly in his arms. "I am never there when you most need me. I would give everything I possess for the right to be with you all the time, though I have given you no reason to believe me," he added bitterly. "Does Charles know? What have you told him?"

Katy felt the excessive warmth of Kerry's body through her thin wrappings and knew him too ill to be out of bed. His words came from a state bordering on delirium, and she dreaded his reaction to what she had to say, but it must be done. "He believes the child is his, from a time before you left for Charleston. I will not tell him otherwise," she said firmly and clearly, pulling back from Kerry's arms so she might look him in the eyes. "This child is the only thing that eases his pain. It makes him happy to believe he has finally sired an heir, and the prospect of the child's birth is the one thing that may get him through this winter. We owe him this, Kerry, and as much as it may pain you, I am asking you to give up all claim to it. Do you understand me?''

Anguish deepened the lines on his brow as Kerry stared back into clear violet pools, seeing her reasoning clearly through the haze of his own. He kissed her cheek and let her go. ''I understand and will respect your wishes. I suppose it is the least I can do after what Charles has done for the both of us. But you are right, I don't like it, and if it were in my power to do so, I would claim the child for all the world to know. And this time you will not keep me away; I wish to watch him grow and to be there when he comes.'' His hand strayed to the small swelling of Katy's abdomen and he smiled as he caressed its growing curve. ''So find some excuse for me to camp on your doorstep, for if I keep no other promise in my life, I will keep this one, my darling Katy.''

Tears formed in Katy's eyes at his tender touch and all the calm control she had maintained through the last harrowing hours dissipated, leaving her open and defenseless and relieved that someone else now shared her terrible burden. Pressing his hand where it rested, Katy looked up into the angular face she so dearly loved, and touched Kerry's hot cheek. ''Then you must go back with me tomorrow, and I shall assign you an invalid bed of your own. Jake tells me you have been ill.''

A dark shadow passed over Kerry's face, and he caught her hand in his as he shook his head. ''No, my love. There are things I must do here first before I can join you. Besides, it would not look well if Charles learned I was freed immediately; he would want to know how you did it, and you cannot very well tell him, can you? Just go back and tell him you have the governor's word that he would investigate the matter more thoroughly, and I will show up in a week or two before he can worry again. Can you do that for me?''

Unconsciously Katy dug her fingernails into his hand, and a feeling of terror swept through her. ''Kerry, I do not know what you are planning, but don't. Come back with me tomorrow; we will find some explanation for Charles, and then, when you are feeling better, you can come back here. You are not well now, and I cannot leave you here.'' Unreasoning fear edged her voice and she clung to him as if afraid to let go.

''I know what I am doing, Katy. I cannot let any rumor touch you or your family. Go home, take care of them; I will take care of myself. Now it is late and you are supposed to be sleeping; give me a kiss and I will say good night.'' There was sorrow in Kerry's voice and eyes as he took in the faerie figure in front of him, knowing he had to part from her again. As she moved into his arms and he stole one last kiss, he stored the memory of this moment to hold through all the empty days to come. If he had only known how many they would be, he would never have let her go.

Leaving Katy sobbing into her pillows, Kerry stepped outside the door, and face pale and set with fevered determination, confronted the waiting governor. ''I am ready when you are.''

The older man bowed his head reluctantly. ''You know I do not like this,'' he muttered, taking Kerry's elbow and leading him to the stairwell.

''It is the only way I can protect them. After Katy's fainting spell and the doctor's call, it will be all over town tomorrow that she is with child again. The rumors about us have all but died down since her marriage, but if you should free me now, they will all be dredged up again, and even her husband will find it hard to disbelieve them. I do not intend to take that chance. Lock me up and use this time to follow up on the information I have given you on Halberstam. He is the man you're looking for, but I warn you, he is dangerous. By keeping me behind bars you will divert his suspicions until you can verify my statements. It is the only sensible plan I can see, short of murdering him myself.''

''Then you would be hung for certain. I don't suppose you have told that little girl upstairs your plans?''

''I am relying on you to keep it quiet and get me out before she hears of it. She has too many problems as it is without laying another one at her doorstep.'' Setting his strong chin firmly, Kerry stepped out into the flaking snow and gave himself up to the prison guard awaiting him.

November 1737

KATY came down to breakfast half-expecting Kerry to be waiting for her. Dressed in her freshly cleaned and pressed gown, she swept into the dining room to find only the governor's lady in attendance. Hiding her disappointment, she took her place and exchanged casual conversation until the meal ended. After extending her gratitude for all the help she had been given, Katy asked to see the governor before she left.

The governor's wife looked mildly startled and a trifle worried, but she led the way to the study where the governor spent his early-morning hours. He looked up from his papers with surprise, but stood and smiled graciously in welcome as the two women entered the room.

"Good morning, Lady Stockbridge. I trust you slept well and feel no ill effects from yesterday's cold journey?"

"Very well, thank you, sir. I have come to extend my gratitude for all you have done for us and to make one small request, if I might." Katy clasped her hands nervously in front of her. She had been more than presumptuous in everything she had done since she came here, and these kind people had taken it all in stride. Now she might be taking one

step further than her rank or privileges might permit, but
Charles had made this request and she would respect it,
whatever its purpose.

"By all means, make your request, and I shall attempt to
do all within my power to grant it." A guilty conscience
made it easy to be affable. The thought of Lord Kerry once
more in that stinking prison, though now comfortably reposing in a cell of his own with sufficient rations and privileges,
made the governor uneasy.

"Am I to presume Lord Kerry has been officially pardoned
from all accusations of wrongdoing?" Katy sensed the undercurrent of tension in the room, catching the quick glance that
sped between husband and wife at her question, and her
apprehension grew.

"Of course. He has confirmed the alibi you have provided
and given names of other witnesses to prove his whereabouts
at the time."

Katy breathed more easily. For a moment she had worried
that Kerry's sense of honor had forced him to deny the entire
story, but the governor's reply set aside that suspicion. "Then
might I ask for a copy of his official pardon? Sir Charles
requested that he receive one, and I feel it might make him
rest easier to have it. He regards Lord Kerry much as the son
he never had, and he has been overworried on this account."

The governor looked uncomfortable. "Did Lord Kerry not
ask you to delay telling your husband of this matter?"

Katy gestured impatiently. "Yes, of course, and though it
is nonsense, I will abide by his wishes, and if Lord Kerry
should appear before a week is up, I will never have to show
my husband the paper. But should there be any delay, for
whatever reason, it will ease Charles's mind to see that piece
of paper. You can understand my reasoning, can't you?" A
growing sensation within her told her the pardon might be
more important than she had believed, and the longer they
argued, the more determined Katy became to have it.

Something of this thought apparently communicated itself
to the governor, for he abruptly gave in. "Yes, of course, I
am sure you know what is best. If you will wait, I will write
out a copy myself." He gestured for the women to be seated
as he returned to his desk and took up quill and parchment.

The governor's wife gave her husband a piercing glance, then patted her young guest's hand sympathetically. Whatever the men were up to, she was siding with Katy. They waited in silence as the quill scratched out quickly the words guaranteeing Kerry's freedom.

When he was done, the governor blotted the paper carefully, then reached across his desk to hand it to Katy for inspection. "I hope this will set Sir Charles's mind to rest."

"Should it not have some official stamp or seal on it?" Katy inquired, no longer perturbed by her presumption. She would have Kerry's freedom signed, sealed, and official before she left this house. It was a poor substitute for Kerry himself, and beneath her calm exterior lay an undercurrent of worry about his whereabouts and health, but these were things that had to wait until immediate business was complete.

The governor began to look annoyed. He sent a glance of appeal to his wife, but found her as immovable as Katy.

"She is right. You always put your official stamp on important documents. Why do you delay? Lord Kerry is certainly worth whatever trouble it causes you." The older woman rejected her husband's look implacably.

Resigned, the governor posted his stamp to the parchment, signed it with a flourish, folded and sealed it, and returned the pardon to Katy. "An ironclad agreement, Lady Stockbridge. I believe I am beginning to understand why his lordship never married."

For a moment Katy was confused; then, at his friendly smile, she colored prettily. "I am afraid I do not rate very high in his reasons, but thank you. If you should ever be in Georgetown, please let us return your splendid hospitality."

"That I will be certain to do. Give my regards to Sir Charles." Standing, he dismissed them.

Mahomet was surly and silent for the entire ride home, tempting Katy to pry into his mood. But his muffled grunts to her first tentative bids for conversation prevented her from prying far, and she respected his taciturn attitude as a plea for privacy. Only her suggestion that Mahomet persuade his master to return to Georgetown as soon as possible for the sake of his health received any acknowledgment, and his grim agreement was so unusual that Katy lapsed into silence for the remainder of the trip.

Charles waited expectantly for her return, notified of her arrival well in advance by the noisy welcome below. Katy's cheerful demeanor told him immediately that her news was good, and he breathed an inward sigh of relief. It grew more difficult with each passing day to avoid the opiates the doctor prescribed, but he was determined to keep a clear head until he had one last talk with the young lord. From Katy's expression, his wait was almost at an end. He waited for her to sit beside him on the bed before speaking.

"I was afraid the charms of Charleston would prevent your return, but I see the call of motherhood was stronger." Charles lifted a weakened hand to gesture toward the toddler cuddled in her mother's lap. "Was the trip difficult? Did Junior give you any trouble?" He placed a hand over Katy's belly much as Kerry had done the night before.

Katy's joy was too abundant to let this thought oppress her, and she covered her husband's hand with her own. "You may thank Junior for whatever success I may have had."

Charles raised an eyebrow. "That makes him just a trifle precocious, does it not?"

"No, I think it was at just about this stage that Maureen had the same effect. At our wedding, if memory serves me correctly." Katy grinned mischievously.

Beginning to follow the drift of her words, Charles smiled incredulously. "Surely you did not persuade the governor to release Kerry by fainting?"

"No, but it certainly captured his attention quickly." Her spontaneous laughter drew a smile from Sir Charles and set Maureen to giggling delightedly. Lost in the intricate paths of adult conversation, Anna managed a tentative smile and waited for further word of Kerry.

"Remembering my reaction to it, I can well imagine the governor's. Are you certain you did not plan it that way?"

"I am not so smart, but your son seems to be. Anyway, it brought me an audience and the governor's agreement to put Kerry in more suitable quarters while he personally conducts a complete investigation. He promised immediate action, and I am confident he is a man of his word. Will that suffice to label my journey a success?'' Katy dared not show her anxiety as the merry words slipped past her lips. Charles must be reassured at all costs, even at the price of her honesty, which she had already forfeited in any case.

If Charles's pain had been any less, he might have noticed the uneasiness behind his wife's too bright laughter, but her presence was too welcome for him to search below the surface.

''If it has eased your worry, I will certainly call it a success. I have never doubted your persuasive abilities, my lovely Katherine.''

Their happiness extended into the week, and Charles even felt well enough to entertain a few visitors. When a week passed and no word came from Charleston, from either Kerry or Jake, Katy's own edginess caused her to bring out the parchment to reassure her husband that everything was well and that surely it must be Kerry's illness and poor weather preventing his arrival.

Another week passed without so much as a note or a letter, and Katy felt the first stirrings of panic. If Kerry were seriously ill, surely Jake or Mahomet would let her know? Could the governor's reluctance over the pardon have some ulterior meaning? But she had seen Kerry for herself, and he had promised to come to her. Surely both men would not have lied? He had to be free. A dozen times a day she sat down to write a hasty missive to Kerry's Charleston house, until common sense and prudence made her tear them up. He would come, he had said he would, and she would not doubt him.

Boating on the river was sluggish this time of the year, and isolated as they were by Charles's illness, they heard little of the happenings in Charleston. So the news was a week old when it reached them, and then only by the special efforts of a seriously distressed Jake.

Katy knew nothing of Jake's arrival until she came in from the kitchens to hear the children chattering volubly, particularly Anna, who had grown withdrawn and silent over the last months of her father's illness and Kerry's absence. As Katy listened, she heard her adopted daughter pour out more words than she had said aloud in a month, and not until she heard Jake's answering rumble did her heart leap to her throat, and she abandoned any pretense of a leisurely entrance.

"Jake, what are you doing here?"

Anna's mouth fell open at Katy's unexpected rudeness, but Jake's reply was even more disturbing. He stood abruptly, dumping Maureen on her stocky little legs, bringing their welcoming session to an end by ushering both children from the room and closing the doors behind them. Such decisive action from the slow and amiable sailor was more startling than gentle Katy's rudeness. Anna ran to her father for comfort.

Unaware of the consternation he caused, Jake reached out to grasp Katy's cold hands.

"What is it, Jake? Tell me before I go mad. You look like death itself." Katy blanched at her own words and fear flew across her face, widening violet eyes into black hollows.

"The governor is dead, Katy, a week ago. Halberstam is now acting governor." The grim tones of Jake's voice bespoke worse tidings to come, but he had not yet the words to form them.

"My God." Horror-struck, Katy sank onto the nearest chair, still clutching at Jake's hands. "How could he be dead? I just spoke with him two weeks ago, and he was well and hearty then. It is not possible." At Jake's answering silence, she stared up at him, panic ripping inexplicably from the compartment where it had hidden since Kerry's last farewell. "But Kerry is safe, isn't he? He's been with you and Betts these last few weeks, hasn't he? Hasn't he, Jake?" Hysteria tinged her words and her voice rose at Jake's brief negative shake of his head.

"He made us promise not to tell, but you've gotta know. He and the governor made a deal. He went back to jail to keep rumors from spreading about you and to give the governor a chance to cover his actions honorably by finding the real traitor. Lord Kerry had a notion who it was and expected to be released within a week. Instead, the governor died—of heart trouble, they say—and Halberstam has thrown Lord Kerry back into the pits again." Jake spoke cuttingly, his voice almost cruel as he watched Katy crumble before his eyes. What rumors Kerry wished to suppress, Jake could well guess, and Katy's behavior confirmed it. But he was incapable of maintaining his coldness in the face of Katy's sobbing despair.

"No, he can't do that!" she cried desperately, wringing Jake's hand desperately. "The governor pardoned him, set him free; he promised to be with me. He *promised*, Jake!"

Suddenly she grew very still, her face whitening to a ghostlike pallor as she stared up at Jake. "Why has it taken you a week to come to me? Have you seen Kerry? Is he well?" In contrast to the hysteria of moments before, her tone grew cold and calm, a chill of fear creeping into the marrow of her bones as she found her answer in Jake's eyes before he could reply out loud.

Jake's tongue felt swollen and lumpish as he gazed into the black pools that had once been sparkling violet waters. He had been driven here in a frenzy of jealousy, anger, and anguish, too furious to gain control of his actions, and now Katy was paying the price of his recklessness. How could he find the words to tell her the rest?

"I'm sorry, Katy. I did not mean to break the news to you like this. I have been beside myself these last few days, and I don't know what I'm saying. Maybe I should talk to Sir Charles first."

"Oh, no. No, you don't, Jacob Horne. You stand right there and tell me what you came to say. I don't care what you think of me, accuse me of anything you like, but for God's sake, tell me what's happened to Kerry!" She nearly screamed the words, reading Jake's expression all too easily.

Jake looked away and began reciting mechanically words practiced and thrown away a dozen times on his ride up here. If being a gentleman meant repeating any more of these cruel reports, he would prefer to return to sea.

"It's taken me this week or more to find Lord Kerry and get to him. When they came to throw him back in the public cell and he found out about the governor, they say he went mad, nearly killed the guards with his bare hands. When they threw him back in with the others, he started a riot. They had to separate him, and not very gently. I finally found him in a cell of his own, not much more than a rat hole, but he's beyond noticing. He's raving, Katy, I can't get any sense from him at all. One minute he's threatening to kill Halberstam and the next he's calling to you, telling you he's coming. He don't even recognize me."

Jake's voice dropped off as he heard the quiet sobs and choking gulps of breath beside him. He knelt down before her, still holding her hands helplessly, not knowing what to say or how to calm her. He had heard about Katy's pregnancy, though Kerry had made no mention of it, but he was no expert on such things and too embarrassed to question her. Yet, if it were the truth, he had no right to upset her like this. It was one more guilt he laid to his own account. At least he had had the sense not to mention the extent of the wounds inflicted in removing Kerry from the cell, but they were only incidental to his madness, and Jake hung his head in despair.

Katy couldn't calm the racking sobs shaking her frame; they grew in magnitude with each passing moment as Jake's words ground deeper and deeper into her imagination, bringing forth vivid pictures of Kerry as she had seen him last, knowing he could not survive much longer. The effort of driving out such thoughts took all her strength, leaving none to dry the tears.

The drawing-room doors slid open and hastily closed again, distracting Katy into looking up. "Charles!" she whispered, horrified, then cried his name out loud again, "Charles!"

Whereas once she had been paralyzed with anguish, now she leapt into action, running to her husband's side so he might lean on her, guiding him to the nearest seat with a gentle concern completely dissipating the hysteria of moments before. "Charles, you shouldn't be down here. What do you think you are doing?"

"Not sitting on that bloody sofa, for one thing," Charles said dryly, avoiding the offending chair and aiming for his favorite. The scene he had walked in on had wrenched his heart, but he was not prepared to expose his own emotions to these two children. Anna had told him of Jake's arrival, and he had lain in his room too long listening to the sounds below. Katy's wails of distress had been more than he could tolerate. Gruffly, to Jake, he said, "The only way to handle hysterics is to give them something to do. Works every time. Remember that and save an old man a lot of trouble next time." He patted Katy's hand affectionately and avoided giving her a worried look.

"I'm sorry, sir. It's all my fault. I shouldn't have spoken

like I did, but Katy's not ever taken on like this before. I
didn't mean to . . ." Nervously Jake jammed his big hands in
his coat pockets, staring with dismay at the emaciated old
man who was all that remained of Katy's tower of strength.
He gulped, and avoided Katy's eyes.

Charles waved his hand impatiently. "She's been under a
great strain, and you have apparently added more weight to
the burden. In her delicate condition, that was neither healthy
nor wise. So now shift the weight to my shoulders—they
have been idle too long."

Despairingly Katy sank to the floor at his feet, leaning
against her husband's knees and burying her face in her arms.
It was not a ladylike position, but there was no comfort in
being a lady when her entire world was crumbling apart
before her eyes. The rumble of voices above her head was so
much meaningless noise in the midst of chaos.

As Jake's story tumbled out, Charles rested his hand on his
wife's fair head. He was exhausted by the exertion of travers-
ing the stairway, the pain in his chest seemed to inundate the
entire fiber of his being, but he hid what he could and
concentrated on Jake's words as a palliative to pain.

Jake repeated his tale, not in its entirety, for the benefit of
Sir Charles. Having some suspicion of Kerry's reason for not
wanting Katy's husband to know of his earlier release, Jake
eliminated that detail without harming the truth. Katy's agony
was too real to be ignored, and Jake's loyalty still too strong
to betray her with his suspicions. Not generally given to
reflections, he wondered briefly at the immensity of wrongs
created by something so right as love, but he did not follow
up the thought.

"You say Kerry's solicitors have impounded the governor's papers in an attempt to find evidence of his investigation of Halberstam?"

Jake nodded. "I told them everything Lord Kerry told me
before the governor died, but by the time they got to it,
anything that was there was gone. It's only my word against
Halberstam's, and you know how that looks."

"Am I to take it you are implying Halberstam is somehow
involved in the governor's death and the disappearance of
those papers?" Charles looked troubled. He had in his pos-

session a signed, sealed document freeing Kerry. It must have been written shortly before the governor's death, and he must have written it for a reason. The fact that Lord Kerry had not been released after its posting seemed likely evidence to Jake's suspicions and meant he was holding a highly explosive and potentially dangerous document.

"I ain't sayin' nothin' but that I know Lord Kerry's innocent and he thinks Halberstam is guilty and it's mighty suspicious that as soon as the governor takes a personal interest in the matter, something happens to him," Jake answered doggedly.

"Halberstam means to kill Kerry. I have always known it, I should never have let him stay," Katy whispered tonelessly, not lifting her head from her arms.

Both men looked at her, startled and half-alarmed. Sir Charles spoke first. "I think you have had too much of a shock, my dear. Let me call one of the maids to see you to your room."

Katy raised her head sharply. "I am not going to my room. It is entirely my fault Kerry is in that man's hands, and if it is proof they need to free Kerry, it is proof I shall give. We have the governor's pardon. I will take it to Charleston for all the council to see. I will tell them everything, and let's see Halberstam untangle himself from that one!" Her voice was shaky but triumphant as she related her plans, but the wild gleam in her eye succeeded only in further alarming both men, particularly Jake, who had a better idea of what her words meant than did Sir Charles, though Jake knew nothing of the pardon.

Charles spoke soothingly, not questioning the meaning of her words. "You will give that pardon to me, Katy. If what you say of Halberstam is true, it is too dangerous to have in your possession. I think it is time for me to take charge. Immediately after you hand that pardon over to me, Katy, I wish you to send a dinner invitation to young Halberstam."

That caught Katy's attention, and she stared at her husband with incredulity. "An invitation? Even if I should be so mad as to send one, he would never accept it."

"I think he will have to. If he is the guilty party, he has no idea how much you or I know, or what Kerry and the governor have told us. He will have to come to satisfy his curiosity, but not only that; if your description of his character is correct, he will *want* to come."

Katy glanced to Jake for confirmation she was hearing right, but he was listening intently to Sir Charles and did not see her question. Gathering her wits together, she tried again. "Why should he want to come anywhere near us?"

"Because of you, my dear. Your invitation will regret that your husband will be unable to dine with him but will ask his company after dinner. He will be expecting you to make a plea for Lord Kerry, and such an attractive tête-à-tête will be an open invitation to a man like that. Since I gather he is well aware of Kerry's fondness for you, he will jump at such an invitation, the better to rub salt in old wounds. He will come."

Jake's intensity had turned to horror. "Sir, you do not know this man! Katy will be at his mercy, and he has none. You cannot mean what you are saying!"

Charles looked at the lad with some amusement. Jake's new gentlemanly exterior gave him the appearance of a man-about-town, but did not disguise his touching lack of experience with women.

"If Katy has been capable of holding off a man of Lord Kerry's temperament from the time she was a child of fifteen, she is certainly capable of restraining this young pup through dinner. After dinner, I will demand his company, and after that he will be in no mood for romance. What do you think, Katy?"

The remembrance of her last encounter with Halberstam widened her eyes with horror, and she was not so certain as her husband of her capabilities, but if this must be done to free Kerry, she would do it.

"I cannot believe he will have any interest in a woman five months gone with child, and I shall have exceeding difficulty remaining civil to him if he should attend, but other than that, I am not worried." She spoke calmly, hiding her fears.

Jake collapsed into a nearby chair. His innocence had long since been laid aside, but he felt a green amateur in the face of these revelations. That Charles knew of Maureen's paternity, Jake realized, but that he should so calmly speak of

Kerry's repeated attentions to his wife was a concept beyond
Jake's comprehension. That he now offered Katy for the
prurient attentions of a madman for Kerry's sake was beyond
belief. Did he perhaps also know of the probable paternity of
the child Katy now carried? For Katy to so calmly accept
these plans was the final blow. Jake was outmatched and
undone.

Resignedly Jake asked, "And where do I come into the
scheme of things?" He didn't dare ask sarcastically if he
would be allowed to seduce Katy too; he was no longer
certain he even wished to try.

"I believe Halberstam to be too much of a coward to harm
Kerry directly, but we must offer him some protection anyway. Bribe, threaten, or intimidate his jailers into allowing
Mahomet back there as his guard until we can get Halberstam
up here. On that night and for as long as it takes afterward,
have a man and a sturdy carriage waiting outside the jail. As
soon as Kerry is released, get him into that carriage and back
here without delay. There will be no further interference this
time."

"You had better set the date of that invitation soon. I don't
know how much longer he can live like that." Or for that
matter, how much longer Sir Charles would be able to last,
Jake thought gloomily, watching the older man's shaking
hands and seeing the pain and exhaustion in the lines of his
face. Soon Jake might find both his rivals gone, and then
where would his plans to save Katy from herself be? The
thought of the two innocent girls upstairs softened his disgust;
they would need protection even if their mother did not. For
them he would agree to this insane scheme.

Jake returned to Charleston that same day, much to the
children's disappointment. Katy was too worried about her
husband's health even to notice Jake's absence or contemplate Kerry's danger. After Charles returned to bed, his labored breathing worsened, his ashen pallor sending Katy in a
panic for the doctor. There was no time for guilty thoughts or
self-condemnation as she worked around the clock to keep
her husband alive, while the doctor came and went, shaking
his head in despair, convinced Sir Charles's life hung on the
thread of his young wife's willpower.

But the invitation went out as Sir Charles directed, and as the days passed and the immediate crisis came to an end, they began to wait nervously for some reply. Their only report from Charleston came from Jake, a dour note telling of Mahomet's infiltration of the prison and Kerry's continued fevered madness. Knowing his own time to be limited, Charles felt an anxiety nearly as great as his wife's as each day came and went without reply to their invitation.

When the expected answer finally arrived, its stately formality was almost a hysterical relief. Stating that the acting governor would be pleased to renew the acquaintance of Lady Stockbridge and make the acquaintance of Sir Charles, he would accept their invitation for dinner two days hence. Katy handed the heavy vellum with its hated signature back to her husband, her color a shade whiter than before.

"Will you tell me now for what reason we are bringing this monster into our home?" she asked.

"If he is the coward you say, to terrify him into releasing Lord Kerry. It should not be too difficult a task. Once, I would have been able to do it on my own, but in my present state I am not too terrifying a figure. That is why I am asking your collaboration, unpleasant as it may seem to you."

"If you can succeed in terrifying that madman, I will gladly do anything you ask, but if he is as dangerous as Jake claims, are you not endangering yourself in this enterprise?"

"No, my powers are too limited to warrant eliminating. I simply need you to put him in a mood more receptive to terrifying, else he will storm in here determined to bluff it out with me and be on his way. A pretty girl and too much wine will weaken his defenses sufficiently for me to penetrate them."

Charles lifted his hand to his wife's fair cheek. A sudden draft of sorrow swept over him at the thought of how short a time he had been given to enjoy her loveliness. But he had led a long life and a relatively happy one, and he was leaving a small part of himself behind; no man could ask for more. He was not one to indulge in self-pity. He gave his wife his best smile and watched her go.

December 3, 1737

THE NIGHT OF THE DINNER, Katy paced nervously up and down the drawing room, her green velvet gown swishing quietly behind her. She had chosen the gown for the bulk of its mantua, effectively hiding the telltale bulge of the silken underskirt, but there was no disguising her thickening waistline. Unconsciously Katy stroked the spot where Kerry's child lay hidden, drawing some comfort from this small contact with him.

Half an hour after the appointed time, a maid interrupted Katy's wandering to announce the acting governor's arrival. Katy grimaced and nodded for his admittance.

The tall, pompous figure entering was more portly than Katy remembered, the eyes more reptilian, and she almost recoiled at the cold touch of Halberstam's hand on hers, steeling herself with grim thoughts of Lord Kerry just in time to quell the reflex.

"Good evening, Governor." She smiled sweetly, giving him the benefit of a title he did not deserve, knowing it would please his arrogant pride.

"Good evening, Lady Stockbridge. It has been a long time

since we met." He continued holding her hand, his icy gaze freezing her in place.

"I have not sought to make it so, milord, but circumstances warranted it." Smiling coquettishly, violet eyes sparkling invitingly, Katy dipped a modest curtsy. If he thought her whore, whore she would be; determination hardened her heart.

The ploy was working. Icy eyes melted slightly as they rested thoughtfully on creamy shoulders and wicked wheels turned in his mind. "Then shall we correct the circumstances? May I call you Katherine, your ladyship?" His tone was insinuating as his gaze raked over his adversary. The advantage was all his.

"I would be honored . . . Joshua," Katy murmured enticingly, eyelashes lowered demurely in Belinda's best mannerism, while she secretly gritted her teeth at the sound of that hated name passing her lips.

Halberstam warmed quickly to his role as his hostess poured sherry, keeping his glass well supplied while hovering close, giving him ample glimpses of her resplendent bosom. He was not fool enough to believe this display entirely for his benefit, but he knew when a bargain was being offered, and he was confident of getting the better of the exchange. The thought of possessing Kerry's woman produced a glow warmer than the wine's, and his smile grew increasingly appreciative.

"You have grown more beautiful since last I saw you, if that is possible," he commented. "Kerry always did know how to pick his women." His eyes roamed slowly over her velvet-draped figure, hardening at the evidence of Kerry's bastard growing within her, but otherwise appreciative of her frail daintiness.

"That is because he truly enjoys women." Katy fought to still her nausea throughout this inspection. She could endure almost anything, but it would be simple torture if she must listen to Kerry's name on those despicable lips. But she hid her thoughts behind a deceptive smile.

"As do I. 'Tis a pity we have not had the opportunity to see more of each other. You would soon learn the magnitude of my admiration." Halberstam's hand rested on her bare shoulder as he pressed suggestively closer.

With relief Katy greeted the maid's announcement of dinner. She was too revolted to eat, but it would put the width of the table between them. "Perhaps this subject would best be discussed after dinner, my dear Joshua. Shall we?" She took his arm gaily, brashly flirting her eyelashes as she gazed up at him. Belinda would be proud of her now.

Wine poured freely throughout the meal, but Halberstam was too far enraptured with his lascivious plans to notice. Already tasting the fruits of victory, he allowed the wine to slip down untasted. By the end of the meal, all trace of icy unpleasantness had disappeared; only the flush of triumph lingered in his eyes.

"Since there are only the two of us this evening, would you care to join me in the drawing room? We can have drinks served there." Katy stood coolly. She had drunk little, and as her guest had grown more trustingly warm, she had grown more noticeably colder, but Halberstam was too far gone to observe the change.

"Most satisfactory thought." He shoved his chair back, staggering slightly as he attempted to rise, but recovering rapidly. Well accustomed to long evenings of wine and liquor, he was still well out of reach of the point of inebriation. Wrapping his arm familiarly about Katy's shoulders, he followed her willingly back to the privacy of the drawing room, away from the prying eyes of servants.

Though he was not drunk, his tongue was sufficiently loosened to forget its place. As his hand dropped daringly to Katy's waist, he commented, "Too bad Kerry is such a prolific bastard. Must have cost him a pretty penny to buy that husband of yours."

Katy stiffened. Such talk might be acceptable in the salons of London, but if she had a sword in hand, she would gladly run it through him now. Remembering her game, she replied sweetly, "No price should be too high for the pleasures of love, don't you agree, my dear?"

Halberstam chuckled at this confirmation of his suspicions. "Anything offered in the open market is subject to bargaining, my sweet."

"But rare commodities should bring a higher price, should they not?" Katy moved away, pouring a stiff drink from the decanter on the table and praying her faithful maid would put in an appearance soon.

Halberstam followed her, accepting the drink and gulping it down rapidly. "Oh, I'll grant that. And stolen goods are sweeter, too. But don't you think a sample is needed to prove its worth?"

As he set the glass down to reach for Katy, the salon door slid open, and he casually let his arm drop back to his side. Katy breathed easier.

"Sir Charles asks if he might have the honor of making the acquaintance of Governor Halberstam?" The little black maid stood demurely in the doorway, hands crossed in front of her, dark eyes dancing with laughter. Whatever the master and his mistress were up to, it surely wasn't going to make this gentleman happy. Katy had offered her a large reward to enter at just the right time, and to be paid to listen at doors seemed downright sinful. Tess would gladly have done it for nothing, or just for the sight of this gentleman's face when she threw the doors back. He had pinched her sharply earlier, and she was greatly pleased at so successfully foiling his fun.

"Of course," Halberstam replied dourly. "My dear, will you excuse me while I give my regards to your husband?"

Katy bowed her acquiescence silently, drawing on her reserve to keep hysteria at bay. Tess's laughing eyes had almost been her undoing.

"You will wait here for me?" he asked imperiously.

It was almost more than she could withstand. Biting her lip to control the laughter that so easily could turn to tears, Katy replied solemnly, "Willingly." Then she moved toward the settee, lounging gracefully against its pillows, while an enticing glimpse of ankle peeped from beneath her skirts. When he was gone, she buried her face in the pillows to prevent the sound of her violent eruption from his ears.

Upstairs, the two men faced each other grimly, the younger more confident than ever of his powers as he gazed upon the withered remains of Katy's wealthy husband. With both Kerry and this relic out of the way, Katy would be fair prey to one of his standing, and who knows? If her wealth was great enough after her husband's death, he might consider marrying her himself. She was certainly tempting enough to rate consideration. He would have to keep Kerry alive long enough to squirm at his mistress's fate. The idea began to tickle him, and well pleased with himself, Halberstam offered his hand in greeting.

"Sir Charles? It is a pleasure to meet you at last."

Charles scorned the proffered hand. "A man in my state hasn't time for pleasantries. I wish to come directly to the point, since surely you have deduced you were not invited here to renew old acquaintances." Charles smiled to himself as the man's eyebrows shot up. If he had assumed he would be dealing with Katy, she had done her job well. He did not care to imagine how well. Already he had caught his guest off balance.

"The previous governor received numerous communications on the matter of imprisoning without trial a member of one of his majesty's most noble families. Are you familiar with these communications?"

"I am not, sir. In case you are unaware, the solicitors have impounded all the governor's privileged communications, and I have been denied access to them," Halberstam answered coldly, throwing off the aura of well-being brought on by the amount of alcohol consumed during the evening. If this old man intended to dupe him, he had chosen the wrong opponent.

"Then I will tell you now of their essence. Doubtless you know Lord Kerry has proclaimed his innocence. The governor and his solicitors had been provided with sufficient evidence to convince the governor of the worth of that claim, and he issued an official pardon releasing Lord Kerry from his incarceration. You, sir, are holding an innocent man."

Halberstam almost laughed in his face. Any evidence the governor may have had was long since destroyed, and any pardon was no longer in existence. "That may be so, sir, but I have been given proof of none of this. Let Lord Kerry's solicitors produce the evidence, and I will see to the required justice."

"We can do better than that, *Mr.* Halberstam." Charles emphasized the title. "At the time of Lord Kerry's incarceration, a letter of protest was sent by his family to his majesty. Upon receiving sufficient evidence to release his lordship, the governor immediately sent a copy of the official pardon to his

majesty, to the Duke of Exeter, and to myself. Your imprisonment of an innocent man can only lead to your immediate
removal from office and possible charges of incompetence,
misuse of powers, and improper authority, once the circumstances are revealed to the proper authorities. And I can
assure you now, a letter fully describing these charges is
already in the hands of a competent ship's captain, waiting to
be posted if he does not hear from me otherwise within
thirty-six hours."

Halberstam considered these charges thoughtfully for a few
minutes, wondering how much of the old man's statements
were truth or bluff. Tentatively he decided on testing them.
"There is no need to be so harsh in your judgments, Sir
Charles. As I have stated, I am more than willing to consider
your evidence, and if it was sufficient for the former governor
to issue a pardon, I am sure I can do the same without
consulting the council."

"You will do better than that, Mr. Halberstam. Here is my
copy of Kerry's pardon, officially signed, stamped, and sealed
by the governor. No other evidence is needed." He removed
the document from its hiding place and handed it over.

Halberstam's blood rose at the receipt of the one piece of
paper that had escaped his destruction, convincing testimony
in any court of law. His hand itched to destroy it.

Sir Charles, spotting the nervous tic and divining his motives, interrupted his reverie. "If you are thinking of removing that document, don't. My man in there will break your
arm at a single word from me."

He nodded in the direction of the small dressing room Katy
had appropriated for herself, where one of his sailors from the
shipyard now waited, grinning from ear to ear at the thought
of legal decimation of one of his majesty's loyal officers.

Halberstam muttered a low curse and threw the paper on
the bed. "You may call off your dogs, Sir Charles. Southerland
will be released as soon as I return to Charleston. Far be it
from me to act against the governor's last wishes."

Carefully folding the paper with some satisfaction, Charles
replied nonchalantly, "I hope you have a speedy return; there
will be just sufficient time for word of his release to reach me
and prevent that letter from sailing."

"You can be certain of *that*," Halberstam spat out, swing ing on his heels and striding to the door without furthe ceremony. Before leaving, he shot one last word of farewell "I should think you would have been glad to see the last o that cuckolding bastard. He must pay you well." Then h swung out.

Katy was right about the man's dangerousness. Even though Charles knew the truth of Halberstam's scandalmongering character, the first poisonous seeds of doubt were sown, an Charles cursed as the door closed behind him.

Downstairs, Katy hid in the refuge of the darkened study a the sound of footsteps on the stairs, but some soft rustle of her gown must have betrayed her, for Halberstam found he without hesitation.

"That was a splendid trap your husband laid for me. I wa ensnared no matter which way I moved," he hissed, moving closer to her shadowed outline until he could see the flicke of fear on her pale face. "But you will regret acting as the bait to lure me here, my sweet."

His hand gripped the low neckline of her bodice, his fingers slipping beneath the protective material and harshly pinching a tender crest. "If I had the time now, I would give you a sample of what I mean, but after a winter of nursing a madman and a diseased husband, you should be more recep-tive to my approaches. Till then, this will serve."

He withdrew his hand and cracked it sharply against Katy's cheek. As she crumpled to the floor, he strode out.

Crying as much from disgust as pain, Katy huddled on the floor until she no longer felt his hated presence; then fear for her husband sent her flying to his room.

The sailor had already departed when she entered. Sir Charles lay in the darkness of one lit candle, his face looking old and gray in the single light.

"Charles, are you well? Halberstam was in a terrible tem-per. I thought maybe he . . ." she whispered fearfully.

Charles looked up at the flushed face of his young wife and closed his eyes wearily, not noticing the harsh mark forming along her jaw. "I can still take care of myself, Katherine. Lord Kerry should be free in the morning and with us by tomorrow night. Now, if you do not mind, I think I would like to sleep.''

''Of course, Charles.'' Instead of retreating, Katy stepped forward and bent over her husband's still figure to kiss his cheek. ''I love you,'' she whispered, and left.

Charles lay awake long into the early hours of morning, nourishing the pain in his chest and cherishing the moistness on his cheek.

December 1737

THE NEXT EVENING, Jake and Mahomet gingerly carried in the limp figure of a barely recognizable Lord Kerry. Beneath several weeks' growth of beard, his haggard face lay pallid and lifeless, and beneath the tattered remnants of his clothes, his body was a discolored network of bruises, burning feverishly to the touch. Only Mahomet's sleeping potion kept him resting quietly while they bathed and dressed his wounds; he raved and fought them deliriously whenever he woke.

Grim determination was the only emotion discernible in Katy's face the next day when Emma Stone's dark form appeared in the hallway. Finding Kerry installed in the room on one side of Katy's small dressing room and Sir Charles on the other, Emma shook her head despairingly.

"I don't suppose you are going to tell me that cot in the dressing room is for the nurse and that you intend to obey doctor's orders and rest in the guest room?" she demanded.

Katy laid down the basin and compresses that betrayed her intentions and shook her head. "No, Emma. I owe them both everything I have, and I can do no less than give everything I can to restore them to health, or at least," she faltered, still unable to face the inevitable, "make them comfortable. I will do nothing to harm the babe. I promise that much."

"Then let me help in whatever way I can. You should not be running up and down those stairs in your condition." The minister's wife took up the heavy basin of water and started toward the stairs.

Gratefully Katy watched her descend, then returned to the room where Mahomet waited. Kerry lay still now, sleeping from the potion administered by the black giant, his face pale and emaciated against the pillows. Their attempts to pour liquids between his parched lips had come to naught; he had fought their every move until, in desperation, they surrendered. Now he lay resting, deathlike in his stillness.

"I am going to leave the running of the household in the hands of Mrs. Stone. So if you wish to eat and rest, go down to Bertha—she will look after you. I will stay here awhile." Katy addressed Mahomet, but her eyes lingered on the still figure on the bed, her hands absently straightening covers and smoothing a fevered brow.

The black man watched a moment with thoughtful concern, then nodded his head and slipped away. It would be hours before Kerry awoke; he would be back by then.

Charles was aware of Kerry's state, but after the previous night's exertion, he had taken a turn for the worse and slept most of the day under the doctor's sedation. It was the first time he had consented to the drug, and Katy followed his labored breathing with sorrow. It did not seem possible that one day she would wake and find the wisdom of her husband's eyes closed forever, but the doctor had warned her to prepare for the worst. Sometimes his pain seemed so obvious, she was amazed at her own selfishness in wishing him to live, but the finality of death frightened her, a remnant of the terror caused by her father's, and she clung to any shred of hope, refusing to believe she could not accomplish the impossible.

Twelve-year-old Anna entertained Maureen quietly in the nursery while Katy spent her time between sickrooms. Charles had tried to explain to Anna that one day he would be going to join her mother in heaven, but like Katy, she could not believe she would be separated from this final link to her

past. She clung with a child's faith to the hope that Katy
could save him, and she did her best to help by keeping
Maureen occupied so Katy could spend her time nursing the
invalids.

Only in the mornings were the two children allowed in to
see Charles. Awakening after a lengthy sleep, he would share
tea with Katy, then welcome the frolicking of his daughters
for half an hour or so, until the pain became too difficult to
conceal, and he would hug them both and send them on their
way. To Katy, these morning sessions were the best time of
her day, and as she watched the joy in her husband's eyes as
they rested on the children, she could almost believe he was
recovering. But when the children were gone, he would
clutch her hand and talk of their future without him, desperately staving off the moment when he would submit to the
oblivion of opiates. As Katy administered the drug when
requested, tears streaked down her cheeks, and she remained
with him long after the drug took its effect.

For the remainder of the day, Katy stayed with Charles
only long enough to see that he rested comfortably and took
his meals when awake. The other hours were devoted to the
other sickroom, where Kerry continued to linger on the bor-
der of life, his active mind lost to the delirium of fever.
Sleeping drafts soothed his restlessness, but as they wore off,
his cries for Katy quickly echoed through the hallways, and
he became fierce in his efforts to escape the confines of bed.
Not until she was by his side did he seem to calm down,
soothed by her touch and the sound of her voice. She fed him
nourishing liquids and healing herb mixtures whenever he
gained consciousness, but with every passing day it seemed
more like an exercise in futility.

But in mid-December, the day finally arrived when Katy's
efforts were rewarded by a glimmer of sensibility in Kerry's
eyes as they flickered open. She held her breath until green
eyes focused and found her. Then, taking his hand, she
basked in the slow smile emanating from Kerry's drawn face.

"Katy?" His voice was weak, but the smile grew strong,
hovering behind his eyes and lighting the dark hollows of his
cheeks. "You are real? I am not dreaming?"

Katy stroked his forehead lovingly, her soul singing with

joy, but she did not let her excitement escape. "You may be dreaming, but I can vouch for my reality." Only a hint of a soft smile revealed her happiness.

"No dream ever spoke like that, only my Katy." Kerry closed his eyes with contentment, clinging to her hand until he drifted into a normal sleep.

After that, the spells of lucidity grew longer, and when awake, Kerry developed a voracious appetite, building up the strength he needed to fight the fever. In a household that no longer seemed to eat many meals, he endeared himself to Bertha by asking for seconds, and she soon cooked solely for his pleasure.

Coming in on one of these repasts, Katy touched her hand to his forehead to test for fever, and instead found it captured in Kerry's firm one.

"Sit down and talk with me. You flit in and out like a hummingbird afraid to light. I see you more in my dreams than when I am awake."

Unclouded by fever, green eyes gazed seriously at the loved figure beside him. Her delicate frame still seemed incredibly small to him, but he knew from Mahomet that it was nearing Christmas, and she must be past her fifth month of pregnancy. With a worried look, he searched her face for the well-recognized signs of strain.

"That is because you need me more when you are fevered than when you are not," Katy replied, perching on the edge of the bedside chair.

"Well, I am better now and need you when I am awake. Now, sit down properly instead of preparing for instant flight, and tell me when you had your last meal. Or do you eat like a bird, too?"

"I eat when I can, and at the moment, I am not hungry." She winced as a kick from their child found a tender area.

Kerry grinned. "You may not be, but my son is." With gentle curiosity, he extended his hand to touch the spot where his child lay, feeling the fluttering kicks through the layers of clothing protecting him. The lines of stress on his face melted away and the carefree Kerry of old emerged. "He is not quite starved yet, I see, but would probably like some of this pudding Bertha sent up. Sit back and eat it while you tell me what has been happening.''

Touched by the change that had occurred in his eyes, Katy settled herself more comfortably and accepted the dish he gave to her. For a few minutes it would not hurt to remove the weight of the world from her shoulders and allow herself to pretend they were free and friends as before. With a lighthearted chatter she had forgotten she was capable of, she told of the girls' Christmas preparations, created funny tales of Maureen's antics, and spoke of none of those things weighing heaviest on her heart.

As she talked, the weariness left her eyes, leaving the sparkling pools of violet Kerry so well remembered. Her smile brightened and gaiety returned to her gestures, reassuring him that her spirit remained undaunted despite the heavy load it bore. He relaxed and enjoyed her company in a way he had not permitted himself to do since her marriage, letting the fleeting memories of enchanted evenings sweep over him. Not until he realized she was rising to leave did he return to cruel reality.

''Don't go yet, Katy. There are things I must talk of. You cannot keep me isolated forever.'' He held her back, his strength not enough to prevent her going, but his touch accomplishing the purpose.

This was the moment Katy had dreaded, had avoided with her busyness. She did not wish to talk seriously, had avoided it even when Emma and her husband had tried to talk with her. Only Charles could touch her, and that was limited to a few minutes a day. And with Kerry, it would be worse, much worse; he knew her too well for evasions to work. She steeled herself against the dread subject.

''When your fever is completely gone, you may have as many visitors as you wish, but I have tarried too long. Let me go, Kerry,'' she pleaded, deliberately misapplying his words.

''My fever is gone. You cannot continue treating me as a child. I want to know what happened. How did you get me out of that hellhole? Was it a dream or did someone really tell me the governor is dead? I seem to remember a tremendous desire to kill someone,'' he added contemplatively, searching through the mists left by fever for the kernel of truth in his dreams.

"The governor is dead. He died a week after I saw you at his house. Halberstam is now acting governor." She repeated these facts in a monotone, avoiding the emotions under them.

Kerry cursed, then searching her face, read the blankness of her eyes. "I abandoned you again, didn't I? You risked your reputation, your marriage, everything, to get me out of there, only for me to turn around and walk right back in. I do not suppose you want to understand why I did it?" There was a trace of bitterness behind his question.

"Oh, I can imagine why you think you did it, and I should thank you for risking your life to save me from scandal and to bring a criminal to justice, but I cannot right now. It is not something I think you will understand or that I care to explain. I am just too tired to think about it. Now, may I leave?" Katy answered wearily, all the burden once more shifted to her shoulders and the moments of magic forgotten.

"No," he replied harshly. "I want to know the rest of it. What did you have to tell Halberstam to get me out of there?"

"I did not have to tell him anything, Charles did. You may thank him for your rescue." The memory of that revolting evening hung heavy on her conscience, and she shivered with fear at its finale. It was as if something cold and rotten had come into their lives from that moment on, and she could not shake the dread haunting her day and night.

"I will do that when you let me see him. But just what did Charles know to tell him?" The hardness in his voice reflected the turbulence of his emotions. He considered Charles a friend, but there was a point at which it became possible to resent owing a friend too much, and Katy still remained a bitter point between them.

Katy looked at him oddly. "He showed Halberstam your pardon and threatened him with everything from your family to the king himself, I believe. It seemed to work, whatever it was."

Kerry relaxed. "My family? And what pardon?"

Briefly Katy explained Charles's insistence on a document and the bluff he had woven around it. She made no mention

of her part in the meeting, knowing intuitively it would caus
Kerry's mood to jolt rapidly from amiable to bitter again. H
would rest easier not knowing it.

"Charles shows incredible insight into the criminal mind.
must ask him about that," Kerry jested when she finished. "
take it his health is improving, to carry out an act such a
that?"

It had been early June since he saw Charles last, an
though he had seemed weak at the time, he had been recover
ing. Despite Katy's worries of a month ago, Kerry felt confi
dent Charles would pull through. He had too much for whic
to live. So it was with shock that he heard Katy's next words.

"He is dying, milord, that is why I cannot spend muc
time with you. May I go now?" Those were the words Katy
had sought to avoid, had not said even to herself, would le
no one else say, but now they were out, and she wished to
run to escape them.

Her cold tones and formality scarcely stung him beneath
the sudden shock of her statement. Kerry grabbed her hand
"Why did you keep this from me? I must talk with him,
Katy. Bring me my clothes."

"I will not. He is asleep, and I will not have you disturb
ing him or risking the contagion of your fever. When he is
awake, I will tell him you asked after him. He has been much
concerned with your health." Katy stood with a stamp of
finality and moved toward the door.

"*My* health!" Kerry replied, amazed. "Katy, wait, you
cannot go and leave me after a statement like that. I must
know more."

She had meant to escape before the tears flooded down her
face, but it was too late. She turned her back on the bed and
rested her forehead against the hard wood of the door, her
shoulders shaking with sobs as she clutched her elbows,
crossing her arms over her breasts in an age-old gesture of
despair.

"Katy!" Kerry cried with anguish. "You had best lock
that door if you are to continue like that, for I am about to
climb out of this bed, and you would not wish Emma to come
in on us when I do," he warned, attempting to untangle
himself from the multitude of covers.

"I will save you the trouble. I am leaving." And Katy fled, leaving Kerry to pound the pillows with frustration.

Katy left Mahomet to tend to him the remainder of the day and Emma to ask after his needs and attempt to answer his bewildered questions. There was little Emma could add to what Kerry already knew or guessed, and he was forced to accept that he had exhausted Katy's loyalty with his constant demands. Now her loyalty lay entirely with her dying husband, where it belonged. Kerry expected no less from a character as strong as Katy's.

That evening, as Katy prepared for bed, Charles awoke and called for her. Dressed only in her heavy winter shift, she came to his side, smoothing back his graying hair with tender hands.

Charles pressed her hand to his cheek and admired her proud bearing, even as the burden of pregnancy grew more noticeably heavier. "You are carrying this child lower than the last. Does that mean it is a boy?"

Katy smiled, the tears of earlier safely concealed in his presence. "It is definitely a Charles. I have held long conversations with him."

"A Charles, huh?" He smiled despite himself at this conceit. He had allowed Halberstam's words to cut too deeply, a foolish thing for a man of his age. What mattered now was Katy's love and the child she carried within her, and one way or another, they were both his. "Well, I will admit I like the sound of it, but a Charlotte will suit just as well. Just be certain you take care of him or her."

"I am, and I am feeling fine. There is no cause for you to worry on my account."

"Then what of young Southerland? Has he come to his senses yet?"

Katy's smile disappeared. "What is left of them, at any rate. He was asking after you today." Her tone was expressionless as she released his hand and began straightening the sheets.

"Don't tell me the first thing you have done is quarrel with him? If he is in any condition to argue, he must be improving rapidly." Charles trapped her hand, stopping her nervous fidgeting and pulling her down on the bed beside him.

"The only time Kerry cannot argue is in his sleep, and I am not certain that always holds true," Katy complained.

Charles read the sadness in her darkened eyes and stroked her bare arm thoughtfully. It was not Kerry she had the quarrel with; she fought an unvanquishable foe in arguing against death. She would learn soon enough, and he did not envy Kerry's task in sharing the result.

"Do not be so hard on Lord Kerry. You must have realized by now that you are the products of two different backgrounds and can never hope to agree on many things. Kerry has had everything given to him and must fight continually to prove his riches have not made him soft. It is his nature to do the risky thing, take the more dangerous route. Surely you have learned this by now?"

Katy nodded. "From the first, but right now it is rather difficult to accept."

Of course. To almost lose both her men at once must have put a strain on her nerves, particularly now, when she most needed stability. But she must be made to realize she would soon be on her own and could not rely on either of them.

"Well, I did not bring your young noble here for you to argue with. I want to speak with him as soon as he is able."

"That should be as soon as he finds his clothes and staggers from his bed. We have taken the precaution of hiding everything so he cannot surprise us by falling down the stairs one day." A small grin strayed across her lips.

Charles quirked a quizzical eyebrow. "By 'we' are you including the saintly Emma Stone? Or is she aware of your propensity for nursing undressed males?"

Katy giggled at his affected satiric tone. "You and the 'saintly' Emma have little to fear from Kerry. He is terrified Emma will walk in on him unclothed, and will not stir from his bed until appropriately attired." She grew more serious again. "Though I doubt he could take two steps if he should rise."

"But the fever has gone?"

"Since daybreak." Katy sighed and rested her head upon his shoulder for a brief moment. It had been a long, emotional day, and she was weary from the ups and downs.

"Katy," Charles whispered softly, waiting until he felt her

head turn toward him. "I am growing tired and cannot fight this battle much longer. I wish I could know you will be all right when I am gone. You will be a wealthy woman with three children to raise. What will you do? Have you thought about it?"

Katy heard herself speaking clearly, but could not remember thinking the words. Yet they came easily and untroubled, and when they were out, she knew they were the truth.

"I will do whatever you would have wanted me to do. I cannot go far wrong with advice such as that." Miraculously, there were no tears; his calm acceptance gave her the strength she needed.

"And if all else fails, my love, follow your heart; it has not made a mistake yet." Charles brushed the golden strands back from the clear blue of her eyes and knew he was right. Love burned brightly in their dark depths, and whatever she was or might be, love would continue to guide her course.

Katy remained doubtful, but cherished the thought. There would be a time when she would need it and would see his face as he spoke the words and know he would approve. But that time was yet to come.

December 1737–January 1738

WITH MAHOMET'S AID, the next day Kerry donned breeches and robe and took the first few steps from his sickbed. Using the black man's support, he traversed the few yards of hallway from his room to Charles's and entered without ceremony.

The windows were heavily shuttered, the bed fully curtained, and in the semidarkness Kerry thought Charles asleep. With dismay he looked down upon the frail remains of his once stocky friend, the paper-thin skin of his face and hands now white and lined, with no resemblance to their former healthy ruggedness. The seven months since he had seen him last had stripped Charles of all that remained of his former presence, and sorrow creased Kerry's eyes as he lowered himself to a nearby chair to rest before returning to his own room. He should have listened to Katy and not disturbed the dying man.

A moment later, Charles's eyes flickered open, and their clear blue intelligence restored the familiar features of his countenance. He had refused his medicine since the night before, wanting to keep his mind clear for Kerry's appearance. He was thankful the young lord had come so quickly. The pain was almost beyond endurance now.

"I will wager Katy does not know you are up. She would prefer to make invalids of the both of us so she can know exactly where we are at all times." A ghost of a smile whispered across his face.

"She is usually right, though, and I will regret my foolishness, but she mentioned you wished to see me, and I owe you too much not to come as soon as possible. Katy told me you were responsible for my freedom, and for that I shall be forever grateful." Kerry motioned for Mahomet to depart, settling himself more comfortably in the chair.

"I was counting on that, for I have a large favor to ask of you. But first I want to know if you intend returning to England.

Kerry's surprise was genuine. "Is there some reason why I should? My home is here now, and other than business trips, I cannot foresee any event to force me to return."

Charles looked relieved as his shaky hands picked aimlessly at the covers. "Halberstam will not let you live in peace. He has endangered your life once, and it will not take much reason for him to try again."

"I am aware of that. I had not realized his enmity had grown so strong or I would not have given him the first opportunity. I promise you it will not happen again. You have not said anything to Katy about this? I would not have her worrying on my account."

"I have said nothing, but some things she knows instinctively. She has a very strong sense of survival and knew at once Halberstam's menace. Do not underestimate Katy's anxieties."

Kerry leaned back and nodded thoughtfully. His face softened as he remembered the little girl dressed in her first evening gown warning him so seriously of the petty fop's danger; he had taken her words lightly, just as he had ignored her fears of only a month ago, and learned to regret his foolishness. He would have to pay more attention to her concerns now, though he doubted if he would have acted differently.

"I have always thought she possessed a little of the powers

of a sorceress, but they were only part of her charm. I did not think of them in terms of survival, but I see now that you are right. She has always had that ability.''

"There is no magic to it, and she is not invulnerable. That is why I wished to talk with you." Charles regarded the young lord seriously. Kerry's prison confinement had paled his normal tanned good looks, and the wasting fever had left his normally lean frame drawn and emaciated, yet a fiery strength still burned bright in those green eyes, and Charles felt confident in his choice.

"I have little time left for the niceties. You can see with your own eyes that Katy will soon be a widow, though up until yesterday she refused to admit it."

Kerry remained silent and thoughtful, waiting, and Charles nodded his approval. There was no sentimentality between them, and that made his task easier. "The favor I wish to ask is a common-enough one, but in your case, I fear it might be difficult. You have already agreed to look after my financial interests in the selling of the shipyards, but I have other interests much closer to my heart that will need even more careful tending."

"You know you don't have to ask, Charles. There are none closer to me than Katy and your children."

"Perhaps, but you have a life of your own to live, and it cannot always include a young girl and three children. She is still so very young yet, Kerry. I had not counted on leaving her so soon. She has not yet had time to build up her defenses, she is as vulnerable now as she was when I married her, perhaps more so for a while. The wealth I will leave her will be as much liability as protection. I could ask my brother to take Anna and execute the estate, but if I know Katy, she will not wish to be parted from Anna, or Anna from her. If it were only Katy and Maureen, I would say let nature take its course and I would not worry, but they are a family now, Kerry, and need to be looked after as a family. Do you see what I am getting at?"

Kerry saw. Charles wished him to look after them as adviser and family friend and nothing more. He was asking the impossible and knew it.

"I see well what you mean," Kerry replied, hiding his

esentment. "You have nothing to fear. I love Anna as I
would one of my own. I have learned from past mistakes,
Charles. I would not risk driving Katy to another man's arms
again by putting her in a scandalous situation."

He hesitated, uncertain whether to continue, but his emotions got the better of him, and impulsively he added, "As a
matter of fact, with your blessing and at an appropriate time,
I hope to ask Katy to marry me."

Charles registered no shock at this revelation. "She will
not marry you, Southerland, she loves you too much to
alienate your family with such a proposal." Suddenly tired,
he leaned back into his pillows and closed his eyes. "I was
not certain how you felt until now. I had hoped you would
find a wife and act only as adviser, freeing Katy to marry
again. As it is, I doubt if she will ever look for another
husband, her loyalty to you is too strong. I trust she will not
be driven to marry for convenience as she did with me."

A trifle grimly, Kerry replied, "You need not worry about
that. I was fool enough once to let her go. It will not happen
again." Calming himself with the knowledge that Charles
knew nothing of Katy's surrender to him and the parentage of
the child she bore, Kerry did not continue the argument.
"Charles, I give you my word of honor that Katy and the
children will be taken care of as you would wish. Whatever
else I might be, I am a man of my word."

Charles opened his eyes and allowed himself a small smile.
"That is what I wished to hear. You make it easier for me to
rest now. Thank you, my friend."

Sir Charles died two weeks later, on the eve of the new year.
With Katy six months pregnant and Lord Kerry still confined
to the house, the minister agreed to simple services held in
the Stockbridge home. But there was no avoiding the large
crowd that gathered outside to follow the casket to its final
resting place. With Emma and Anna on either side for support, Katy led the way to the graveyard, refusing to allow
Kerry to risk pneumonia by accompanying them.

As the first clods of dirt marked this final separation from
her husband, Katy turned and hurried away, leaving all but

Emma and Anna behind as she entered the refuge of Charles' home, now hers alone. While Emma led the weeping child upstairs, Katy sought the solace of the study, hoping to find the comfort of Charles's presence there.

Kerry had stationed himself at the front window to watch the procession and for Katy's return. Now, as she entered the door, he turned to her, his arms going out to her misery. Wordlessly Katy fell into them, her tears dry now, but needing the comfort of human warmth to fill the gaping hole left by Charles's death. With time, Kerry and the children might grow to fill and heal the wound, but for now there was only the bleeding emptiness to be stanched, and Kerry applied the pressure needed. He held her chilled body close to his warmth and rested his chin on top of her golden head, his eyes closed in silent prayer.

The month of January was cold and miserable, but Katy sought to warm the emptiness within by devoting her time to the two girls she had neglected over the past weeks. Anna, in particular, clung to her as the one safe harbor in a bewildering world that had left her stranded and all alone just as she was standing on the verge of young womanhood. It was a confusing time for her, but Katy reached out with all the love and affection she had bestowed on the girl's father, and the time slowly passed.

Kerry grew gradually stronger, but tactfully kept his distance as the little family banded together to heal their wounds and mourn their loss. Discreetly he enlisted the services of Emma and her husband as chaperons, installing them in the guest bedroom without a questioning word from Katy. Not that there was any question or need of chaperon, with Katy heavy and far gone with child and Kerry too weak to move far from the house without resting, but he had promised to avoid all hint of scandal, and the Stones were more than willing to protect the innocent.

But by the end of January, Kerry's growing strength made him restless and eager to return to Twin Oaks to account for the losses and gains of his untended harvest and to salvage what he could for the upcoming spring planting. When the doctor pronounced him well enough for a short journey, and a warming thaw in the weather broke through the chill and ice, Kerry announced his intention to make a tour of inspection.

Katy had not thought she would notice Kerry's absence so deeply, but the dinner table was empty that night without him, despite the fact the Stones stayed on at Kerry's request. Katy knew she would have to accustom herself to the loneliness of an empty household soon enough, for Kerry would return to Twin Oaks permanently by spring and the Stones would have to return to their own home, but she was not ready to contemplate the thought. Instead, she turned herself out to make the Stones more at home.

The week passed more slowly than Katy thought possible. Charles had left her with more than sufficient income to support them, and under Emma's guidance, for the first time in her life she found herself in a position to share her bounty with others. Under doctor's orders to stay off her feet, Katy could not join Emma on her parish calls, but she saw to it that Emma left the house each day with a basket full of necessities the poorer families of the town needed to survive the winter.

In the intervening time, while both her friends were out, Katy knitted woolen garments for Emma to distribute later. Unproficient, as always, at this task, she found her mind once again creating pictures and images begging to be applied to paper. Katy had not touched charcoal or watercolors for months, but now her fingers itched to return to them. The process of healing had already begun.

Expecting Kerry's return the next day, Katy prepared to retire early, sending all the servants but young Tess off to bed after the Stones retired to their room. The candles had been snuffed and the fires banked as she prepared to follow Tess's candle up the stairs, when a sudden rap at the door brought a startled halt to their progress.

The two young women exchanged frightened glances. Only once before had Katy known what it was like to be without a man's protection, and it had been a terrifying experience. Since Kerry had come into her life, she had moved within the circle of security he provided for her, but now she was totally on her own. Nervously she glanced up the stairs where the Reverend Stone presumably lay sleeping; then, straightening her shoulders, she moved toward the door. No neighbor would call at this hour unless there was trouble.

"No, ma'am, let me do it." The young maid ran down the stairs ahead of Katy, candle flickering in the draft her movement created. Under Katy's tutelage, Tess had grown from a giggling young housemaid to Katy's right hand, and pride in her position kept her from allowing the mistress to open the door herself.

Standing back out of the door's draft, Katy could not see their visitor, but his deep voice echoed clearly down the hallway to where she stood. "I am Lord Burlington, come to see Sir Charles Stockbridge. Is he at home?"

Katy gasped and flew to the door, sending her maid off in a flurry of instructions to raise the fires and fix tea as she ushered in their distinguished visitor. Showing him into the study, she hurriedly began to light the candles and stir the recently banked fire.

"I am sorry if I have intruded at an inconvenient time, but I have traveled straight up from Charleston and am anxious to hear of my brother. When I saw the crepe on your doors . . ." Hat in hand, the tall stranger watched carefully every movement made by the golden-haired figure before the fire, knowing immediately who she must be, though taken somewhat aback at the obviously advanced state of her pregnancy.

Katy quickly dropped the poker, turning to relieve the marquess' anxiety. "Lord Kerry is recovering well. The crepe is for my husband. I am sorry I did not introduce myself earlier. I am Katherine Stockbridge." She curtsied slightly as she introduced herself, then indicated a chair she had drawn up before the fire. "You must be chilled after such a long journey. Sit down and warm yourself while my maid fetches tea. I cannot begin to apologize to you enough for bringing you all this way . . . I never dreamed . . ."

"It is I who should apologize, springing myself upon you at a time like this. I had not heard about Sir Charles. I am so sorry. I did not know him well, but he was one of the few friends of Kerry's that I trusted. You must forgive my intrusion. If you will direct me to the inn, I will come back in the morning at a more appropriate time." He spoke politely, his face a reserved mask as he moved purposefully toward the door.

"I will not hear of it, milord. Lord Kerry would never forgive me if I should treat his brother so shabbily. Give me your hat and coat, the tea is coming now." Katy took the garments from the reluctant stranger, staring at him with long-aroused curiosity.

The duke's elder son was taller than Kerry, closer to forty than Kerry to thirty. The marquess' well-made frame did not have the muscular gracefulness of his younger brother's, a product of a more sedentary life, but there was an underlying strength in his movements as he crossed the room to the chair Katy had set out for him. His dark hair was styled fashionably, but he had abandoned the powdered wig in deference to the travails of weather and travel. His features were even, if not so ruggedly handsome as Kerry's, but his polite expression and the lack of warmth in his eyes deprived him of any great beauty.

Katy handed the garments to Tess after the tea tray was set out and returned to the fireside to act as hostess.

"Where is my brother . . ."—Burlington's tongue hovered over her formal title; she had not introduced herself as Lady Stockbridge, and he had some misgivings about doing so— "Lady Stockbridge?"

A twinkle of amusement flickered in Katy's eyes as she poured the tea. She had noticed his hesitation and understood his objections to addressing her as one of the nobility. It was the reason she had refrained from using her title in the first place. Kerry had not exaggerated in his descriptions of his brother's staid correctness. "Please call me Katherine, or Katy, as your brother does. The title does not quite suit, *n'est-ce pas*?" Her long-abandoned accent crept back as a reminder of the past; it was something she could not forget under those uncompromising eyes. "Lord Kerry has returned to Twin Oaks for a few days. We expect him to return tomorrow. So if you would care to rest here with us, you will save yourself the trouble of journeying farther."

"Kerry resides with you? How did you gain his freedom? In your letter, you sounded quite frantic." Burlington made no pretense of picking at his food; shipboard fare had been quite limited compared to the assortment Tess laid out, but his eyes seldom strayed from the delicate face smiling back at him through the flickering firelight.

Katy carefully sipped her tea and answered his questions one at a time. "Kerry has been ill and unable to leave the house these last months. Now that Sir Charles is gone, and I"—she made a delicate gesture indicating her present state—"unable to get about, he is acting as my protector once again, under the pretense of allowing me to nurse him back to health."

She smiled gently at Burlington's wry look, acknowledging his brother's deceptions. "I am sorry if my letter has caused you to make a fruitless trip. We wrote it after exhausting all other possibilities when we were in dire fear of Lord Kerry's death. I am afraid he would not have lived much longer if Sir Charles had not resorted to more drastic measures. It is Charles you have to thank for your brother's freedom." A shadow of sadness crossed her face, and she withdrew into the protection of darkness, leaning against her high-backed chair where the light could not reach her.

"I do not think I have wasted the trip. When I learned of Halberstam's involvement, I took the precaution of obtaining the king's commission to investigate matters in the Carolinas and to accompany the new governor on his journey. Unfortunately, the long journey was too much for a man of his age, and he died en route—leaving Halberstam as acting governor again, I presume. That is the reason I came directly to you without stopping in Charleston. If talk of your husband is painful, I will not ask you to go into details, but I would like to know what has been happening."

For the first time that evening, a glitter of warmth appeared in the visitor's eyes, and he relaxed to a degree. Unless she were a consummate actress, her sorrow over her husband's loss was genuine, and Burlington did not need to explain his relief at this discovery.

"Lord Kerry would be better equipped to explain the politics of the situation, but I must admit Charles used your family name as a weapon in ensuring Kerry's release." In her weariness, Katy let slip the familiar address and was rewarded by a small frown from her guest. She bit her tongue and resolved to be more careful in the future.

"If he succeeded in releasing Kerry, he must have wielded it well. I only wish I could thank him personally. Kerry may be something of the family scapegrace, but we have all been quite frantic after receiving your letter. Kerry has been most prolific in singing your praises, and we trusted your judgment implicitly. I trust Kerry wrote to his mother upon his release so they will no longer be worrying?"

"I believe he has written just recently. I sent a letter as soon as he was brought here, for at the time he was in no condition to do it himself. I trust that puts his family's mind at ease. I must admit, his lordship's talk of all of you has taught me to respect you as he does. I never thought I would make your acquaintance, but I can see now he has understated your character. I can only hope you think half so well of me as I do you." Katy bent forward into the light again to set her saucer on the table, the fire's flames shooting golden sparks across her hair as she moved.

Burlington gave a curt laugh. "Knowing my brother, I am not so certain I should take that as a compliment, although I appreciate your politeness in wording it in that manner. I had believed his talk of you to be exaggerations to excuse his behavior. You will forgive me if I am a trifle disconcerted at finding he spoke the truth?"

Katy flushed, knowing too well to what behavior he referred, and that this tall stranger did not know the half of it. What would he think should Kerry decide to tell him the rest? But he had promised he would not. She would have to remind him of that promise. This child would be Charles's as far as the world was concerned.

"Lord Kerry and I have been thrown together at some very unpropitious times. I hope you will not judge either of us too harshly. Now, if you are quite warmed, you must be tired after such a long journey. Let me show you to your room." They stood together, Katy barely coming to the man's shoulder as she carried the candle and led the way.

As they reached the stairway, Burlington took the candle and offered his arm for support, his tone growing softer when he spoke. "I can only wish I could see my wife as you are now, Lady . . . Katherine. It must have been a great pleasure to Sir Charles to know he was leaving such a legacy behind. I believe I would give all my estate for the chance to leave the same.''

"Lord Burlington, I wish I could aid you and your wife, but in all my knowledge of herbs and medicines, there is none to hold a child. Where I come from, the opposite was more frequently needed.'' If there were a trace of bitterness in her voice at these unbidden memories, Katy quickly hid it. "I am sorry, I should not have said that. Kerry reminds me frequently my bluntness is not always ladylike.''

There it was again: the familiar form of address, as if she were accustomed to calling Kerry by name and not title. This time Burlington shrugged it off; the manners of the colonies were not those of England. Instead, she made a more interesting point he preferred to follow up. "You have a thorough knowledge of medicinal herbs?''

"Not a thorough one, only of those herbs useful to a lonely old lady in the back streets of London. One of Lord Kerry's slaves has a knowledge equal to or greater than mine.'' Katy's skirts whispered along the hallway as she led Lord Burlington to the remaining guest room at the end of the hall.

"May I answer your bluntness in kind? You do not have to answer if you choose not to.'' Burlington turned to face her porcelain loveliness, holding the candles high to better see into her violet eyes. She waited expectantly, and he continued. "You had the means to rid yourself of Kerry's babe and did not? Why?''

The darkness of Katy's eyes widened as she looked up into Burlington's. His question had been asked mildly, but there was a penetrating quality to his gaze while he awaited her reply. She could offer him no less than the truth. "It never occurred to me, Lord Burlington. I have never used that particular piece of knowledge and doubt that I ever shall. Does that answer your question?''

"Most admirably. I am looking forward to knowing you better. I must admit, you have piqued my curiosity.''

Katy's smile returned. "And you mine, milord. Until the morning, then?'' She bowed her head, and at his nod, slipped quietly into the darkness of the hallway, leaving the bemused lord to stare after her.

Katy and Maureen were playing a noisy game of tag the next morning when the tall stranger strode into the room, a look of amusement on his face that had not been there the night before. He looked rested and refreshed, and the twinkle in his eye changed his plain appearance to one more reminiscent of his brother. The game came to an abrupt halt at his appearance as Maureen stopped stock-still in front of the intruder, and putting her chubby hands on her little hips, demanded to know his name.

Burlington threw a plea for help to the laughing golden goddess behind the green-eyed tyke, and Katy bent to scoop up the youngster, making the formal introductions. "This is Lord Kerry's brother, Lord Burlington. I want you to be polite and wish him good morning."

Maureen eyed the stranger suspiciously, and Burlington attempted the first overtures with his young niece. Offering his finger for the chubby youngster to grasp, he bowed politely and said, "I understand you have a fondness for sweets, Mistress Maureen. I usually carry a few in my pockets. Do you think you can find them?" To match his words with actions, he began an exaggerated search of his pockets until he turned up a small piece of horehound, offering it to the suspicious child.

At the mention of sweets, Anna came shyly out of her corner to stare openly at this performance. With a wink at the older girl, this once proper gentleman began another diligent search until another piece of candy miraculously appeared. Both pieces were accepted with alacrity as the children cautiously eyed his pockets, wondering if more would be forthcoming. It was the bold Maureen who—after sucking the candy thoughtfully and finding it to her taste—leaned forward and held out her arms to be taken so she might inspect more closely the pockets of treasure.

Triumphantly Burlington took the little imp in his arms and immediately his pockets began to produce more miraculous candies for both eager girls. With a wide grin of pleasure, he looked over the girls' heads to Katy.

"It is a trick I learned with Brigitte, the most suspicious tyke that ever walked. She and Kerry are much alike, and I figured Maureen to be the same." He laughed as the little girl's sticky hands wrapped around his neck in a hug, and he squeezed her tight before setting her back on the floor to run to Anna to compare treasures.

"You have a way with children, as does Kerry. 'Tis a pity between the two of you you should not have a dozen by now." Katy moistened a corner of her handkerchief in the washbasin and scrubbed a piece of candy from Burlington's coat, her eyes sparkling with laughter and joy. She had been afraid of the proper lord's reaction to her very improper daughter, but now she felt relaxed in the man's company. Her estimate of Burlington's character had not been far wrong.

The marquess accepted her ministrations easily, then gave her his arm as they left the now quiet nursery. "So our father thinks. He is threatening to find Brigitte a husband who will change his name to ours so there may yet be a chance of having another Duke of Exeter." Burlington's laughter showed his lack of distress over this possibility. "If Kerry has repeated as much of our family history as I suspect he has, you must have a strange opinion of us all."

"Enough to know that Brigitte would never be satisfied with a husband willing to change his name for a title," Katy laughed. "Kerry has told me much of his sister's strong opinions. I hate to imagine her reactions to that suggestion."

"You are quite right. She has sent me here with a valiant plea to save Kerry's life and marry him off at once so she might pursue her own romance without further threats. Selfishness has always been a famous Southerland quality."

Laughing, they entered the dining room, where the Stones waited with curiosity to meet the unexpected guest.

For luncheon Anna insisted on returning Lord Burlington's treat by entertaining him in the nursery. Katy did not think he would consider this much of a treat, but to her surprise, he accepted, leading Anna into the nursery on his arm as he would any hostess. In deference to Katy's condition, she was allowed the room's one normal-size chair, a rocker, leaving Burlington to fold up his large frame into one of the child-size chairs as Anna helped lay out cold meats and cheeses and

served tea and milk. Maureen's one contribution was to
giggle helplessly and pass the cakes, the one dish she had any
interest in.

Maureen's giggles were infectious, and they were all laughing uproariously at their attempts to manage the meal in their
laps when a loud cough at the door swung their attention
around. Barely concealing his grin at the scene which greeted
him, Kerry stood in the doorway, arms akimbo, in much the
same stance as his daughter's earlier, as he took in the sight
of his lordly brother bent and folded into a child's chair while
he balanced plate and cutlery on his knees.

With a screech of delight, Maureen dropped her plate on
the floor and flew to Kerry's open arms, giving Burlington
time to untangle himself and come forward.

"What in hell are you doing here, big brother?" Setting
Maureen down, Kerry reached out to grasp his brother's hand
and shoulder in an affectionate embrace, his grin spreading
wide across his face.

"Having luncheon with three charming ladies, as you can
see. You are not the only one in the family who has a way
with women." Burlington returned the embrace more awkwardly, not accustomed to showing affection as openly as
Kerry, but pleased at his welcome.

"I can see that, but these are *my* women you are trying to
steal. Anna, are you the hostess here? Do you have room for
an extra guest?" As he asked, Tess entered carrying a tray of
additional food sent up from the kitchen at news of Kerry's
arrival. "Anna, you are a brilliant hostess, thank you." He
made a gallant bow in the direction of the pleased girl, leaned
over to kiss Katy's cheek, and settled himself on the floor at
her feet, appropriating the low serving table for his own use
while Maureen complacently crawled into his lap.

As Kerry talked and ate, he fed tempting tidbits from the
table to his daughter, who promptly fell asleep in his lap
before the cakes were served. Burlington watched with some
envy at the manner in which his brother made himself at
home with the small family; there was no mistaking the look
of love which Katy bestowed upon him, and though Kerry
had his back to his ward, the genuine fondness among the
four of them was evident. There was no need for Kerry to

start a family of his own when he obviously felt so welcome in this one.

Maureen was carried off to bed and the small party broke up, leaving some cakes for when she woke. While Anna and Katy cleared away the dishes, Kerry led his brother down the stairs to the study, where they could smoke their pipes in peace.

When they were gone, Anna turned anxiously to Katy. "Has Lord Kerry's brother come to take him back to England?"

Katy straightened slowly, looking at her stepdaughter through eyes clouded with worry. "He may have, Anna, but I don't think Lord Kerry is likely to be leaving anytime soon."

"If he does, will we go with him?" Anna's anxiety was too painful to bear. She had been uprooted in one manner or another too many times in the last few years, and her uncertainty was obvious.

"No, Anna." Katy shook her head firmly. "This is our home here, and I expect we will stay in it for a long time to come. In a few years, you will be old enough to look around for eligible bachelors and you may be the first to leave here for a home of your own." Attempting to change the subject, she asked teasingly, "Do you have any men in mind yet?"

Instead of laughing, Anna answered quite seriously, "I do, if you do not get him first."

Startled into almost dropping her dishes, Katy asked inadvertently, "Who? Lord Kerry?"

Anna gave her a scornful look. "No, of course not, he is old enough to be my father." Then her face lit up. "Why don't *you* marry Lord Kerry? Then we could live at Twin Oaks and I would not have to worry about you getting in the way."

Katy smiled at this childish ingenuity. "I am not ready to be talking about marrying anyone just yet, Anna, and I certainly cannot marry Lord Kerry. He must marry a lady with titles and family as good as his, because someday his children may be lords and ladies too. I think you have little to fear from my marrying, love, and if I should ever consider it before you are married, I will be certain that you approve of my choice. How will that be?" Carefully avoiding inquiring again into Anna's choice of suitors, she picked up her tray and swept from the room.

Unobserved in the darkness of the hallway, Lord Burlington watched their retreating backs thoughtfully; then, retrieving the tobacco pouch he had come in search of, he returned to the study.

February 1738

LORD BURLINGTON left for Charleston the next day, well supplied with information from Kerry and ready to carry out his commission to the detriment of anyone who stood in the way of his majesty's best interests. Promising to return within two weeks to visit longer and see Twin Oaks, he accepted Kerry's offer of the use of his town house, but refused his offer to accompany him.

"You look in no shape to be traveling, little brother. You had better stay and let your harem take care of you awhile longer. It will be better if we are not too closely associated, though it is hard to hide the relationship," he added cheerfully.

Kerry had not been eager to leave Katy's side, and he agreed easily, watching his brother off with some relief before returning to the contentment of his "harem." Though Katy could not be expected to return his love so soon after her husband's death, she had awakened from the torpor Charles's absence created, and Kerry sought eagerly to renew their friendship. With a little time and patience, he was confident he could win his desire.

In the weeks following Burlington's departure, Katy be-

came more aware than ever of Kerry's presence. At the
dinner table, he entertained the Stones and other friends—
often planters from outlying plantations who had stopped to
see Kerry—drawing Katy out of her silence with grace and
ease without bringing attention to himself.

After dinner, when all but the Stones had departed, he
preferred to sit quietly next to Katy, boots propped on the
hearth while he smoked his pipe and contentedly listened to
the flow of conversation around him, his eyes seldom leaving
Katy's awkward figure. If his hand occasionally strayed to
tuck a golden tendril behind a shell-like ear or reached out to
touch an idle finger, the Stones pretended not to notice, but
Katy felt the closeness of his thoughts and was reassured.

During the days while the Stones were out on errands,
Katy would enter the nursery to find Lord Kerry down on the
floor drinking tea from tin cups with the girls or telling them
a bedtime tale, and her heart would swell with love, and if it
were possible, she knew she loved him more than before. He
became a constant, tangible part of her life, directly and
indirectly. The servants deferred to his wishes, friends called
on both of them, and together they attended church on Sun-
days. He watched in amusement as she drew rapid sketches,
only to wad them up and throw them at him. He showed her
how Sir Charles kept his books, explained what income she
had and how to take care of it. When he noticed her growing
charitable contributions, he joked about the price of avoiding
scandal, and showed her how to include the expense in her
budget. He was always there, and Katy began to wonder what
she was going to do when he was not.

Kerry came in one day to find Katy reclining on the settee
Sir Charles had so often cursed, skeins of wool strewn about
her and a frustrated expression on her face. Examining the
scattered remnants lying about, Kerry raised an amused eyebrow and inquired, "I trust this was not intended for the
baby?"

"No, for a little boy down at the docks. Emma says he has
no warm clothes at all." Katy's expression was one of resignation as she took up her needles once again.

"I do not remember seeing any youngsters down there with
one arm a foot longer than the other. That is, if these are

sleeves?'' He held up the two mismatched pieces with mounting amusement.

Katy jerked the offending pieces from his hands and hid them behind her back. "Quit laughing at me when I am trying to be useful."

Leaning one arm against the back of the settee, Kerry rested his other hand over Katy's where they lay on her well-rounded abdomen. "You are only useful when you are doing things you are good at doing, and you are good at many things. You have a talent for drawing, you love children, and you run this household more efficiently than many women with years of experience."

His voice softened to a caress as his eyes drank in her beauty, not daring yet to touch what he saw. There would be time enough after the child was born to arouse those passions that would bring them together again; for now, he would satisfy himself by accustoming her to his presence.

"And you, milord, grow more forward every day." Katy struggled to sit, but Kerry laughed and held her in place.

"Rest. If I am disturbing you, I will leave. But I am not being forward, I am simply communicating with our son. I do believe that is what you specified this time, was it not?"

"It is, and his name will be Charles Edward," Katy said laughingly, then grew serious. "But you have promised you will tell no one of his true parentage. This is Charles's child so far as I am concerned."

Kerry frowned, the hard line of his jaw tightening perceptibly, but he remained in control of his temper. He had too much to lose by giving in to his impulsiveness now. "If that is the way you want it, kitten," he replied mildly, but could not help adding warningly, "But Charles need no longer be protected. The child is ours, and I am proud of him. I do not regret one moment of the time that conceived him."

Katy stared at him wonderingly. That brief period of adultery had led to his imprisonment and near-death; how could he not regret it and look back on it as a time of immense folly? But Kerry had never lied to her before, and the intensity of his gaze told her he did not lie now. Uneasily she skirted the subject. "I know I am being selfish about this babe, but we both owe Charles a debt we can never repay. I do not think it

is too high a price to pass on his name and title as if the child
were his. If you do not wish me to use the Edward, I will not,
but Charles Stockbridge he shall be.'' Seeing the frown remain between Kerry's eyes, she added sweetly, ''You may
name her if it is a girl.''

That broke the frown, and he laughed. ''I shall start thinking on it at once, but Charles Edward I fear he shall be. The
name is a fine one, and I have no objections.'' He studiously
avoided the ''Stockbridge.'' If he had his way, that would
soon be changed; it was just a matter of time and patience until
he won her around.

Lord Burlington returned the third week of February and
the entire household turned out to greet him. Tucking Maureen under one arm, Burlington laughed as she began rum-
maging through his pockets, and turned one inside out to
empty into waiting hands. He gave Katy a brotherly peck on
the cheek and jested with Kerry over his ''harem's'' care, but
when all was said and done, he resolutely appropriated both
study and Kerry, and they spent the remainder of the day
embroiled in serious discussion.

When dinner was over and the children in bed, the marquis
unfolded part of his plans to Katy. ''I am going to ask a large
favor of you, Katherine, but it is for Kerry's safety as well as
possibly your own.'' He watched wide violet eyes look up to
him in alarm as she sat comfortably settled in her favorite
chair in the salon. She appeared more fragile than a Dresden
figurine, but Kerry had assured him she had a will of iron. At
the moment, Burlington wasn't thoroughly convinced.

''You yourself have called Halberstam a dangerous man,
and all I know of him assures me you are right, but I have not
been able to locate any positive proof that will put him out of
harm's way. I have even investigated your young Jacob's
theory that Halberstam was responsible for the governor's
death, but although the governor's wife admits Halberstam
was the last man to see him alive, she also tells me the
governor had a long history of heart infirmities. I have followed all Kerry's leads and found nothing; Halberstam has
covered his tracks too well. If the governor had any evidence,
it is gone now. I have only rumor and supposition to report to

London, and nothing to remove him from the colonies permanently, as I had hoped to do.''

Katy clasped her hands tightly in her lap, staring back into
the marquess' clear brown eyes. He was a practical man, this
lord, and he would not understand her premonitions, yet he
seemed to share her fears for Kerry's safety. She prayed he
had more than fears to share.

"So he will remain here as acting governor until his majesty sends a replacement?''

"I will see that he is replaced immediately upon my return,
but that means several months of waiting. I wish to borrow
Sir Charles's tactics and frighten him into submission for
those few months.'' Burlington stood before the fireplace,
leaning against the mantel as he looked down on the blue-
velveted figure of his hostess, ignoring Kerry's impatient
pacing in the background. He waited for some sign of
understanding.

Katy nodded reluctantly. "It worked once, and your appearance makes it less of a bluff than before, but I do not see
how you can catch him so easily by surprise this time. He
must know your purpose here.''

"I do not need to surprise. I have power and he knows
it—that is more important. It is difficult for me to flaunt my
power outside the environs of England, but if you will give
me some of the trappings, I will do my best to be convincing.
I wish you to give a dinner party in Halberstam's honor.''

Katy's look of horror surprised him, but he hurried on. "I
know you are officially in mourning and that your condition
rates privacy, not publicity, but I will leave the choice of
guests to you, and if they are close friends, it should not
mean so much discomfort for you.''

Kerry's violent objection to this plan was overruled by
Katy's cautious agreement and Burlington's promise of protection. With a growl, Kerry finally conceded the match, but
a vague uneasiness gnawed at his innards, put there by Katy's
obvious reluctance. He had no liking for this evasive diplo-
macy. It would be simpler to call the man out and put a
sword through his black heart. This thought caught and hung
like a small thread on a thorn bush, there to unravel at length
as time went on.

The invitations were sent, not to a small circle of friends, but to a glittering assortment of the colony's most influential and wealthy residents. The names of two lords and the acting governor would be sufficient to draw the acceptances of everyone able to attend. It would be a social event to rival Charleston's summer season, and should create the setting necessary to impress indelibly on Halberstam's mind the power he was up against and what he stood to lose should he oppose it.

Kerry and Burlington returned from Twin Oaks the day of the dinner. Encountering the hectic activity of last-minute preparations, they hastily retreated to the study with a bottle of Sir Charles's good wine until the time came for them to retire to their respective rooms to dress for the evening. To venture out unwittingly into the whirlwind of preparations would have been more than their lives were worth.

After sending Emma off to dress for dinner and making certain everything was running smoothly, Katy returned to her chambers to bathe and dress. While both girls ran in and out in a fever of excitement, Katy dressed, with Tess's help, in the new gown she had purchased for the occasion. With the help of the neighborhood seamstress and the memory of a French fashion doll she had once seen, Katy had designed a gown that made the best of her no longer slender waistline. Instead of the usual tight-fitting bodice, she had substituted a simple band of white ribbon snugly fitted beneath velvet-clad breasts, leaving the gown to billow out in a cloud of diaphanous black lutestring over a silken underskirt. The neckline was low, but not daringly, yet the off-the-shoulder flare of sleeve bared an extravagant amount of creamy fair skin, broken only by a narrow black ribbon at her throat.

Tess helped to pile silver-blond curls in a staggeringly elaborate coiffure that effectively added inches to Katy's height, a style she had learned in London but seldom had the occasion to use. Still, she refrained from the final fashionable touches of powder and paint, as much in preference for naturalness as out of respect for her state of mourning.

Katy sent Tess out with the children to prepare trays for their nursery repast while she adjusted the final hairpins and made one last critical inspection. Hearing Tess's voice in the hallway and the opening of the door, she expected the maid and called out, "How does it look now?" while she twisted a final curl in place.

The sound of a deep male voice behind her instead of Tess's melodic one made Katy drop her comb and spin around.

"Bewitching, as usual." Kerry grinned mischievously at her surprise. The week at Twin Oaks had returned some of his color, and the seamstress had taken in his dark gray coat to meet his narrower figure so that once more he presented the elegant sophistication for which he was known. Already his broad shoulders were straining at the seams of the alterations, and the looser light gray breeches did not disguise the muscularity of long legs. The lack of color in his attire provided a splendid foil to Katy's light and dark, creating a chiaroscuro effect that would stand out in the crowd of bright colors of their guests.

Katy stared in amazement, startled into silence by Kerry's unexpected appearance. Her gaze longingly took in his immaculate attire, from the subtle silver buckles he affected instead of the elaborate garish ones of fashion, to the burnished copper of his tightly bound hair above the craggy handsomeness of his smoothly planed face. Almost overcome by a sudden longing to fling herself into his strong arms and feel them once more around her, she took a moment to quell her emotions.

"*Magnifique, monsieur,*" she whispered, realizing she was staring but unable to think of anything else. He had never invaded her room before, and his presence left her flustered and nervous.

Amusement tilted his mouth, but it was appreciation that lit the green lanterns of his eyes. Giving Katy his hand, Kerry brought her to her feet, his gaze sweeping over the porcelain loveliness clothed in its ephemeral cloud, lingering longingly over polished shoulders curving delicately upward to reedlike throat and the barely concealed lobes of pearly-shelled ears. His hand reached out to trace their fragile outlines, then halted abruptly.

"I have brought you something I thought might go well with black, a gift to thank you for everything you are to me."

Kerry produced from his pocket an elongated velvet box of old green velvet, pressing it into her hands without taking his eyes from darkening pools of violet.

Nervously Katy tore her eyes away to fumble at the box's clasp, nearly dropping it when the top swung open. Prismed blue fire flashed back at her from the dark recesses of its interior, and she dared not touch the contents.

"Kerry, I can't . . ." she murmured, distressed. Never in her life had she seen anything so miraculously beautiful. To touch them would be to crave them forever. Her eyes reflected the sparkle of the diamonds as she turned her gaze back to Kerry.

"You will." Firmly he unfastened the ribbon at her throat and replaced it with the delicate filigree of diamonds, his fingers brushing lightly against her back and shoulders as he worked the hook. Tiny tearlike droplets were next, fastened to the pink shell ears that had captured his imagination, knowing they formed the perfect setting for his gift. The diamonds caught the flicker of firelight and reflected it in a thousand tiny dancing fires, ringing Katy's loveliness with its enchantment.

"There," he whispered hoarsely, unable to fight a sudden surge of desire. "A fitting charm for a sorceress. I will take my thanks now."

The hands that had been touching her so lightly before now became more demanding, gripping her shoulders painfully as they drew her to him. Kerry's mouth closed down on hers, and their lips met in a fierce conflagration, parting greedily to slake their hungers with every precious morsel of life-giving breath.

Katy felt herself weakening, her backbone melting in the intensity of the blaze conjured up by his kiss, and her hand clung tightly to him for support, tears springing to her eyes as his hands gently released her shoulders to caress her back. As their lips parted, she managed to gasp, "Kerry, please . . ." but his hands firmly held her in place, only now his eyes, instead of his lips, sought her face.

"I was only wondering if pregnant ladies still have the desire to procreate," he murmured, green eyes twinkling devilishly. "I think you have satisfied my curiosity quite nicely."

"Kerry, I swear . . ." She tried to slip from his grasp, but he held her tightly.

"I know you do, my sweet, and you really shouldn't. What if the children should hear?" He was laughing now, diverting her refusal with his teasing.

Katy knew his ploys too well, and she relaxed, allowing his hands to rove where they would. "I cannot accept such a gift, Kerry, and you know it," she replied adamantly.

"Then accept them as a loan, my kitten. It would be criminal to remove them from such a flawless setting." His fingers lightly traced the line of the necklace as it dipped into the hollow of her neckline.

Katy's fingers touched the glittering hardness of the stones, and timidly she turned to find her reflection in the mirror. The ice-blue gems sent a ripple of light across her skin, shimmering against the velvet blackness of the gown. Cautiously she touched the delicate pendant at her ear.

"Kerry, how can I? They are so beautiful . . ." Reverently she stroked one small stone of the necklace. "So costly."

Kerry stood behind her, wrapping his arms about her thickened waist as he whispered against her ear. "Nothing is too beautiful for the mother of my children. Wear them, Katy, they are yours."

Smiling at his reflection in the mirror, she reached up to rub his cheek, enjoying this moment of intimacy. "I will wear them tonight to impress your guests. Perhaps they will distract them from my impending motherhood." A teasing glint appeared in her eyes as she saw his mock resignation in the mirror, and she turned her head to kiss his chin lightly. "I shall need a bodyguard all evening to protect your valuables. Do you know anyone interested in the job?"

Firmly tucking her small fingers in the crook of his arm, Kerry bowed gallantly. "I have no other purpose, my dear. I find your body well worth watching." And pressing her fingers more tightly against his arm so they crushed the cloth, he led her from the room.

None of the guests had yet arrived when they entered the salon, but Emma and her husband were entertaining Lord

Burlington while they awaited Katy's appearance. As the
doors opened, all three looked up in anticipation, and their
stunned admiration at the couple framed in the doorway
satisfied all Katy's expectations. Her smile lit the room as
Lord Burlington approached first, bending over her hand as if
she were a duchess.

"You are magnificent, Lady Stockbridge. I have never
thought black to be becoming until you opened my dull eyes.
The effect is positively enchanting." He straightened, his
eyes finally coming to rest on the string of diamonds at her
throat. Without comment he gave his dauntless brother a
pithy look, then kissed Katy's fingers lightly before returning
her hand. "Kerry has told me of your bewitching qualities.
Now I fully understand him. I can only hope your charm
works for all of us throughout the evening."

"If charm is all you need, you do not need my aid, milord;
yours should be sufficient for everyone's needs. Although I
will admit, all the charm in the world might not be sufficient
to quell our guest of honor. I trust you are preparing something more efficient for him?" Katy could not understand the
sudden tension between the two brothers, but valiantly she
attempted to dispel it.

The Stones came to her rescue, and as the first guests
arrived, the brothers' personal differences were set aside to
form a united front of graciousness building up a solidarity
that their guest of honor would not dare confront. Halberstam
arrived late, not irritating anyone as he had hoped to do, but
giving all their guests an opportunity to meet the heirs to the
Southerland estates and gossip deliciously about their hostess.
That Katy had pulled off a coup with this evening was
evident, and the beautiful widow's name was already being
noted on a number of mental guest lists.

When Halberstam finally arrived, he barely had time to be
introduced to the first few guests when dinner was called, and
Katy and Kerry exchanged malicious glances over his annoyance. He was partially mollified by being seated at the head
of the table on Katy's right while Lord Burlington was reduced to her left and Kerry even below that, but his satisfaction ended there. Katy proved a most unsatisfactory dinner
partner, answering each question coldly and formally and

venturing none of her own, a far cry from the gracious companion she had proved on an earlier occasion.

Flanked on either side of the table by Kerry and Burlington, Halberstam could wreak no revenge and was reduced to conversing with the elderly lady on his right, who turned out to be either deaf or senile. It was not an auspicious beginning to what he had hoped to be a celebratory evening, for in Katy's invitation he had seen the capitulation of the two lords to his colonial powers. An uneasy suspicion murmured in the young acting governor's ear as the dinner progressed.

Katy looked down the glittering table at her resplendent assortment of guests and remembered a time she and Jake had grudgingly been allowed at the bottom of this same table. At the time, she had measured the distance between herself and Kerry by the number of bejeweled wigs and smoking candles dividing the polar distances of their seats. Now Kerry was near at hand, smiling reassuringly at her whenever he caught her eye, and she was part of the animated conversation that always flowed around him. How had such a thing happened? She belonged upstairs in the nursery, not down here with the lords and ladies. But as she looked down the rows of be-wigged and painted men and women, some small part of her began to relax its rigidity, and when Kerry's eyes next rested on her, she gifted him with a brilliantly confident smile and an anticipatory gleam that sent his spirits soaring.

With the meal over, the guests began to roam about the open salons, but frowns of consternation began to appear when it was realized the two principal guests did not appear. Speculation was rife, but Kerry and Katy ignored it as they finally found a moment together.

"Are you feeling well, my love? You look pale." There, in the center of the room, with all eyes upon them, Kerry could not reach out to caress a golden curl or smooth Katy's tired brow, but the softness of his voice had the same effect.

Katy brightened and touched his sleeve as if to remove a stray thread. "I am just a trifle tired. The strain of being civil to Halberstam was almost more than I could bear. How did you fare after dinner? Is he sufficiently impressed by the money and power your friends wield?"

"His greedy eyes were shining like gold coins. Burlington should be pelting him with less pleasant prospects by now; do not expect him to return in quite so magnanimous a mood. Let me help you entertain your impatient crowd while we await their return. I will try to stay close by, but keep your lady friends around you if you can. I have no wish to give Halberstam a chance to wreak his ill feelings on you."

"Do not worry. I intend going no farther than this chair, and there isn't much he can do in full view of a roomful of people. Circulate for me and make the ladies happy." She smiled ruefully, knowing most of the women eagerly awaited a word from the colony's most eligible bachelor, and she had no claim to hold him back.

"There is only one lady I wish to make happy." Kerry took her hand and squeezed it, making a pretense of bowing formally over it. "I will be back." He meandered off after making certain Katy had company to entertain as well as protect her.

Katy was not without admirers of her own, young men attracted by her beauty or wealth or both, but they produced little more than pale compliments and uninspiring badinage, and Katy paid little heed to them beyond the duties of hostess. The Reverend Stone, overcome by his hostess's generosity in inviting him to an evening that opened up numerous possibilities for his parish and his own advancement, assiduously attended to her every need until she laughingly accused him of neglecting his wife, dismissing the young pastor to further his charitable causes.

Finding herself momentarily alone, Katy decided to check on the children and started to struggle awkwardly from her comfortable seat. A hand went out to help her, and she grasped it gratefully, accepting the support as she rose and not attending her helper until she was standing. To her horror, she found herself gripping the hand of the man she feared most. Halberstam glared balefully at her astonishment.

"A pleasure to be of service to you, madam," he said mockingly, when it became obvious Katy intended to offer no thanks. " 'Tis a pity I cannot stay longer to accept your gratitude, but I have urgent business that calls me to Charleston this night, and I must be leaving. I have just come to offer my farewell and mention my appreciation for the delectable dinner.'' A glimmer of hatred in icy gray eyes made a lie of his words.

Katy glanced around nervously, finding Kerry nowhere within sight as she attempted to remove her fingers from Halberstam's. ''Please to release my hand, *monsieur*,'' she replied, haughtily hiding her terror. The French-princess act had worked effectively on overeager swains before, but this was no young simpleton.

''When I am ready,'' Halberstam answered in French, a malicious gleam burning as he grasped this opportunity. Continuing in the same language, he added, ''I came expecting your trap this time, my little bait, but this one was a good deal more subtle. I do not accept my fate easily. Expect to see me again when you have rid yourself of Kerry's bastard.'' He glanced disdainfully at Katy's protuberant figure, bowed swiftly, and departed.

Katy blanched, visibly shaken by his parting remark. There was no way that man could know, could even guess . . . It was just another of his scandalmongering retorts. With relief, she felt Kerry's arm reach out to support her, but his first words offered no comfort.

''What did that scurrilous vermin say to you, Katy?'' His deep voice was insistent, his features hard and demanding as his fingers tightened about her arm. ''I can tolerate no more of his insults. Tell me what he said, Katy, before he can get too far. I am putting an end to this once and for all.''

Katy stared up into the frightening glitter of emerald eyes, terrified by the murderous gleam she found there. ''He said nothing that is not the truth, Kerry. What do you mean? What are you planning to do?''

''Never mind. I just want to know exactly what he said. I intend to cram every word of it back down his throat when I catch up to him.'' Kerry was too furious to understand the implications of her words. Already, in his mind, he had located sword and called out his man and horses. He had but to act to be on his way.

His murderous intent was clear without being spoken, and Katy felt her heart quake. Kerry's swordsmanship and courage in duels were well known, but illness had sapped much of his strength. She could not allow him to go out after that evil man who would like nothing better than an excuse to murder. She gathered her strength and jerked her arm from Kerry's hand. "If you leave me here tonight, Kerry, you will never step back through that door again." Violet eyes blazed with determination.

Kerry stared at this usually obedient faerie creature with furious amazement.

"Don't defy me, Katherine!" He spoke in an undertone to prevent being overheard, but his mood remained thunderous. "With or without your aid, I intend to put an end to his persecution. I will call Emma to take you to your room, but I am going."

A soft voice from behind Kerry brought the discussion to an end. "You are going nowhere, little brother, if I have to knock you to the floor in front of all our guests."

More thoughtfully, measuring up his younger brother with his eyes, Burlington added, "I am still bigger than you and your strength is not what it should be after your illness. It should not be too difficult, but I would rather not disturb Katherine if I can avoid it."

Turning to Katy, he took her hand and quickly searched her pale face. "I apologize for not coming sooner. If Halberstam has harmed or insulted you in any way, I will take the necessary measures to stop him. Is all well?"

His reassuring voice did not ease Katy's distress as she observed the determined lines of Kerry's face. It would take chains to prevent his seeking out his tormentor unless she could convince him otherwise.

"I am fine. Halberstam merely came to say good-bye. He caught me by surprise, that is all." She spoke to Lord Burlington but her eyes pleaded with Kerry.

"Katy, you never were a convincing liar. You had better tell us all, for one way or another I intend to put an end to his dirty career." Kerry was adamant, ignoring her pleas and his brother's threats.

"Kerry, I cannot tell you," she said, begging his understanding. "He said nothing that was not the truth. You cannot call him out for that."

Burlington studied the eloquent debate being carried on

without words between the young widow and his brother. They understood each other well, in a way most people did not, unless they were lovers. His eyes narrowed thoughtfully, but the shadowed, widened eyes in Katy's frighteningly pale face told him it was time to end the debate.

"Kerry, you cannot do anything without endangering this child's health—just look at her." He gestured toward Katy's quivering figure. "Take her upstairs and see her settled; then I would have a word with you." To Katy he added, "If you wish to make a complaint against Halberstam, I will see your honor protected without involving Kerry. Shall I send someone to stop him?"

Katy's pleas had finally registered with Kerry, and he frowned, trying to think what truths might upset her as these had. There could only be two that he knew of, and he cursed inwardly. Robbed of his excuse for challenging Halberstam, he now realized the danger of Katy's condition, remembering too well the doctor's admonitions about her frailty. Taking her hand in his arm, he answered for her.

"It is too late now to stop the coward. Let us cover up this little scene before rumors start flying without Halberstam's help. James, find Emma and have her make Katy's excuses. I will see her upstairs." And giving his brother a grim look, he added, "If you wish to speak to me about anything, it will have to wait till morning. I do not believe our guests deserve another disappearing act tonight."

Upstairs in the bedroom, Kerry quickly took Katy by the shoulders and examined the blue stains under her tired eyes. "Shall I call Dr. Jackson? Are you going to be all right?"

Katy nodded wearily. "I need nothing but rest." Then anxiously she clutched his hand. "You will not go after Halberstam, will you, Kerry? Promise, or I will not rest at all."

Soothingly he agreed. "I promise, Katy. I will not drag your name through the mud, as I surely would should I go after him now. I take it he spoke of the children?"

"Not of Maureen. He has never seen her. It was just conjecture, Kerry, he was trying to be insulting. I don't see how he could have any idea of the truth, but it startled me so . . . I am afraid I will never make a very successful actress."

"I would not want you to be, my love, but you have left me some fancy explaining to do with James. Or perhaps it is my temper that has made him suspicious. Will you let me tell him anything, Katy? I would rather he knew."

Hungrily Kerry searched her face for some sign of willingness to release their secret. He wished he could proclaim to the world that Katy was his as much as the child, but to reveal the truth to just his family would at least ease the pressure they were bringing to bear on him.

Katy swayed lightly under his hands, and he gently led her to the bed. "I would rather you did not," she murmured, but before she could say anything more, Emma hurried into the room and took over, chasing Kerry out with horrified exclamations, leaving the subject undiscussed.

March 1738

THE NEXT MORNING Katy slept late, the household tiptoeing around her room while she obtained the rest she so badly needed. When she did rise, she went directly to the nursery to describe the past evening to the impatiently waiting Anna while she combed little Maureen's hair. By the time Katy left the nursery in search of breakfast, Kerry and Burlington had been closeted in the study for nearly an hour.

"Kerry, you have given me no suitable explanations at all. I cannot go back home and tell them nothing—the duchess would have me in the dungeon and our father would cheerfully put me on the rack until I confessed everything. What do you want me to tell them? That you are not married, that you are not coming home to marry, that, as a matter of fact, you have given the diamonds intended for your wife to the woman you are living with?"

Burlington's dark eyes were tired as he wrestled with the problem of his younger brother. He had spent a sleepless night constructing this interview, trying to find ways to talk sensibly to this temperamental half-brother of whom he was so fond. When he had thought Kerry in danger of dying, he had vowed not to mention the subject uppermost in his family's mind, but circumstances had voided that vow.

"She sent them back to me last night," Kerry stated flatly, staring out the window with his hands jammed in his pockets. "She insisted on taking them as a loan."

"I have always told you Katy shows more sense than you. Your mother might be amused by the girl's drawings and the tales you tell of her, but I can assure you she would not be so pleased with your giving her diamonds to a girl from the streets. Would you care to give some explanation of last night's little episode? I take it Halberstam was being his usual offensive self, but was it enough to challenge him? And what truth did Katy speak of, or should I guess?"

Kerry swung around, eyes flashing emerald fires. "Damn you, James, what is this? An inquisition? I am not some prep-school lad any longer. I needn't explain my every action to you."

James sighed. The blowup was inevitable. He had been badgering Kerry for almost an hour now and was no closer to the truth than before, but he would have it before he left. "I am simply trying to obtain some rational explanation for your behavior. It is not difficult to understand why you might insist on staying with your ward through a difficult period after she and her husband saved your life, though I am not quite certain yet how they obtained that pardon, but duels and diamonds and your explosive temper over trivial matters are not so easily rationalized. Would you care to explain to me what part your ward plays in your life?"

"No, I would not," Kerry replied curtly, not for the first time that morning. "You see how we live here. We are completely chaperoned, there is nothing going on between us that you cannot see with your own two eyes. Now, why don't we drop the subject?"

"Then explain why you have made no further moves toward finding a wife. Was I mistaken in thinking you had some plans in that direction when you left England last? I had assumed you had said as much when the duchess gave you her mother's jewels."

"My mother considers herself prescient; actually, she was just hopeful. I never said anything of that nature to her."

Kerry adopted an attitude of nonchalance, but his tempe[r]
seethed. James was a fair man and had always been a goo[d]
sport, but his pompous righteousness was irritating beyond a[ll]
relief at times.

James slammed a fist on the desk and swung around i[n]
Charles's old desk chair to face Kerry. "Our father is ill, no[t]
seriously so, perhaps, but enough to make him realize hi[s]
time is limited. He wants heirs, he wants grandchildren, h[e]
wants to see a little bit of himself in the future. Surely yo[u]
can understand that? Believe me, Jenny and I have tried t[o]
gratify his wishes. I would give anything just to have tha[t]
little girl you have upstairs. But Jenny cannot carry a bab[e]
full term and your bastards will not solve the problem. Wha[t]
do you intend to do about it?"

Kerry stared at him coolly, his expression unsympathetic.
"Do you really wish an answer to that?"

From Kerry's expression, James knew he did not, but he
had learned perseverance long ago and did not give up now.
"I would not have asked you otherwise," he replied with a
trace of defiance.

"I intend to marry Katherine." Kerry stood back with
arms crossed and waited for this to sink in, a glimmer of
interest on his face now that the news was out and he could
watch his brother's reaction.

James sank back in the chair and stared, understanding
instinctively that this was not one of Kerry's amusing pranks.
He was serious, and the repercussions of this decision seeped
slowly through his thoughts.

"You are insane," he finally choked out; then, grasping at
straws, he demanded, "Has she agreed?" A flicker of uncertainty in Kerry's eyes answered that, and James breathed
easier.

"She will," Kerry replied bluffly, with a certainty he did
not feel.

"Then go ask her. If Katy has half the sense I think she
has, she will refuse, and you know that as well as I."
Burlington spoke confidently, with some satisfaction. He was
finally getting somewhere with this obstinate brother of his,
though the direction was one he had not expected to take.

"There is more to it than that, and you know it. She has

ust lost a husband of whom she was genuinely fond, as was
. I cannot insult his memory that way," Kerry protested.

"Blame it on me. Tell her I insisted on knowing so I can
eassure our father one way or another. He is an old man and
mpatient. I would like to tell him he will have heirs instead
of bastards. Tell her anything. If you are convinced she feels
he same as you, she should give you some answer to satisfy
an old man's whims." James prayed his intuition had not
ailed him. Kerry's own impatience for an answer played
against his reluctance to rush Katy, and the matter would
soon be settled, if Katy answered as James thought she
would. If she did not, there would be all hell to pay, but at
east he would know where he stood and could work from
here.

Kerry's anger and impatience warred with his better in-
stincts and won. He would know for a certainty that Katy was
finally his, and the months of waiting she would surely
impose on him would be more easily endured. And at the
same time, he would put an end to this infernal questioning.
"I will go see if she is up yet."

He moved toward the door, but James rose ahead of him.
"No, you will wish to talk to her in private. I will have her
come here." He quickly left the study in search of Katy.

Finding her idling over a cup of chocolate and a muffin at
the table, Burlington stopped to compose himself. It seemed
incredible to him that the bewitching enchantress of the night
before and this simply dressed young girl could be one and
the same, but there was no denying the beauty of either of
them. 'Twas a pity that aristocratic profile and air of good
breeding were not backed up by a pedigree to match, but the
fact remained, Katy was a street urchin, a governess at best,
the widow of a colonial, and entirely unsuitable as the wife of
a Southerland. Carefully he did not reveal his thoughts as he
greeted her.

"Good morning, Katherine. I trust you are feeling better
this morning?"

Her smile lit the room like morning sunshine when she
looked up. "Good morning, Lord Burlington. I had wondered where you and Lord Kerry had wandered off to."

"We are having a rather serious family discussion in the

study and would appreciate your company. I fear our discus
sions nearly inevitably end in disagreements, and we require
your aid in resolving this one. Are you almost through here
or could I call someone to carry a tray to the study so you
may join us?''

Katy studied this tall, dark man's serious demeanor. Burlington was unfailingly polite, but she had thought these last
few days he had grown somewhat warmer. Now she could
see he had retreated to the cool, aloof attitude of his arrival.
Whatever the discussion, it had not been to his liking.

"I am finished here, milord. I do not know how I might be
of any assistance to you, but I shall be more than happy to
try.'' Adapting her manner to his, Katy laid aside her smile
and accepted his arm with a gravity she did not generally
exude.

"I am relying heavily on your sensibility and judgment in
this matter, Katherine. Kerry has always been the reckless,
intemperate type, he reacts more often than he thinks, and in
this case I can certainly understand why, but when he has
calmed down, I am afraid he will regret his rashness, and I
need you to provide the cool thinking he lacks right now.''
Dark eyes fastened unfathomably on Katy's petite form as
they stopped before the study door.

"I am not certain that I can be of any help if that is the
case, milord. I have yet to calm Kerry when he is in a
temper. I have found it easier to let it pass.'' Katy searched
the inscrutable face above her, finding no clue to his thoughts.
His facade relaxed a little under her scrutiny, allowing some
warmth to seep through.

"I am afraid this will not pass, and I am the impatient one.
Go in, talk to him, I will be waiting across the hall.''
Burlington opened the door for her, bowing slightly in the
direction of Kerry's stiff figure, then departed, leaving Katy
alone to face the problem.

"Katy.'' Kerry came forward, took her hands, led her back
to the sunlight of the window, where he seated himself next
to her on the window cushions. Golden curls were pulled back
in a simple knot this morning, but a silver fringe of hair
escaped, forming a haloed frame for wide violet eyes staring
up at him, puzzled.

"Lord Burlington says there has been some disagreement he would like resolved, but I cannot imagine how I can be of help. What is wrong, Kerry?" Her voice was soft and gentle in her questioning, sensing some disquiet behind the confident gleam of emerald eyes. The air of excitement about him clashed with the hard set of the angular lines of his jaw. The boyish grin she loved was not there, but a trace of it lingered about the firm lips of a determined man.

"Is that what he told you? If it is a disagreement, then it has been going on for longer than I care to remember, and yes, with one word you can put an end to it." That an entire new set of disagreements would open up, Kerry did not reveal. There would be time enough for that later, after he had what he wanted. "It is not something I wish to confront you with just yet. I know you have had too many other things on your mind, and I would prefer to wait for a more appropriate time, but James has his reasons for wanting it resolved now, and I will admit to a certain impatience of my own."

Bewildered, Katy waited for him to continue. Kerry's hands were strong and warm as they held hers, and she drew strength from their firmness. Their knees touched on the narrow width of ledge, and she was close enough to see the fine network of wrinkles formed by laughter around his eyes, but they were not laughing now. She wished she could smooth them, but did not dare remove her hands from his hold.

"You do not have to give me your answer today, I know this is too sudden for you to comprehend all at once, but for you to just tell me you will consider it will ease my mind."

Katy's eyes widened in panic. Just the inflection of his voice told her she did not want to hear this, not now, not ever. She had no wish to resolve anything, she wanted everything just as it was without a word being said, she wanted to make no decisions, say no hated phrases, nothing between them that would warp what they had now. She wasn't ready for this, whatever it might be.

"No, Kerry, please, do not say anything. I do not think I want to hear this. I am not up to giving answers right now. Please . . ." She tried to pull her hands away but he held them firmly.

"It is not what you think, Katy. I would never do that to

you again. I have told you I love you, and I think you still
feel the same for me, though it may be masked by grief right
now. I do not say these words lightly, I have spent a lifetime
looking for a woman to whom I can say them, and now that I
have found her, I do not want to lose her again. Katy, I want
the right to have you and our children at Twin Oaks with me
permanently, I want you to be my wife. Tell me you will
think of it and give me your answer when you are ready.''
Eagerly Kerry waited for the surprise in her expression,
praying he would see some joy there too, but her eyes only
darkened in mounting panic.

"No, Kerry, I asked you not to." She whipped her head
away from his searching gaze, unable to free her hands but no
longer able to face the pain she would find in his face.
"Please, take it back, do not make me answer you." Tears
sprang to her eyes as she felt his grip tighten on her fingers;
she could not bear to see his eyes.

"I won't take it back, Katy. I never believed the chance
would come so soon. I was prepared to wait a lifetime, but
now that the opportunity is here, I have no intention of
passing it by. You are my wife in every way but name, and I
wish to change that. I want you and our children to bear my
name, I want to tell the world you are mine, and I do not
think I will take no for an answer."

"But no it must be, milord," Katy whispered miserably.
She knew now what Burlington had been telling her. Kerry
had divulged his intentions to his brother, and his brother
disapproved. That was all the warning Katy needed to fortify
her resolve, but it made the words no less painful. She felt as
if her heart were being cut from her with the wrong end of a
knife, the bludgeoning pangs of its incision rending the very
fabric of her soul.

Horror-struck, Kerry dropped her hands and forced her
face up to meet his gaze, reading all the anguish in the
bruised violet of her eyes. "Why, Katy? Why must it be
no?" he asked hoarsely, the force of his words grating on the
edge of his voice.

"You know why, milord. Your brother can tell you why as
well as I. Let me go, do not make me say anything more to
come between us," she pleaded.

"No, I want to hear it from you. Why, Katy? You tell me you love me, you bear my children willingly, but you will not marry me. Tell me why, Katy." His voice rose with his anger. He knew her reasons but wanted to hear them from her lips, torment her with their foolishness. He wanted to strike out at something, rip away the barriers obstructing his desires, destroy everything in his path, but all he could see was Katy.

"I do love you. It is because I love you that I cannot marry you. Another woman would not think twice before saying yes, but I am not that other woman. I love you too much to hurt you. I would have spared you this hurt, but you would not stop when I asked it of you." Desperation forced the tears from her eyes, and Katy faced him proudly, wanting nothing more than to be held by him but knowing she never would be again. She was driving him back to England as surely as if she had put a ship beneath his feet.

"That is nonsense, Katy. If you love me, you will marry me. You know how much I have wanted it, you cannot deny me now with this double talk." His fingers were leaving whitened marks on the delicate skin where he gripped her jaw, but he could not let go.

"It is not double talk," she replied softly, absorbing the flash of fine green eyes rimmed with heavy lashes, wishing to memorize the long line of cheekbone as it jutted into the plane of his jaw. It was all over now, she might never see him again, but the loss could not touch her so long as she could see his face.

"To marry me would be to cut yourself off from your rightful home and family, from your friends, from the estates you could expect to inherit one day. You would be an outcast, as my father was. I have grown up with that label and do not mind it, but you have not, and I will not ask it of you. Perhaps my father was not so strong as you, but neither are you so foolish as he. Sooner or later you would grow to resent what I brought upon you—perhaps during a bad year, or a series of bad years when the crops fail and the livestock die and your ship is laid up and there is no one to turn to for help. You may fight it out, you may cut your losses, but you will resent it. I will be to blame, whatever happens, and you

would be right, if I were fool enough to hear you now. But
am not, and I will not. I want you for my friend, I will no
destroy what has been between us, and if you choose to leave
me now, I will have only good memories when you are
gone." Sobs choked her throat and she could not go on
Tears wet her lashes, and she blinked them away.

A roar of fury and rage exploded in Kerry's throat, blinding him to her tears as he flung her face aside and threw
himself to his feet, pounding the floor with murderous rage as
he crossed the room to the door. Before he could fling it open
and storm out, Burlington quietly entered, calmly shutting the
door behind him and leaning against it, halting Kerry's
departure.

"I gather she has given you your answer," he commented
dryly, throwing an anxious glance to the wilted figure in the
window seat but keeping one eye warily on Kerry.

"God damn you to bloody hell and back, James. What did
you tell her?" Kerry's arm swung out to indicate Katy, but
his rage had found its focus in his brother's face. His anger
boiled over, steaming and frothing in the flames of his words.
"What did you threaten her with? What in bloody hell do you
think you are doing interfering in my life? Dammit, will you
get out of my way before I throttle you?"

Ignoring Kerry, Burlington deliberately turned to Katy.
"Excuse my little brother, Lady Stockbridge, he has always
been inclined to temper tantrums. It will pass." Then, slowly
turning to face his brother, he lifted a sardonic eyebrow. "I
take it the answer was no?"

Kerry's fury flared from white-hot to icy cold. Through
clenched teeth he muttered, "Did you have any doubt?"

"One or two, but if she had accepted, I would have had no
compunctions about shredding her reputation or offering
bribes," he replied calmly. "As it is, I regret what I have put
Katherine through. She deserves better treatment than what
you, and now I, have given her."

Deftly avoiding Kerry's threatening stance, he crossed the
room to Katy's huddled, silent figure. "I am sorry, Katherine. I come from a cynical world and was not certain whether
your love was real or feigned; now that I know, I am sorrier

than ever for both of you, but you have chosen the wiser course. Shall I have someone assist you back to your room?''

''No!'' The word thundered and echoed around the room, rattling the fragile windowpanes with its bellow of denial, roaring with a raw pain that throbbed in the ears. Kerry's hands were clenched in massive fists at his hips as he faced the room's two occupants, blocking any escape. ''No!'' he repeated. ''She is the mother of my children and she is not going anywhere until we hear from your own lips what you intend to do if we marry.''

His anger was such that Kerry paid no attention to Katy's shocked gasp and her blanched face, but Burlington had not only heard the incriminating word but also caught Katy's reaction confirming it. Trying to maintain his cool demeanor, he asked, more of Katy than his brother, ''Children? More than one?'' Dark eyes searched for confirmation in Katy's paled face, finding it there and in the rapid deflation of Kerry's anger.

''Kerry, you promised . . .'' she cried mournfully, in a low voice. It was an unexpected blow, following hard on the heels of the first one, rocking her senses and leaving her shattered. Stripped of her pride, she crumbled visibly before their eyes.

Stricken, Kerry rushed to her side, catching her hands in his and pleading for understanding. ''I am sorry, Katy, I did not mean to break it like that, but he has to know. Can't you see that? I cannot let my family come between us and destroy both our lives.'' Gently he touched her cheek, rubbing at a solitary tear, but she flinched and turned away.

Burlington sank into the desk chair and sat quietly observing this scene, all his mental resources quickly reevaluating the situation in this new light. Deciding he did not have enough information with which to work, he interrupted their colloquy. ''I take it this means the child she carries is yours, Kerry?'' His tone was cold, but his eyes remained thoughtful.

Kerry did not raise his eyes from Katy's painfully averted face. With firm assurance he replied, ''It is.''

''I presume you have no Indians to blame this time?'' Burlington could not resist asking dryly. Katy's pain was obvious, and he did not dare turn his questioning to her.

"No Indians," Kerry agreed. "Sir Charles was an invalid, and I took advantage of Katy's weakness; she has few, but I know them all." He smiled bitterly, rubbing a rough knuckle down the line of fair cheek presented to him. This time, she did not flinch, but neither would she look at him. "Everyone assumed the child was Charles's, and because she hoped to gain time from her husband's illness, Katy continued the charade, hoping to prolong, or at least ease, his last days. Charles was no fool and Katy no liar, but I think she succeeded, nevertheless. Charles was content, and nothing else mattered."

Kerry's voice lowered, and he no longer talked to his brother but to Katy, his hand opening up to cup Katy's chin gently, turning her face to meet his gaze. "But now, my darlin' Katy, it is time to admit the truth. It can no longer harm Charles, but it can help me. Katy?" Quietly pleading with his eyes, Kerry begged her forgiveness and acceptance.

"Is the child Kerry's, Katherine?" James asked softly, unable to tear his gaze from the golden-haloed silhouette at the window.

Weakly Katy smiled down at Kerry's anxious face. He knelt at her feet in an unconsciously classic pose, and her hand automatically went out to stroke his worried brow. "It is, milord."

"Forgive me for asking, but is there any proof of this? You were a married woman, after all . . ." Burlington ended lamely.

With mild reproof, Katy looked away from Kerry and up at his brother. "The governor released Kerry on the basis of my word; the child is due nine months from the time Kerry left Charleston—my doctor will vouch for that." She added with a rueful smile, "Sir Charles's condition being what it was, Dr. Jackson has always doubted the child's parentage, but is too good a man to mention it."

With relief, Kerry sat beside her, putting an arm about her waist as they faced Burlington. Capturing a tendril of her hair, he whispered in her ear, "Am I forgiven, then?"

"No," Katy replied calmly, "for it changes nothing. The child is Sir Charles's heir, and there is nothing you can do to change it."

Kerry swore vehemently, but Burlington agreed with some relief that Katy would not use this new admission to further Kerry's cause.

"She is right, Kerry. The child has a name, and I assume Sir Charles left a sufficient estate to support both wife and children, although it might be appropriate if you contributed to the child's maintenance as you have to Maureen's. There is no reason to change the status of things."

Kerry was on his feet in an instant, his hands belligerently forming fists once more. "Would you like to make a wager on that? Shall I give you reason enough besides the fact that Katy is the woman I want and that she is the mother of my two children?"

Burlington crossed his hands thoughtfully under his chin and waited for his intemperate half-brother to continue.

Kerry obliged forcefully. "You tell me our father is ill and wants heirs, that the title and estates are liable to revert to the king should we not produce a claim to them, and that you have not yet been able to do so."

There was an air of threatening menace in Kerry's eyes as he repeated their earlier conversation. Burlington nodded uneasily in agreement.

"Then you can go back and rid yourself of Jenny and find another wife to produce those heirs, because I am here to tell you now, if I cannot marry Katy, I will never marry at all, and all my rights I shall will to my bastards. Now, make what you want of that." Kerry flung his lanky body into the nearest chair and glared defiantly at both Katy and James.

"I see." Burlington's assurance paled slightly as he made a tent of his fingers and slipped into thought. He loved his wife despite the frustration of her childlessness. It might be possible to dissolve his marriage on the basis of her inability to bear, but he doubted it. Yet he knew that was not what Kerry was getting at. Kerry was asking him to give up the woman he loved for the heirs the title needed; he was reversing the situation, making him see what was being asked of him. And Kerry was right. Burlington sighed. It would not go over well at all at home, but Kerry was right. The family could not expect him to give up not only the woman he loved—for Burlington doubted not for an instant that Kerry

had at long last surrendered his heart—but also his children
for the sake of the family name. It was not to be expected of
this half-wild Irish brother of his. There was no questioning
this time that Kerry meant what he said.

"I think he means it," Burlington commented conversa-
tionally to Katy, whose strained expression did not change at
his nonchalant remark. "I do not suppose there is any way
you can persuade him otherwise?"

Katy's violet eyes flew to Kerry's frozen face and back to
his brother's relaxed one. If she had not known this serious
man better, she would imagine she saw a twinkle of amusement behind his dark eyes, but that was not possible. Kerry
was threatening to throw away thousands of years of noble
heritage for a woman he found in a whorehouse. Burlington
could not possibly find that amusing.

"I have tried before, milord, without success. I should
never have told him the truth about this babe. I am sorry to have
created such a scene, it never occurred to me—"

Burlington waved her into silence. "Kerry can still count.
Sooner or later he would have figured the child to be his,
particularly if it turns out anything like Maureen." The twinkle of amusement grew as he turned to his brother.

Now that he had no choice in the matter, he not only saw
the humor in the situation but also was relieved to be rid of
the burden of keeping these two apart. If fate ever intended a
match, it was between this reckless, hot-blooded Irish brother
of his and the demure, half-French little sorceress with the
will of iron. They deserved each other. A half-smile flickered
on his face as he spoke to Kerry.

"You don't leave me much choice, do you, little brother?"

Kerry remained silent, clenching his teeth to prevent further outbursts until he knew what Burlington had decided. He
willed his gaze to remain on the desk and not stray to the
diminutive figure at the window, knowing Katy's unspoken
pleas could weaken his determination.

Burlington shoved back his chair and rose to move around
the desk, sitting down beside Katy on the window seat and
taking her fragile hand. For a moment he studied the wide
brow and overlarge violet eyes set in the finely boned frame

of her small face as if seeing her for the first time. She quivered slightly under his scrutiny, and relented.

"May I welcome you to the family, Katherine?" he asked quietly.

A burst of joy exploded inside Kerry's head, and he felt free of shackles at last. A tremendous light-headedness hit him, and he felt as if he could float across the room, sweep Katy into his arms, and dance out on a beam of sunlight. The day seemed suddenly brighter, though the weak winter sun had not changed. An idiotic grin crossed his face as he looked from James to Katy, disappearing abruptly when he noticed the slow shake of Katy's head.

Bewildered and disbelieving, Katy continued to shake her head negatively, emphasizing her words visually. "No, it cannot be. Kerry has blackmailed you into this madness. I cannot be Lady Kerry, my children cannot be lords and ladies and someday dukes or duchesses or even barons. I have no wish to return to England, ever. I want my children to grow up here, not tied to estates and titles but free to be as they choose. I do not *want* my son to be a duke," she cried, desperately searching for a way to make them understand. She could never marry Lord Kerry, heir to the Southerland fortunes, only the man she had known in the cabin, the farmer who worked in his shirt sleeves to earn his own living, and not the elegant gentleman his family knew. But how could she make them see this?

Bemused, Burlington turned to his brother for aid, standing up and moving out of the way as Kerry bore down on them with the intent of a madman.

"Katy, you are a snob." Kerry threw himself into the seat vacated by Burlington. "If you were not so damned awkward to get hold of right now, I would give you that spanking I should have given you years ago."

As if to carry out his threat, Kerry ripped off his coat, throwing it on the floor and loosening the snowy white cloth at his throat. Katy began to move away fearfully, but Kerry threw the cloth down and caught her wrist in his hard grip, forcing her to look at him.

"There, now I am plain Kerry Southerland, gentleman farmer, and you are my wife, for I intend to make an honest woman of you. Our children will not have titles. Such things mean little in this land. Our children will have two grandparents and aunts and an uncle who would dearly love to see them, and when you are well enough to travel, we shall go to England to visit, but we will stay only long enough to deck you out in all the fine gowns I have longed to see you in. Then we shall return here and live as we have been. You may draw and paint to your heart's desire, indulge the children, teach an entire school if you like, but you will be there waiting for me when I come home at night because I will think of nothing but you as I ride the fields each day. Why worry about a time that may never come when we can have it all now? James may have a dozen children yet. He will probably live to be a hundred. Our son will have half a dozen children of his own before there is any possibility of his becoming a duke. He will be old enough to make his own decisions by then; you cannot deny him that choice, Katy. It should be his right to make it, not yours. Now, quit being such a bigot and give me a smile. For all you know, you may be the granddaughter of a count or two yourself—you have no right to look down on me.''

In Kerry's smile Katy found the man she had grown to love as a fifteen-year-old child: the cynic, the bored rakehell, the thoughtful guardian, and the serious businessman, all blended together now in the familiar planes of lover and friend, green eyes insistent and demanding as ever, but not hiding the extent of his desires. The man she had looked up to and admired all these years, the unobtainable lord, was just a man, a man with wants and needs that included her. It seemed incomprehensible and too sudden to absorb, but it had to be true. Unbelieving, Katy reached out to touch his cheek, and found herself captured by the intensity of Kerry's gaze. Their combined gaze excluded the room's other occupant, but he succeeded in interrupting their reverie with a polite cough.

"I trust this means everything is settled? And may I ask where a count comes into the conversation?'' Burlington stood over the two lovers with an air of embarrassed curiosity. There was much more to be gone over yet, but these two seemed to have slipped into another world. There would be time enough for that later. Now that his decision had been made, he wanted it acted upon.

Kerry smiled vacantly, unconcerned with petty details while basking in the warmth of Katy's loving look. "Romantic theory, fairy tales from the past," he murmured incomprehensibly, wishing his brother would dissipate so he could take Katy into his arms and begin the lifetime of kisses he anticipated.

"There are a few minor matters needing to be cleared up, if you two would come back to earth for a while." Deliberately Burlington continued badgering them. Left to themselves, they would muddle along hopelessly forever—that was totally apparent.

"Go away, big brother." Intent on violet eyes, Kerry ignored the towering presence in front of them, but Katy pulled back slightly from his questing hand, her gentle smile and sidelong glance indicating she felt Burlington to be an obtrusive presence to further relations. Kerry scowled and finally turned to stare him down. "A man's got a right to privacy when he proposes marriage, you know."

Imperturbably Burlington agreed. "And as soon as I make a few minor points, I will remove myself. First, I cannot guarantee our father's reaction to the marriage, though I have a strong suspicion your sister will heartily endorse it and the duchess find it amusing, as she usually does with your escapades, once they are over and there is no preventing them. Which leads me to point number two: it will be better if I return to say the deed is done and there is no undoing it. The prospect of an immediate heir will somewhat soften the blow. And that is point number three: I am not certain of the legal ramifications involved in adopting children born to another marriage, but I would suggest it would somewhat alleviate the problem if this child should be a male if you were to be married before it is born. The child will automatically take on the Southerland name at birth and the lawyers can work out the remainder of the details."

Floating on a higher cloud, aware of little more than the pressure of Kerry's hand on hers, Katy scarcely understood a word said, but something in Burlington's voice and the movement of the man beside her caught her attention and the last few sentences punctured her cloud, bringing her to earth as Burlington had desired.

"Not so soon! We cannot possibly do that! I will not degrade Charles's name by remarrying so soon. It is preposterous!" Her face flushed with indignation.

Burlington admired this additional coloring and the hot sparkle of dark-lashed eyes. If their children were anything like their parents, he was almost relieved there would be an ocean between himself and them. Emotional, but never boring. "Calm down, Katherine. I have the greatest respect for Sir Charles myself, possibly more so than you two evidently did," he added bluntly, "but I am certain there is some way this can be arranged. Perhaps Mr. Stone can make some suggestions. The marriage need not be made public until you are ready to do so, but I would like to attend so the family will be represented, and to be certain all the official documents are properly recorded so there will be no disputing the child's rights. Other witnesses will probably be needed and sworn to secrecy in the interval."

"Katy, it will be fine. I will stay with you as I planned until the child's birth. The Stones will be here. No one will ever know the difference. You will not be able to travel for months yet; when you are ready, we will simply announce our intentions of marrying, and by that time everyone should be quite accustomed to the idea of our living together." Kerry kissed her brow, smoothing away the worried wrinkles.

"And what of Anna? She should know what is happening. She will be uprooted once again by all this."

"We will tell Anna. She is old enough to keep a secret. She will be thrilled to live at Twin Oaks with her beloved horses, and our marriage should make her a wealthy woman."

Both Burlington and Katy looked at him questioningly. Kerry smiled and shrugged. "Charles left me as executor of the estate and Katy as his sole heir, except for the house, which is to be Anna's upon Katy's death or remarriage. He trusted Katy to do what was right by all the children, knowing Maureen was already provided for, and giving her the option to treat their unborn child as it deserved. Under the circumstances, I think Charles would have wanted all his estate to go to Anna, since I am well able to provide for Katy and our two children. Don't you agree?''

"You are leaving Katy without a dowry. I hope you are so rich as you claim,'' Burlington pointed out.

Worriedly Katy looked up to Kerry. As a younger son, his wealth was not great, and depended much on his making a successful marriage. Twin Oaks must have made a sizable hole in his worth; Charles's money would go a long way toward mending it. But he was right, the money rightfully belonged to Anna.

"We will get by. The plantation is already showing some small profit, though I have not been available to watch over it as closely as I would like. With Katy there, I think I will be less likely to stray. That is all the dowry I need.'' Kerry tilted Katy's chin so that her eyes met his, and their smiles once more shut out the intruder.

Having elicited the information needed, Burlington surrendered the futile battle for sense and discreetly removed himself from the study. As the door closed behind him, Kerry was pulling Katy into his arms for the long-delayed seal of their betrothal.

March 15, 1738

THEY KEPT the wedding ceremony simple and private, holding it in the Stockbridge drawing room with the Reverend Stone presiding, Lord Burlington standing up for Kerry, and Emma with Katy. Jake and Anna were the only guests. When the ceremony ended with the final words, not a dry eye remained as Kerry tenderly took his heavily pregnant wife into his arms and gently kissed her. The words "to love and protect" silently echoed in the ears of their audience.

Tears were quickly dashed at the sight of the wedding repast Emma had conspired with Bertha to produce. As the wine flowed freely, so did their spirits, leaving Katy to look fondly around the room at the small group of friends and family she had accumulated, all thanks to Kerry. She gripped his hand tighter beneath the table as her gaze went from face to face, resting on Anna's last.

Anna had been allowed to dress and dine with the adults for this occasion and Katy smiled, remembering their earlier conversation as they both dressed for the wedding.

Anna had seated herself beside Katy at the dressing table, gazing adoringly at Katy's reflection while she tucked the last

pins and golden curls into place and arranged the gift of
pearls from Kerry around her throat. Watching Anna's wistful
gaze, Katy had been moved to ask, "What is on your mind,
ma petite? You look so sad."

Anna gathered her own brown tresses up in both hands and
twisted them in a lump atop her head. "I was only wishing I
could look like you when I grow up, then maybe Jake would
look at me more often. Do you think I will ever be pretty?"

At this astounding declaration, Katy bit back laughter.
Anna was going on thirteen and not too young to think of
such things. After all, Katy herself had been in Kerry's bed at
the age of fifteen, so nothing was impossible. Remembering
the scrawny tatterdemalion she had been then, Katy allowed
herself a smile.

"Someday you must ask Kerry what I looked like when I
was only a few years older than you. He called me, if I
remember correctly, 'a scrawny, plain wench' with hair the
color of his spaniel's." Her eyes slipped far away, reminisc-
ing, remembering the towering, frightening devil of a man
she had seen before the fire that fateful night. As only a child
could, she had learned swiftly the hard facade hid a tender
touch and the angry green of his eyes could soften into
gentleness. She shook off the reverie, Anna's eagerness for
more forcing her back to the present. "You are already way
ahead of me at that age, pumpkin. Someday you will make
the heads of all men turn."

Shyly Anna studied their reflections in the mirror, trying to
find some hint of the beauty Katy promised. Her hair fell in
lank brown tendrils from the crown of her head where she
still held them in place, and she saw only the snub nose and
plump cheeks and not the long lashes and misty blue of her
eyes, nor the healthy cream and pink of her complexion. "If I
could only make Jake's head turn, I would be happy," she
replied miserably.

Commiserating with the agony of early heartache, Katy
took a decisive hand in the matter. With nimble fingers she
brushed and combed, pinned and curled, and styled the girl's
hair into a startlingly adult fashion. A few ribbons intertwined, a gold chain about her creamy throat, a pinch to both
cheeks, a sparkle of delight in her eye, and Anna was trans-

formed from child to young woman, the small breasts of her childishly plump figure just an enchanting detail. When Katy dabbed a spot of perfume behind her ears, Anna hugged her ecstatically.

"Will you mind awfully if I take Jake away now that you have Lord Kerry?"

"Not so long as you take good care of him, *ma petite*. Being a woman is a big responsibility," she whispered warningly, then sent Anna delightedly on her way.

Now, as she sat watching Jake and Anna talking animatedly at the foot of the table as she and Jake had once done, she felt a little sad at the past she was leaving behind, but the pressure of Kerry's fingers and the warmth of his concern as he looked on her brought the present back to pleasant reality. She smiled up at him, the love in her wide violet eyes so deep that he was reassured.

"Why so pensive, my love?"

As Katy quickly related the morning's episode, Kerry's gaze moved down the table to the young couple, and he smiled in agreement with Katy's words. Jake had undergone a transformation in this past year, determinedly learning the ways of a gentleman under Kerry's amused guidance. Through the months of illness and imprisonment, Jake had proved himself a reliable and astute business manager, but he would not be ready to provide for a family of his own for years. With a little help from Kerry, it might be in time for Anna's coming-out. The thought of those future years with Katy by his side made Kerry's smile broaden, and as he returned his gaze to Katy's expectant face, the love between them was so patently obvious it raised a conspiratorial smile between the table's other occupants. The wedding was definitely a success.

Sitting alone in her bedchamber later that evening, brushing flaxen curls into a shimmering nimbus of pale gold, Katy remembered Kerry's smile and pondered on the strangeness of a wedding night without a groom. Their need to keep the wedding a secret prevented them from informing the servants of their new status and continuing the pretense of separate bedchambers and chaperons. Not that there was any question of consummating the marriage anyway, Katy thought ruefully, giving her pear-shaped figure a sorrowful glance, but it was difficult to believe those few words made her married when there was no man by her side. Still, it would probably be better once she had regained her slender waistline and could make love to her husband as he deserved. She was of no use to him now, like this.

Sighing, Katy rose from the table and moved toward the curtained bed, throwing back the coverlet before putting out the candle. With a frown, she stared at the sheets beneath. The house contained an ample supply of linens, some plain, others embroidered, but these she did not recognize; indeed, they did not even appear to be linen. The edges were crocheted in a fine white lace of the most exquisite design Katy could ever remember seeing, and as she ran her finger across the creamy, smooth surface, she smiled gently at another memory. Satin. Once, lying on a rough wool-covered bed of pine boughs, she had been promised satin sheets.

Her fingers smoothed the luxurious material lovingly, but sadness tinged her violet eyes. It would be better to have the pine boughs back if she could only have Kerry with them.

Watching silently from the darkened doorway, Kerry could almost feel the look of longing on her face, and his heart lurched at the strength of the emotion she betrayed. Seldom had he seen her expression so unguarded, and he felt as if he were prying into her innermost thoughts, which, in effect, he was. Hastily he stepped into the circle of candlelight.

"Kerry!" Katy swung around, startled, delicate-boned hands flying to her lips in surprise. The fine lawn shift she wore to hide her shapeless figure was nearly translucent against the candlelight, and her movement emphasized the shadow of her breast so clearly outlined against it.

Kerry smiled in appreciation of the picture she formed, then solemnly produced a bottle from behind his back, bowing gallantly as he offered it to her. "Champagne, I believe was ordered." With his other hand he produced two crystal goblets, setting them on the nightstand. "Will there be anything else?" He raised a quizzical eyebrow as he awaited her reaction.

"Kerry!" she repeated wonderingly. "What are you doing here?" Too stunned to move, she drank in his half-dressed figure, robe wrapped loosely about his broad-shouldered torso, the light mat of hair on his chest a darkness against his skin, auburn hair pulled back from his face as he bent his head lovingly over her.

"You did not think I would spend my wedding night alone, did you? That would certainly set an awkward precedent for the future. From now on, my love, you are at my tender mercies, and you had better become used to it."

He gathered her in his arms and smothered her face in light kisses, feeling her trembling response as her hands crept about him. It would be months before he could take her as he wished to do, but for now he would be satisfied with these intimacies. Kerry's lips were gentle as they found hers.

Katy gave up asking for explanations. He was here, he was with her, and nothing else mattered. Her tongue slid teasingly to meet his, and his embrace tightened, his need for her mounting uncontrollably until finally he broke away with a laughing gasp.

"You are a wanton woman, Lady Kerry, and if it were not for the delicacy of your condition, you would find yourself ravished before we reached the champagne, but as it is"—he swung her up in his arms and planted a kiss on her brow before depositing her in the silken warmth of the bed—"we had better consume champagne instead of each other." He filled their glasses and handed Katy one before joining her in the cavernous darkness of the bed.

"Champagne and satin sheets. You are a lascivious man, Lord Kerry, and you should be repaid in kind." Eyes brimming with laughter over the rim of her glass, Katy sipped the tingling beverage.

Propped up on his elbows, Kerry grinned back at her. "Did you have anything in particular in mind?"

"I do indeed, milord, but I am new to this business and need another glass of champagne to fortify my courage."

He chuckled and poured the requested glass, replenishing his own while admiring the curtain of silver-gold hair brushing partially covered breasts. "I am afraid your only business right now, midear, is to produce that healthy son of ours and get well as quickly as possible. Then we will be better able to negotiate terms." His hand gently covered the spot where his child rested, feeling the restless life within, thrilled once more at this visible proof of her love for him.

"Would you like to place a small wager on that?" Katy murmured softly, returning her empty glass and rearranging her pillows so she rested more comfortably on her side, her fingers tracing patterns on the skin exposed by his robe.

Kerry put the glasses up and blew out the candle, sliding deeper under the covers until they lay side by side. Gentle fingers removed his robe, and he shrugged it aside, allowing his hand to wander wonderingly to her breasts, finding their tips hard and eager for his touch. "Katy . . ." he muttered hoarsely, feeling her fingers unerringly find the rising bulge of his manhood.

Her lips were hot against his as her hand traced patterns of fire down his loins.

"There is one point we must clarify now, milord," she whispered against his mouth, brushing it with her words.

Kerry pulled her into his arms, settling her more comfortably against his side so he could feel the pressure of her breasts against him. "And that is?" he asked with curiosity.

"I do not intend to share you with another woman and will never give you any excuse to stray." Slowly, lingeringly, her mouth moved from his lips to his throat and on down his hair-roughened chest, her hands working their magic with incredible ease.

Understanding her intentions, Kerry grasped a handful of hair and pulled her back up until their breaths mingled in a deep kiss. Then, snapping her head back so she could see the glittering emerald fires of his eyes, he breathed harshly, "I have no intention of giving you any excuse to turn to another's man arms, milady. I am yours, I wish no other."

Lips curled in a smile of satisfaction, Katy freed her hair from his grasp and returned to her pleasure, gradually increasing the intensity of light kisses and gentle pressures, working to achieve his ultimate release. Freed from months of abstinence imposed by his own will as much as by the confinement of prison and illness, Kerry uttered a muffled cry of joy and gave in to the intoxicating sweetness of her lips and touch, sighing her name with delight as molten tides of heat swept his loins.

When the last explosive shudders passed over him, Kerry drew his bride gently into his arms and began to teach her the final lessons about her own sensuality. Overjoyed at discovering how far she would go to bring him pleasure, he was painstaking in his application of the same principle, treating her body as he would a finely tuned instrument, bringing her to a sensitive pitch with the touch of his lips and tongue and fingers until it took little more than the slightest of pressures to secure her release in shivering ecstasies.

Feeling his wife drowsily satisfied against his shoulder and his child's impatient kicks against his side, Kerry gave a deep sigh of contentment. "I knew you would make an excellent mistress, kitten."

Sleepily Katy murmured, "I will make an even better wife, milord."

Kerry grinned. "It should have occurred to me earlier that one woman could be both wife and mistress. Look at the advantages of not keeping two households, the money and time and travel saved between Twin Oaks and Charleston. You have turned out to be the best investment I have ever made, Katy."

"Remember that the next time I ask you for money, milord," Katy whispered before drifting off to sleep.

Kerry lay awake longer, drinking in the satisfaction of having finally obtained his long-awaited goal. Not only a wife, but Katy; his happiness defied the fates.

March–April 1738

BURLINGTON left within the week, carrying among his personal effects copies of the documents of Kerry's marriage, fresh sketches of Maureen, letters from both Katy and Kerry to his parents, and a long report on the state of his majesty's colony in Carolina. Any reference to Halberstam was safely carried in his head, to be divulged only in the privacy of court chambers.

With assurances they would write when the child was born, Kerry and Katy waved him off with a mixture of regret and relief. The marquess' presence had been a bittersweet one at best, and they needed more time to establish their future together before they could fully welcome such links with the past. In their joy, they turned to each other, binding a spell of happiness about the entire household.

During the day, their routine did not waver from that before Burlington's arrival. With the return of Kerry's health, he was able to ride out to Twin Oaks to direct spring planting, but he seldom stayed long, preferring to leave Mahomet and the overseer to carry out instructions while he returned to the luxury of home and Katy's arms.

But at night Kerry continued to defy propriety, and under the judiciously averted eyes of the Stones, he repaired to Katy's chambers as soon as the servants retired for the night. With little more than a month before their child's expected birth, there was little passion spent in these nights together, but neither could bear any unnecessary moment apart. They had been separated too long to permit it easily now.

So it was when Katy felt the first pangs of birth in April, Kerry lay beside her in the bed, and she had only to reach out and touch his hand to be reassured all was well. She smiled inwardly and allowed the ache to roll over her. If her experience with Maureen was anything to judge by, there would be a long wait between this first pain and the final one; he would need his rest.

She had not counted on that unspoken communication between them: even as the second pain began, Kerry was leaning over her in the early-morning darkness, eyes filled with fear and concern as he gripped her hand.

"What is it, Katy? Should I get Bertha?" Anxiety tinged his words as he felt his hand squeezed convulsively while the pain held her in thrall. Although Dr. Jackson had offered his advice throughout Katy's pregnancy, Katy insisted on a midwife for the moment of birth. Bertha had assisted in the birthing of many of the children in town, and once or twice Mahomet had called for her assistance at Twin Oaks. Katy trusted her, and nothing else mattered.

As the cramp dissipated, Katy smiled weakly. "There is no need to wake Bertha yet. She will need her strength when it is time for our son to arrive, and that will not be for a while yet."

Not knowing whether to crow with excitement or frown in anxiety, Kerry pulled his young wife into his arms and buried his face in her hair. He remembered too well Charles's description of how they almost lost her with their first child. He could not bear to contemplate such a possibility now, not so soon after finally winning her.

Katy understood some of his fears and tried to soothe them, running gentle fingers down his back. "I am quite healthy this time, Kerry, there is nothing to fear. You have given me too much to live for to give up now."

Her words struck a chord and Kerry pulled back to study her face. "Is that what happened last time? Did you give up because I deserted you?"

Sadness darkened her eyes as she stroked the worried wrinkles on his brow. "It was a wound that would not heal. Even I had no idea of its depth. I grieve now over causing Charles so much pain at the time, but it does not matter any longer. We are together, and there will be no repeat of my illness. I intend to be healthy and strong very soon."

Silently acknowledging his part in the debacle that very nearly took her life, Kerry held her close and comfortingly, vowing never to allow anything to come between them again. He had spent too much of his life wandering aimlessly in pursuit of one challenge or another; it had almost lost him a child and the woman he loved. Never again. If he had spoken the vow aloud, Katy would have warned him he defied the fates with his thoughts, but as it was, neither had any warning of what was to come.

With the next pain, Kerry could no longer remain mute. Holding Katy until it passed, he then rose and swiftly dressed, leaving Katy momentarily alone while he went to rouse the Stones.

One look at Kerry's anxious face told Emma all she needed to know, and she sent him back to the bedroom while she dressed and went to fetch Bertha. To her sorrow, Emma had never borne a child of her own, but she had assisted with many of those of her husband's poorer parishioners and knew what had to be done. First item on the agenda was to keep the husband occupied, and hand-holding was the best occupation at this stage.

So Kerry remained at Katy's side while the women went about their multitude of tasks. This child threatened to come much sooner than the first, and by midmorning Anna and Maureen were sent off to neighbors, out of the hearing of Katy's muffled groans.

Kerry tenderly wiped his wife's brow and held her hand while she struggled through each succeeding agony. His helplessness in the sight of her suffering was almost beyond endurance, but he managed an outward calm, knowing she needed his strength more than his fears.

By early afternoon the pains were increasing in frequency and intensity, but the babe was no closer to coming than before, and Katy felt inclined to wipe Kerry's brow in return. When Tess interrupted with the message of a visitor below, Katy encouraged Kerry to leave, finding some relief in not having to hide her agony in his absence.

Below, Kerry's strained face showed only worried concern as he met with Jake in the drawing room. "You picked a god-awful time to appear. What do you want?" Unceremoniously dropping into the nearest chair, Kerry gestured for his guest to do the same, but Jake remained standing.

Glancing nervously above, where Katy's muffled cries could be heard, Jake fingered his hat and searched for words. He had been the bearer of bad tidings too often before to expect to find words to soften the blow. Postponing the inevitable, he asked uncertainly, "The babe?"

Kerry nodded wearily. "Anytime now. So for God's sake, hurry up. What is the matter now?"

Jake gulped and prepared to take the blow. It was the worst possible time to bring bad news, but he'd rather tell Lord Kerry than Katy. Still, he offered one last evasion. "Perhaps I'd better come back later; there's not much that can be done now."

Kerry stared at his young aide suspiciously. "If it was so important you had to come all the way from Charleston, you had better spit it out now. I do not need to spend the rest of the day wondering about it."

Jake sighed and blurted out, "It's Lord Burlington, sir. His ship was waylaid by pirates."

Kerry's eyes blazed as he flung himself from the chair. His wife could be hovering near death's door and this young pup came bearing fairy tales of pirates! How much could one man bear?

"There haven't been pirates on this coast for over a decade! Why bring me this drivel? It is preposterous!" Kerry stormed across the room to pour himself a drink from a decanter.

"So I thought, until I finally located one of the men spreading the story." Jake looked longingly at the drink in

Kerry's hand but said nothing. His employer's uncertain temper needed no igniting today.

Too caught up in his own worries, Kerry missed the lad's look, but poured a second drink out of habit, handing the glass to Jake as he once more sank into a chair. "All right. Let me hear the tale, but do not expect me to believe it."

Jake swallowed the drink gratefully, then proceeded to tell his story. "Some of your men brought me rumors of a ship stopped at sea by pirates. The tales ranged from mass plundering to kidnapping, but the only thing certain was the ship, and it's the same as your brother sailed on. So I've been trying to trace the rumors to their source, until I finally found a couple of the deckhands that started the tale."

He drained the glass and set it aside while Kerry frowned expectantly. "It seems these men were on a ship bound for Charleston when it was flagged down by your brother's ship. Messages went between the captains, but you know how the hands are when they get together, they told as how they were come up on a couple of weeks out by a maraudin' frigate that had them outgunned. When the pirates came aboard, they stripped the passengers of their valuables and took a hostage for 'safekeeping,' they said. The hands couldn't tell me who the hostage was, but said he was an important noble on his majesty's business and the captain raised an unholy fuss. But the pirates insisted on the noble and said if the captain didn't aim right on for England with their ransom demands, they would deep-six the hostage and that it would be on the captain's head if that happened."

Kerry closed his eyes and pressed strained fingers to his temples. "Ransom?"

"The men didn't know too much about that. Just said the pirates gave the captain some sort of message and insisted the ship better not turn back. It was only sheer luck they crossed the path of a Carolina-bound trader and so could pass on the word. The men claimed the captain took the tale to the governor to warn of pirates in the area, but I ain't heard nothin' official about it, and no one's lookin' for them."

"No, of course not." Kerry's head sank back against the chair and lines of pain and worry deepened across his brow. His youthful smile gone, laughing eyes shuttered and closed, he looked his thirty-four years and more. Happiness was only a fleeting illusion at best. A harsher cry from upstairs broke his reverie, and reluctantly he took command.

"Halberstam is behind this, one way or another. Those were no pirates. Get my ship prepared to sail, load it with supplies for at least two months, find men who are familiar with the coastline from here to Georgia. Lord only knows what their ransom demands are, but with any luck, they will keep Burlington alive long enough to carry them out. That should give you at least two months to locate him before the ransom comes through or they dare kill him."

"Me?" Jake had been taking mental notes until jogged loose by the equivocal pronoun. He had assumed Kerry would take charge of this expedition.

The light in Kerry's eyes had gone out as he nodded tiredly. "You and whatever men you trust. I cannot leave Katy, not now, not like this. I have done it to her too many times. My brother's life, and in a sense, my own, will be in your hands, Jake, so take care."

Jake quickly helped himself to another drink without asking. This was more responsibility than he cared to assume: the Marquess of Burlington, heir to the Duchy of Exeter—the ramifications were tremendous if he should fail. And in all that varied confusion of islands and inlets up and down the coast, how could he possibly not fail? His misery grew as the profusion of possibilities increased. If anything happened to Burlington, Kerry would be the heir, and Katy . . . It did not bear thinking.

"Milord, even Katy should understand your need to find your brother. It is unlike you to—" A mournful wail from the second floor interrupted his plea and both men turned to look up the stairs, finding no clue to answer their prayers there.

Kerry gestured upward and replied harshly, "How can you listen to that and deny Katy needs me more? My brother will have to look after himself. If you do as I say, your chances of finding him are as good as mine. Go to it, you should be able to set sail within three days. Keep your sailing as secret as possible to prevent Halberstam from interfering. I am going back to Katy."

Slamming his glass down, shattering the fine crystal into

tiny pieces, oblivious of anything but the sounds from above, Kerry hurriedly left the startled young man behind.

Between the pains of her labor, Katy saw Kerry enter, nearly panicking at the look she encountered on his face, but overcome by another wave of agony, she could not react, grasping his hand gratefully as the wave broke over her. Both Emma and Bertha shook their heads disapprovingly over Kerry's reappearance, but neither would deny him entrance. Only Katy had the authority to overrule the young lord.

When the pain subsided, Katy looked up anxiously into pain-dulled green eyes, and her worst fears were confirmed. "What is it, Kerry? Who is down there?"

Kerry shook his head and smiled sadly. He could conceal nothing from this prescient little brat, even in the midst of pain. "Jake is down there, and it is nothing that cannot wait. Concentrate on producing our son, madam." He stroked her brow tenderly, irregardful of the others in the room, though Bertha's black head nodded knowingly at this admission to fatherhood.

Katy accepted his words as truth, too involved in the rigors of labor to be more than half-aware of her surroundings. Clinging to Kerry's strength for as long as possible, choking back her cries to prevent scaring him worse than she knew she had done, Katy struggled through the remainder of the afternoon, sending Kerry away only when she could no longer hold back the screams, knowing the birth to be imminent.

Stumbling into the study in a daze of fear-filled anguish, Kerry filled a tumbler with brandy and gulped it down before realizing Jake had followed him.

"What in hell are you still doing here, man? I thought I sent you out hours ago." He splashed more liquor into the glass, and at a second thought, shakily poured a tumbler for Jake. "Here, looks like you could use some of this," and he shoved it at the white-faced young seaman.

"Can't do anything till morning. If I ride all night, I can still make it. How's Katy?" Jake gulped the fiery liquid gratefully. Hours of listening to mysterious cries while waiting helplessly below had left him shaken and unnerved.

"Damned if I know. How in hell did Charles stand two

days of this?'' Kerry sank into the desk chair, carefully
keeping brandy and glass close at hand.

"Why do you think his hair turned gray?'' Jake hiccuped
uncertainly. The brandy on top of the wine stolen throughout
the afternoon had a strange effect on an empty stomach.

Kerry grinned at the thought of the stalwart baronet growing gray overnight and ran his hand through his own burnished locks. ''Shear our hair like Samson's, that's what they
do, drain our strength.'' He took another large gulp of brandy,
and at another wail from above, took a second drink for
additional fortification.

''You gonna get drunk, you keep that up.'' Jake swayed
above him thoughtfully, abruptly sitting down in the window
seat a moment later.

Kerry help up the fragile stem of the brandy glass, admiring the dying firelight through the amber liquid. ''Never get
drunk now. Katy don't approve of it, says I make an ass of
myself.'' He sipped the liquid more carefully, hoping the
buzzing in his ears would drown out the cries from above. He
had eaten little or nothing all day—he couldn't remember.
''She's right, I'm an ass, and I'd willingly let her ride me any
day.'' He chuckled at his muddled joke, but Jake didn't catch
it. He, too, was staring at the brandy glass Kerry dangled in
midair.

The piercing scream from above wailed and echoed endlessly, and Jake just managed to stumble forward to remove
this second glass from certain destruction before Kerry's
tightened fist could snap it in two. They stood gaping at each
other, Jake with both glasses in hand, as the cry reverberated
one more time, and then fell silent.

Shakily Jake set the glasses down, but Kerry remained
paralyzed, straining to hear sounds from above, fists clenched
and face immobile, willing one more wail or cry to speak of
life. When it came, it was not what he expected, but a silly
grin of relief spread across his face at the weak cry of an
infant. Sinking back into his chair, he accepted the brandy
offered by Jake and drained it abstractedly.

Then, rising from the desk, Kerry stood in the hallway
waiting for someone to appear on the landing above. Vowing
to storm the citadel if no one appeared within the five minutes

t would take the clock to strike the hour, he was momentarily
staggered when the bedroom door opened just as the first
chimes struck.

Emma carefully carried the bundle to the stairs, but Kerry
had already reached the top before she could touch the first
tread. Gently poking into the blankets to find the reddened,
wizened face of the babe, damp auburn curls plastered against
its tiny head, eyes scrunched closed and sightless, Kerry
looked questioningly to Emma.

"A son, milord. Already he looks like you." Emma fondly
stroked a tiny fist.

"And Katy?" Taking the bundle gently into his arms,
Kerry waited anxiously for her reply.

"Resting fine, there was no problem with this birth."
Emma watched with concern as the young husband lurched
toward the bedroom, then shrugged in Katy's manner. Katy
would take care of him.

Slipping into a bedside chair, Kerry waited until his wife
opened her eyes, then held the bundle out for her to hold.
"May I present the Honorable Charles Edward Southerland,
my love?"

Accepting her son, Katy smiled wanly. "We have already
met, but have never been properly introduced. It is nice to
know I have produced something honorable." Scanning Kerry's tired face, she asked anxiously, "Will you tell me now
what is wrong?"

Kerry grinned ruefully. "I am more than a little drunk and
frightened half out of my wits and my hair will probably be
white by morning, but there is nothing else that you need to
know for now. Go to sleep, your son will be needing you in
the morning."

"And you will be in no state to heed his cries." Katy
reached out a gentle hand to trace his lined cheek. "I love
you, milord."

"And I you, my lovely Katy, more than any man can
bear." Kerry leaned over her then, gently gathering her into
his arms and hugging both mother and child to his breast
before laying them back against the covers. A faint glimmer
reflected in his eye as Katy leaned back happily, a small

smile of satisfaction on her lips, and he watched anxiously
until she fell into an untroubled sleep.

Belatedly remembering Jake, Kerry returned downstairs to
show off his newest offspring and to give the good news of
Katy's health. Then, sadly slapping him on the back, Kerry
sent the young seaman on his way to begin the journey
affecting so many lives.

April–May 1738

UNABLE TO SLEEP, Kerry rose early from the lonely bed he had returned to in deference to Katy's health. Stalking Tess's movements to the nursery, where he stood in the way in his fascination with his wailing son, Kerry followed her out again when she carried the child to Katy.

Looking up at the sound of their entrance, Katy smiled at the sight of father and son, but after Tess departed, the smile faded. Kerry's restless uneasiness warned that all was not as it should be.

Kerry watched as Katy tenderly took the infant to her breast, and he knew his joy at this sight should be fulfillment enough, but it was not. The infant's dark head against the pale background of silver-gold curls and creamy skin produced a longing to touch and be touched, and he reached out to move a stray curl from his son's clenched fist.

"He is much like his father, is he not, milord?" Katy asked with a teasing gleam to her eye.

"No man can resist such lovely tresses, my love, but there will be no denying he is my son. My mother's traits are very strong indeed." He gently stroked the light fringe of aubur hair glistening against his son's small head.

"Will you blame your mother for your hot-tempered wil fulness also?" she asked curiously, searching his face fo some sign of the trouble bothering him.

"No, for that I have my father to blame. Have I been s very bad these last few months?" Kerry grimaced ruefull and sat back in the chair. His head pounded wickedly fron the liquor the night before, but not so much as the pain of hi decision.

"No, milord, you have not, but I believe the strain i beginning to show. Will you tell me now what is wrong? promise I am quite well enough to hear the truth."

Kerry gazed at her doubtfully, the frail prettiness cast u against the pillows, her now slender figure outlined agains thin sheets. She always appeared so delicate, yet she ha withstood all the trials and tribulations he had showered upor her, and he could not keep the truth from discerning viole eyes.

"Jake brought some tale of my brother's kidnapping b pirates. There is evidence of some truth to the tale, though believe it will be found the pirates are more likely to b Halberstam's men."

Katy absorbed this information thoughtfully, seeing the meaning behind the new lines etched across his brow. "An what do you plan to do about this? We cannot go to Halberstan and demand Burlington's release under such circumstances."

"Jake is supplying my ship to start a search. With an luck, Halberstam will not hear of it until too late, and there i every chance Jake and his men will trace the pirates' patl through rumors or talk in taverns up and down the coast. Such goings-on do not go unnoticed—these colonies are stil too scantily populated."

With resignation Katy faced the inevitable. Removing the now sleeping babe from her breast, she wrapped him care fully in his blanket. "When are you sailing?"

"I am not. Jake will go in my place." Kerry took the infant from her arms, studying it carefully. He was a married man with two children now; he had responsibilities to them first. He remembered too well Katy's injunction about his family coming first; this was his family now.

Shocked, Katy stared at his bent head. "You are jesting surely, milord?"

Kerry looked up then with a sad smile. "No, my love, I am not. Jake is a capable young man and knows these waters better than I. If anyone can find James, it will be he."

"And what will he do when he does find him? Jake is no soldier. I doubt if he has ever held pistol or sword in hand. What will he do to rescue your brother from a band of pirates?" Katy demanded.

"Are you suggesting I am better prepared to take on a band of pirates, or do you merely concern yourself with Jake's safety?" Kerry asked with curiosity.

Slowly Katy began to understand, and her eyes widened. "You are staying because of me, are you not?" A few expressive French curses slipped by her lips at Kerry's reaction before she calmed down. "You are mad! It is hard enough for me to sit here helplessly, unable to do anything while one I love is in danger, but to ask you to do the same is bordering on insanity, and you will drive everyone else to the brink of it if you do not go. Get Tess to pack your trunks and get out of here before that ship sails. I will not have the health of half the town on my conscience."

Kerry smiled wryly at her outrage. "I promise I will not be so bad as that, but I cannot go. As you have said yourself, I have left you too many times before. I will not leave you again."

Tears of frustration sprang to Katy's eyes, and she tried to swing out of the bed, but Kerry rose and sat down beside her, effectively trapping her beneath the covers. Laying the babe down beside her, he took her in his arms. "You are my family now, Katy, I cannot leave you," he whispered softly, kissing her hair lightly.

"You are such a fool, Kerry Southerland." Katy curled up in his arms and rested her head against his chest. It hurt to let him go, she needed the comfort of his love and strength, and it was too soon, far too soon, to send him off again. But his brother needed him more than she, and neither of them could survive the results should anything befall that lord.

"Burlington is your family too, and you must do the same for him you would do for me. I do not want you to change for me, Kerry. I married you as you are, and you must act as you think proper. Go, find Burlington, then come back to me as swiftly and safely as possible. I will still be here, I promise."

Kerry clasped her tighter, resting his chin on her hair. Through the black clouds of trouble brewing in his breast shot a sudden shaft of sunlight in the form of a silver-golden head, and his love expanded to new dimensions. There was so little he knew about love, and so much to learn.

"My lovely Katy, you have just borne me the son I have always desired, and I love you more than life itself; I cannot bear to be parted from you. You have only to say the words, and I will stay, but if you release me, you know I must go with Jake, and it may be months before I see you again. I do not like leaving you alone."

Two tears trickled down Katy's cheeks, but she hid them against his shirt, her fingers wrapping themselves tightly in the linen material as if never to let go. To be totally alone with only her children about her suddenly seemed more terrifying than the months after her father's death when she walked the streets of London. But she was older now, with the wealth to support a family, and friends to protect her. She must let go.

"Go, Kerry, you would never forgive yourself or me should anything happen to Burlington. Find him safe and well so you may remain a gentleman farmer and my son may learn to be a Carolinian and not an English lord. I beg of you to do nothing foolish, but you must go."

With fiery desire, their lips met and meshed, clinging in a volatile conflagration that should consume mere mortals, leaving burning embers long after. Not so long as that ember lived could they be kept apart, and when Kerry left that evening, he took part of Katy with him.

With Kerry gone, the Stones had no need to linger, but out of anxiety for Katy's health and well-being, they stayed another week. By that time their young hostess declared herself well enough to be out and about, despite the urgings of doctor and friends. It was useless to dissuade her, and leaving her in the care of Bertha and Tess, the household kept in order by the housekeeper, the Stones returned to the parsonage.

Idleness made the days grow longer, but Katy had not yet gained the strength to undertake major cleaning tasks, and the housekeeper directed all others. Bertha's proficiency in the kitchen left little to do in that quarter, and Katy threatened to reopen her school for the sake of filling empty hours. Only activity could serve to drive out thoughts and worries of Kerry, but there would never be enough to begin accomplishing that.

Weeks passed. April became May without word of Kerry or Burlington. No further reports of pirate attacks were heard, and the brief skirmish faded from the minds of all but those most affected. Anxiously Katy awaited Halberstam's next move, but none came. Time hung in suspension, marked only by the growth of the babe she had come to call Chad in combination of both his names.

Kerry's overseer had been left in charge of Twin Oaks, with instructions to follow the planting directions given earlier and to refer to Katy any question involving house and staff. Not certain of the extent of Katy's authority, the manager deferred to her as he had Sir Charles and called upon them as he did before whenever he came to town. Mahomet was frequently his driver and a visitor to the Stockbridge kitchens, and all news passed through both households in this manner better than any other. What little Bertha did not know of her mistress, Mahomet guessed.

But it was no ordinary visit he made one midnight in early June. Katy was preparing to retire as the remainder of the household had already done when Bertha intruded on her dark thoughts. Startled to see the large cook in the front of the house where she seldom appeared unless summoned, Katy looked up apprehensively from her book.

"What is it, Bertha?"

"Dat big black man here. Say he see you. Told him he crazy man but he sez you come." Worried, Bertha twisted at her apron, trying to portray Mahomet's urgency to the delicate figure of her mistress. Katy looked tired and drawn these days, and the cook dreaded adding to her already worrisome burden.

"Mahomet is here?" Katy's eyes widened and her face paled. There could be no good reason for the slave to risk coming this far at this time of night without the company of a white man. Had the Indians returned? Surely he could not have heard from Kerry?

Slowly laying aside her book, Katy rose reluctantly to follow the cook, a gloomy cloud of dread encompassing her thoughts. Whatever had brought Mahomet to her door in the dark of night could not bode well on the future, and she had had enough of black worries and their resultant perils. Only let Kerry be safe, she prayed as her feet trod lightly through the hallway to the back rooms of the house.

Mahomet's huge blackness in the small back foyer would be ominous under the best of conditions, but in the candlelit midnight gloom, he presented a shadow of darkness covering the diminutive figure bravely confronting him.

"What is it, Mahomet? Has something happened at Twin Oaks?" Katy held her candle higher, trying to read the black man's impassive eyes.

"Sojers say house belong to big man now. Told Marster Davies to go, give him papers say he no longer work there."

Davies was the white overseer, and Katy's mind flew rapidly over the possibilities unexpressed by Mahomet's taciturn message. Soldiers at Twin Oaks. Big man. Removal of the only figure of authority at the plantation. Halberstam. Katy's heart lurched painfully.

"How many soldiers, Mahomet?" Cautiously Katy tried to slow the pounding of her anxious pulse and think clearly. Without Charles's wisdom or Kerry's strength, she was on her own, and the thought frightened her as much as Halberstam.

Mahomet held up six fingers. "Said more come tomorrow with big man. He live there now. People belong to him."

Kerry's slave population had gradually increased with the growth of the plantation and now included a number of women and children who tended the house as well as the fields. Katy had heard too much of the practices at some plantations to do anything but shiver at the thought of randy soldiers let loose in a houseful of unprotected women. "The women and children, Mahomet? Where are they?"

If it were possible for the black man to smile, satisfaction curved his lips now. "Gone to woods. Heard what sojers say to Marster Davies, and all hide."

"Well, they can't stay in the woods until Kerry returns. Get as many of the people to neighboring plantations as you can. I will give you a letter asking for their help. I think they will take them in." Many of the women had come from those same plantations, and it would be something of a homecoming for them. And surely the neighbors could not complain too strenuously about free labor, although Katy had no possible means of answering the questions her request would surely raise. One thing at a time. She tried to calm her feverishly racing thoughts.

"If you can, try to keep the young, strong hands with you. The plantation will need working if the soldiers will allow it, and Kerry will need their strength should he return soon. Where is Davies now?"

"My place. He not move fast enough. Sojers push him down steps. Leg mebbe broke." Impassively Mahomet awaited further instructions.

Katy pinched her eyes shut and covered them with her hands. That poor doddering old man. There wasn't a rebellious bone in his body. That served to show the type of soldiers Halberstam had sent. Thank God the women were gone. All these thoughts flickered rapidly through her mind as she tried to concentrate on more relevant ones. But none came. She bade Mahomet sit while she went to fetch quill and paper.

"I do not know what else to tell you to do," she said, coming back and handing the slave the letter she had hastily scribbled. "The people are most important, see to their safety above all. Protect Twin Oaks second, in whatever way you deem sensible. I am certain I will soon find out what this is all about, but without Kerry, I am powerless to act. You have heard nothing from him?" she added wistfully.

"Indians in woods. No time to talk wit' dem. May see him, ask next time." The terse words were dragged from him. He was eager to be off, before sunrise found him missing.

Katy frowned slightly at the thought of Indians so close to the plantation where Kerry swore they seldom strayed except in winter when food was scarce. But at the moment, she was certain Halberstam posed a worse threat than savages. Sending Mahomet on his way, she slowly made her way to the empty room she called her own, there to worry the night away in dread of what the morrow might bring.

June 1738

THE MORROW came soon enough, and with it, Katy's thoughts cleared from the fogging clouds of fear. If Halberstam thought Kerry and Burlington safely out of the way—not dead, she prayed, please, not that—not only was Twin Oaks in danger, but herself, and thence, the children. Unless Burlington's papers were intercepted, and she had no reason to believe they were, Halberstam could not know of their marriage, and he could not know for certain the parentage of her children unless he saw them. His hatred of Kerry would lead him to destroy all things Kerry's, and this she must avoid at any cost.

Flinging herself swiftly from the bed, Katy roused a startled Tess and began hastily packing a bag for the children. A sleepy but puzzled Anna aided in gathering the basic necessities and took the letter Katy quickly scribbled to the Stones. Maureen and Chad slept through the confusion until a bewildered Emma came to lead them away.

"Katy, I do not understand why you are doing this. Halberstam cannot do anything to harm you or the children even if he should want to. You are surrounded by friends here; they would let nothing happen to you. I think your imagination has run away with you.''

Katy shook her head impatiently, keeping her thoughts on the imperative and away from this separation from her children. ''It would be better if that is the case, but I cannot take chances. He can reach me through the children, and that I cannot allow. If he comes, I will be alone and will have only myself to protect. That is the safest thing I know to do. If I hide, he will come looking for me and that will only endanger others. Please, Emma, I cannot begin to explain now. You will have to find a wet nurse for Chad, I do not dare leave the house until I know for certain what is happening. You can do nothing else but pray for us.''

Katy hugged her friend before lovingly lifting the infant to her arms one last time, kissing each of the children before consigning them to the care of Emma and Tess.

With her most precious possessions safely out of harm's way, where Halberstam could not gaze upon telltale emerald eyes or auburn hair and guess their true father, Katy had only to pass the long hours away. Perhaps she was being foolish, overreacting to the upsetting midnight call, but she could not shake this premonition of danger, and it was better to act than do nothing at all.

Hours dragged on interminably, even longer in not knowing what she awaited. Halberstam's threats of revenge had not been specific, but that he meant them had become certain. There would never be a better time than now, while she sat alone and unprotected. Katy cringed at the thought of facing him, almost lost courage and wished she had the woods in which to hide, but the thought of Halberstam's rage on finding her gone and its effect on children and friends deterred her panic. If she could do nothing else for Kerry, she could protect his children with her life.

Morning passed into afternoon and Katy was almost ill with fear before the first sounds of a carriage in the street reached the darkness of the study. Katy had retreated there, feeling the comfort of the presence of both Charles and Kerry in this masculine refuge, but even that comfort escaped her now with the carriage drawing up outside.

Nervously she tugged at the high collar of her gown. She

had dressed as modestly as possible, leaving off panniers and heavy petticoats to make movement easier. If there were any chance of escape, she would find it, but she was not overly optimistic of her chances. Standing at the study window, she watched the detested figure of Halberstam descend from a coach attended by two militiamen. She assumed these were more of the "soldiers" Mahomet had referred to, and her prospects diminished further.

With fatalistic tread she entered the hallway and opened the door alone. She had commanded the remainder of the servants to stay out of sight unless called upon.

Halberstam's jeering gaze took in her dowdy attire and one eyebrow quirked mockingly. "You evidently did not expect callers, Lady Stockbridge."

Katy's fingers tightened on the knob of the door, and only a great effort of will kept her from flinging the door shut in his face and fleeing. "No, sir, I did not. To what do I owe this honor?" She made no move to let him in, but spoke simply to avoid antagonizing him.

"What, Katy? You do not beg me in as in the past? You were not always so unsociable. But no matter, I have come to return your hospitality. Today you will be my guest. I could prefer you wore a more appealing gown, but it is too late to rectify the error. Come, I have a surprise for you." He held out his arm and commanded her compliance.

"You surely cannot expect me to drop everything and run off with you? I am a respectable widow with many responsibilities, as you surely must know. If you wish to tell me anything, there is no reason you cannot tell it here." Katy refused his arm, pulling herself up haughtily to her full diminutive height.

"Madam, I wish to *show* you something and it cannot be done here. Fetch your maid for chaperon if you wish, but I have not come all the way from Charleston to be refused." The impatient irritation of his tone brooked no delay, and he clearly looked capable of carrying her off if necessary. Though he would scarcely soil his own hands for so menial a task, thought Katy spitefully.

Not wishing to endanger any more of the servants than already reported by Mahomet, Katy reluctantly acquiesced.

"If you promise it will not take long. I have other things to do this day and will be missed if not back by nightfall."

Her spirits sank as she realized she was walking with full knowledge into his trap. To refuse would only make him angrier, and Halberstam was quite capable of sending his men to carry her out, with little regard for her person in the interval. Not that she expected much regard in that respect. She remembered hot fingers searing her skin and the hungry gleam of his gaze in previous encounters, and her entire body contracted at the thought of coming in contact with him.

With a malevolent smile of satisfaction, Halberstam agreed. "Whatever you say, madam. Are you prepared to leave?" He was willing to agree to anything, so long as he had his prey where he wanted her with a minimum of fuss.

Sensing his attitude, Katy felt a flutter of panic but quenched it quickly. She had chosen to bait his trap deliberately, like a mother quail diverts the hunter from her nest. It was no time for second thoughts. For a moment her mind flew involuntarily to Kerry, and she begged his understanding; then with trepidation she accepted the arm so repellent to her.

The ride was tedious, the usual jolts and lurches unsoftened by any familiar shoulder. Stoically keeping her balance on the seat opposite Halberstam, Katy made no attempt at friendliness, and Halberstam seemed content in watching her discomfort with an occasional smug smile, the cold gray of his eyes warning that his was the upper hand now, and he would choose the moment to act. When Katy made no effort to respond to his desultory conversation, he lapsed into satisfied silence.

Their destination was soon apparent, but Katy showed no sign of recognition or surprise, denying him any pleasure he might derive from her plight. It would be nightfall before the coach would reach Twin Oaks; that Halberstam had lied to her came as no shock.

Their arrival at the plantation aroused no bustle of servants or welcome greetings. A lone militiaman sauntered around the corner of the mansion at the sound of the carriage, giving an uncertain salute as Halberstam descended to the drive.

With angry impatience the acting governor demanded an explanation for this dereliction of duty and upon further

conference with his aide, ordered a full report of their activities and a complete tour of the "traitor's" confiscated property. As an afterthought, before searching out the officer in
command, Halberstam ordered his passenger to be shown to
appropriate chambers.

While Katy delicately found her way to the ground without
the aid of any of the men standing idly about, Halberstam
studied her for any sign of reaction. A quick glance had
already told her the place was seemingly empty. That being
her major concern, she remained silent, waiting for some
indication from Halberstam as to whether she were prisoner
or if he had some other design on her.

Frustrated of his gloating by her silence, Halberstam curtly
sent her after the appointed guide, leaving Katy to guess at
her status here. He had been traveling since the dark hours of
the morning and was in no mood to exchange sarcasms with
his recalcitrant passenger. She would discover soon enough
his intentions. Stalking after them, he surreptitiously surveyed his prizes: Kerry's elegant whore and the mansion to
which Halberstam could never have hoped to be invited.
They were his now, and his spirits lifted.

To Katy's amazement, the militiaman shepherded her to
the end of the upper hallway, to Kerry's inviolable quarters,
where, so far as she knew, no one ever entered but himself
and a maid. These were the rooms intended for their marital
chambers, should Kerry ever return to rescue them from
grasping hands. Katy had no doubt these would be the most
magnificent rooms in the house. Why had they not been
assigned to Halberstam? The possibility that these were
Halberstam's rooms made her skin crawl with disgust.

The rooms were empty, and as soon as she entered she had
a better understanding of why she had been placed there
without definitive word from the plantation's new "owner."
Demanding to be brought water for a bath, she dismissed the
servile soldier and stared at the place above the mantel.

A full-length portrait in vibrant oils graced the place of
honor, and with awe Katy approached her own likeness.
Wearing the royal-blue velvet she had first worn to the opera
in London, the figure in the painting bore a startling likeness
to the young girl Katy had attempted to portray in her minia-

ture. The portrait must have been commissioned during Kerry's last sojourn in London and the artist had relied heavily on the miniature watercolor Kerry carried with him everywhere. It was an amazing likeness, and Katy suspected the artist to be one of the young gallants who had haunted her box that brief winter of desolation and enchantment. Still, for Kerry to have had it commissioned then, while she was still married to Charles and he supposedly looking for a bride . . . His love and his sorrow must both have been very deep. Reverently she touched the gilded frame, and tears sprang to her eyes.

Looking around to shake the memories threatening to destroy her composure, Katy found her collage of kitten sketches on another wall. With a smile, she wandered over to caress it casually, remembering Kerry's face when first she gave it to him. Curious now, she circled the sitting room, lovingly touching the elegant appointments he had chosen with her in mind. They were all of the finest quality and craftsmanship and reflected Kerry's simple good taste more than any of the other rooms. Cautiously she approached the bedchamber, uncertain whether she dared this sacrosanct interior without Kerry by her side.

At first glance, the room was merely the spacious, airy chamber she remembered, surrounded by the trees and fields depicted in the bank of windows at the rear. A large poster bed dominated one wall; washstand and wardrobes completed the suite. It was simple to the point of severity, the windows providing the only adornment. But Kerry's presence was reflected here more than anywhere else in the house, from his love of the land and plantation to his love for her, as Katy quickly discovered.

Feeling the urge to be closer to this man she called husband, Katy swung open the door of the first wardrobe, expecting to discover familiar coats and waistcoats that she could touch, their masculine scents an ever-present reminder of Kerry. But instead of the male attire she expected, she was faced with an assortment of women's apparel, elegant satins and velvets in a rainbow of colors, with the predominant shade of violet-blue Kerry favored on her.

Without taking one out, Katy knew they would fit better

than any she owned, that their workmanship would be designed to suit a woman of her stature and attributes, and that
their style would not so much reflect the latest fashion as the
wearer's looks. They were pure Kerry, and tears poured
down her cheeks as she remembered their first day together
when he had chosen her entire wardrobe, instinctively knowing the appropriate materials and designs to suit a young girl.
Lovingly caressing a rich maroon velvet, Katy steeled herself
with new resolve.

She *would* escape, immediately, before Halberstam could
so much as touch her. She would rather risk the perils of the
forest again than have that man touch her. Now that he was
safely diverted from the children, she would run.

As if to cement her resolve further, a knock pounded at the
door. Praying it was the bath she ordered, Katy hastened to
open it, greeting the familiar figure on the other side with a
muffled cry of joy.

"Mahomet? Oh, bless you, dear man, come in." Urging
the towering giant into the room, she shut the door behind
him, gesturing for him to set aside the huge buckets of hot
water he carried.

He regarded her with a puzzled frown at first, then slow
understanding. Not only did the "big man" claim Kerry's
plantation, but Kerry's woman. His frown grew ominous.

"Mahomet, I have got to get out of here now, before
Halberstam comes back. Can you find me some boy's clothes,
some my size? And a big floppy hat, something I can pull
down over my face? It is dark and the disguise might work
long enough to get me to the shelter of the trees." She
gestured, indicating her needs, and the slave nodded thoughtfully. "You must hurry, please!"

Since getting his master's woman out of this place had
been his first thought on finding her, Mahomet agreed readily, disappearing in the darkness of the hallway with a warning to bolt the door until he returned. With relief Katy did as
she was told, then hastily stripped herself of women's garments and hid them in the wardrobe, praying Halberstam
would think her still about the house should he find her gone
too soon.

Mahomet reappeared quickly, handing in the clothing and

standing guard uneasily outside the door. The soldiers were
lax in their attention to slaves and "prisoners," more interested in tending to their own needs than those of others, and
without competent leadership to rule them. But this same
laxity that made it simple to move freely, posed dangers in
other forms. News of Katy's youth and beauty would soon
circulate this all-male stronghold, and in combination with
the strong drink the soldiers had imbibed, it did not take a
man of much sophistication to guess the result.

Dressed in loose linen shirt and overlarge duck trousers
tied at the waist with a length of cord to keep from walking
on them, Katy peered cautiously around the door, relaxing
slightly to find Mahomet still waiting outside. His bemused
expression at the sight of her petite form dressed in such
outlandish attire gave her little confidence, but bravely she
shouldered one of the braces of wooden pails he had used to
carry water, now empty of their contents.

Pulling the large hat down to hide her face and hair, Katy
motioned for him to take the other brace, and silently they
stole along empty hallways, wary of any noise. Katy's heart
pounded against her ribs as they neared the rear door and the
sound of Halberstam's voice echoed down to her, but she
hesitated only a moment. Slouching her shoulders, shuffling
in a barefoot gait, she shoved open the door and meandered
idly out into the darkened courtyard, the heavy buckets
bruising her hips as they swung from the length of ropes.

The night was clear and starlit and it was impossible to
escape unseen. Out in the yard, a soldier spotted them,
yelling incoherent phrases as they moved across the yard.
Katy halted, keeping her face averted as she rested her weight
on one leg in an awkward stance while Mahomet made some
obedient reply. Seemingly complying with the man's orders
for water for the governor, they ambled on toward the kitchen
and well, praying Katy's absence wasn't soon discovered.

Once on the farside of the wall, out of sight of the house,
they hastily dropped their buckets while Mahomet shouldered
a large sack tucked away in a flour bin. Then, noticing the
outline of Katy's white linen against the night sky, he let the
sack down again and glanced quickly about. A burlap sack
caught his eye, and grabbing it up, he ripped a hole in the end

vith his knife. Lifting Katy's hat from her hair, he whipped
he sack over her head, completely encompassing the glaring
vhiteness of Katy's clothes. Another swift movement and her
golden hair was once more concealed beneath the felt head-
gear. Nodding his satisfaction, he again shouldered the sack.

Indignantly Katy tried to move her arms within the confines of the scratchy material, but her protests were stifled by
Mahomet's stealthy pace. She had to run to keep up, dodging
behind the low shrubberies of the gardens, bent over to
conceal their movements in the darkness of the night. Around
them came the filtered sounds from the house and stable
yards, the restless tamping of hooves and low mutter of
voices, the myriad whines and clatters of insects, but their
own noise as they moved along the grass edging the garden
path was soundless. Katy swallowed her protests.

Safely reaching the edge of the garden, they were then
faced with the open swath of lawn edged in the distance by
virgin forest. Too close to the house and too far from the
river for cultivating, Kerry had left the natural growth at this
edge of the lawn. In that stretch of pine and hardwood Chad
had been conceived, and to its concealment of underbrush
and overhanging branches they must escape now.

Catching their breath with a quick gulp of cool night air,
they slid silently into the open lawn, flitting like shadows
across the verdant grasses, hoping no one would glance out
an open window to see the odd movement in the side yard.
Mahomet's dark, unshirted back blended into the landscape,
his patched and dirty trousers only a smudge against the
backdrop of grasses and trees. Burlap hindering her movements, Katy skittered awkwardly behind him, blood pounding
through her veins, sweat breaking out on her brow as they
neared the far edge of the field. Almost there. No excited
noises or sound of chase behind them. Grass whispered about
her thong-clad feet, mosquitoes buzzed in the air about their
heads, and the breeze grew suddenly cooler. The forest reached
out to engulf them.

Ecstatically Katy dashed into the blackness of the under-
cover, pulling futilely at the entangling burlap. They were
free! Halberstam's men could never find them in here at
night; they did not possess the skill of Indians. As Mahomet

jerked the cumbersome sack from her head, Katy threw u
her arms in joy.

Halberstam could not possibly involve her friends or chil
dren now. The whole town would know she had gone wit
him; he could not admit she had run away. Neither woul
there be any object in doing so, since they obviously coul
not know where she had gone. She was truly on her ow
now.

Katy's joy dimmed. Her breasts ached with untouche
milk. She was free only as long as she stayed away fron
home and family. Once more she was thrown out upon th
world alone, and this time there was no convenient Lor
Kerry to rescue her from her fate. Where would she go? Wha
could she do? How would she ever find Kerry and warn hin
of what awaited? Bleakly she looked to Mahomet's stoic fac
for answers.

But the black giant moved purposefully between the trees
following some unmarked path deeper into the darkness
farther away from threatening civilization. Katy meekly fol
lowed. Before long she had the eerie feeling they were n
longer alone, though her ears could detect no sound but th
hooting of owls and the hum of insects. She followed close
on Mahomet's heels, but the feeling nagged until it was mor
than just a feeling. A quiet movement in the corner of he
eye, the flash of a homespun shirt, crackles of twigs not troc
by their feet, and she knew there were others in the trees
around them. Panic caught in her throat, but Mahomet seeme
oblivious of danger. He continued swiftly down the unseer
path as if it were clearly blazed and in full sunlight.

Now the sounds were no longer just sounds, but shapes
forming in the darkness. Darker blacknesses against the out
lines of trees moved suffocatingly closer, words whispered
around her, and she glimpsed clothes much like her own bu
dirtier and more tattered. And then, suddenly, Katy realized
she was caught in the midst of a dozen black men, slaves
assuredly, most likely the men she had ordered Mahomet to
keep behind to protect the plantation.

But what were they doing here, silently following their
leader into the wilderness, further away from their home?
They could not possibly have known of her arrival and been

prepared for her escape. And the sack? She had assumed it
contained food, but Mahomet could not have prepared it in
the time he had discovered her presence and they escaped. He
had already been prepared to flee. But why? Were they running for their freedom from slavery and taking her with them
as hostage? Mahomet wouldn't possibly do that, would he?
She had the urge to run to him to ask, but he moved too
swiftly ahead, and she was caught in the center of the herd,
held back by the press of bodies around her.

Oddly, their numbers seemed to be increasing. No distinct
shapes were visible, but the sounds seemed to be growing,
the edges of the band expanding to include more than the
dozen shapes she had first assumed. And then a sudden
halting of footsteps opened ahead of her. Katy stepped through
the thick night air, hemmed in by the press of bodies, eyes on
the ebony giant towering head and shoulders over the others.
Mahomet was her friend, she would be safe at his side.

But when she stepped out into the open glade to confront
him, she let out a gasp of fear and glanced quickly around for
means of escape. Nearby stood the Indian Tonga, and in the
glade around them, a host of other savages, multiplying the
number of slaves into a small army. There was no possible
means of escape. They had joined forces, and she was truly
alone, totally at their mercy. There had once been a night
when she stood all alone in front of a room full of savages;
how much difference could there be between these red and
black ones and their white counterparts? Shivering with terror, she walked boldly up to Kerry's companion.

"What is the meaning of this, Mahomet? Where are you
taking me?" If her voice quaked slightly, the proud tilt of her
fine head denied it.

The thoughts of the two leaders were impossible to determine from their impassive countenances, but Tonga's hand
was gentle as he touched a silver-gold strand of hair escaping
from Katy's hat, and he grunted a few unintelligible words
approvingly.

Mahomet's eyes gleamed in the darkness as he replied
tersely, "Red man know where is Marster Kerry. We find."

Katy gaped at him, astounded; then her eyes flew back and
forth between the two stoic savages and her heart filled with

disbelief and joy. They were taking her to Kerry! It seemed
incredible, but these savages were more friend than foe, and
if she dared, she would hug them all. But then she remembered the sack and the men hiding in the woods, and a
gnawing worry grew.

"You were going before I came. Why?"

"Tonga says bad men in the woods. Marster needs help.
We go." Deciding this was sufficient explanation, Mahomet
shouldered his sack and swung off down the path, the little
band of men obediently falling in behind him.

Tortured by a multitude of emotions, Katy fell in step with
them, no longer fearful of her own safety. She was certain
these men were her friends as well as Kerry's, although she
could not describe the basis of that certainty, accepting it
unconsciously. What worried her was the necessity for this
march and the distance it might entail before they reached
Kerry. Would he still be there? Had he been hurt? Had he
found Burlington or run afoul of Halberstam's men? Her
jubilation at the thought of being reunited with her husband
was tarnished by her frustration in not being able to demand
answers to these worrisome questions. That, and thoughts of
her children created a subdued mood as she marched beside
her odd assortment of protectors.

Unhampered by long gowns or petticoats, Katy was able to
move with relative ease in her male clothing. Without the
heat of their previous Indian march, she was able to keep
their pace comfortably. But the night grew long and the
disquiet in her heart made the time and distance even longer,
and she was grateful when they stopped to rest just before
dawn.

Mahomet dispersed his rations frugally, but Katy felt little
hunger, though she could not remember her last meal. Her
breasts ached for Chad's greedy suck and her mind was
weary with unanswered questions. Taking advantage of this
respite from their march, she curled up beneath a tree and fell
exhaustedly into slumber. Mahomet propped his back against
the tree and sat cautious guard. None dared risk Mahomet's
immediate bulk or the prospective wrath of the sun goddess's
lover, and she rested safely.

Their trek through virgin forest continued throughout the

next day. Toward evening the timber seemed to thin and the land was frequently marshy, cut by trickling inlets of waters, the shade broken by frequent sight of blue sky. The heat intensified accordingly, and Katy wished she had the freedom to remove her sticky shirt as the men around her did. Sweaty, unwashed bodies kept her protectively in their center, and she found herself wishing fervently they were not so cautious. She would prefer trailing along behind and breathing cleaner air.

Near sunset they stopped to rest along a babbling brook, and Katy seized her chance to cool her aching body. Signaling to Mahomet her intentions, she slipped farther up the creek bank in the concealment of some bushes and quickly divested herself of what little clothing she wore. Sinking delightedly into the swift-running water, she let the cool motion massage away the journey's aches, soothing fair skin irritated by heat and insects. She wet her hair and let it dry in the wind, blowing tendrils caressing unclothed skin as she basked in the last rays of golden sunlight.

When she made her way back to camp, she found both Tonga and Mahomet carefully guarding the path she had taken. The Indian remembered well her penchant for bathing at sundown. If the sun rose in the great waters in the morning, it stood to reason it must sink in them somewhere at night. The sun goddess's predilection for water was easily explained in sacred terms, and her prestige expanded accordingly. The Indians were thoroughly convinced they were walking in company with a piece of the sun, and if she were symbol of the golden dawn, her lover was the fiery sunset, and they had felt his anger once too often. The tale of the lovers' sojourn with the Indians had passed into folklore. To appease the gods, they must swiftly bring the two together again. And in this prospect, Mahomet encouraged them.

They moved on through the cooler night air. The forest became sparse now, the ground more treacherous. A wind picked up off the Atlantic and Katy could smell the salt in the breeze, though she could neither see nor hear the magnificent waters she had once sailed. With beating heart she prayed they were closer to their destination. They had been moving steadily southward and must be somewhere near the bound-

aries of Georgia by now. She had heard wild tales of the
pirates settled there, criminals sent to man the colony from
the dregs of London's jails. It was not a stable place to be,
and she hoped they would not go much farther.

The night sounds changed. No longer did she hear the
hooting of owls, but the occasional harsh cry of a scavenging
gull. The mosquitoes hummed thickly, but above the murmur
of insects she detected a lower murmur, and as they moved
closer, the murmur developed a distinctly human flavor. The
band of men around her dissolved slowly into the darkness of
the underbrush, moving silently on sandy soil, leaving her in
the company of Mahomet and Tonga as they moved toward
an open firelit glade.

An unobtrusive bird call broke the silence, and to a man,
the band of slaves and Indians stepped into the circle, completely surrounding the white inhabitants. Into the ensuing
stunned silence walked the black giant and the Indian guide,
their small companion between them.

One of the seated figures at the fire's side rose, flames
flickering red against his light breeches, casting copper glints
through burnished hair, and without a word being said, the
slight form in male attire broke free from her burly bodyguards, running into the circle of light to cast herself into the
lone standing figure's arms.

The glade erupted in a cacophony of consternation, but as
Katy's hat flew off and golden ringlets cascaded down her
back, consternation turned to merriment and laughter rang out
while the two figures at fireside clasped each other in passionate embrace, unconscious of their audience while their
lips clung in emotional reunion. Two months' separation was
stronger than embarrassment.

Totally bemused by Katy's appearance in this wilderness,
Kerry pulled her tightly against his chest, the feel of her
slight weight against him good after so many months of
abstinence. Burying his face in the mass of curls at her nape,
his body overcome by a sudden hunger, he quelled his desire
with thoughts of what peril brought her here. Instantly his
mind unfogged, and he set her back on the ground.

"Katy, what happened? What are you doing here?" His
eyes went over her head to the two men accompanying her,

but they remained silent, leaving the speaking to Katy. Fearful, his gaze once more focused on darkened violet eyes. "Where are the children?"

Disbelieving his reality, Katy stroked his stubbly cheek, rejoicing in the touch and smell of him while jumbled explanations poured out unbidden. She was aware of Jake appearing at Kerry's side, and the crowd of sailors pressing closer to hear her tale, but her eyes were only on Kerry, all her senses attuned to his presence so that she knew his every move and thought before he made them. Even their fingertips communicated as his curled around hers.

As she spoke of her abduction at Halberstam's hands, Katy could feel the violence of his tension, his frown terrible in its menace, and she hastened to explain her escape. But disbelief lingered as Kerry clenched her hands tightly, his eyes seeking out Mahomet for confirmation. At the slave's reassuring nod, the tension relaxed, but Kerry's frown remained fixed. His concern over the possible loss of his entire plantation did not come close to his concern for Katy, and the thought of Halberstam's reptilian hands on her person raised bile in his throat. He had despised the man before; now he was prepared to personally throttle the bastard. Unconsciously he pulled Katy closer into his protection, barely hearing the remainder of the tale until she spoke questioningly, inquiring after Burlington.

"We have found him. The problem is in freeing him without harm. Now that you are here with the men I need, we can find a plan. Have you eaten?" His eyes scanned her face anxiously, finding only a glowing happiness at his assurances.

Suddenly struck by a ravenous hunger, Katy nodded her head, and Kerry directed that food be provided for the newcomers. While Katy ate, Kerry seated himself in a position to watch with mounting amusement his petite wife's voracious appetite, at the same time lending an ear to the discussion as Jake described Burlington's plight to Mahomet and Tonga. At some word from Mahomet, Kerry raised his eyebrows slightly, tilting his head dubiously as he studied Katy's male-garbed figure. Nodding his head in thoughtful agreement, he spoke a few words, but eagerly turned from their circle when Katy completed her meal.

As Kerry took Katy's hand and helped her to rise, his gaze roamed hungrily over her scanty attire. "Those clothes are somehow more striking than I remember. I trust your health did not suffer from this expedition?"

"Other than a dire need for Chad's greedy habits, I am enormously healthy," Katy replied demurely, feeling the searing fire of his eyes and trembling in their heat. Her own desire blossomed and grew in their radiance.

"Chad?" One brow quirked inquiringly. With her explanation, Kerry grinned. "It seems fitting that two such illustrious names should be reduced to a diminutive in this land. Chad it is, then. He will make his own name. Now, it seems we have more important things to discuss in private, if you will accompany me?" His lopsided grin told of the subject in mind as he tucked her hand into the crook of his arm.

A dazzling smile was the only reply he received.

All heads turned to follow them as the couple drifted from the circle of light, swallowed up by the darkness. Knowing looks were exchanged, but no man moved to disturb their privacy.

While Kerry spread a blanket in the protection of a circle of shrubs, Katy teasingly unfastened her loose linen shirt, allowing the lapels to flutter enticingly over bared breasts.

"It seems you have grown overfond of colonial soil, milord," she commented ambiguously, eyeing his makeshift bed askance.

Reaching out to grab her, Kerry found himself holding only the scrap of linen that had covered her, and soft laughter tauntingly filled his ears.

"You speak in riddles, my little minx. My fondness is certainly not for soil." Hands on hips, he allowed his gaze to roam greedily over the lovely vision now exposed to his gaze, but made no further move to catch her. "I have never made love to a woman in breeches before, but stand willing to correct that lack."

Katy pointed at the rude bed he had made. "You do realize both our children have been conceived on a forest floor and not once have we properly made love on anything but rough wool? Am I forever doomed to be Lady Marian to your Lord

Robin?'' Following his avid gaze, she swung around and presented him with her back.

Kerry chuckled. ''It is only fitting we consummate our marriage the way it began.'' Moving softly so as not to frighten his elusive prey, he came up behind her, his arms gently capturing her in their embrace while his hands filled with soft breasts.

''When we return to Twin Oaks, we shall experiment with every room in the house until we find the setting you consider suitable. I shall make love to you among the flowers in the sun room, on the carpet in the drawing room,'' his voice murmured sensuously in her ears as his fingers kneaded tender nipples, ''and if that is not sufficient to satisfy your curiosity, we will repeat the experiment continually until you have decided on your preference.''

Katy giggled quietly, leaning back against the hardness of his chest and succumbing to his ardor. ''I have no objection to your experiments, milord, but I have already decided on my preference. I wish to be made love to in a high poster bed overlooking my favorite plantation, under a portrait of my lustful husband to match the one of his loving wife in the sitting room.''

She freed an arm to reach up and pull his head down to hers, her lips tasting the sweetness of his kiss with mounting longing, feeling again the scrape of unshaven cheek, scenting the sharp masculine smell of him.

''There is no portrait of your lustful husband, my dear, and I see you had time enough before your escape to spy upon my private retreat. Curiosity has its price, kitten.'' Kerry pulled her around then, catching her up in his arms to better brand her lips with his own, pressing her against the full length of his body before lifting her onto the blanket and covering her with his weight.

''There will be a portrait of him so I might remember his face when next he darkens my door again. And it is not curiosity killing this cat at the moment, milord.'' Katy pressed urgent lips to his, her arms circling his broad shoulders as he lay against her. She could feel the tightening in his loins through the thin material of their breeches and her body cried out to welcome him. It had been such a long time, such a

terribly difficult long time. She smothered a cry as his hand
loosed her waistband and found its way to the empty achingness
between her thighs.

"I will not let you die of this malady, my love, nor will I
let you forget my face for need of a portrait or otherwise. I
think we shall begin our experiments tomorrow in a ship's
bunk, the next evening in my town house in Charleston, and
after that . . ."

With each word, Kerry's lips found a new and more sensitive area to caress until he had worked her trousers down and
laid her fully exposed to his gaze.

"After that, we shall try satin sheets in Georgetown." His
tongue flickered over the warm moistness of her entrance,
while his fingers rapidly removed his own clothing with
Katy's eager aid. "And then move on to those places I spoke
of at our favorite plantation." His mouth moved upward,
lightly teasing, until his hard nakedness completely covered
her.

Frantic with the desire to possess and be possessed, Katy
scarcely heard his words and had no time to wonder at them.
Tomorrow was tomorrow, but tonight she was his and needed
the brand of his manhood to prove it. As he braced himself
above her and she felt his heat between her thighs, she arched
her back eagerly to meet him, groaning with the pleasure of
his quick penetration. Then they were wound in the spiraling
swirl of their passions and words were meaningless. Straining
to fill the emptiness of three hundred aching nights, their
bodies collided with the impact of their need, heating with the
intensity of their union until they exploded and melted together in the completion of their passion. It was a satisfying
sweetness beyond all that had gone before, and fulfilled, they
collapsed in each other's arms, no shadow of wrong to hover
over them and dim their happiness. They were one, at last.

June 15, 1738

WITH THE DAWN came cold reality, and Kerry pulled his sleeping wife closer to the warmth of his body. He did not like the plan they had conceived the night before, and after the sweetness of Katy's lovemaking, he was even more reluctant to carry it out. At one time he had feared she would come to shun all men, and he had certainly done his worst to cement that fear, but despite everything, she had blossomed beautifully and was now as fully eager as he for this joining of their bodies. To expose her once more to the taunting jeers of an audience of lascivious men was tempting fate too far. If anything should happen to her . . .

He shook that fear off. He had to free James and get all of them out of this place. The quickest, most practical method was the one suggested last night; he would let nothing happen to mar their happiness. Kissing Katy's nose lightly, he roused her carefully.

She peered sleepily out at him from behind one half-open lid, closing it again to squirm closer to his warmth. "Hold me, I am cold," she demanded.

Kerry laughed and moved away. "I am no blanket for your

convenience, Lady Kerry. Get yourself up and dressed if you wish warmth. We have work to do this day if you wish to move from hard, cold ground to the relative comfort of ship's bunk by nightfall." He jerked on his breeches and fastened them before handing Katy hers. "I cannot say I wholeheartedly approve of your attire, but it should certainly take less time to don."

Katy indignantly wrapped herself in the blanket and glared at Kerry's laughing expression. " 'Tis not for you to jeer, milord. If it were not for the likes of you, we women would soon adopt the freedom of these clothes and reject the silly furbelows you men insist upon as a symbol of femininity." Katy jerked the offending garments from his hands and pulled the blanket over her head before dressing herself in them.

Admiring the well-turned length of an uncovered calf, Kerry was almost forced to agree. Why should it be the men who showed a pretty leg when there was much more to be seen beneath the multilayers of women's petticoats? Reluctant to concede the point, Kerry bent and tickled a dainty instep. "We only wish to make the chase more difficult. The prize is that much sweeter when fought for."

Throwing the blanket over Kerry's head, Katy stood up, the linen shirt falling well below her knees as she pulled on her trousers. "If fighting with stays and petticoats is that desirable, you may have all of mine," she taunted him, laughing in spite of herself as he tugged the blanket belatedly from his shoulders in time to catch her tying the final knot in her makeshift belt.

"I *have* all of yours. Everything you possess is now mine, my witty wife, including that precious seat of yours." He moved as if to pinch the mentioned part, and Katy skittered away, laughing over her shoulder as she ran back in the direction of the camp.

Kerry loped after her, hoping the day would end so merrily as it began.

Kerry's explanations of Mahomet's plan left a sour taste in his mouth, and he could tell he was not alone in his reaction. Jake had protested it the night before but had not been able to find a better one in the duration, and now he sat, frustrated, watching as Katy dubiously agreed to it. Mahomet and Tonga remained impassive, but several of Kerry's men had already offered to storm the kidnappers' hideout and take their chances rather than to hide behind a woman's skirts, or breeches, as the case might be. But no one could guarantee Lord Burlington's safety during the attack, and Katy, more than the others, remained adamant about that. She would take no chances on the legacy of the Southerland estates falling on Kerry's shoulders. Her children would grow up here, without the stigma of their mother's birth to hamper them, if she had to risk her life to do it.

It was not her life so much as her person Kerry worried about as he watched Katy's brave figure saunter brashly down the dusty path, her linen shirt unbuttoned seductively to reveal her womanly charms, golden mane floating in the breeze. He intended to remain within shooting distance of her at all times, but he would have to rein in his temper unless she fell in obvious trouble, or their cause would be lost. He ground his teeth and made the most of it. He would get his revenge soon enough.

The sun sailed overhead when Katy first caught a glimpse of the abandoned settlement the "pirates" had claimed for their own. Her eyes quickly searched and found the outbuilding Kerry had determined held his brother, and she looked for some sign of life, but not even a guard barred the door. Bolted from the outside, it stood clear of the other shacks on the far side of town. Her gaze veered back to the first buildings, their roofs sagging in disrepair, the chinked logs crumbling and decayed. They looked abandoned, with no visible signs of habitation, but unless they had been deserted during the night, they held at least a dozen of Halberstam's hired criminals.

Steeling herself for what was to come, she bit her lip to bring some color to it and threw her hair back from her face. Nervously she fingered the low décolletage of her unbuttoned shirt, but she must prove she was no stripling lad. All their schemes counted on her womanly wiles. Straightening her shoulders, she strode confidently down the remaining road, knowing Kerry and the others were in the bushes all around.

As she approached, a bent figure appeared on the porch of the first house. Closer inspection revealed a flannel-shirted, potbellied excuse for a man, one finger idly scratching at his crotch as he squinted nearsightedly in her direction. Several weeks' worth of beard stubble studded his jaw, and greasy, unkempt hair hung in lank tendrils about his shoulders. Katy gagged at the sight, forcing a smile to her lips as she waved gaily to attract his attention.

"Yoo-hoo, mister." She moved into a trot, causing her breasts to bounce tantalizingly beneath the thin linen.

The man came to attention at that, throwing some remark over his shoulder to an unseen companion as he moved down the broken steps to the road. Determinedly Katy came on. It was her duty to flush out all twelve of the kidnappers, and she was not off to a good start.

"Mister, you wouldn't happen to have something to quench the thirst of a maiden in distress, would you?" Katy brazenly called out, slowing down now as she came within hearing range. Hips swaying jauntily, she gave her would-be rescuer an apraising once-over. It was a part she was ill-prepared to play, but the only one to get the results she wanted, and she drew on her recollections of another type of woman she had known before entering Kerry's rarefied circles.

"Might have. What kinda distress ye in?" Potbelly grunted agreeably now that he seemed certain the newcomer was definitely female and a comely one at that.

"I just rid myself of a bunch of damned renegades, and I'm parched for whatever you have. I'm so desperate I'll even take water." Katy turned on a wicked grin, full of the worldliness she had learned as a fifteen-year-old.

The first man was joined by a second and third, each seemingly filthier than the last. They grinned appreciatively as Katy cast them interested looks and one returned obligingly to the cabin for a dipper of water. Potbelly was more forward. Flinging a friendly arm about her shoulder, he attempted to steer her up the stairs.

"Why don't ye come in and rest a spell? Ye can tell us all about it and mebbe we can help. Ye do somethin' for us, we do somethin' for ye, mebbe."

One rough hand played suggestively with her breast and

Katy caught her breath, slipping out from under his posses-
sive arm to sit complacently on the ramshackle porch. Accepting the dipper from the returning man, she glanced
surreptitiously about, noting with satisfaction the advance of
several more men from other buildings, not daring to glance
at the distant outbuilding.

"That's mighty friendly of you, kind sir, but I am not
much interested in coming across that crew again. Who's
your friends here? Ain't there any women about this place?"
Batting her eyelashes with happy surprise at the latest arrivals, she smiled enticingly at her first companions. They moved
in closer around her, cutting her off from the latecomers. The
first seeds of agitation were sown, and Katy smiled inwardly.

"We ain't seen a woman in more days than we can count,
and there's a goodly amount of spending gold mounting in
our pockets." Another man approached from behind, and
Katy swung around to meet his hungry gaze. He was leaner
than the rest, bronzed muscles sweating vigorously beneath a
leather jerkin, and his sharp black eyes literally devoured the
slim form perched temptingly on the porch.

Katy moved instinctively from this one, rapidly trying to
count heads as she casually twirled about, her glance falling
on a youngster with soft down still upon his cheeks. "Why,
what have we here?" She stroked an unshaven cheek to a
chorus of laughter, moving suggestively closer to the lad,
away from the more dangerous one. She was almost certain
all the men must be out now, but they kept shifting around,
and she couldn't see them all at once.

One of the larger men spun her around, grabbing her tender
breasts roughly as he forced a slobbering kiss against her lips.
Katy spit defiantly in his face and jerked away, only to fall
into the grasp of another while Potbelly put a knife to the
throat of her attacker.

"I seed 'er first. Ye'd better keep yer hands off."

Hot, bored, restless, and irritable, the "pirates" needed
little excuse for argument, and Katy provided the spark needed
to decimate what little discipline they maintained. A chorus
of jeers and curses followed Potbelly's words, and Katy
rapidly found herself embroiled in a melee of fists and knives
until a rock-hard arm caught her about the waist and carried

her to the edge of the fray. The stink of sweat filled her nostrils, and she clutched at the arm in fear.

"We'll let them old buzzards fight it out. You're too good a wench to waste on the likes of them. I know what a whore like you needs . . ." the voice went on monotonously, detailing the obscenities he had in mind as he edged her farther from the fracas, keeping her pressed hard against the length of him. Holding one muscular arm beneath her chin, he pressed her head back against his chest, but Katy did not need to turn to know this was the lean one, the one with the look of madness in his eyes, and her knees turned to water. His lewd suggestions poured by unheard as his hands played freely with her body, fevered fingers stripping back soft linen to rake the delicate creaminess of skin untouched by sun. She was back in a room with a hundred hungry gazes stripping her naked, shouting obscenities, pinching tender parts, while destroying her soul. . . . Glaring sunlight darkened and spun backward.

"Release her or I'll blow a hole in your back as wide as the one in your head."

A familiar voice cut through the mists of time, causing Katy to stumble back to consciousness at the same time the grip about her neck loosened in surprise. With startling agility she dropped from his grasp and darted out of the way as Kerry's pistol went off before her molester could free his from its belt. In horror she saw the lean body topple to the ground, and then she was dashing for the safety of Kerry's arms, quivering with terror and disgust.

Kerry caught her up with both arms, throwing aside his smoking pistol as he held her to his chest, not needing to signal to his men to finish the job he had begun. The peaceful street lay deserted no longer, but was filled with screaming men and muskets, Indians, black men, and sailors rampaging through the streets with vicious delight, seeking Katy's molesters. Kerry watched with satisfaction as one by one the kidnappers surrendered, outnumbered and outarmed. He kept Katy safely out of the field of fire, holding her tightly, soothing all fears.

Fastening the loose shirt to cover Katy's tempting bosom, Kerry kissed his wife lightly. "In all my times at Drury Lane,

I have never seen such a performance. I did not know whether to murder you or your besotted admirers."

Katy shivered and burrowed closer. "I hope it was worth the effort. I would not care to repeat it. Is Burlington safe?"

"He is halfway back to the ship by now, and the only time I want to see you repeat that performance again is behind our bedroom doors." A hint of steel tinged his voice, and Katy glanced up quickly to catch the gleam of emerald fires. "If that is the means you used to entice Halberstam to free me, it is no wonder he is half-mad to have you. If I had known you were such a wanton, I would have claimed you long ago. Why is it I have never been given the benefit of your more-than-ample wiles?"

Kerry's teeth were clenched as he stared over her shoulders, seeing again Katy's bold wantonness as she blatantly displayed her wares. He had never been so jealous in his life, and his heart seethed with anger at another man's hands on his wife. One lay dead already, guilty of that crime, and he would not hesitate to slay the rest single-handedly should the need arise.

A slow smile flickered about Katy's lips as she idly traced a finger down the expanse of bronzed chest bared by her husband's half-open shirt. She, and she alone, had driven the careless Lord Kerry to jealousy, and she was not above gloating at her power.

"If you will recall, milord, I had need of all my wiles to persuade you in the opposite direction. You have always been much too eager without need of my deliberately enticing you. But should your spirits ever lag . . ."

Her teasing tone and playful caressing had their expected effect. Kerry bent with mischievous grin to nibble at her ear. "You will know that I am quite beyond your reach," he completed her sentence. "So long as there is breath left in my body I have no intention of giving you excuse to find another. You are condemned to a lifetime of monogamy, my dear."

"Then I shall just have to practice my wiles behind bedroom doors, will I not?" Gleefully she threw her arms about his neck, all fears flown as he lifted her free from the ground and captured her with kisses.

But there wasn't time for dalliance. Regretfully Kerry returned her to the road and surveyed the scene of battle. All Burlington's captors had been subdued and bound and lay waiting for Kerry's disposal. A few of the men had wandered off to dig a grave for the battle's only casualty, and Kerry gazed at the body with distaste. He had killed before in the heat of battle, but never with the blood lust of this one. He hoped never to have to do it again, but Halberstam still lurked as an obstacle on the horizon.

Katy interrupted his gloomy thoughts. "What will you do with them?"

He blinked, coming back to the present with her words. "Tonga recognizes some of them as the swindlers that precipitated the uprising we almost suffered. I have agreed to let him take them as his prisoners. The others will sail with us to give evidence against Halberstam."

"What will the Indians do with them?" she asked almost fearfully. Her own fate at the Indians' hands had been momentous enough; she did not know if she wished a worse fate on these men.

"Do not worry. Tonga will keep them alive should I need them for further witness. Sometimes civilization is more savage than our uncivilized friends. They will at least see that their prisoners receive sufficient food, adequate shelter, and healthful exercise. A short term as an Indian slave should make them consider honest toil in a better light." Kerry chuckled, covering up his bitterness at his own treatment as a prisoner of white men.

But Katy heard it and respected it, confident he would use his experience wisely and not allow the bitterness to fester. The worst would soon be over, and she would make it right again. The fates owed it to them. Taking his hand lightly, she swung it between them as they made their way through town and down the path that would take them to the ship and civilization.

Kerry watched with amusement as Katy's happiness bubbled over, inundating his men with her effervescence. She teased away Jake's scowl, bringing him to lighthearted merriment while flitting from one spot to the other, discovering delicate flowers hidden beneath bushes, and later, as they neared the ocean, crowing over common shells she found and tucked away about her person or anyone else's in the vicinity. She was like a child freed from a tiresome term at school, and Kerry appreciated this return of her kittenish behavior. She had been through a long, hard struggle, a bleak period they would both prefer to forget; it was time her mourning ended and she began to live again.

The ship lay hidden in a cove pointed out by one of Jake's sailors, a man whose past would not bear close scrutiny but whose knowledge of these coastlines could not be denied. As they worked their way through sand and scrub grass, Kerry caught up with his straying wife and threw her over his shoulder like so much baggage, much to the amusement of his men. As Katy beat her fists futilely against his broad back, they heard him bellow while long strides carried them off, "Your wanton days are over, madam. I have a berth aboard that ship for the likes of you," and they exchanged gleeful glances. It mattered little to the seamen whether their captain's bedding was sanctified by marriage or not; they were only glad to see an end to his simmering anger and this tedious journey, and his joy was theirs.

Burlington awaited them on deck, and despite the filthy tatters of his clothes and the fact he had clearly not had a bath in months, Katy immediately threw herself into his arms once Kerry returned her feet to the boards. Smothered with kisses, Burlington could do no less than lift her up and chuckle with amusement as he observed his brother's glare over her shoulder.

"If I had known sisters-in-law could be as sweet as this, I would have demanded you find one much sooner." Carefully setting her down again, Burlington held her off and surveyed Katy's unusual attire with a quizzical eye. "Kerry has not smuggled you to Twin Oaks as one of his slaves, has he? I seem to remember the women wore skirts—has that changed?"

"You are not one to talk, my fine lord. Since when have England's nobility ceased to bathe?" Katy held her nose and laughed delightedly at the rueful expression on the face of the once cold nobleman. There was a touch of Kerry about him as he implored his brother for respite.

"Below with ye, ye swab," Kerry crowed gladly, vastly amused by this chance to order his brother about and to even

the score. "We will have explanations later. I'll not be havin'
my ship smelled up with the likes of ye."

Ordering water hauled below for the purposes of bathing
their noble passenger, Kerry claimed his victory and his
prize, spiriting his bride off to the captain's quarters. For
once, Burlington would take his place in a berth below his.

Later that evening, after the ship caught the first fair wind
for home and the captain's bunk had been fairly tested for
comparison with forest floors, the three of them dined more
tranquilly about Kerry's table, exchanging tales of their
adventures.

Burlington looked somewhat cleaner for a bath and a shave,
but not his usual sartorial self in shirt and breeches made for a
smaller, leaner man. Katy was forced to stifle her giggles at
the sight of breeches made for Kerry's narrow hips pulled
snugly across Lord Burlington's much larger posterior. She
would never be able to look upon him as on a pedestal again.

Burlington stared in growing wonder as Kerry regaled him
with the tale of Katy's aid in his rescue, finding it hard to
believe the demure young maid with graceful blushes, her
golden curls now neatly ordered in a knot at her nape, could
dare the advances of a dozen lustful cutthroats. That she was
a sprightly nymph at times, he knew well now, but a courageous wanton? Looking at the delicate cheekbones caressed
by the curve of long dark lashes shyly lowered to hide
embarrassment, Burlington declared the thing impossible.

"Look at her! Despite her manly attire"—Burlington waited
for Katy's giggle to subside: her trousers had become a point
of jest between them—"she would shame the fairest ladies in
the land. I love my Jenny, she will make a noble duchess
someday, but even she could learn a few things from yon
lass. If you had not told me otherwise, I would think her
descended from a race of princes, but I will not believe she
lured those bloodthirsty varlets from their hiding places."
Burlington slapped his wineglass down for emphasis.

Kerry's lips quirked at Katy's downcast eyes and rosy
blush. She looked as innocent as a virgin maid, but the
afternoon's pleasures dispelled any such conviction in his
own mind. He had taught her the delights of passion well,

and now she returned them fourfold. His grin grew wider at the memory.

Nonchalantly sipping his wine, Kerry replied, "Believe what you will, but without her, your chances of being here now were mighty slim, and you may tell our father he would be without either son if it were not for a certain charming kitten. For myself, I need no convincing, I have long been sold on her value." Green eyes danced as violet ones clashed with his. "And for good measure, you may very well be right about the line of princes. It is rumored her father was the descendant of a noble house of France, and you know how royalty mingles in their blood."

Burlington glanced at him suspiciously, then studied Katy as she bit her lip and kept silent. "You have mentioned some such before, but I received no satisfaction from it. Perhaps I could get more sense from your wife. Katy?"

Katy shook her head, the remark about being sold having curled her tongue with the eagerness to let loose at Kerry's taunts. " 'Tis only a childish fable, milord. I am a bookseller's daughter, nothing more."

Taking pity on her embarrassment, Burlington covered her small hand with his own large one. "You are Lady Kerry, and much, much more. Will you ever forgive my conceit in thinking you not fit to wear the Southerland name? You have earned it far better than any of us, and are far more deserving of it than any maid at court. You will ever be welcome at Southerland House, and anyone who would slur your name must be answerable to me. If you cannot forgive me now, I will work to earn your favor. I owe you my life and my thanks."

Kerry's pride was half-scornful as he watched his arrogant brother woo his willful Katy. There was little for Katy to forgive, for she had been of the same opinion as Burlington, and wryly Kerry was forced to admit that at one time he had been in agreement. What fools these mortals be, he quoted glumly to himself.

"That is a very pretty speech, milord, but highly unnecessary. There is nothing to forgive, and my actions were entirely selfish. I only wished to see you safely returned to England so I might keep Kerry here to myself."

Honest, forthright Katy, Kerry reflected wryly. So much for speeches and turning pretty heads. Out loud he added, "A toast, my brother. To your life in England and mine in the colonies. We shall see which makes the better of it." He held up his glass, and James struck it willingly.

"You are two children ahead of me already, but I will see if I cannot rectify that soon. But you will have to tend your estates more closely than this if you wish to exceed mine."

Relieved that the subject had turned from her, Katy asked, "If he should have any estate at all. What will become of Halberstam? How do you intend to remove him from Twin Oaks?"

The two brothers exchanged glances, and Kerry opted to let his brother speak. Burlington was as eager for revenge as he.

"I believe my testimony and that of our prisoners will be enough to convince the council of their acting governor's treachery. They have not the power to remove him, but with the king's commission, I believe I can persuade them I have the power to lead a force of militia to regain Twin Oaks and put Halberstam in chains. Whether it is within my powers or not, I will see him aboard ship for the jails of London before I leave this place. Only then will I be satisfied justice has been served."

Katy's gaze flew fearfully from one stern face to the other. "Militia? You are not both thinking to lead troops to Twin Oaks? Halberstam would like nothing better than to have you shot as insurgents."

Kerry shrugged at his brother as if to say: What did I tell you?—then took Katy's hand to soothe her fears. "With the council's backing, we will be the law and Halberstam the insurgent. Once his men see the proof of our power, they will not remain loyal long. Twin Oaks will be given up without a fight, I promise."

Dubiously Katy frowned at him. "And you will promise not to call him out or do anything to give him cause to draw his sword on you?"

Kerry sighed with amused exasperation. He could not deny the thought had crossed his mind more than once. He felt entitled to dispatch his own justice, but she reminded him he was no longer the carefree courtier free to risk his life at a whim. He must become used to more civilized ways.

"I will stay entirely out of his sight if that will make you any happier. A tour in the hold of a ship and a spell in jail should be a better lesson for him." Kerry relaxed at Katy's dimple of happiness. He was not certain who had won, but they were both satisfied with the outcome. And there were much better pleasures than fighting. His grin widened as Katy caught his eye and blushed; she hadn't lost her ability to read his mind. He sat back and waited for the moment they would be alone.

Hair blowing free in the ocean breeze, Katy stood silently at Kerry's side while they watched the pattern of waves slap against the stern in the darkness. Hand at her waist, Kerry had fallen into thoughtful silence as the wind blew them on a course to their future.

"You do realize I have no intention of letting you out of my sight once we reach Charleston?" Kerry's low voice broke the quiet as he turned to Katy, catching her hair and restraining it with his fist.

"I believe you mentioned that thought in your inanities last night," Katy replied calmly.

"While Halberstam remains free, I cannot risk your safety for the sake of propriety, and will not give up your company for the opinion of gossips. You will stay with me at my town house until we can have our nuptials made public." A thread of determination hardened his voice as if he expected argument.

"Just as long as the children are with me," she agreed easily.

"No objections to appearing openly as my mistress?" Kerry could not keep a trace of astonishment from his tone.

'None, milord." Katy smiled quietly, turning to face him. "While you are by my side, nothing can befall you. Nothing else matters." She held up her arms to him, and Kerry bent slightly to let her fingers slip about his neck.

"And I thought I had the upper hand," he whispered

ruefully as sweet kisses rained upon his cheek. Then, taking matters well in hand, he gripped her tightly, parting her lips with the force of his own, and the ship sailed on without the benefit of watching eyes.

July 1, 1738

EVEN AT THIS early hour of dawn, the humidity had the power to steam the shirts to their backs and wring sweat from their brows. The horses, too, stank of sweat and breathed heavily from the long march.

Kerry swatted with irritation at a nagging fly and urged his tired mount on. Twin Oaks was just around the bend and the heat of anger burned more fiercely then the Carolina summer night.

Burlington kept up with him with some difficulty. They had stopped in Georgetown only long enough for the small band of militia to rest their horses and for Katy and Kerry to be reunited with their children. The memory of that happy reunion and the sight of the two-month-old Chad had stirred pain as well as happiness within the young marquess. It would be worth giving up a dukedom for children like Kerry's. Burlington sighed and dug his heels into his horse's sides. These last months of enforced idleness had not prepared him for this jaunt, and painful memories did not ease the task ahead.

Kerry brought the group to a halt in a thicket of trees just out of sight of the river. Some of the neighboring plantation owners had promised to join them and he awaited their signal impatiently. He wanted the place surrounded, with no chance of escape. The thought of the reptilian Halberstam inhabiting the house he had built for Katy irked Kerry, but the man's audacity in actually kidnapping his wife created a thirst for revenge even Katy's admonitions could not quench. Pistols and swords would not suffice this time. He wanted his bare hands around the bastard's neck!

Kerry caught the hooting signal and the shimmer of metal in the sun's first light and pointed out the other band of men across the clearing to the commander of the militia. They returned the signal and the men began to move in, spreading their ranks in a circle that would soon surround the clearing.

The gleaming magnificence of the porticoed mansion rose abruptly before them, catching the rays of dawn from the east while the south side from which they approached remained in the shadow of towering oaks. In the heavy heat, the Spanish moss hung limp and lifeless from the ancient spreading branches.

Kerry halted his stallion at the edge of the woods where he had once questioned Katy's happiness before returning to England to seek his own. He knew now his happiness lay here, in these fertile river lands, with the bookseller's daughter at his side. And the despicable Halberstam stood between him and this happiness.

Burlington glanced worriedly at his half-brother's grim expression. Kerry had sworn to Katy he would do nothing rash, would leave this action in the hands of the government militia, but Kerry's notions of "rash" often differed from others'. Burlington saw no likelihood of change at a time like this.

As the remainder of the men spread out to surround the house, Kerry scanned the scene below. No breakfast fires smoked the air. All the slaves had departed, leaving the renegade soldiers to fend for themselves. It seemed none had taken a liking to cooking.

A lone figure staggered from the barn wearing nothing but soiled breeches and straw in his hair. Kerry chuckled grimly.

Burlington glanced askance at this unexpected sound and

Kerry gestured to the drunken weaving of the man below. "My larders may not be depleted, but I wager my cider kegs have been tapped to the dregs."

Burlington grunted a sour agreement. Kerry had a liking for challenges and seemed to gain energy just at the prospect of one. Burlington, on the other hand, would rather be in a ship's bunk right now—on the way home to the comforts of the Southerland House.

The man below stopped to relieve himself on some of Kerry's newly planted shrubbery. Kerry gritted his teeth, then caught his breath as the man looked straight at them. They had been sighted.

With a whistle to signal the commander of the militia and his neighbors, Kerry motioned for them to proceed. The mounted army slowly drew the noose tighter, advancing into the clearing, loosening their scabbards and lifting their muskets. The drunkard dashed into the protection of the house, his aching bladder apparently forgotten.

The house sprang to life. Faces appeared at the windows. Dismayed figures appeared on porches, gazed upon the armed band of men, and hastily retreated. Muskets appeared here and there from upper-story windows, but no organized defense appeared imminent.

Kerry gauged the situation swiftly, then sidled his mount closer to his brother's.

"Halberstam has no defenses, but he will attempt to bluff it out. Coward that he is, he'll choose a position safely out of our range to make his stand. That balcony over the front entrance should suit his purposes nicely. Keep him occupied when he appears."

Before Burlington could question, Kerry had spurred the stallion onward, skirting the edge of the woods beyond the line of men, edging closer to the house and the cover of the oak trees.

A raised musket fired into the air, commanding full attention from all within hearing. The officer in charge of the militia followed this salute with a loud hailing of the inhabitants of the occupied mansion. By the time Burlington diverted his attention from this tableau to follow Kerry's progress,

Kerry had disappeared. Riderless, his stallion rested in the shade of the towering oaks, his tail idly switching at flies.

Burlington grunted his displeasure at this unexpected development, but advanced into the clearing to take his place beside the militia officer.

"Halberstam, as a representative of his majesty, King George the Third, I hereby order you to present yourself for questioning by the royal authorities. You have no choice, man, give it up!"

Burlington's stentorian tones rang true and clear in the dawn air, causing consternation in Halberstam's ranks. Several windows went up and curious heads appeared when no gunfire resulted.

"The council has acted to declare this appropriation of property an act of rebellion and demands that its duly sworn militia return to their ranks and cease and desist from any further support of such acts. Any men returning to their ranks at this summons shall be exonerated."

The commander read this speech from an unrolled document which he carefully folded upon finishing his presentation. Then, glancing up at the idle soldiers leaning from the windows, he yelled, "Get your asses out here, now! That's an order!"

Before any immediate reply could be forthcoming, Halberstam's tall, stocky figure appeared behind the parapet of the balcony, just as Kerry had predicted. Burlington glanced again in the direction in which his brother had disappeared, but found no sign of him.

Garbed in immaculate white breeches and linen, his gold-braided waistcoat gleaming in the rising sun, Halberstam glared down at the offensive army below.

"How dare you address a governor of his majesty's colonies in such a manner! I will have you stripped of your commission and whipped for this audacity!"

He scarcely batted an eyelash in recognition of Burlington's presence. Garbed in the righteous dignity of his exalted position, Halberstam acted the part of outraged monarch well. The marquess glanced down at his own travel-worn and sweat-stained clothing and grimaced wryly. Perhaps clothes did make the man, upon occasion.

Then a movement among the trees caught his eye and he studied it surreptitiously, ignoring the pompous speeches of the man on the balcony. Burlington abhorred violence and had forbidden bloodshed, but Halberstam seemed prepared to force the issue. So what in hell was Kerry doing in those trees?

Auburn hair glinted momentarily at the end of a long limb two stories above the ground. Burlington held his breath at a flash of white breeches between the leaves, then groaned inwardly as Kerry's lithe figure flattened itself against the roof's sloping tiles. The bloody fool was climbing over the roof now! Damn, but what he would give to shake his teeth until they rattled!

But he almost licked his lips in anticipation. Halberstam's bombastic oratory had brought the battle to a standstill. Under orders not to shoot unless told, the ring of farmers and milita stood helplessly in the growing blaze of sunlight, listening to their governor's meaningless rhetoric. Even Burlington felt the helplessness of having his hands tied by his own orders. Yet he could not order one of his majesty's civil servants shot down in cold blood. Kerry's daring traipse across the rooftop just might prove the solution. If he did not get himself killed first.

Others became aware of the bold figure crawling across heated tiles. The horses, sensing their riders' tension, pawed nervously at the grass. Rifles still aimed from various windows, and fingers itched edgily on triggers as ranks began to close around the house, but only Halberstam's demonstrative speech split the air.

The man's mad, Burlington thought, not bothering to define which one: the resplendent acting governor on the balcony or the furious Irish lord perched on the roof over his head. Varying degrees of madness existed.

Kerry held his breath and gritted his teeth as he cautiously crawled the remaining few feet. Halberstam stood just below him, but he could not let his eagerness spoil the element of surprise. He had no means of knowing how many men waited in the house below with guns trained at the intruders. His only hope of safety was catching them off guard.

"Lay down your arms and return to your homes! Let this

matter of policy be settled by the council, where it belongs!''
Halberstam shouted, encouraged by his audience's evident
powerlessness.

"To hell with the council! We'll settle it now, Joshua."

Kerry dropped feetfirst from the eaves, the sudden landing
jarring the breath from his lungs but not disturbing his re-
flexes. As Halberstam swung furiously to confront this unexpected invasion, Kerry ducked and came up swinging.

The explosion of his fist against Halberstam's jaw brought
a satisfying crunch of bone against bone and sent the yard and
house into pandemonium. Screams of fury and fear erupted
all about them, men attempted to join them on the balcony,
but unseen forces held them back. Kerry took no notice of
anything but his adversary.

Halberstam recovered slowly, wiping the back of his hand
across his bleeding lip as he glared at Lord Kerry's blazing
emerald eyes. No sooner had he returned to his feet than
Kerry's fist flew again, aiming for a softer target.

Better prepared, Halberstam attempted to evade the blow,
but his larger, slower figure presented easy game. Kerry's left
hand flew up to hit where the right had missed. The acting
governor made a satisfying grunt of pain before striking back.

Halberstam had no intention of fighting fair. Apparently
deserted by his bodyguards, he took advantage where he
found it. Bent double from Kerry's blow, he came up fast
with his fists clasped together, driving hard at Kerry's jaw.
Kerry's swift sidestep prevented all but a glancing blow, but
sufficient to knock him off balance while Halberstam grabbed
for a heavy clay pot on the railing.

The pain in his jaw only served to fuel Kerry's anger. With
a roar of rage, he drove his head like a battering ram into
Halberstam's soft paunch. The pot flew from the railing as
the portly Halberstam crashed against it, and grappling wildly,
the two men rolled to the floor of the balcony.

Burlington held his arm across the doorway, preventing
interference from the men behind him. Eager to join the fray,
the militia halted grudgingly and watched the battle over the
marquess's broad shoulder. Their thirst for action whetted but
not satisfied by the brawl with Halberstam's men, they wished
to join this much more interesting fracas.

Silently begging Katy's forgiveness, Burlington allowed the fight to continue. Each blow Kerry struck expressed the vengeance within his soul. One blow for Halberstam's insults to Katy, the next for his imprisonment of Kerry, the next for his assault upon Twin Oaks, the next for Burlington's own kidnapping . . .

Kerry's repeated blows had their result. Though the larger man, Halberstam fell with a groan to his knees and did not rise, despite his opponent's pleas to the contrary.

"Get up, man! I'm not half done with you!" Frustrated of full vengeance by his adversary's cowardice, Kerry urged Halberstam to fight, unable to bring himself to strike a man on his knees. Halberstam had done so more than once, figuratively as well as literally, but Kerry could not lower himself to his enemy's standards. He clenched his fists in frustration over Halberstam's panting figure.

"Captain, arrest that man and put him in chains!"

Burlington stepped forward, ending the moment of decision and ignoring his brother's baleful look as the militia marched in and jerked Halberstam to his feet.

"Damn you, James, this is my fight! Let me finish the cad as he deserves!"

Gasping for air, his jaw already swelling and one eye half-closed, Kerry glared as the marquess ordered the prisoner carried away.

Finally turning to gaze upon Kerry's battered face with a certain grim amusement, Burlington shrugged nonchalantly. "I thought to save your neck and my own from that wife of yours, little brother, but judging from your appearance, it may be too late. 'Tis a pity Halberstam could not stand up like a man, but now I fear we must face Katy's wrath instead. You did mention something to her about not taking chances . . . ?"

Managing to look both contrite and wryly sheepish through the rising swelling of his face, Kerry muttered an expressive expletive and stomped after the retreating militia, leaving Burlington to do likewise.

The sun sailed past the horizon as they mounted their horses. In the distance, tobacco plants shimmered dark green and ripe. As the soldiers marched from the field of battle, a low song of joyous thanksgiving floated from the woods beyond.

Kerry turned his horse toward the source of the sound, and with pride observed the rich lands that he had conquered on his own. His gaze met that of the giant black man emerging from the woods, followed by his loyal people, and pride became something else—a deep feeling of attachment for all this new country represented, and the people who inhabited it. Kerry's heart swelled with the love Katy had taught him, and a promise fired emerald eyes as he saluted the black slave and turned his horse toward home.

Epilogue

KERRY FOUND her in the sun room, a half-finished painting waiting on an easel, and a sleeping infant Chad on her lap. Gentle October sunlight dappled the floor, polishing the golden strands of Katy's hair. His hand strayed automatically to the softness of her curls while he gazed fondly at his cherubic son.

"Is not a bed a better place for sleeping?" he asked softly, touching one finger to a chubby fist.

"I have sent for Tess to take him up," Katy replied calmly, turning her face up to his, smiling at the kiss he bestowed upon her. "Did the sloop bring good news from Georgetown? You are itching to tell me something, I can tell."

"I could not keep a secret from such a sorceress, I know." Kerry waited for the maid to remove his infant, then pulled Katy from her seat and deposited himself in the chair, pulling her down on his lap. When her arms flew about his neck as much for balance as for affection, he kissed her thoroughly, running one hand down soft curves with a loving gesture of possession. It was a constant delight to him that he was now able to do so freely in the eyes of the world. They were publicly man and wife, and he was wont to flaunt it proudly.

"There is an invitation from the new governor to Lord and Lady Kerry, to attend the wedding of one Amanda Lyttle and friend, and a host of similar items, as usual."

"And as usual, you will ignore the lot of them to tend your horses and spend your nights in your own bed." Katy squirmed unconcernedly in his arms; she had no objection to his choice. "But that was not all there was, was it?" she asked pointedly, nipping at his ear when he pinched a tender spot.

"No, my prescient witch, it was not." Maneuvering one hand around to reach his coat pocket, he produced a familiar vellum stationery with the Southerland crest. "We have here, at long last, an epistle from that dilatory brother of mine. Not to mention additional notes from the entire family with appropriate ecstatic greetings."

Satisfied to let him give the news in his own way, Katy did not take the letter from him. Settling down comfortably in his arms with her head against his shoulders, she demanded, "What did he have to say?"

"For one, the big news of the day, he is now the proud father of a son, named James Edward Southerland, born August 3 at a most inconvenient hour of the night—as always." He beamed with delight as Katy threw her arms around him again, smothering him with kisses.

"The duke has an heir? And poor Burlington finally has a child of his own to spoil. Thank the Lord for that. Now I may safely keep my own without sharing him." She grinned impishly.

"Selfish brat," Kerry agreed. "It seems his wife gave birth the day after he arrived home—most thoughtful of her to await his arrival, though from experience, I must say it would have been easier on the poor chap if she had delivered while he was gone." He dodged Katy's slap. "Anyway, he's crowing over his success, and now that our father has two more heirs to boast of, he cannot complain of our lack of offspring any longer and now complains that he will never see all his grandchildren together if we do not repair to England at once."

Katy wrinkled her nose. "I suppose that means we will be on the next ship sailing from Charleston."

"I had thought it better to wait until our own ship could be loaded with the plantation's harvest and sail in the relative comfort of home, if you think you and Chad healthy enough for the trip."

"And just when might that be?"

"Within another month or so, depending on how quickly we work."

Katy frowned, and behind his head began counting on her fingers, her lips moving silently as she eliminated each consecutive digit.

In bewilderment Kerry watched her. "What is that for? Is there some time limit we must obey?"

"Nine months," she muttered. Then, satisfied with her calculations, she looked up to his startled face. "It seems to be a habit with us, there must be something about the months of July and August. But if we are home before April, I suppose Chad and I will be healthy enough. Just don't expect to show me off in too many new gowns while there."

Kerry looked as if he had been felled by a particularly large oak. His bewildered expression gradually turned to one of bemused but delighted joy. "Our third? My God, Katy, you will make an old man of me yet. After watching my brother go childless for so many years and siring no bastards of my own, I had thought there was more difficulty in the process than this. I cannot believe . . ." At her knowing grin, Kerry stifled his absurdities and crushed her ecstatically to his chest. "My beautiful fragile Katy, we will sail anytime you wish or stay home should you desire. You may have anything you want. I would see this child born in peace and harmony, without the pain of the others."

"Milord, if such a thing were possible, there would be more bastards in this world than are already there. Childbirth without pain would be like giving candy to a baby." She deliberately chose to misunderstand him. "If your family is not too wrathful over your marriage, I am quite willing to make this journey once to meet them. Just do not expect me to be too eager to repeat it."

Laughing heartily at her pugnacious air, Kerry hugged his whimsical wife again. "Wrathful, indeed! After the tales Burlington must have wove, they are ready to worship the ground you walk on. Your head will be so swollen by the time we leave, it will rival your belly."

Katy's laughter chimed in to join his at this image, and their laughter filled the room and spread through the mansion via the open door. Black faces exchanged merry glances at the sound; the household had not been the same with the arrival of their new mistress and the children, and they were glad of the change. Even Bertha, passing through the back of the house to the kitchens, smiled. Since her mistress had moved to Twin Oaks, she was able to enjoy the company of her "big black man" every night, and now that Kerry had given Mahomet his freedom, she enjoyed the prestige of being a freeman's woman. Twin Oaks was a lucky place to be, and as she went out the back door, she began contriving the special meal she would cook for the master's dinner tonight, and her smile broadened.

"But there is one thing more Burlington adds in his letter. He claims it as his reason for delaying writing." Kerry sobered, though a small grin flitted about his features.

Katy worked her hand beneath his shirt and began playing sensuous patterns against his chest. "It better be very important. The children are napping, and I am expecting a pressing engagement in our chambers."

A wicked gleam rose in Kerry's eyes as he tasted bewitching lips. "Very pressing indeed. We have not yet tested the sun room . . ." His voice trailed off expectantly as his fingers found a rosy crest beneath her bodice, the other hand sliding up a stockinged leg.

Katy squealed and fled his lap, readjusting her bodice. "Your ardor must wait until we are behind closed doors, milord. I will not risk being spied upon. What else does your brother have to say?"

Kerry rose stiffly, the gleam in his eye not quenched by her tactics. "It seems he made a few inquiries at court while he was there seeing to Halberstam's justice."

Interest flickered in Katy's eyes as she continued to back

away from her irrepressible husband. "What justice did he find?"

"A long, long term in the Tower is my guess. Halberstam's father was lucky enough to buy his life. But that is not what I wished to discuss."

"I can well imagine what you wish to discuss. But what of Burlington's inquiries, you were going to say?" Katy retreated behind the greenery, peering through the foliage to discern his intentions.

Kerry patiently stalked his prey. "It only takes a few proper connections to unfold mysteries. He took copies of your baptismal certificate and your parents' marriage papers with him. There were those at court who remembered them well."

Startled, Katy forgot their game and stood still, her eyes widening with amazement at her husband's words. "At court? They knew my parents at court?"

With little difficulty Kerry reached out a hand and pulled her from her hiding place. "They did indeed. Your mother did not quote fairy tales. She was, as she said, a bastard—but she did not also mention that she was a ward of the court, which is the only way a French nobleman could have met her."

Katy tried to absorb these words but there were too many points left open to take in at once. She remained tongue-tied.

Taking advantage of his wife's unusual silence, Kerry continued. "Her mother died, unwed, at childbirth, and the court took in the orphan. The only reason they would do such a thing is that she was of noble or royal blood and had father or family in influential position. According to Burlington's sources, your grandmother was of good family, and the man who fathered your parent, of royal blood. Burlington prides himself on knowing good stock when he sees it, and uses this as an example. Whether you believe it or not is up to you. But he did not stop there."

Kerry hesitated, waiting to see if Katy understood the implications of his words, if she wished him to continue. When she said nothing, he finished his tale. "The sources at court well remember the scandalous romance between the visiting French nobleman and the royal bastard. Theirs was a

passionate affair, doomed from the start, they claimed. The
Frenchman was a younger son sent to find an English heiress
and your mother lived on charity. In turn, the English court
frowned on any alliance between a royal ward and a Frenchman,
and forbade the liaison. One night the young couple disappeared, and were never seen again. It is well known that one
day's scandal is soon replaced by another, and little was ever
done to find them. Many assumed them dead or gone to
France.''

The air seemed to leave Katy's lungs and she collapsed
against Kerry's comfortingly hard chest. It was like discovering her parents' existence after a lifetime of orphanage. The
fact that she had a past and some claim to family was nothing
less than miraculous. Though she might never learn exactly
who that family was, it was good to know they weren't
cutthroats or thieves.

Kerry held her tightly, his voice rumbling deep in his chest
as he continued. ''Burlington wasn't satisfied with these few
tidbits. He has a passion for genealogy and sought further,
through friends, into the court of France and traced your
parentage to the noble house of Devereaux.''

Again widened eyes sought his face, and he smiled slightly,
brushing a soft kiss across her forehead. ''If Burlington is to
be believed, there exists now a Comte de Devereaux who had
three sons. The two eldest have died without issue, the
youngest disappeared in England well over twenty years ago.
A search was made with no result for this son, and the count
resides, a bitter, ancient man, in a crumbling estate in the
south of France. An estate, midear, that could very well be
your own if you wish to claim it.''

Tears welled up in Katy's eyes at Kerry's soft words, and
she kept her face hidden against his chest, clinging desperately to his coat for support. She had wanted to know the
details: now she had them, and they were tearing her apart.
There existed, somewhere, a lonely old man who could very
well be her grandfather; she, who had claimed no family,
now suddenly had not only a family but also a name and
possibly an inheritance. It was incomprehensible that after all
these lonely years on her own, with no other constant in her

ife than Kerry, she suddenly had a past to claim. The incredibility of it overwhelmed her.

Her tear-streaked face and glistening eyes moved to search Kerry's noncommittal expression. "Would you have me be a *comtesse* with estates in France?" she asked weakly, uncertain of his reaction to his brother's news.

"If you should choose to return to seek your inheritance and your family, I will do all I can to aid you," he agreed a rifle grimly. It was an occurrence he could easily understand, and for that reason had reported the news immediately, the better to avoid thinking of it.

Katy gave a shaky laugh. "After all my complaints of your name and titles, it is I who come closest to gaining them. All the world would surely approve our marriage then—titles and possibly wealth also. Surely that will please your family."

"Will it please you, Katy? Do you wish to have a title and a name so you might hold your head up high? A grander title than baron to pass on to our children, since I am no longer in line for a dukedom?" Green eyes lost their sparkle as they encountered hers.

His words had the ring of the ridiculous to them, and Katy's lips began to turn up of their own accord. "Will you have to call me 'my lady' and kiss my hand and bow courteously before me? How does an English baron fare before a French *comtesse?* Would you practice on me awhile so I might get the feel of it?" Impish lights danced behind violet pools as she moved from his arms and spread her skirts regally.

Delight flared once more in his eyes at her mocking words. "Practice on you, madam? I would gladly practice on you." Kerry moved closer, the hunger in his gaze making mockery of his promise.

"I can see that." Instead of retreating, Katy moved within the circle of his arms and once more fingered the fastenings of his shirt. "Would you think less of me if I said I wished to remain Lady Kerry and hope my son has no title grander than 'honorable' attached to his name?"

"No, I would think my kitten has remained true to her nature and I would love her the more for it. I consider I made

an excellent match from the start and have no need of titles or
dowry to prove it. You are all I need to prove my worth.''

Katy melted against him and felt his arms tighten at her
waist. She sighed contentedly. "Your pretty phrases warm
my heart, milord, but not my body." As he moved to correct
that malady, Katy stayed him with one hand. "Still, I think
some effort should be made to let that poor old man know of
his son's fate. What did Burlington suggest?"

Kerry buried his face in fragrant golden tresses and muttered, "I suggest we repair to our chambers and discuss this
later, but if you must know, my inestimably proper brother
has already informed the count of your existence. With any
luck, he will be there to greet you when we reach Southerland
House. Now, may I practice on you?" His hand caressed a
soft curve while his other arm pulled her waist closer, so that
she bent hard against him. A warm gleam heated his eye.

"All my spells and enchantments, and I have yet to teach
you patience. Practice as you will, milord," Katy sighed,
flinging her arms about his neck and allowing herself to be
pulled from the floor.

"At last you admit your witchery, Lady Sorceress,"
Kerry whispered against her ear.

"Never denied it, milord." She smiled, seeking and finding the lips of which she would never tire.

About the Author

PATRICIA RICE, who was born in Newburgh, New York and attended the University of Kentucky. She now lives in Mayfield, Kentucky with her husband and her two children, Corinna and Derek, in a rambling Tudor house. Ms. Rice has a degree in accounting and her hobbies include history, travel and antique collecting.

Romantic Reading from SIGNET

(045

☐ **THE VISION IS FULFILLED** by Kay L. McDonald. (129016—$3.50)
☐ **DOMINA** by Barbara Wood. (128567—$3.95)
☐ **JUDITH: A LOVE STORY OF NEWPORT** by Sol Stember. (125045—$3.25)
☐ **MOLLY** by Teresa Crane. (124707—$3.50)
☐ **GILDED SPLENDOUR** by Rosalind Laker. (124367—$3.50)
☐ **BANNERS OF SILK** by Rosalind Laker. (115457—$3.50)
☐ **CLAUDINE'S DAUGHTER** by Rosalind Laker. (091590—$2.25)
☐ **WARWYCK'S WOMAN** by Rosalind Laker. (088131—$2.25)
☐ **THE IMMORTAL DRAGON** by Michael Peterson. (122453—$3.50)
☐ **THE CRIMSON PAGODA** by Christopher Nicole. (126025—$3.50)
☐ **THE SCARLETT PRINCESS** by Christopher Nicole. (132696—$3.95)
☐ **WILD HARVEST** by Allison Mitchell. (122720—$3.50)
☐ **EMERALD'S HOPE** by Joyce Carlow. (123263—$3.50)

*Prices slightly higher in Canada

Buy them at your local bookstore or use this convenient coupon for ordering.

NEW AMERICAN LIBRARY,
P.O. Box 999, Bergenfield, New Jersey 07621

Please send me the books I have checked above. I am enclosing $_____
(please add $1.00 to this order to cover postage and handling). Send check
or money order—no cash or C.O.D.'s. Prices and numbers are subject to change
without notice.

Name_____

Address_____

City_____State_____Zip Code_____

Allow 4-6 weeks for delivery.
This offer is subject to withdrawal without notice.